RESURRECTION IN MAY

Other Novels by Lisa Samson Include

The Passion of Mary-Margaret

Embrace Me

Quaker Summer

Straight Up

The Church Ladies

Tiger Lillie

Club Sandwich

The Living End

Women's Intuition

Songbird

RESURRECTION IN MAY

LISA SAMSON

THOMAS NELSON
Since 1798

NASHVILLE DALLAS MEXICO CITY RIO DE JANEIRO

Published in Nashville, Tennessee, by Thomas Nelson. Thomas Nelson is a registered trademark of Thomas Nelson, Inc.

Thomas Nelson, Inc. titles may be purchased in bulk for educational, business, fund-raising, or sales promotional use. For information, please e-mail SpecialMarkets@ThomasNelson.com.

Scripture quotations are taken from the American Standard Version of the Holy Bible, public domain.

Publisher's note: This novel is a work of fiction. Names, characters, places, and incidents are either products of the author's imagination or used fictitiously. All characters are fictional, and any similarity to people, living or dead, is purely coincidental.

Library of Congress Cataloging-in-Publication Data

Samson, Lisa, 1964–
Resurrection in May / Lisa Samson.
p. cm.
ISBN 978-1-59554-544-2 (soft cover)
1. Young women—Fiction. 2. Older men—Fiction. 3. Death row inmates—Fiction. 4. Intergenerational relations—Fiction. I. Title.
PS3569.A46673R47 2010
813'.54—dc22 2010016055

Printed in the United States of America

10 11 12 13 14 RRD 6 5 4 3 2 1

For Jarrod, pastor of the ether,
cherished friend and soul brother

PART 1

Only a life lived for others
is a life worthwhile.

—Albert Einstein

• I •

Spring 1993

He wasn't sure how he'd got to the far end of his life, or how he'd begun finding himself some mornings driving down to Natural Bridge and ending up on top of the great stone expanse. The vista of the earth far beneath his feet spread out wide, treetops like so much broccoli out in the distance.

Since Claudius was a farmer, everything ended up looking something like a vegetable in his mind. His mother had favored paisley prints, and he always thought of them as summer squashes. Whenever he saw a picture of a flying saucer—pattypan squash. Beads on necklaces, depending upon size, were either peas or cherry tomatoes.

He'd always lived right around this spot of Kentucky. And it was not that his own fields and woods weren't enough anymore, but this vista did something for him he couldn't even voice—he just knew he enjoyed it, the freewheeling breeze, the small pebbles lining the precarious sandstone path with no guardrails, even the tourists who liked to sit on the edge and dangle their feet into that same expanse of nothing but air.

But he'd lived close to the bone of his existence. Sitting on the bridge, he asked God in his usual easygoing way if maybe, now that time had whittled his life down to most likely just a few remaining years, if that same God, who'd always taken good care of him, would speak to him somehow. Other people at church heard directly from the Spirit, but Claudius had only seen the face of God in the world around him. Maybe hearing God would quiet the restlessness in his soul.

He took the words back immediately. For seventy years Claudius couldn't remember a single day he wasn't grateful, and he wasn't going to change that today.

So, he said to the good Lord Jesus, he'd take whatever God was willing to give. No less and no more.

As he slowly drove back home down Route 11, old knees aching from the climb—he sure couldn't do things so easily as he used to—he pulled his white Galaxy over to the shoulder for the hurried modern man or woman to pass along to a life obviously more pressing than his, which was fine with him, by the way. He patted the steering wheel in time to some mountain music on one of those stations lower down the dial. He'd taken good care of his mother's old car for years, driving it around when Violet no longer could, changing the oil and filters regularly, rotating the tires. He'd have made a handy husband had some woman wanted him. Too late for that now.

He realized he'd forgotten to collect yesterday's eggs from the coop; he also realized he'd become nothing more than the old guy people waved to on the street or chatted with at the gas station, but who hadn't had a lot of visitors in the ten years since his mother died.

Well, unless you counted his pastor, but pastors were paid to do that, and Claudius had called him and asked him to come out so he could talk about willing his land to the church once he passed, a little over forty acres, along with the house and the outbuildings. He hadn't had to wait but two hours for that visit to be arranged!

Claudius pulled his car over once more for a man in a battleship gray Taurus, just an undercoat of paint slathered over its panels, and he turned his head to wave a finger or two and nod.

"Ah!" he cried out, realizing someone was crawling up the

road, right in front of him on the verge. He jammed on the brakes, his midsection slamming back against the seat, and oh my Lord in heaven above! He reached in his pocket, then wiped his forehead with a gray bandana.

A young woman crawled along the gravel, her head hung down like an old sick dog's, swaying from side to side. He suspected she didn't even feel the edged gravel pushing into her palms and knees, because she barely realized he was there when he knelt in front of her and placed his pecan-colored hand atop her head.

Finally, when he said, "Whoa there, young miss," she looked up, squinted against even the pale morning sun that caught the gun-metal slick of her eye shadow, and sat back on her haunches.

"Mmm . . . ?" She closed her eyes, swayed, then righted herself. Opening them, she rubbed away long, straight blonde hair matted with throw-up. "You're a light brown man," she said. "And your eyes are so blue." She smiled and swayed again. Too far.

He reached out and righted her and remembered those punching-bag clowns kids used to play with. *Blam* and down they'd go and then they'd pop right back up for more punishment. Like the human race in general.

Well, his mother never had prepared him for this, and he thought about that prayer atop the bridge. He hadn't really asked for this. The girl was packaged in a watermelon-colored dress that had clearly been cut from the vine before it had been allowed to grow all of its skirt—I need to get a TV. Maybe I wouldn't be so shocked by young people.

Then he realized girls were dressed like this all the time in Lexington, where he took his produce to the farmers' market once a week. He just wasn't used to seeing them mid-Monday mornings along Route 11. That was it. A matter of context. He certainly didn't want to think of himself as a judgmental old coot. It wasn't like he didn't know what a hangover felt like. Now that was something a fellow remembered even though many rings had accumulated on the trees in the woods since.

She leaned over and heaved on the roadside grasses.

Claudius wasn't much affected by what bodies did. Or said, for that matter. He pulled out his bandana again from the back pocket of his gray work pants while waiting for her to finish. He'd get her a Coke. A cold bottle of that worked miracles, and there was that liquor store just around the corner. They tried to call it a convenience store, but it was only convenient if you were trying to buy a case of light beer.

When she straightened, he wiped her face. "You look like you've had a rough time of it."

She nodded and moaned softly. Even amid the gravel and the hard night before, the effects thereof sadly evident, he pitied her. So young and lovely, and here she was. Side of the road. In her pretty party dress. Not from around here. Poor thing. Couldn't have been much past twenty years old.

"I'm sorry," she said.

"Let me help you up." He guided her to her feet, his knees feeling that stiffness again. "Come on, I'll get you back to my farm, and you can sleep it off. Then we'll see who you are."

Limply following his lead, she handed him a small purse that had been hanging crosswise over her shoulder, tanned arms and legs putting Claudius in mind of the weeping willow his father planted for his mother when Claudius was only eighteen. She didn't argue, which made sense considering what she was doing in the first place.

—She probably needs to argue with life a little more than she does. Well, don't we all.

It wasn't as if his life had made much of a difference to anybody but his parents. And the animals.

And the land.

There was that, of course.

He helped her into the passenger seat, smelled the sourness of her breath as he buckled her in, thankful for her sake he wouldn't hurt even a garter snake, glad he'd found her before someone else had, someone of dubious intent. He settled her purse next to her then wiped the gravel from her knees and her palms. Maybe he'd sneak in a word or two that she might want to be more careful in the future.

Once at the farmhouse, the bungalow-style place where he was born—just big enough for mother, father, and himself—he led her upstairs to the room the evangelists, traveling preachers come to cause revival once a year, used to stay in when they came to Beattyville. Violet Borne made ample use of her gift of hospitality, which in the early days meant good food and a quiet room with sheets that smelled like the breeze off the Kentucky hills or a little lavender if she went the extra mile.

His stepfather, Garland Borne, possessed the gift of the gab, and many's the time Claudius, sitting there while Garland told jokes to Violet or the traveling preachers, would compare his own light brown skin to the pale Irish complexion of Garland and realize afresh he really wasn't the man's child. The blessing was, most days he forgot. His stepfather was kind, a person who looked you in the eye and listened to every word you said, who could actually make you feel better with a little joke and a glass of overly sweet tea.

He'd sacrificed a lot to marry Violet, who never would tell Claudius, or anybody else for that matter, how he'd come about. And he was her biological son—they had the same facial structure, although once more their skin colors merely coordinated. His was the skin of the walnut, hers its flesh.

After throwing back the yellow quilt and the mint green sheet, Claudius lowered the young woman down onto the mattress—getting her up the stairs hadn't been as easy as it would have been even a few years before. Oh, Lord have mercy on his back. It wasn't giving him too much trouble yet—except when he chopped wood or lifted hay bales—but he couldn't count on that much longer.

He tucked the covers up under her chin, thinking how vulnerable she seemed. Like a little girl wearing her older sister's party dress and the older sister always seemed to take things a little too far and the mother would die if she saw her baby trying to emulate the child she'd been trying and failing to rein in since she was ten years old and realized that boys liked her for some reason. Of course she figured out why by twelve.

"Just keep 'em alive 'til they're twenty-six," he whispered. His father, a church deacon, would pass on this crust of wisdom to parents who sat at his table wringing their hands over their wayward offspring. He hoped somebody had thrown a similar crust to this girl's parents.

Her parents.

He jostled her shoulder. "Do you need me to get word to your home?"

She shook her head and moaned. "Have my own apartment."

"All right. I'll be back in a moment."

He went downstairs to mix up the hangover concoction his mother had made him drink a time or two. A few minutes later he slipped back up the steps, lifted her head off the pillow and cradled it against his upper arm, and made her drink up. She protested a little with screwed-up eyes and a grimace, but he was patient, knowing the ginger would cut the nausea. He settled her back down and wiped her chin with a clean napkin.

She pulled her arm out of the covers and rested it atop the spread.

Interesting. He'd never seen a person with a tan like that. She looked somewhat carrot-colored. Not exactly. But close enough. He wondered if she had some kind of bizarre medical condition. He hoped not. Life was hard enough for young people nowadays. So much simpler when he was young.

Claudius sat in a straight chair until he heard the girl's breathing steady up. He laid his hands atop his thighs for support as he stood.

Her purse. She might be concerned if she woke up. He hurried down to the kitchen and brought it back up, arranging it just so on the seat of the chair so she could see it there right away.

So, the chores needed doing as always. You could always count on the farm giving you something to do. He snapped shut the curtains in the small square window beneath the eaves and stepped softly down the narrow steps and out into the early May sunshine.

His farm spread before him, its faded outbuildings yellow against the electric green of new grass. He'd mow some after taking care of the animals. But maybe not. It might wake her up. That wouldn't be good, to wake a person so sick before she was ready.

At seven that night, figuring ten and a half hours was a good amount to sleep off a hangover, he poked his head in the door. "You up now?" he whispered.

She scooted up a little in the bed, the covers pulled up around her chest and tucked under both arms. "Yes. I don't know what happened."

"Not many people do. Even when they're sober." He chuckled a little. More from nerves, he realized. He hated that about himself. Always had. Put him in a room with a pretty girl and he felt like Bozo the Clown.

"Where am I?"

He told her, edging into the room with a tray, the frayed sleeves of a blue-and-green plaid cotton shirt swinging from his elbows. He'd been needing to do some laundry and was sorry now he'd put it off.

"I'm glad nobody come over that hill and hit you. Lordymercy, them fellers from Lexington come up here in their sports cars and think they're driving Formula One or something."

"Thank you. I don't know what I was thinking, coming all the way out here graduation night."

"Got some chicken soup. Made it fresh. And an aspirin and some sweet tea."

"I'm hungry. I should be sick." Eyes bluer than the periwinkle vines beneath the oak tree out front blinked.

His father had eyes just like them. Light and friendly, not aloof like some blue eyes. A tiny scar ran for a quarter of an inch just below her bottom lip on the right-hand side.

"You probably don't remember getting my surefire hangover-proof concoction before you drifted off."

"Sorry, no. But I appreciate it." She tried to smile, the corners of her mouth pushing up soft cheeks. "It sure beats Tylenol and a big glass of water."

There wasn't anything harsh about her face. No protruding cheekbones crescented beneath her eyes, jaw soft and feminine, almost childlike. She looked like a Hollywood star from his own times, not nowadays, if the bony-faced girls he saw on the magazines at the grocery store were indicative of the fashion. Not that they weren't pretty now. Just not much to his liking.

"It was my mother's recipe. She said her mother made it for my uncle many a time. And I have to admit I tasted it more than once or twice myself when I was a youngster."

She scooted up yet further against the pillows, her dress rumpled beyond any pretense now, its pink creases running in several directions, fabric flattened and folded. Her hair was stuck together in some places, flyaway in others, like a chick that's losing its down while growing its feathers.

—My, how ugly and pitiful those birds look at that stage.

Claudius set the tray on her lap. She grabbed the spoon right away, dipping into the bowl. Her hand shook a little as she raised the spoon to her mouth, then slurped off the soup. She closed her eyes in what appeared to be a kind of relief. "This tastes better than anything I've ever had."

"Food's better when you know who it was laid down its life so's you could live to see another day," he said.

"Is this"—she looked out the window toward the barn—"one of your chickens?"

He nodded. "Parma-Jean."

She sucked the sweet air of the room into her chest. He'd opened the window when he checked on her earlier, releasing the alcohol stink, not to mention the odor of throw-up still clinging to her hair.

"It don't matter none at all." He pulled over the straight chair, hiked up the knees on his green work pants, and sat down nearby. "Parma-Jean was a sweet chicken. A Golden Comet with a right nice-sized comb atop. She was getting to the end of her prime anyways. I always need a better reason than me to send the girls on their way, so in a manner of speaking, your comin' did me a favor."

The sun, on the wane, eased through the old window Claudius knew needed replacing soon, and illuminated half his head, its light showing his lobeless right ear.

The girl noticed, touching her own ear.

He lifted the right side of his mouth. "A dog got me. Dang thing. Run off into the woods and never saw him again. Guess he got a fine meal offa me. Didn't affect my hearing, as you might could suspect."

She spooned up the warm broth, laying a hand on her throat. "It's been a long time since someone's fixed me soup to make me feel better."

"Me too. And there's nothing like it when you're . . . well, a little tender inside."

"But why? Why soup? Why not a turkey bacon club?"

Claudius didn't know.

She reached for one of the hot biscuits dripping with butter he'd churned earlier that day. Well, not *churned* exactly. He always made butter in Violet's old Sunbeam mixer.

The girl sighed as she chewed.

Lordymercy! What did young people eat these days, that chicken soup and a biscuit forced out such a response? He felt a little sorry for her even though her gold jewelry looked real and her hair musta been done at a fancy beauty parlor, because surely that color blonde wasn't God-given.

At least this girl still recognized what was good. You couldn't say that for everybody.

"When I was a little boy I always wished that warm buttery taste would never end," he said.

"I can see why. It's not that I generally use food to comfort me—but maybe your food is magic or something."

"My mother always told me that somebody caring enough to make it made a real difference. She believed intent makes the difference in just about everything."

"My mom says that. Although she always says 'It's the thought that counts.'"

That wasn't exactly what he meant, but no bother.

"Sounds like a wise woman."

"She's a music teacher."

"That so?"

She took another bite, a mannerly bite. "Yep. She has kids coming in and out of the house all day. She grew up going to the symphony, and she took up the violin when she was five. She's really good. She also plays a mean fiddle."

"What does your daddy do?"

"He teaches sociology at UK."

"My daddy graduated from the university. So you're from Lexington?"

"Yes. Born and bred."

"Any brothers or sisters?"

"Nope. Only child."

"Me too."

She set down her spoon. "Advantages and disadvantages, you know?"

"And I'd agree with you."

"My grandparents are all dead, and my parents weren't close with their siblings. Most of them moved out of state after they graduated. I always thought having a big family would be neat."

"I did too. But it was just us around the place."

"We live in my mom's parents' old house. It's too big, but it's been in the family since my grandparents bought it in 1940, and it's hard to let go of that, you know?"

Boy, did he.

While she ate, she asked questions about his farm.

He pulled his bottom lip together between thumb and

forefinger, then let go. "It's just a small farm. Forty acres. I grow food for the farmers' market in Lexington, mostly. Some people here in Beattyville like my tomatoes and such. It doesn't make much, but I don't need but little. Got a milk cow, some chickens for eggs, a goat. Just need to keep the lights on and the belly full."

"Do you have a horse?"

"Just an old mule named Bill. Bill on the Hill. Can't get rid of him, though I probably should. Sentimental value more'n anything. Sometimes I hitch him up to the wagon when I harvest pumpkins. Usually I use the tractor, though."

"Do you grow flowers?" She popped the last bite of biscuit into her mouth.

He pulled on his lip again. "You like flowers?"

She nodded. "I've never grown them, but I used to take pictures of them a lot when I was in high school. I don't know why. It's not like the world needs more flower pictures, but I took them anyway. They just made me happy."

He liked flower pictures. What was wrong with a nice picture of a flower?

"I just grow some marigolds to keep the bugs away. My mother loved flowers, though."

She set down her biscuit and picked up her spoon. "Are you married, Mr. . . ."

"Claudius Borne. Just call me Claudius, though."

"I'm May Seymour."

He laughed. "May come in May." He examined his work-rough hands on his knees, then began to pick his nails clean with his pocketknife. "Naw, I ain't married. Not that I didn't want to be. Seems to me some of the men that would make the best husbands are the most overlooked by the women. And there weren't nothin' I could do about that."

"Here, here," she muttered. "I've overlooked my share. That's college for you."

"And maybe I was too behind the times. Just wanted to stay

on here. Farm, live a simple life. After the war, most the gals had set themselves to moving to Lexington and what not. They say Beattyville's a fine place to be *from*."

She smiled.

"But I'd die in such straits. Now it's a little late to go finding me a wife. And we do fine here, May. I got me a German shepherd, Scout's his name, who's been a fine friend. You got a pet?"

"I do! I love animals. Her name's Girlfriend. A miniature English bulldog. She's probably going crazy back at my apartment."

"Then let's get you back to Lexington, May-May." He never called her hardly anything else after that. "Can't have that Girlfriend messing all over your floors now, can we?"

"Nope." She threw back the covers, straightened her dress, then circled the room with her gaze twice, examining the place.

He hoped she didn't think he had improper designs. It seemed evident to him this wasn't his room, that nobody stayed here regularly amid the wallpaper Mother picked out in the early eighties, with its pink cabbage roses and ribbons in shades of rose and green. The tops of the golden oak furniture held nothing but yellowing doilies beneath old milk-glass vases and lamps with frilled pink shades.

"It's pretty up here."

Nothing had been dropped or cast aside. No mugs or saucers sat forgotten on the downstairs trip to the kitchen, no ball of Kleenex or paper had missed the trash can. And yet, despite the fact it had never really been anybody's room, Claudius cleaned it regularly, the old pine flooring still glowing with the blurred reflection of the windows, the pale green curtains thin and soft and fresh.

Only two dime-store pictures in cheap document frames hung from hooks on the walls—the old mill house and the guardian angel guiding children on a bridge. He'd moved them from his own bedroom downstairs after his mother died. For some reason, he liked the thought of guardian angels.

"I've always loved that picture," May said. "Do you believe in guardian angels, Claudius?"

"I sure do. I even talk to mine, but just one time I'd like the angel to show himself and at least say hello."

"I believe in them too. I used to see mine."

"You did?"

She nodded and turned to a small corner bookshelf holding a few of the fanciful novels he liked to read, like *Scaramouche* and *The Three Musketeers*, their cloth covers dappled with age, their pages golden.

Her back to him felt so decisive, he couldn't ask the follow-up questions: How did you know it was an angel, and what did this angel of yours look like? And then he'd ask, but not until he knew her better, could you see my angel too?

"I like it here." She turned to face him, her arms hugged across her waist.

The girl looked like she could use a round of meals like his mother used to serve.

"It's pretty. And very peaceful."

"It is that."

"I already feel so much better."

"Well, good. I'll get this tray back to the kitchen. You sure you finished? Only one biscuit?"

"My stomach is still a little . . ."

"Say no more."

He backed out of the room with the tray.

As they pulled onto Route 11 just north of Beattyville, May, still hugging her midsection, asked, "What's the name of this farm?"

"Borne's Last Chance."

"I love that! Who named it?"

"My great-grandfather, when he bought it well more than a century ago."

"There's got to be a story behind a name like that."

"Oh, yes indeed. Apparently his family was well-to-do back east. Maryland, they say. And his son, my grandfather, was on his way to bankrupting them if he didn't end up in jail first. So Great-granddaddy Borne found this farm, plunked down the money, then plunked down his son and headed back east quick as he could. They never spoke again, far as I know."

"I see he must have done all right with the place." Her eyes glimmered with hopefulness.

"Naw. He moved on after two years, leaving his new and pregnant wife behind. When my grandmother got notice of his death a few years later, she wrote a letter to my Great-granddaddy Borne and told him everything. The great man arrived two months later with the deed in his hand and a tear in his eye." He turned toward her. "That's how my father always described it. He gave my grandmother the farm and stayed in close touch. No wonder my father was such a good man. How my Great-granddaddy sired my grandfather, now that I don't know."

"It's hard to say with some kids." May rooted around in her little pink purse. "And it can be all mixed up. Like, I'm hardly the perfect girl. I date too much, drink too much, smoke too much, but I just graduated with a 4.0 and I love animals and little kids. People are a little of this and a little of that sometimes."

He passed what might be the slowest woman in the county, at the wheel of a green Gran Torino. "Well, my grandfather seemed to be . . . hardly complex."

"Lucky for him, then." She put some kind of bright blue rubber band on her wrist.

Even from the side he could see a sadness glistening over her eyes, a sheen of exhaustion from trying not to let life get down too deep inside.

"You think so? Lucky?"

"Sure." She turned to face him. "It's like, imagine not really having a conscience. Or caring that other people suffer. Wouldn't that be a great existence?"

Claudius had to admit he didn't do too much that would make other people cringe. But caring about suffering? Well, he was too busy running the farm, he guessed. He *cared*, in his heart, and when the ladies' group at church had a special drive he always helped out, but he didn't think that was the type of caring May was talking about. "Hmm," he said. "What got you thinking about suffering?"

"I'm leaving for a trip to Rwanda soon. Working at a medical mission. Probably an everything mission."

"For how long?"

"A couple of months."

"So you'll be going with a church group or something?"

"Just me. Believe me, I'll just be helping out. I'm no missionary."

The way she said it sounded like she thought being a missionary was a bad thing. But Jesus said to go to the lost, didn't he?

"Then why are you going?"

"Not to force my beliefs on someone, that's for sure."

Oh. "Then what for?"

"Father Isaac needs help in the village. I like kids, and I don't mind pitching in and doing what needs doing."

"I'm sure you'll have a good time."

They continued along in silence, May dozing on and off, then drove down Mountain Parkway, Claudius wondering what Ruthie must have thought when they whizzed by her as she was pulling out of the Shell station near the exit. Honest to goodness, he'd never had a woman as pretty as May in his car, and Ruthie—Sister Ruth as the folks at church called her—had been bugging him for at least thirty years about his marital state. Not that she was up for it herself, but people can always see what's wrong with other people's lives before their own. Ruthie had always been a good friend, the asparagus of friends, planted deep and coming back year after year.

May woke up completely when the rumble strips buzzed as they pulled onto the exit for I-64. She braided her long blonde hair as they drove along, then tied it off with the blue rubber band. She'd brushed as much throw-up out of it as she could when he'd showed her the bathroom before they left. Washed her face, too, and brushed her teeth.

"I hope Girlfriend's okay. She's probably already messed all over my apartment."

"How long you had her?"

"Seven years. My parents gave her to me after I finished up ninth grade."

"You got a dog just for finishing ninth grade?"

"It was a terrible year. I got acne, lost my best friend to the cool group, and was given the model citizenship award, which is the death knell of any chance at popularity. I figured the dog was well deserved. You know something's wrong when your parents think you so unable to make friends, they buy one for you."

He laughed out loud. Seemed May was more introspective than she looked. He glanced over with a reassuring smile every once in a while, and she returned it. He didn't know what to make of her. She seemed sweet and kind, but the way she talked about her life, about boys, well, he just couldn't wrap his mind around it.

"Looks to me like you don't have to worry about being popular now."

"No offense, Claudius, but you've lived on a farm in Beattyville all your life. How could you know what cool is?"

"I get to know all kinds at the Lexington farmers' market."

She raised her eyebrows. "Okay. I'll totally give you that."

"Why, thank you. And I'll take it."

"Let's just say I learned to put on makeup, dye my hair that sorority girl blonde, and not let people get to me."

"That the key to life?"

"For some of us. I'm sorry you never got married," she said as they passed Winchester. "You seem so nice."

"Sometimes it just doesn't happen."

"Well, nowadays it seems that decent men like you are so hard to find. And would I even recognize one? Are they the ones who hang out at the computer lab or work hard in the cafeteria kitchen? Probably. And everybody knows May Seymour has no time for boys like that, little fool that she is."

She must still be a little drunk, or she fancied herself as a modern-day Daisy Buchanan. Claudius shook his head. "Do you always speak so frankly about yourself? Daisy?"

She barked out a laugh. "You got the reference!" She put her hand up, facing him, palm flattened.

He had no idea what to do, so he grabbed it and shook it a little.

She laughed even more. "No, I don't speak like this often. You must have put something magic in that concoction of yours."

"I just have that kind of face. Always have."

"I hope you don't think I'm crazy."

"We're all a little crazy, May-May. The sooner you recognize that about yourself and the rest of the world, the more relaxed and the better off you'll be."

"It's just guys, Claudius. I don't know how to handle them. I don't know when to say yes, when to say no. Who's the right kind of guy, who's not. I have no sense about them, like . . . well, it's like this. There are people with math brains, right? And so math comes easy to them."

"I was one of those."

"Me too. But then there are people who don't have a math brain, right? And you know they'll never ever be sitting next to you in calculus."

"But they might could write a poem better than we could."

"Oh, yeah. True. That's not what I'm saying. No offense to the non-math people at all. I'm just saying that when it comes to guys, I'm like people with no math brain. I just can't get it. Them. Whatever."

He reached out and gave her his hand to shake. "That's me with women. Right there." They shook hands this time, and he chuckled. "Well, at least we both know there's somebody else out there like us. And it sounds like the boys at least like you. I just hope you'll figure it all out better than I did."

"How's that?"

"I ended up living my life on my farm."

"Gotcha. You know, it's still not inconceivable you might find a woman, live a little, go out beyond your borders."

"Oh, May-May! I'm seventy-one years old. I think my time for adventure is done and gone."

She waggled a finger at him. "You never know."

Well, she was right about that. Maybe a woman would come into his life. And maybe his tomatoes would grow to three pounds apiece and his pumpkins as big as a house. That could happen too.

Claudius stayed to make sure she got in okay before he drove away. A young man came to the entryway. Though he felt bad for thinking it, Claudius thought he looked as though he got through all his exams by lucky guesses. He reminded him of the Neanderthal man's good-looking younger brother. Why did women find that animal sort of fellow so attractive? He'd never figure that one out. Maybe May was right about her lack of understanding with men.

With a knit brow and a wave of his sun-browned hand, he pulled away. Scout sat in the backseat, pink tongue swaying. He gave a good-bye yap.

May waved back, then stooped to scoop up Girlfriend. She held the dog's paw and made it wave too.

Such a nice young lady. Too bad men were her Achilles' heel.

"Wouldn't be the first time a woman lacked that sort of judgment," he muttered, turning right onto Rose Street. Then he said to Scout, "This was a pretty good day. What do you say we have ourselves a big time and stop at the Dairy Queen in Clay City?"

Scout looked agreeable, as always. Claudius treated the dog to a couple of burgers while he sat at the picnic table outside the restaurant eating a chili-cheese dog and a side of onion rings. He still enjoyed drinking a cold Coca-Cola from a straw, the cold of the soda, and that slurping sound when he reached the ice.

The lights in the parking lot flickered on, and he realized it was later than he'd thought. Almost nine o'clock.

"Wanna hike to the Bridge and see the world in the dark?"

Then he remembered the park closed at dark. He scratched Scout behind his ears. "I guess we'll leave the fast living to May-May and the young people, right, boy?"

Scout stayed by his side as Claudius tossed the empty containers into the red trash can and walked slowly over the cooling blacktop to the Galaxy, his hands deep in his pockets. "And my knees don't need another one of them climbs today, I suppose."

Scout looked baleful and sympathetic, as if he knew that Claudius was telling the truth of the matter. But he would be too kind a sort to tell his master he was slowing down.

Borne's Last Chance sat silent in the moonlight, the animals at peace, the fields at peace, the trees at peace. Claudius climbed the stairs and looked around the guest room. A shard of moonlight bathed the nightstand next to the bed. It was May-May's room now. He didn't know how he knew that. He just did. He remembered that prayer he'd prayed earlier in the day. He'd said he'd take whatever God wanted to give him. Well, the Lord knew best. Claudius had known that for a good long time.

2

Claudius decided he'd go ahead and get the broccoli planted, since he'd prepared the bed a couple of days before. The seeds had sprouted well under his grow light in the corner of the barn; the young plants looked strong enough to make it out in the wide world. He wondered about May, if she needed more time under the grow light. Though a week had passed since they parted, there wasn't a day went by he didn't think of her and hope she was all right.

"Here we go now, little greens."

He loaded up his old Radio Flyer wagon with the tender sprouts and was just passing by the coop when he heard a car pull up and the driver cut the engine.

Claudius dropped the handle at the sight of May extracting herself from one of those little convertibles that would crush like a ripe plum if it ever got in an accident. "Hey, there!" he hollered, hurrying over.

"Claudius!" She reached into the back of the bright blue car and pulled out a box about the size of two shoeboxes put together. The top was striped with white and gold, the bottom a girly pink. It said *Victoria's Secret* on top. Claudius had no idea who Victoria was or how she expected to keep her secret by advertising it on the lid of a bright cardboard box like that one.

"What kinda car is that? Spiffy little thing."

"A Miata."

Must be one of them Japanese models.

"You must have yourself a good time in that."

"I do."

"How did you find your way back here?"

"I'm one of those people who remembers how to get back to wherever she's been."

"Like a cat."

"Exactly."

"Was never one for cats, but I won't hold that against you." He reached her and took the box from her hands and tucked it beneath his left arm.

"Me either. Dogs all the way."

He pointed to Girlfriend, sitting in the passenger seat. "Bet she enjoyed the ride."

"Uh-huh."

"Cute little thing."

May let the dog out, and it immediately ran up to Claudius, rearing up and placing its paws on his knee.

"Hello there, Miss Girlfriend." He leaned down slightly to scratch the wrinkles over her eyes.

"Isn't she sweet?" May patted the box under Claudius's arm. "I wanted to say thanks."

"For what?"

"Being my knight in shining armor."

He had to laugh at that. "You do have man problems, May-May. Why, I'd think honorable men would be lined up at your door."

—Not like that blond caveman in your apartment, but that's none of my—nevermind.

"Remember what I said about the math brains?"

"Yes, I do. Care for a glass of sweet tea?"

"I'd love it. Then you can open the box inside."

She'd pulled her hair back into a ponytail, and he thought she looked so much nicer in just those simple dungarees and the light yellow UK Wildcats T-shirt. Younger, too, without that makeup running down her face.

He showed her in through the back kitchen door, set the box on the oak hoosier to his right, then got out the pitcher of tea he had chilling in the icebox.

He handed her a glass ringed in shades of red, orange, yellow, and green. The pitcher matched, only it included citrus slices on its surface. His mother had loved that iced tea set, and he recalled the way his father's Adam's apple would bob up and down when he chugged down the tea after an afternoon in the field. He'd hand the glass back to his wife with a sigh and say, "I thank you, Violet, honey."

May took a sip. "This is wonderful. As sweet as can be, and just the way I like it."

"You're such an agreeable sort. If you'll pardon me for saying so, your sensible manners don't seem to add up to the clothes the other day, the fine little car, and the trek up Route 11."

—Or that fellow in your apartment, but that'll slide.

She sighed. "I'd like to think this is the real me. But I don't know for sure. And I got the car secondhand, cheap, with the money I saved up from photography jobs of professors' kids and families and all. It's easy enough to look like you have more than you do if you buy just a few good things and put your nose up high in the air."

He chuckled.

"Anyway, open your box!" Her white teeth flashed in her tanned face.

He lifted up on the white-and-gold lid. Well, goodness. The box was filled with framed photographs. "Did you take these?" He lifted a picture of a park somewhere in the spring, bulb flowers in curved beds striping the view with reds and yellows mostly, some whites as well. "Tulips and white daffodils?"

"Uh-huh. I love spring flowers."

"These are pretty, May-May. You have a real eye."

"I just thought you'd like them, for some reason."

He nodded. "Nothing like the art of nature, even when people help it along a little bit."

About ten frames held photographs of flowers, leaves, close-ups of blooms and their striped veins. "Don't you just appreciate the way a plant works?" he asked.

She laughed. Really laughed. Musical and quite loud. "I do! Stamens and petals. And ovaries. I mean, ovaries? How crazy is that? So, I thought you might like to have these," she continued, and he was glad for it. "A lot of people in the journalism department don't appreciate a picture of a nice flower, not edgy enough, but I thought you'd like them. I'm clearing out my apartment before Rwanda."

"Let's sit out on the porch and you can tell me more about your trip."

He led her to a door to their right and into the bungalow's living room, painted a dark gold and furnished with his mother's old walnut coffee table and side table and an old leather couch.

"My mother loved her pretty things, but before she died there wasn't a butt-worthy seat in this room. A man needs to rest himself after a day's work. I found that couch alongside the road in Lexington one day and strapped it right to the top of my car!"

"I don't have any trouble believing that."

"My mother had the room seafoam green. I just never took a shine to seafoam green."

"Me either. It's a sickly color, like grass green caught a virus somewhere."

He pointed to the wall opposite the kitchen door. "There'd be a fire going over there in that fireplace if it was winter. I heat this place with that, and the woodstove in the kitchen."

"No central heat?"

"Nope. Or air-conditioning. Somehow we survive."

"It must be nice."

He opened the front door, painted a brick red, contrasting with the whitish gray of the stone. Two pine rockers sat side by side, tan wicker seats soaking up the sunshine.

"So tell me about this trip you're going on." He eased himself down. "You said you're not going to be a missionary to the people, so why are you going?"

She began to rock, a quick jiggle of a rock. "I was waiting to hear from a magazine in New York about an internship. I was a journalism major, photography minor. There's still no word, and I can't just sit around doing nothing. The priest at our parish, Father Stan, has a good friend who's a priest in Rwanda. So I'm heading to his mission because, to be honest, I've been all the way through college and I don't know what I want to do anymore. It's like I got it all out of me in school! Like school ruined me!" She laughed nervously.

—Hmmm, sounds incomplete.

"Did that crawl down Route 11 have something to do with that?"

"Big time." She tapped the wide arm of her chair. "But my father told me not to worry; Africa would probably change all that anyway. He says Africa is always a good place to begin a journey."

"When do you leave?"

"The beginning of August. But I've got to get out of Lexington. That boy you saw—"

He wondered if they were living together.

"—and then my parents are going away for the summer. I don't do well by myself. I just don't like it. My mom said I followed her around all the time when I was little. I still do! When I'm home."

"I could use a hand here on the farm until then. How about staying on? Would your parents mind?" He couldn't believe he said it so easily. What was wrong with him? You'd think after seventy-one years—

"They pretty much let me do what I need to do, so long as I don't do anything totally stupid or get arrested or something."

"When can you come?"

She set her drink on the porch boards. "Are you serious, Claudius?"

This was his chance to make a joke of it. But, "I don't know why not," he said.

—So much for that!

"You seem to love flowers, so it stands to reason vegetables won't be much of a stretch. They start out as flowers. And I won't work you too hard. You can walk all over the place and take your pictures. Read a little F. Scott Fitzgerald."

"Wow." She fell back against the back of her chair, sending it into a deep rock. "Wow."

"Aww. I'm sorry, May-May. I mean, why would you want to stay here with some old coot? I don't know what I was thinking."

"No! It's not that. I mean, like, what would really keep me from doing it?"

"The fact that you don't know me much?"

"Maybe." She grinned, raising one foot to rest upon the seat of the chair. "But I'm a journalist, sort of. I know how to find out if you're who you say you are. And let's face it, it sure beats my job hostessing at Buffalo Wild Wings."

He liked her spunk.

"Tell you what, then. You go on home and find out if it's all right to come. Then when you do, how long do you think it'll take you to get back out here?"

"Three days to get everything packed up and stored at my parents'. Will that be okay?"

"Fine by me. I got nowhere to go."

Claudius waved her and Girlfriend off half an hour later, mumbling "My goodness" to himself over and over.

Scout ran up, a dead rabbit in his mouth, dropped it at Claudius's feet, and wagged his tail.

"Good boy. Good boy. Let's go hang up those pictures."

Scout plonked himself by the cold stone fireplace as Claudius carefully measured the frames, then the wall, marking just the right spots for the nail holes, right there above the mantle.

"Just seems right," he said out loud.

3

When she showed up three days later she only had two suitcases, her dog, and a box of books. "I picked these up for you."

Costain, Dumas, and an assortment of other writers of the adventure ilk.

"You don't miss a thing, do you, May-May? You noticed my bookcase, I'll warrant."

"I wish to goodness I did miss things sometimes."

He picked up a book from the bottom. *Tender Is the Night* by F. Scott Fitzgerald. One of the authors with which he departed from his norm. The other one? Evelyn Waugh.

"Well, you just leave your worries right at the door. We got all we need right here." He swept an arm across the barn, the fields, the coop, and finally the house.

She laid a hand on his arm.

He looked down. Her once-perfect, bright pink nail polish was already chipping away. His mother was never much for nail polish. Now, Sister Ruth was another story. Somehow that woman even made yellow look okay on her fingertips. Little sparkly chips too.

May's hand seemed almost childlike, it was so small and soft. Not that she was a small woman. Claudius figured she probably stood a few inches shorter than his mother, maybe five foot six, but no more than that. She sure was thinner! But not angular. Violet Borne never was one to watch her weight, not with all the good food they grew on their farm. And she could cook it too. He'd have to show May his mother's "receipt book" as she had called it, a speckled composition notebook where Violet wrote down her own recipes over the years.

"Thank you for letting me come, Claudius."

"Don't even mention it. Now you just settle in upstairs, and I'll have dinner ready in a couple of hours. Tomorrow you can start helping, but today, just settle in."

He hadn't felt this zingy in a long time. A long time! He figured he'd fry up a chicken, and the arugula was ready to pick—nothing like baby arugula with its buttery-tasting, pale green leaves. There were some potatoes left in the cellar too. Mashed potatoes. Every young person liked mashed potatoes, didn't they? And old people did too. He still could sit down with just a bowlful, butter melting on top, and call it a meal. Salt and pepper. A nice glass of tea.

It was going to be a fair summer. He wouldn't work her too hard. Maybe just hoeing under the weeds and taking care of the chickens. Yes, he'd let her take care of the ladies. He had a feeling she'd like those sweet little gals. Maybe they'd help her forget that caveman in Lexington. He didn't usually take such an immediate dislike to people, but that fellow . . . well, he didn't even say so much as a hello to May when she entered that apartment!

Tomorrow night, maybe they'd have cheese omelets and some of the sausage he'd bartered some eggs for. Oatmeal for breakfast though. He'd been starting off with that for years. It got you through the morning better than anything else.

After he'd slaughtered the chicken, cleaned it, and had it soaking in buttermilk in the fridge, he called up the steps. "May-May? How about letting Girlfriend outside? You think she'd be okay to run around?"

"Let's give it a shot!" she called down.

Soon they were standing in the backyard, both of them with hands jammed deep in the front pockets of their pants, watching Girlfriend, her stocky little sausage body running from bush to bush. Peeing, pooping, having the time of her life.

"Now that one knows how to live!" he said.

"She's like a little kid."

Claudius squeezed his lip. "Well, we'll just hope and pray nothing happens to change that for her."

May sighed and hugged herself, looking at the sky. "If only humans could have a life like that."

Scout watched Girlfriend from a shade tree, and when she found him, he didn't mind.

"Will she go far if I just leave her?"

"I doubt it," Claudius said. "She seems to already think of this as home. What are you going to do with her for the trip?"

"I don't know. I can't afford a kennel for that long. I was hoping one of my friends would volunteer, but so far no go."

"Well, you could just leave her here with us old guys."

"Oh, Claudius, really? That would be wonderful. She'd have a lot more fun here than in somebody's apartment. Thank you."

"Okay, back to the kitchen for me. You settling in all right?"

"Yes, I am. And I love what you did with my photographs. You're so sweet!"

He held open the door for her, feeling his face flush. "Oh, and I'll drive you to the airport if you'd like. Since your parents will be out of the country. The dogs and I would enjoy the trip."

"Thank you. It sure beats having Aiden drive me."

—Aiden? What kind of a name is that?

"That your beau I saw?"

"Yes. That's Aiden. Only he's not my beau. Not even close."

Claudius scratched a circle in the grass with the toe of his shoe.

"You want to ask me what he was doing there, but you're reticent."

"Well, now. You got me there."

"He was a date. That's all. Just a date."

Seemed to him May had a lot of dates. Lucky for her, he guessed. Maybe it beat ending up alone on a farm in the middle of nowhere. Now there were a lot of folks whose shoes he could imagine himself stepping into, but May might as well have been from a foreign land. Then again, the farm had begun feeling a little foreign to him too.

That night, when the chickens had long since settled into piles of feathers at the back of the coop and all sat as still as the rocking chairs on the front porch, he whistled to Scout and headed the Galaxy down the road to the great stone bridge.

The park had closed long before. He shouldn't be there, but he didn't really care. What was the park ranger going to do to an old man like him? Tell him to leave? Well, then, fine. That's what he would do.

Standing in the wind, the trees in darkness, the still pond of the sky above him brimming with lights, he felt his mortality. It was why he stood here, he guessed.

"Why, we live so close to Natural Bridge," Violet Borne used to say, "and we never go up there."

He just didn't want to leave the world without having seen this view as much as the tourists did. That just didn't seem right. It was really their bridge, after all. His and all the people, their families, who'd lived around here for only the Lord knew how many years.

And he felt tall here. Maybe God could see him a little more clearly. He wanted to make sure God remembered him, what he looked like, when he stood on an even higher plane.

It wasn't but the next day after May arrived that Sister Ruth made her presence known. Claudius knew he couldn't escape her eagle eye for too long.

Sister Ruth was a longtime teacher of history and sometimes English at the local high school, and an even longer-time widow. She'd been widowed so long she seemed like a spinster to everyone who hadn't grown up with her. She fancied brightly colored blouses, pressed slacks, and gold jewelry. And though slender, Ruthie was hardly graceful, and when she walked across the wooden floors at church, it sounded like Brother Albert, who was at least four hundred pounds—if he'd been wearing high heels to service, like Sister Ruth always did.

Claudius always wondered who she was trying to impress with those shoes. One time he asked his mother, and she said, "Well, now, honey, sometimes women dress up like that just for themselves."

"Not for the men?"

This was about twenty years ago, and Sister Ruth had just left their house. She'd helped put up tomatoes so she could take some for the winter, and she looked like she was ready for an interview on the television.

"No." Mother set the jars in a wood crate. Her gray hair had escaped its French twist. She always wore her hair like that. When she was a teenager she'd gone to France. But she never told him why.

"She doesn't want the men to find her attractive?"

"Of course she does. She wants men to want her even though she doesn't want them. It's complicated."

—Good thing I never did get married, I guess.

Now Sister Ruth climbed down out of her old red Suburban. She was rehearsing something, Claudius figured, the way she was mumbling to herself.

May was setting the table for a quick lunch of saltines, egg salad, and canned peaches.

"You're my distant cousin," Claudius said as he peered through the window on the kitchen door, pulling aside the lawn curtain barely an inch.

May looked up. "What?"

"Sister Ruth is coming up the walk. I just don't feel like explaining the situation. She goes to my church. We been friends since before there was dirt."

"Uh-huh. Okay. Mom's or Dad's side?"

He pulled at his bottom lip. "Dad's side. They're obscure, remember?"

"Got it."

Sister Ruth's knock vibrated the door.

Claudius let her in. "Mornin', Ruthie."

"Good morning to you, Mr. Borne."

—Oh dear.

She crossed her arms, brown hands with all their gold rings resting on her bloused forearms. The woman sure did like magenta. She looked from Claudius to May and back again, and again, her spine stiffer than a fence post, neck back a little, looking down her nose at the both of them. Her black hair was pulled back into a fake bun she clipped over the nubbin of real hair. Claudius always thought Sister Ruth had long hair, but one day she was slain in the Spirit, threw herself onto the carpeted aisle, and her fake bun got caught on Brother Ben's sleeve button and off it came. She didn't even realize it, which meant she really must have been overcome by the Spirit of God, Claudius always figured.

"I'd like you to meet a cousin of mine. From my father's side of the family. Three times removed. She was doing family research and found us."

He'd never been slain in the Spirit, and he wasn't quite so sure that was a gift from God he wanted anyway. Just the sweet stirrings as he plowed were enough. And he doubted he would even have any more of those with the lies that were flowing from his mouth like milk from Eloise's teat.

"Ohhhh! A *cou*sin!" Sister Ruth threw up her hands and became more like a field of flowers than the briar patch she was when she walked in. "Well, hello there! I'm Ruth Askins."

"May Seymour. Such a pleasure to meet you. Claudius has such wonderful things to say about you." May held out her hand and they shook, once, ladylike.

—She's a smart little thing.

Sister Ruth shot a look at Claudius. "How long are you staying, May? And can I have a glass of your iced tea, Claudius? He does make the best iced tea around."

Claudius busied himself. Thankful.

"Until August. I just graduated from UK." She told the short version of her tale.

Sister Ruth gasped. "Africa! I always wanted to do something like that. Now, isn't Rwanda in a state of unrest?" She narrowed her eyes again. "Should you be going now?"

Claudius handed her the glass. "May-May, Sister Ruth keeps very current with the world."

"I certainly do. I'm a schoolteacher." She sipped her tea, then set it on one of the place mats that had been around that linoleum-topped table since 1972, the year Garland Borne took Violet to Florida for a winter vacation.

That was a big time for them. Avocado green ovals woven from some sort of grass, Claudius didn't know what kind, and *St. Petersburg* embroidered in glossy tan straw. The dye had faded around the edges, leaving a warm tan to match the letters.

He listened for a few moments while the women held a discussion about the Hutus and the Tutsis, and wondered why he never cared for much more than what he had right here on this farm. Their voices settled into a hum in his eardrums as May talked and scratched little Girlfriend's ears as the dog sat in her lap.

Without a word or even a conscious thought, he found his feet drifting out the door and toward the barn to Eloise and her full udder. Old Eloise. There was just something about a big, gentle beast that made you feel comforted. Press his cheek up against her flank, and she might as well have been his armchair in front of the fireplace on a cold night.

May had so much to learn. He did, too, but now, well, it was her time. His was gone, lost in the overturning of earth and the feeding of creation and time passing. Always the time passing and work to be done, or the earth returning to the wild.

He couldn't tell May much about the rest of the world, but he could show her what makes good earth and good animals. And all that good food and sunshine and fresh air and love would do the same for people over in Africa too. He had a feeling what she learned on the farm would stand her in good stead over there.

Over the next few days he wished he was better at carrying on a conversation. His life seemed so humdrum.

They ate entire meals saying only "Pass the salt" or "Would you like a napkin?" He wished he could scratch down inside his mind to unearth good topics for discussion. But she seemed happy enough. They read the evenings away. She'd read bits aloud and so, then, would he. She loved Kurt Vonnegut, and Claudius had to admit the man had a way with humor. He would like to try time traveling like that Billy fella.

But sometimes, usually when they were out working in the field or shoveling out the barn, she'd ask him questions nobody ever had. He chalked up the personal nature of them to the fact that she was naturally curious and a little bit bold. She'd have never been a journalism major if she wasn't.

She asked him if he'd made a lot of mistakes in his youth. He said yes. Did he have a girlfriend? Well, no, not those kinds of mistakes. He was always a little too shy around the women. Why? He couldn't tell you. Did it have to do with his mother? He didn't think so. He was just grateful to her, was all. Wasn't such thankfulness a little extra, though? May was thankful she was born, but that was her mother's choice, not hers. He guessed so, but May, you couldn't understand the sacrifice of my mother and father, raising a little black boy all those years ago.

She had to agree with him there.

Why didn't she give him up for adoption? He didn't know why, he just knew his mother loved to love people and was good at it. She tried to find him girlfriends, but he just never could seem to find his voice around them. May said she knew boys now just like him.

They were sorting seeds in the barn, sitting on a bench near the potting table.

"And you know, the girls at church and school didn't want to marry into a white family. At least I guess that was the case."

"You never know." She sighed, counting out envelopes and laying them on the table. "Well. They missed out."

—But so did I.

"I don't know, Claudius. It just sounds like there was more to it. Did you ever ask your mother about your father?"

"The man who sired me?" He slipped the list of seeds and a pencil from his pocket.

"Yes."

"Write each of these on an envelope," he said. "I did ask her. I even went behind her back and talked to my stepdad. Shoot, I talked to everyone in town who might have known something."

"What did they say?"

"Nothing. Nobody knew anything. Said she went away to college and then came home as pregnant as you please one year, I can't remember which, junior or senior. She never said nothing to anybody. Maybe to my grandmother. But whatever she said was damaging enough to get her kicked out of her home for good."

"You're kidding me!"

"Nope. My grandmother never talked to her again. Her brothers and sisters didn't. Nobody."

"How did your father's family feel about him marrying her?"

"My father was his own man. His family was back east, but I'm sure he wouldn't have needed no approval from them. He was going to do what he was going to do, and if they didn't like it, well, tough luck."

As the conversation ended, the various tomato seeds lay in tiny piles, ready to be started under the grow light next spring. A shadow fell across them from the doorway.

Claudius stood up. "Eli!" He thrust out his hand and shook the visitor's outstretched one.

"Cousin Claudius!"

"You heading out for basic now?"

"Next week."

Claudius pulled May to her feet. "This is my cousin Sassy's son, Eli. He just got out of college, too, and is heading into the army."

May shook his hand.

—Oh, but they look nice together.

Eli had always been a looker—tall, sunny blond hair that curled above his eyes and ears, and those greeny-gold eyes, like a field of grass just as it begins to dry out to hay. And strong.

"He played football for UK," Claudius said.

"You just graduated?" May removed her hand from Eli's large grasp.

"Yes."

The boy reddened. And no wonder. What a cutie that girl was. Claudius didn't blame him.

"Me too."

Eli's major was General Studies. No, he wasn't into anything other than football, and hanging out with his friends.

"I'm surprised I didn't see you there."

"Um, you did." He ran a hand over his hair. "Eli Campbell. St. Patrick's Day?"

Her eyes widened. "Oh." She shot a look at Claudius. "Okay, yes. I remember."

"Well, how nice!" Claudius headed toward the door. "Let's have a glass of tea to honor the reunion of old friends!"

"We'll be right there, Claudius," Eli said. "I just wanna get caught up with May here."

Scout ran up for a good scratch, as did Girlfriend. So Claudius bent down on his haunches just outside the door.

"I'm sorry I didn't remember you," she said. "I mean, I should've."

"We were both drunk," Eli said. "And I never even saw you again on campus. It was one of those things. It's okay."

"Gotta be, right?"

"No hard feelings?" Eli said.

"Of course not. I mean, you know, it's not like I—"

"Me either."

Claudius straightened up and hurried into the house. Things were so different nowadays.

Well, no matter that Eli and May started off under dubious circumstances. People make mistakes, and sometimes, a lot of the times, they actually turn them into something good in the long run. He didn't know if that was virtue or fate. Maybe sometimes it was a little of both, alternating sides of a personality working to and fro. Claudius's mother always said that hate can rest beside love in the same heart, cruelty can hold hands with loyalty and cohabitate with honor. Nobody's singularly good or singularly bad. She said, remember that. It would save him a lot of heartache.

He had to admit he chose to see the good unless shown otherwise.

And what happened between May and Eli's second meeting and when Eli left for basic training was good. Eli figured they were cousins "about twenty times removed," and Claudius didn't know whether or not May set him straight.

It was a beautiful sight, Eli coming over after finishing up work at the garage, eating dinner with them. And that May-May, putting on a pretty dress and sandals for him. Claudius blushed a little himself. He'd never been this close to a budding relationship, and it made him feel a little soft inside too. He thought he might even ask Ruthie to get a bite to eat after church the Sunday before Eli left, but she'd won a few hundred in the lottery—he'd learned not to mention her penchant for the lottery—and had gone off to Lexington to visit a friend for the weekend. So much for that.

That Sunday May and Eli drove into Lexington for a date, dinner, and then maybe a movie or something. He waited up for May until one o'clock, but realized she was an adult, and he wasn't her father.

When she came home the next morning, he was already watering the animals. She waved off Eli, waved to Claudius, then slipped into the house.

He turned off the spigot, figuring she'd sleep the day away.

But no. Surprisingly enough, she reappeared dressed in jeans and a T-shirt, wearing her barn shoes, ready to work, but unwilling to offer up a single explanation.

Things sure were different nowadays.

The day before Eli left, Claudius ventured a conversation as they stirred the compost bins. "So you're sweethearts with Eli, I see. You going to miss him?"

She shook her head. "Not really. Maybe a little. It was just a fun little time, Claudius. But he is a pretty good guy. We just understand each other, is all."

"Oh. I thought maybe you two . . ."

"Were falling in love?" She unearthed a nest of eggs down in the straw. "No. I'm not going to do that right now. There's too much ahead of me."

"I thought people couldn't help themselves. You fall in love, and that's the way it is."

She laughed. "Some people are that way. My mother was. So was my father. Guess it wasn't passed down to me. Maybe my expectations are too high."

"Well, I guess I shouldn't judge. I've never really been in love either. Wait, I jumped to a conclusion. You ever been in love, May-May?"

"Not with anyone that mattered. I have a feeling, actually, I might be too picky. But when I marry, I want it to last for a long, long time!"

"Doesn't everybody?"

"That's the general plan, isn't it? Honestly, though, I just like Eli a lot. And he isn't hard on the eyes either."

And yet, when Eli returned to say good-bye for the final time, she clung to him there in the driveway, just resting her head on his broad chest. Maybe they really were just good friends. Everybody could use a few of them.

Claudius leaned on the hoe and watched as Eli cradled her cheeks in his palms, leaned forward and kissed her forehead, then her mouth. He pulled her to him, and she patted his back.

When he pulled out of the drive, he waved, so did she, and Claudius stood there as mystified as ever.

"May-May!" he called. "How about slicing up some tomatoes and frying some bacon? We'll have BLTs for lunch."

"I'm on it!"

He'd only known the girl for three weeks, and already he was feeling overprotective.

They sat on the back stoop eating ice-cream bars—a Fudgsicle for May, a Creamsicle for him. He loved the way that slightly crispy orange layer surrounded the creamy vanilla ice cream, the way you could smash it up against the roof of your mouth, the way, if it was hot enough and humid enough, it would look, for a split second, like smoke was blowing from your mouth at the beginning of your exhale.

"What I like about Fudgsicles," said May, "is that it's a weird combination of juice popsicle and ice cream, a no-man's-land, sort of."

"I'll grant you that." He nodded. "If it was a beverage, we'd call it a Yoo-hoo."

"Yep. What about your parents? What did they like?"

She asked a lot of questions about his parents.

"Mother liked just the vanilla ice-cream bars, the kind covered with chocolate. Daddy was a Fudgsicle man too."

The dogs sat on the cement walkway leading up to the kitchen door, tongues unfurled.

"I'd sure hate to have all that fur right now," May said.

"Somehow they make it through."

"I think that's one of the things I've learned here. How creatures just adapt to their day. They don't get to turn on the A/C or the heat or whatever. They just have to make do. I guess people used to be like that. Before modern conveniences."

"They sure did. You've been living without air-conditioning this summer, May-May. You've survived."

Just a couple more weeks and May would be leaving.

She gave him a smug smile. "I have, haven't I?"

He nodded.

"See?" She *bapped* him on the leg. "I'm not the softie you thought I was!"

"When did I ever say that?"

"Wait! You didn't! That was me."

They sat and watched the sky deepen from the faded denim blue of the afternoon to something a little more flashy. He liked the way nature turned to gold in the end. Blue skies to gold. Green peppers to gold. Green leaves to gold. And sometimes people did that too. Started out so pinched and immature and then, given the space and the care, spread out to something shimmering and golden.

At least some people, anyway.

"You still want to go on this trip, May-May?"

"Hmm."

"You have to think about it?"

"Oh, I want to go. I'm just trying to think how to explain why."

"Just make a list if you want. No need for prose."

She laughed.

He loved the way she laughed all the time. And sometimes, when she was slicing tomatoes, she smiled even though she didn't realize anybody was watching. Even his mother didn't smile like that. He hoped her parents delighted in her. She deserved that.

She turned the Fudgsicle sideways and sucked that last, stick-clinging bite into her mouth, then set the stick on the walkway.

"Hmm. Okay, so here's one reason. I've never done a big trip like this. I mean, I've seen Europe and stuff, but that was just vacation.

I've lived a pretty sheltered existence, if you want to know the truth. And my dad is a sociologist, so it's not like there's never any discussion around our house about the human condition. But I've never really put myself out there."

"I know what you mean." Yes, he did. Of course, he had different reasons.

"And so, like, before I really go out and get a job and all that, I figure I should see what life can really be like for some people."

"You are going to be a journalist, aren't you?"

She rolled her eyes. "I wanted to work at a fashion magazine."

"You do have a way with your clothes."

Even when doing farmwork, he noticed, she was always, at the very least, color coordinated.

"I love fashion. And it doesn't mean I can't write for a magazine and still do good things on a volunteer basis."

"That's true."

"But it's always good to have a more well-rounded perspective no matter what you do, right?"

"Uh-huh. So it's a self-improvement program of sorts?"

"In a way. But I'd like to think of it as a self-expansion program. I hope there's a part of me that wants to do it for the best of reasons. In any case, I don't have any better place to go."

"So, start where you are."

She leaned down and scratched Girlfriend behind her ears. "Isn't that all any of us can do?"

"I like your honesty. That's a fine start."

"And yet, at the same time, do you remember St. John the Baptist saying about Jesus, 'He must increase, I must decrease'?"

"I sure do." He didn't realize she was religious.

"So, in my expansion, I have to implode too."

He pulled his bottom lip together. "You're going to do just fine, May-May."

"Why do you say that?"

"You understand the importance of a good paradox. I see that all the time here on the farm, death bringing forth life time and time again. A seed is lost in the earth and is found again by the sun and the rain. Maybe you're going to find lost people."

"Maybe I'm going to be found. Maybe the people of the village have more to give to me than I will ever give to them."

He laughed. "You really don't want to be a missionary, do you?"

She leaned forward in her rocking chair, put her arms around him and squeezed. "I'm so glad I met you."

"Me, too, honey. I'm sure going to miss you when you leave."

He washed his face and hands later that night in preparation for bed. While he was throwing his clothes in the hamper, he heard her footfalls through the ceiling, the overhead lamp *clink-clinking*.

· 4 ·

When he dropped her off at the Bluegrass Regional Airport, he figured he knew a little bit about what fathers feel. A heavy heart joined him as he accompanied her to the gate. First she was flying to Charlotte, then to Atlanta, and then to Rwanda. Almost an entire day of travel!

"You'll be exhausted when you get there."

"I know. Father Isaac said he'll pick me up and take me back to the mission where I can sleep as long as I need to."

May was Catholic. "But not a very good one," she'd told him. "I just don't pretend that I am. I've been to church about five times since I graduated from high school."

Claudius didn't know much about the Catholics. Other than they ate vegetables like the rest of Beattyville and they had a nice little church right by the river. His parents would sometimes buy dinner boxes when they sold fish suppers during Lent. Usually whiting, deep-fried to a perfect crisp, homemade coleslaw, and baked beans. And they called that a fast? He had to admit that sounded pretty good to him!

"Good, then. You'll be able to write, I hope. And I'll write you back."

"Okay. Let's write." She laughed and kissed him on the cheek. Her flight was called, and with one of her carefree waves from the middle of the ramp, she was gone.

Scout and Girlfriend waited in the car in the dimness of the airport garage, windows down for air. Claudius pulled out into the sunlight, onto Man O'War Blvd. and finally I-64. Back to Beattyville.

August had just begun.

There were books to read, several titles May had purchased for him at the secondhand store on her afternoon walks into Beattyville, and chickens to feed. A natural bridge made of sandstone from which to view the world he knew so well. He'd thought that world was so small once. But that was a while ago.

~

Claudius grabbed a quick shower after bush-hogging the front two acres and headed over to Cousin Sassy's church in town, his heart heavy. Weddings should be joyful occasions. But this, well now, this didn't seem to be anything but the prophecy of heartbreak and disaster.

Eli, clad in his dress uniform, hurried in through the back door of the church as Claudius pulled his Galaxy into a parking space. The air-conditioning had gone out long ago, and he felt sweaty and large inside his suit.

After taking his seat on the groom's side, after the seating of the mothers, Claudius heard his cousin Sassy in her peach mother-of-the-groom dress bawling her eyes out. Claudius couldn't blame her. Eli was marrying the mayor's no-good daughter. And try as they might to disguise her state of motherhood, even the dim lighting of a candlelit wedding couldn't hide the bulge of the bride's belly or take the edge off the stress on her parents' faces.

It had all just happened so fast.

Claudius thought of May-May over there in Africa, and the three letters she'd already sent. She could write just fine, he realized, reading her vivid tales of the children who followed her around. She always spoke so highly of Father Isaac, how the priest encouraged a sort of awakening of her spirit, and she had been thinking about God for, really, the first time in a lot of years.

Attributing that to Father Isaac, she'd written: *It's powerful when someone's belief reaches all the way to their actions and you're in a state to recognize it. I'm thinking that maybe Jesus was a lot like Father Isaac, only not black, and, according to some of the stories I've been reading in the Gospels, a little more cranky. Or maybe more direct would be a better way to say it. Father Isaac is even nice to the bugs. You might not know about Saint Francis, but Father Isaac is a dead ringer for the man, from what I've been reading. Only Father Isaac is Swazi, not Italian. We even put on plays here with the kids. They love it and so do I.*

She said her parents were still traveling and had even visited her in the village once. *Mom wasn't feeling well. I think the trip's getting to her, but Dad assured me she was going to get a full physical once they return to the States. She hates going to the doctor's. She always has. I'm kind of like that too.*

Claudius could relate.

He asked Sister Ruth about Saint Francis, and she gave him the rundown. "Even a lot of Protestants like that man, Claudius. Sounds like a fellow who'd be hard to hate. You've seen him all the time. On bird baths."

"Oh, the monk with the animals?"

"That's him!"

Now, sitting in the pew at Beattyville Christian Church, Claudius realized he'd raised a ghost of a hope that maybe May and Eli would get together. But then Eli'd gone and gotten Janey pregnant, apparently before he'd reconnected with May. Or maybe he'd been two-timing it between May and Janey. Or maybe he just got drunk and did something stupid with more than stupid consequences. Although he wouldn't put that description on the child itself. That poor thing. Not even born and already behind the eight ball, as the saying went.

He shook his head sadly as they said their vows, promises they had no intention of keeping, promises the mayor and his wife needed to hear because reelection was always just around the corner and even in a town as little as Beattyville, people liked to keep what they worked so hard to obtain. Even at the expense of the lives of their children. If the stories he'd heard were true, that Janey was known for more than just boy troubles. He sure hoped she would sober up now, for the sake of that little baby she was carrying if nothing else.

He saw that fact in the big cars and houses he drove by on his way to the farmers' market in Lexington. He wanted to tell people as they walked by his stall with their kids, the tension twanging, "Your children don't care about those nice clothes you give them. They want times sipping on a cold glass of iced tea or just sitting together in the living room, bored to tears and trying to decide whether or not to play Monopoly for the six thousandth time."

Times came when he was glad not to have had children of his own, not with all the worry that accompanied their presence. He felt bad enough when one of the animals got sick and died. He was already dreading the passing of Scout and felt a little silly about that. That dog would probably outlive him.

No thanks on fatherhood. Definitely not anymore.

—And why are you protesting so much, Claudius?

He was glad May would be gone for a while. Maybe that would get him back on track. He was feeling a little too parental. He realized that one night when he ate a buttered biscuit and began to mist over. May had parents already.

Sister Ruth visited him that night after the small church hall reception of Ale-8 and lime sherbet punch, white cake with vibrant yellow roses, bridge mix, miniature meatballs, and pimento cheese sandwiches. They popped some popcorn and listened to the "Old-Time Radio Hour" that was always broadcast live from the Kentucky Theatre in Lexington. Claudius riffled through the seed catalog as Ruth hooked a small rug, resting over her legs, for the daughter of one of her teacher friends who was getting married.

"You ever regret not having children, Ruthie? Not remarrying?"

She drove the hook into the mesh. "Not really. Especially with all my students. I loved my husband, but I doubt I could have found someone else I loved enough to give up my independence."

Claudius knew Sister Ruth took that verse in Ephesians about wives submitting to their husbands seriously. So, no husband, then. Sister Ruth wasn't capable of living on two sides of one fence.

"Mama and Daddy found the balance, I guess. Nothing like that ever seemed to be an issue. He knew what was important to her, and she knew what was important to him."

"Then they were lucky."

"Or not so bullheaded like you are, Ruthie."

She laughed, then reached for her teacup. "You're right." She sipped. "What about you? Miss having kids?"

"I didn't used to, but then—" Should he admit it?

She threaded a snippet of moss green yarn onto the hook. "May came along, and now you're feeling all fatherly."

"Hmm."

Dulcimer, banjo, bass, and guitar were jangling out a mountain tune from the cream-colored plastic radio. The golden hands on the clock part had stopped for good years before, and black dots threatened to overtake their surface. The Ready Brothers. He did like those fellas.

Sister Ruth laid a hand on his. "Then just enjoy it! She's a special girl, and to tell you the truth, I don't know why. There doesn't seem to be anything particularly amazing about her."

"But there could be!" he cried out, jumping a little in his seat at his own intensity.

"Yes. There could be. I agree. When does she get back?"

"She says she's going to stay awhile now. No use hurrying back, since she hasn't heard from that magazine."

Claudius missed her more than he could say to Sister Ruth. He imagined this was just what fatherhood was like. Wishing they were with you, worrying terribly they wouldn't return, or if they did, they'd be broken beyond anything you could heal or they'd have some no-good in tow who'd give them nothing but heartache, and you nothing but trouble, for years to come.

"You need to be extra attentive to your prayers for May," Sister

Ruth said as she sorted through her wool bag. "The unrest is increasing in Rwanda."

Claudius felt the weave of his stomach tighten. "What's going on?"

"Just the Hutu. Spreading more and more hate about the Tutsi. Convincing people they're not even human and that stomping them out would be like stepping on a cockroach, nothing more. It's complicated."

Like women, Claudius thought.

"There's years of ugliness going on there. The Tutsi, when they were in power years ago, weren't so good to the Hutu either. And believe it or not, it was the Belgians who years ago decided who was Hutu and who was Tutsi. A false delineation that wasn't there before. At least some people say that. It's hard to know the truth from over here."

Claudius felt as if he couldn't hope to understand. He felt tribeless himself, never part of one people or the other.

"Well, it's late," she said, laying down her hook. "I'll tell you more about it tomorrow after church. We should go to Dooley's afterward. In the meantime, you just be praying for that little girl, is all I'm saying."

Claudius promised to step it up. Sometimes prayer was all a man could do.

After he'd washed up the teacups, he took the dogs up the hill and into the woods for a moonlit walk. It wasn't like the climb up to Natural Bridge, but he'd drive over and do that by himself, in the morning, when the sun was rising and the world was just as quiet as it was right then. And it seemed that nothing had really changed after all.

May had mentioned nothing about the tension in Rwanda in her letters. Maybe the news world was just making a bigger deal about it to sell advertising. He'd been told they did things like that.

· 5 ·

August 1993—July 1994

May's first confession in years lasted four hours, due to the fact that she had a good memory—not always a good thing when you're Catholic. But Father Isaac sat there patiently, down at the lake, in a little rowboat so they wouldn't be disturbed. Women washed their clothes at the shoreline, their garments a splash of color against the lush trees behind them. She loved the lake, swimming in the cool waters even when she first arrived during the end of winter.

I feel alive for maybe the first time ever, she'd written to her mother and father.

And yet the tensions were mounting, each day the radio blurting out harsher and harsher invective against the Tutsi. Their village, mostly Tutsi, had already been experiencing hardship, everyone forced to show their cards and declare their race at the school they attended three miles away, being ignored by the Hutu schoolmasters or harshly reprimanded for the smallest infraction.

The two Hutu families in their village were horrified at what was happening, at the radio broadcasts, at the training of militia, boys with machetes and guns, preparing as well. For what? They all could only guess, and their guesses weren't far off the mark.

"We're lucky to be in this village," Father Isaac would say as they huddled around the radio, listening to the mounting hatred. "Our friends would never feel that way about us."

May and Father Isaac, and a dozen or so neighbors, sat in the mission kitchen at night and listened, hate boiling through the mesh grid covering the radio speaker.

"How can they say these things?" she asked him later as they prepared the mission house for the night. She followed him into the kitchen.

He checked the stove, unplugged any appliance. They couldn't afford a fire.

"I do not know. We have no such divisions in Swaziland. You've probably heard talk more like this in your own country."

She clicked off the light and followed him into the gathering hall, where he turned off more lights. "But you grew up near South Africa, didn't you?"

He nodded. "Well spoken. You are right."

They stood in darkness.

"I mean, don't you feel horrible that these are Africans saying it about Africans?"

"Yes."

If she thought racial issues were complicated in the United States, well, they were complicated everywhere.

Maybe she wasn't so surprised at the hate of the Hutu after all.

"You should leave soon," Father Isaac said almost every day, and every day May refused. What did she really have to go home to? She'd been rejected for the internship. Perhaps she'd get a job at the *Lexington Herald-Leader*. Anything seemed better than that.

Then suddenly, the president of Rwanda, a Hutu, was killed. It was all the excuse needed for blood to flow.

The Interahamwe, those calling for the decimation of the Tutsi, began to swarm through the land, locusts eating all in their paths, crunching bones, devouring flesh.

Oh, the prayers she heard that day word got to their village that the Hutu were on the rampage. After months of indoctrination, neighbor was killing neighbor in other towns and villages, the cities too. She prayed prayers of thankfulness they were so remote. Perhaps they'd escape this.

The next day, almost eight months after she'd arrived, blue-helmeted UN soldiers arrived in a dusty Jeep and found her. She wasn't Rwandan, she was a relief worker; they could get her out. But it was now or never.

So far the violence had yet to reach them, but it was coming, they were assured. "Don't think any will escape," the voice on the radio said.

"Believe that," a soldier confirmed.

They could see smoke from the fires in the distance, and relatives from other towns and cities were pouring in for refuge with tales of horror: the dead filling the streets, rape, torture, houses burning. The roads were impassable, Interahamwe patrolling them, out for blood. And now that the fear and bloodlust had spread, neighbor was killing neighbor. "Kill them all, because if you don't they'll turn around and kill you." No Tutsi was safe.

A cousin of her friend Priscilla, who had arrived earlier in the day, said, "A few Hutu are doing the right thing, hiding friends. But it is at their own peril. The Interahamwe are storming houses to find where we are hidden."

The men began to plan, the women to gather food for the inevitable flight. And as the UN Jeep pulled up, they heard gunshots edging closer.

The Hutu among them pledged their allegiance. "We will not kill you."

They all stood in a cluster around the mission well Father Isaac had dug for medical use, fearing the lake water was contaminated. May pictured her backpack on the floor of her bedroom at the mission house. Empty. And no time to pack. No time to make a careful decision. There were but two options.

The children clustered around her. Everyone cried, "Take us! Please!"

The officer barked. "Get in, lady!"

"Can we take more?" she asked. "Father Isaac? What about you?" She turned back to the soldiers. "He's from Swaziland!"

"All right. But get in. Now. We won't be coming back."

She wanted to hate the soldier, but she couldn't. What a hideous job he had.

"I'm not going," said Father Isaac. "I cannot bear to leave my friends now, in their darkest hour."

The soldier rolled his eyes. "Ma'am?"

She looked over at Jeannette, a woman alone, mother of three children, who'd befriended her from the first day. May had listened to her detail her heartache due to a promiscuous husband and desertion. She'd eaten her food and slept on her floor a night or two as well.

Jeannette's eyes brimmed with fear. "Go," she whispered in earnest. "You must!"

"I can't."

"What good will your death do any of us?" Jeannette hissed, her dark, round eyes filled with fear. "Go, May! Go!" Her grip tightened on May's arm as she pressed her forward.

May turned to the officer, knowing she'd rather be dead than disloyal.

"Nobody would ever think less of you for escaping," Father Isaac said. "You've done so much, learned so much. You've grown. What good will your death be?"

She thought of going home, running into her relieved parents' arms, but inside her, a grief and a shame at even entertaining such a thought flared painfully.

"I can't leave. Go on. I'm staying."

The soldier smirked. "Lady, you're a crazy person," he said, Belgian accent thick. "Do you have any idea what's going on?"

"A little."

"You'll die."

"We have faith," Father Isaac said.

"Hope it does you more good than it did the others." The officer nodded to the driver, and they pulled away to the frightened shrieks of the people whose bones seemed to melt inside them.

They all huddled together and wept as the pop of gunfire ricocheted over the green hills.

She'd loved Rwanda so much. It wasn't like the pictures of Africa in books—those long, dusty, parched plains. No. Rwanda was like a jewel, a green, deep gem, lush and filled with life. Down the hill from the mission sat the lake, soaking up the blue of the sky. She thought of splashing there with the children, doing laundry with the women.

She didn't know what she had pictured before arriving in Rwanda. Something more backward. But most of the people were literate, most went to church. And while they didn't have a lot of the modern conveniences, they understood the value of education, of moving forward. Many of the villagers were sacrificing to send their children off to university.

Now they prayed the college kids were safe in their academic enclaves. In the bigger cities it would be easier for them to get out of the country. That's what their families were saying, and May hoped they were right.

That night Father Isaac lit a candle in the kitchen and opened the Bible. The humid darkness settled over their shoulders and down their chairs, flowing onto the dirt floor. Gunshots ricocheted, sounding closer than ever. They were trapped in a womb ready to birth them into a world they had no way of comprehending beforehand.

"You should have gone," he said. "Nobody would have blamed you."

She said nothing. It was done. She was glad, for now that the terror of the inevitable had enveloped her and all possibilities of escape had flown away, she might have jumped in the Jeep. The people in the village had loved her so well. Here she must stay.

The two Hutu families left at Father Isaac's urging. "You will be co-opted to join in. Best to remove yourself from temptation."

Sixteen people piled into a van and a car and headed for the border, hoping to make it into Tanzania without being dragged into the fray.

After praying for their safety, Father Isaac's full lips intoned Psalm 91. "He that dwelleth in the secret place of the Most High shall abide under the shadow of the Almighty. I will say of Jehovah, he is my refuge and my fortress; my God, in whom I trust. For he will deliver thee from the snare of the fowler, and from the deadly pestilence. He will cover thee with his pinions, and under his wings shalt thou take refuge: His truth is a shield and a buckler. Thou shalt not be afraid for the terror by night, nor for the arrow that flieth by day; for the pestilence that walketh in darkness, nor for the destruction that wasteth at noonday . . . There shall no evil befall thee, neither shall any plague come nigh thy tent. For he will give his angels charge over thee, to keep thee in all thy ways. They shall bear thee up in their hands, lest thou dash thy foot against a stone."

They came the next morning, the Interahamwe, a multi-limbed monster with claws of steel. Many of the villagers had joined May and Father Isaac at the mission the night before, and they prayed long into the night that the pestilence of violence wouldn't reach their village. Now the soldiers streamed down the main pathway like a river of machetes and shouts, of gunfire and boots. Most of the village had gathered inside the church, hopeful for some sort of house of refuge, some sanctuary.

Father Isaac began to pray the Our Father and they prayed with him, choking out the words, gagging them out in fear while those who remained outside the walls screamed as they were butchered by people they'd gone to school with, did business with, maybe even loved once upon a time. May huddled with women and children, trying desperately to get her arms around them all, feel the flesh on flesh of them to her, make them one in fear, in pain, in suffering, in death.

—Jesus, help us.

This is sorrow, she realized, acknowledging the ache in her chest. This was not her war, her people, but she was among them, yet not part, not really. This is the ultimate outcome of racial hatred, she thought. This is what that fancy word *genocide* means.

"Why doesn't God step in?" she whispered softly.

Priscilla heard. "Because the evil men must do their evil, so the good men can stop them."

"But you're going to die! Aren't you frightened?"

Priscilla kissed her cheek. "More than words can tell you. But I am ready to see my Jesus."

And the words of prayer rasped on and on. May wouldn't have been surprised if "great drops of blood" had appeared on anyone's forehead. They were going to die. Is this what Jesus felt like, she wondered.

But it didn't matter. The prayers didn't matter and neither did the sacredness of the church walls. With shouts and blood-rage they entered swinging, the machetes growing larger and thirstier with each swing. Limbs were hacked off. Breasts. Ears. Women and girls were dragged outside into the bushes and onto the road. May was one of them. One pair of hands bit into her wrists. One pair pulled up her skirt and ripped off her panties.

When her attacker finished, he reared back and slammed her face with his fist.

The bite of a machete brought her back to consciousness, its edge slicing into her arm, and she prayed she wouldn't lose anything, dear God, don't let them amputate something. Please. She watched a few of the villagers stumble with no arms as they tried to keep living. They soon fell to the ground. She prayed they'd die quickly. Especially the children.

People lay around her in pieces, the thirsty, dry earth drinking the blood that flowed from their wounds. Such dark people. Such bright red blood.

The man whose job it was to kill her was halfhearted about it.

With a rough boot, he kicked the sides of both her knees. She lost consciousness again to the grim bleating of sobs.

May wakened to the darkness and a dog licking her wounds. It was a brown houndish creature who looked as worn and fragile as she felt. Yvette's dog. Yvette ran the village store, a rotund woman who told stories so often she didn't bother to ask if you'd heard them before. The dog whimpered and turned toward the well, displaying a deep gash on his left haunch. Other women, raped as she had been, but shown no mercy, lay beside her, sightless eyes staring out from the pools of blood and flesh their bodies had become.

May shoved back a sob. She crawled toward the mission well where she'd passed the time with her friends, oh, the shooting pains in her arms and legs. The gashes burned and tore with each movement. But she realized having both arms and legs with which to crawl was a miracle.

She drew water, for herself and for the dog, whose name she never could remember. She drank from the bucket, then set it on the ground for the hound.

Somehow she gained her feet, her knees buckling with pain. Back inside the church, moonlight blue through the windows, all was silent. More of her friends lay on the floor, over the benches, strewn like clothing after an earthquake. Oh Jesus, she breathed in deeply, and looked toward the altar.

Bile filled her throat, and she searched for a clear spot to throw up. Nothing. She waited, frantically backing up, but her stomach took the wheel and she ended up spewing on Fabrice, a teenager who had taught her how to make beans. No! Such an insult to that dear girl. Dear Lord, how the shame took root. Her private parts throbbed and ached, the fragile skin torn and abraded. How many had taken her? Thank God she didn't know. Everything was so cloudy.

Were they all dead? So soon? How late was it?

She heard a gasp from the altar.

Father Isaac lay in front of it, clutching the rough tabernacle, holding the Blessed Host to his stomach.

Tears burned as she crawled over bodies toward the man she could call father in more ways than one. A gurgled breath issued from lips that had granted her absolution and taught her how to pray again, lips that had laughed as he told her his stories of hope and humor amid dirt, ashes, and sickness. Hope filled her, then despair when she saw the gashes on his head, the upper half of his right ear sliced clean away, the remainder red with blood.

"Father," she whispered.

"They didn't take it? The Blessed Host?"

He didn't even realize he held the tabernacle in his arms. She was so glad she didn't have to lie.

"No. You still have it."

"I feel numb, May."

"Maybe that's better."

He smiled, baring bloody teeth.

She knelt beside him and gingerly lifted the box from his arms, setting it next to her. Her wounds began to throb with such vigor she gasped.

"Did they cut you too?" he asked.

"Yes." She put his head in her lap, feeling woozy from loss of blood.

"The others?"

She stroked his soft, wooly hair and the dark skin of his cheeks stretched over such high cheekbones. She'd always thought him so beautiful. Everyone did, some saying the love of Christ shone from his face, making him more pleasing to the eye than he would have been normally.

"Everyone else is dead, Father. At least it appears that way."

One hundred and fifty people. Gone.

His last words were silent and wet, and she thought if anybody deserved the martyr's crown it was her dear friend, her spiritual father who dragged her from death to life. They say our tears are kept in a bottle in heaven. But May had to believe some of them were more precious than others.

"Forgive," he mouthed.

She held his hands and laid her head on his chest as his heartbeat slowed further and further. And she whispered to him, thanking him for the good food he made and served with his grand smile, for the prayers of concern he prayed over her, his large hands resting on her head, for the pieces of candy that magically appeared on her nightstand in the mission house. She sang the songs he taught her, songs about Jesus, his great love, his tender care.

When Father Isaac's final breath was taken, she stayed still for as long as she could, until his body began to grow cold. It might have been hours. She gently laid his head on the floor and crawled to the cabinet holding the altar cloths, the only clean cloth she could think of. She ripped them into strips and tied them around the gashes on her arms.

"Let me live."

May tried to do things decently.

The book of the Gospels and the prayer book Father Isaac used during Mass—she didn't know what those books were really called—were missing. So she rummaged through Father Isaac's study and found his Bible, the onionskin pages worn thin, the sides tarnished with years of use among the villagers. But she couldn't find his personal prayer book.

They all deserved a Christian burial, didn't they? They'd loved Christ, built a faith on him, and no wonder, with a man like Father Isaac to show the way. She'd have to wait until nighttime to do it, but she'd try. If she had to do it on her own, she would.

In the mission house she waited, having drawn a bit more water from the well, as the night thickened, hoping the Interahamwe wouldn't return. She knew better than to pray they wouldn't.

Had she been duped?

She found large tubes of antibiotic ointment in the infirmary and some gauze bandages. She shoved them into her backpack. She was smart enough to realize then she needed to keep it with her like a diabetic would keep his insulin.

She cleaned the gashes on her arms. Nine in all. Four on her right arm, five on her left. The water sluiced away the dirt, dragging the particles away, lighting a fire on her nerves where the gashes went deep. With needle and thread she stitched the three most profound wounds together, shaking with the pain. But she persisted. Yes, she'd asked God to let her live, but she wasn't sure he'd heard her. Best to do what she could.

"Oh, Father Isaac," she whispered, thinking how sad her thoughts would make him. Yet he would understand. She knew that too. When news that his mother and his sister, the last of his family, had perished with AIDS, she'd held his hand as he wept.

"The Lord giveth and the Lord taketh away, blessed be the name of the Lord," he had whispered over and over through his sorrow.

"But it's so horrible," she'd said. "How can you stand it?"

"Someday all this will be over, May. All will be made new. It is the only hope I have at times like this."

"You really believe this?"

He'd smiled through his tears. "If I don't, I'm greatly mistaken about my vocation."

Sitting on her bed, she dabbed the ointment on her wounds, then wrapped them. She looked like a mummy. She felt like one.

—I want to go home. I want to go back to Borne's Last Chance. I want to go home.

The hound dog jumped on the bed and threw himself next to her, and she slipped her fingers into the matted fur atop his head as he lay on her thigh with that guttural, doggy sigh. She dozed.

The sun rose and set, and she clothed herself in a pair of jeans and a long-sleeved shirt to keep the bandages together. Barely able to bend her knees, stiffened and bruised from those booted kicks, she began her task nevertheless, slipping into the tool closet in the mission house and finding a shovel. How deep should she bury them? She'd never be able to bury a hundred and fifty people six feet under. Would it be all right if she put several in one grave? Families together? The widows in one place? What about the orphans? She'd bury them with Father Isaac. That seemed right.

She hobbled behind the church and began to dig under a tree in the spot where Father Isaac taught the kids each Sunday before Mass when the weather was fine. She lifted the spade, slammed it into the ground, and cried out in pain, gasping as the wounds, the healing serum they exuded having dried, split open again. For fifteen minutes she repeated her actions, lifting the spade, slamming it to the ground, and she made almost no progress. Only divots, small crescents of earth showed any evidence of her work.

She fell down onto the dirt. "I can't do this," she sobbed.

Voices of the dead whispered in her ears. She ground her palms against her ears, but they remained.

Get used to it, she told herself.

Leaving the shovel to lie where it had fallen from her grip, she hobbled back inside the church and fell asleep next to Father Isaac's corpse.

The next morning they came back, rolling through the village with shouts. Fear, coiled for the night inside her stomach, sprang forward, and May grabbed Father Isaac by his shirtsleeves. She rolled his body on top of her, his face resting on her own. Thankfully, she'd closed his eyes the night before.

—Don't breathe. Don't breathe.

The soldiers came through, kicking bodies, kicking, kicking their way to the front.

—Please. Please.

Barely breathing, she lay with eyes closed, thankful for Father Isaac's head atop her face. They couldn't really get a good look at her that way. Right?

Two of the men joked in their language. "That blonde one might be just as good dead," said one.

"You are a sick man."

"Come, come. What can it hurt? She's dead."

How could she do this? She'd be warm inside. She could lie as unresponsive as possible, but how could she fake rigor mortis? If he lifted her up, he'd know she was alive.

He stood over her and Father Isaac, and May swore she could feel the weight of his shadow as it blocked the sun coming through the round window over the altar.

He *tsked* and ran his boot along her thigh. "Such a shame. You should never have come to Rwanda." Then he leaned down, his mouth next to her ear. "We didn't need you then. Nobody needs you here now."

The voice sounded so familiar. Emmanuel, one of the deliverymen from nearby who'd drop off Yvette's wares to her store? May wasn't sure. She thought so. He'd always been friendly, if a little reserved, but that was the way of some of the Hutu.

Did he know she was alive? And was there some shred of humanness left that felt sorry for the lack of life all around?

She'd never know. But he walked away.

She opened her eyes to a slit. Yes. It was Emmanuel.

When night fell, May decided to try another tack. There was no way, in her current state or even in a healthy one, she could bury the village. She had only two options.

Not knowing if it was something at which the Church would cringe, she felt sure God would give her a pass considering the circumstances. She deserved that. The only other option was to let the bodies rot. She knew deep in her core that wasn't right. These were her grandmothers and grandfathers, her children, her aunts and uncles, cousins and friends. In a village that size, there wasn't one person whose name she did not know, who did not know hers.

She'd laughed with most of them as she learned their language, cried with some as they shared their sorrows, eaten with all.

And so, at the foot of the altar, she piled their bodies side by side like lumber across the front of the church, two deep, then arranged them down the aisle. She grunted, dragging them into position, sweat covering her skin and soaking into her clothing, running down her face and back. She pulled the fifty or so bodies outside indoors. She tried to match up the right limbs with the right bodies, like some grisly puzzle, but it was so difficult unless there was a ring, a bracelet, she recognized. She wept over feet and hands and arms and kept saying, "I'm sorry. I'm so sorry. I wish I could do this right. But I can't. I just can't."

She laid those limbs she did not recognize beneath the altar. She was so sorry.

And though she didn't realize it as she arranged them, when she stood at the back of the church she saw they made up a cross, Father Isaac at the head like a crown of thorns.

As the sun began to rise, she lit a candle and lifted the bowl of holy water from its cradle on the wall by the front door of the church. With a branch from a bush outside, she sprinkled the water over the cruciform of bodies and said the Agnus Dei over and over again.

Lamb of God, you take away the sin of the world.
Have mercy on us.
Lamb of God, you take away the sin of the world.
Have mercy on us.
Lamb of God, you take away the sin of the world.
Grant us peace.

Over and over, candle in hand, making sure she recognized each body for the precious friend it had been, hoping her feelings were wrong, and this wasn't all for nothing, that as Father Isaac liked to say, "In our flesh we'll see God."

And then, oil. She should do something with the oil. In the cabinet to the side of the altar, she found the vial Father Isaac used when anointing the sick, something they did a lot around the village. She loved accompanying him. People felt so loved and cared for, just because of a little oil, a thumb, and Father Isaac's smile and kind words.

She repeated the process of recognizing each person, swiping a cross of oil on each head with her own thumb and saying, "In the name of the Father, the Son, and the Holy Spirit, may you rest in peace."

May figured any bishop worth his salt would shudder at her feeble attempt at a sacrament. But obviously, with what had happened earlier, God wasn't much worried about people anyway, so what could it hurt?

Someone might come back soon. Or not, now that they thought the people were all dead. But she couldn't be certain. And they couldn't either. They would figure some might have fled into the woods. Maybe some did. It was so hard to think about who might be missing. Perhaps some people got away, trying to make it for the border. She hoped so.

The morning sun had crept over the horizon, and fear crawled beneath her scalp, but still she moved on, stumbling among them, waving away flies, making crosses, making crosses.

Finally she was done. Exhaustion overtook her to such a degree, she didn't know if she could continue. Too tired to go back to the mission house, May slid the ointment out of her pocket, pulled off her shirt, and rebandaged her wounds with the rest of the altar cloth. She sat for a while next to Father Isaac. Not planning to, however, she fell asleep and woke up as the sun was setting.

Awoke with a start to the sound of gunshots.

"Oh!"

Her breaths racked her torso.

She balled her hands into fists and summoned the remaining kernel of her will. There. There, now. And she stood.

She removed Father Isaac's red stole from the closet where he hung his vestments, the stole for use on martyrs' feast days, folded it, and tucked it into the waistband of her jeans.

The crucifix, heavy and of thick wood, came down next. And she felt almost like a Roman soldier as she lifted it off its peg, its weight slamming against her chest, a pain ripping through her heart. Is this how Jesus felt? Arms lacerated from the whip? The thought comforted her, oddly enough.

She couldn't hold it, so she placed the cross beam over her shoulder and dragged it behind her to the mission house, the arms of the corpus digging into her shoulder blade. She wondered where to place it and eventually decided to put the crucifix against the wall in the room where they used to teach school and gather to feast. She placed the stole on the small table next to Father Isaac's bed.

She siphoned the gasoline out of the mission's decrepit Rover. Soon a bucket was full, and she lugged it into the church, careful not to let much slosh over the side. Oh, how her wound-ribboned arms smarted and ached down to the bone. By this time May felt like she had dragged the entire world behind her. And the world was pitiful, and it was dead.

She wondered what would be best. Pour the gasoline directly on the bodies, or on the benches and hope it would spread?

Well, the purpose was to keep them from rotting any further. Out of respect for her friends she never would describe the stench. She never did know how she managed what she did.

May decided to pour the gasoline right onto their clothing.

The first bucket took care of the crossbeam of bodies. The second bucket covered the support beam, the limbs, and Father Isaac. She fell to the floor beside him and wept, feeling so full yet so empty, the fumes of the petrol eating at the lining of her nose, but she couldn't move.

Yet in my flesh I shall see God, he seemed to say. *It's all right, May. Be at peace.*

"It's too much to ask," she muttered.

By the time she grabbed the long matchsticks they used to light the gas stove in the mission kitchen, the stars pricked through the fabric of the night to look down. May was glad for the company. Her grandfather showed her some constellations when she was young, and she'd long forgotten their names, save one, the galaxy Andromeda, but they'd remained the same and that was all that seemed to matter.

Standing at the door of the sanctuary that had once lived up to its name so grandly with Father Isaac around to give it credence, she saw it for what it was: a giant, rough-hewn, wooden tomb. She couldn't have known then what was happening all over the country; that people were being burned alive in churches.

"Imagine my thinking it couldn't get any worse than what was happening in our village," she said later. "Ours was very typical."

She'd removed the crucifix, the chalice, the patens, the tabernacle. Even the souls of the people that made up the Body of Christ were gone. It was a crematory, an indoor funeral pyre, yes.

She struck the first match and set it on Father Isaac's chest. She couldn't watch it take root, so turning, she struck the second match at the end of the right crossbeam, igniting the bright green and yellow dress of the first woman she'd called Grandmother, a widow who had cared for her grandchildren upon the death of their mother, her daughter. Third, upon the shirt of the old grandfather who cooked meat in honor of her arrival the summer before. Finally at the foot, she set the burning match to her friend Jeannette, the woman with three children whose bodies were arranged on either side of her, whom she'd gossiped with late into the night.

She allowed some sort of coping anesthetic to soak into the fibers of her brain, heart, and soul, and the part of her that sat in journalism classes rose to the surface and she thought, *Who ever gets to see a sight such as this*?

When her story came out years later, people criticized her for thinking like this, but every writer who wrote to her said they sympathized, pausing to remember their exact feelings as they stood over the bodies of dead loved ones, so that someday they could use the memory to write realistically.

She stood at the door watching as flames spread, eating up disease and pain and death. An all-consuming fire.

Our Father who art in heaven, hallowed be thy name.

Up the aisle the flame ran.

Thy Kingdom come, thy will be done.

Over the cross beam to meet in the middle.

On earth as it is in heaven.

Father Isaac, already a ball of fire.

Who could forgive this? she asked of him.

And she could say no more. It was enough, and it would never be enough, because if this was kingdom come, it didn't seem better than anything else. It was worse.

May subsisted on whatever she could find. She didn't want to risk making a cooking fire, so she ate raw fruits and vegetables, bananas mostly, sweet potatoes, beans and peas from household gardens. Some days she didn't eat at all.

And now, so much death. And the fear! It never left, following her around during the day and crawling in with her at night in the mission house where she slept under Father Isaac's bed. The closest she came to praying was to ask him, "If you can see me, put in a good word."

And no offense to the hound who was still hanging around, and she was thankful for him, but having her own dog's warm body with her, kissing Girlfriend's wrinkled face, would have made bearable this storm in which no cloud break cottoned the horizon.

During the first week of May, after the church had burned, they came back, said, "No bodies left in the road. Somebody did this. They can't be far."

She managed to hide in the bushes, her backpack hastily packed with Father Isaac's stole, bandages, all the ointment she could find, and some clean underwear. Fear that the dog would give her away bit at her straining muscles as she squatted in the foliage.

They searched every home, the mission house, and for spite,

burned every structure in the village to the ground. Now May had no shelter.

The murdering swarm continued for another two months and so did May, though she never knew how. Some of her wounds festered, and she tried as best she could to cleanse them with the water from the well, each dab and wipe excruciating. Only the antibiotic ointment kept them from killing her, she supposed. She didn't know much about that sort of thing, she just faithfully dabbed it on. Some of the slashes had closed up, she noted with a sort of satisfaction. While everything around her was in decay, it was good to know her body could still heal.

There were times she looked at the charred remains of the church, pictured those once inside, and thought how lucky they'd been to have been burned *after* they were dead.

Day ran into day. Night into night. Nights were the most excruciating, every sound magnified in anticipation of their return.

She slept amid the trees, the backpack under her cheek, Father Isaac's stole pillowing her head a little more. Shivering in the evening coolness, only the clothes on her body for covering, and soon they would be tatters. May clung to the memories of the people who had died, telling herself over and over again it was all worth it, to have known them, to have loved them. Some days she convinced herself of this. Others, well, she couldn't no matter how hard she tried.

And the days walked, bringing the nights along on their backs, and May lost count. But she figured several months had passed.

When she heard a motor coming closer one day, which turned out to be early July, she realized this was her chance to end this all formally. Emaciated, infected, aware of the definition of the word *weary* as only a woman in prolonged childbirth understands the word, May stood by the well, arms crossed. It didn't matter what they did to her, it couldn't be worse than it already was. She was ready. She just hoped it would be quick. No more rape. Just a quick chop to the neck and it all would be over.

The roar of the engine and the jangle of the shocks on the pitted roads grew louder, her heart raced, and she broke out in a sweat. There was still time to run—the thought raced through her brain, but her weariness won the contest. Because she had no fight left. There was only one way out of this.

—So be it. You wanted to know what your life should be about, May? Maybe it's about getting to the end and not caring whether you live or die.

Did she have to go through all this to get here, to this, this nothing?

Something whooshed out of her, from the top of her brain, traveling down the length of her spine, her thighs, her knees, her calves, her ankles, and through her toes.

She began to laugh, hugging her sides, as she leaned against the well and slid down, her bottom behind her heels. Wasn't life a trip? Try to do something good and end up worse off than when you were partying and ignoring God at all costs?—Yep, kill me now. You want me to pray, God? How about that? Let me die.

Once again her unspoken hopes fell on deaf ears.

The Jeep came into view, and she saw that the driver and his companion wore the blue helmets of UN troops. She was safe. More or less.

• 6 •

August 1994

Sister Ruth knew before anybody else in Beattyville that the unrest in Rwanda had boiled over in April. They'd prayed every night. And every day, no word from May. Claudius made each action, each breath, a prayer, dedicating it to May's safety. But as the months passed, with no letter or phone call, he began to give up hope. The folks at Harmony Baptist supported him as best they could, but after a while people just didn't know how to keep up the same level of intense concern. So while his fears escalated, their actions waned. It couldn't be helped.

Except for Sister Ruth. She came over every day with reports. None of them encouraging.

"She stayed," he said to Ruth. "I can just feel it."

"Let's hope she was smart enough to get out while there was time."

And while Claudius crossed his fingers, he knew if May had escaped, she would have contacted him.

They held their breath for three months, then four, until he could take it no longer. He and Ruth sat in his living room after Sunday night church, drinking coffee and worrying. "It's been over for a month now. Surely she'd be back by now. We should try and find her parents," he said. "He's a sociology professor at UK."

"I'm on it," Ruth said. "There can only be one sociology professor named Seymour there."

She returned around noon the next day, set her purse on the hoosier, and set the kettle on the boil. "Well, she's home."

Claudius didn't realize how tightly he'd been strung until all the cords of his muscles loosened at once. He grabbed a chair back for support.

Ruth continued. "She was in bad shape, machete wounds on her arms. She was in a hospital in Kenya for a week and then was transported back home. She's been resting there for about three weeks now, and they're getting her into therapy. You can imagine."

He couldn't.

"Is she eating?"

—Now why ask that, Claudius?

He couldn't think of anything else to say. Machete wounds? Lordymercy. Lord have mercy.

"I didn't think to ask that," said Ruth, turning to slide two teacups out of the cupboard. "But he said she won't talk about it. So they don't know the details. Just that she was by herself in that village for three months."

"Oh my, Ruth."

"I know, Claudius. That poor little thing."

"We should go see her."

Ruth shook her head. "Not yet. I asked. Dr. Seymour said he'd phone when she's ready to receive callers."

Claudius walked out of the kitchen into the yard. He circled around and around the chicken coop. Didn't know what else to do.

A week later a lean man with a gray ponytail, dressed in climber's shorts and a gray T-shirt, knocked on his front door.

"Mr. Borne, I'm Michael Seymour. May's father."

Claudius threw the door open wide. "Come in, come in."

He sat Dr. Seymour on the leather couch, then perched himself in his easy chair. It seemed dim in the room, the skies outside promising rain. A downpour soon, if he had to hazard a guess.

"How's May?"

"Not doing well." He rubbed his palms over his thighs. "She's refusing to say anything in her therapy sessions. It's almost like she's made of stone."

"I'm sure it will take awhile."

"She found one of her old school friends, and she's been going out and drinking a lot, getting home late, two or three in the morning."

Claudius nodded. "Stands to reason."

"It does. But she can't go on this way."

"No. I'd guess not."

"She talks about you a lot, though."

His heart jumped. "Is that so?"

"She wants to come here."

"Oh, my!" Indeed.

"I think a setting like this would be better than Lexington and her old haunts. She was a little . . . untamed."

"I gathered that a bit."

"We spoiled her. Only child. My wife had to have a hysterectomy after she was born. I guess we let her get away with too much."

Claudius knew nothing about parenting, what was too much, what was too little. But he knew a little about May. "I imagine it would be hard to say no to that face."

Dr. Seymour smiled.

"And I can't say no, either," Claudius said. "When you going to bring her?"

"I came to ask you first. How about Wednesday?"

It was Monday.

"We'll be ready."

He wouldn't have recognized her if he'd seen her on the street. Dowel thin, her skin stretched over her cheekbones like a latex glove over the knuckles of a fist, she tried to smile when he hurried across the driveway to Michael Seymour's old station wagon.

"May-May!"

She raised a hand, and when he pulled her into his arms, she went limp and whispered, "Oh, Claudius!"

"Now, now, May-May, I'm here. It will all be all right."

Tears filled Michael's eyes as they met Claudius's gaze over May's shoulder. "I'll get her suitcase," he said.

He opened the hatchback and pulled out a bright pink rolling suitcase, a glaring shade of the old May, not this colorless child in his arms.

"Let's get inside," Claudius said, hating to pull back.

The two o'clock sun shone hot, as it always did in mid-August. It would feel better inside.

Michael followed them into the house, gently setting the suitcase by the bottom of the stairs.

"Can I get you something to drink?" Claudius asked, always mindful of the manners Violet taught him.

May shook her head.

Michael stuffed his hands in his pockets, a fatherly defeat written all over his face, the words *I tried* seeming to come from his eyes and the words *I failed* just on their tail.

An awkward silence filled the space between them.

"Well, I guess I'd better go, then," Michael said, running a hand over his head. "Elisabeth—my wife—has a doctor's appointment at four."

"I'll take care of her." Claudius laid a hand on May's shoulder.

"Thank you." Her father turned May to face him. "You going to be okay, shug?"

She nodded, whispering, "Yes."

They said their good-byes, Claudius's heart breaking for the two of them. For himself a little too. He and May watched her dad turn around at the end of the drive and pull away.

"You want to rest?" he asked.

"More than anything."

"Let's get you up to your room, then." He grabbed the handle of the suitcase. She took his arm, and they climbed the narrow, steep stairs together.

At the top she stopped and rested her head on his shoulder. "I'm so tired, Claudius."

"I know, honey. But we've got nothing but time."

He turned down the bed as she found a T-shirt in her suitcase. "You sure you wouldn't rather be home?"

She shook her head. "My mom is sick. She doesn't need this."

"Your father seems like a good man."

"He is. He doesn't deserve this either. He was trying so hard. But I just need to be, Claudius. To rest in peace."

"You can do that here, honey."

Poor baby. He left the room.

Checking on her an hour later, he found her resting on her side, back toward the door. She'd been wearing a long-sleeved shirt and pants upon her arrival, but she'd taken off the shirt, just a yellow T-shirt now, and her arm rested atop the light summer blanket. He ventured forward.

Lordymercy. He thought he might have whispered the word. But then, some prayers go beyond sound and straight to the heart of God. The sleek red lines on her arm were just memories of something gone deeper in, and the skin in-between was still puffed, as if someone had stuffed her arm a little too much with down feathers. Gone were the sculpted lines. He knew her arms were, in some manner, ugly, deformed not so much from appearance as from the intent of those who wounded her. And he felt sad, because he knew women well enough to know she'd never bare those arms in public again. Maybe to the sun. When she was alone. Maybe then.

In the kitchen Claudius slid his mother's old remedy book from a shelf on the hoosier near the door. He'd never concocted her ointment himself. Didn't really have those herbs growing. But he'd find them somewhere, even if he had to drive to Lexington or, heaven help him, Cincinnati. He'd been there once, on a class trip when he was fourteen, and he'd prayed to God he'd never have to go back. So far God had proved himself faithful!

His little freezer was full of dinners, thanks to Sister Ruth, who had made herself useful from the moment he told her May was coming home. No need to kill one of the ladies. Although Frances was ready to go. If he didn't take her soon, she wouldn't even be good for jerky. Maybe she already was jerky, come to think of it. He smiled.

—Okay, let's find those herbs.

Thursday afternoon, May having slept through the last evening and into the night and still not having risen, Claudius expressed his concern to Ruth, who'd come to keep vigil with him.

"She'll be fine," Ruth assured him from her seat in his living room, her lap hidden under another rug she was hooking.

So he piled Scout and Girlfriend in the Galaxy, and off they went to Imogene Meyer's herb farm near Lexington, on a perfectly decent Thursday afternoon too.

May slept on. Through that evening and into the night.

He checked on her every few hours just to make sure she was still breathing.

Friday morning he received a letter from the cardiologist in Lexington. He'd had a spell a few weeks ago, liked to have died he was in so much pain. Claudius had never felt anything like that before, nausea, pain just beneath his rib cage, and the sweat! So he did some tests. Ran around all day with something hanging around his neck. Oh, he really didn't want to remember it all. He never did trust doctors.

The letter held good news, mostly. His heart was fine, but he had a medical condition called Wolff-Parkinson-White syndrome. It wasn't even bad enough to be medicated, and if he ever needed a surgical procedure, it would most likely be outpatient.

Tucked into the envelope, a folded handout was ready to tell him all he needed to know. He tucked it into his pocket and headed over to Ruthie's. She'd make heads and tails of it in half the time it would take him.

"Well, as near as I can tell, it's an electrical problem." She removed her reading glasses and set them on her glass-topped kitchen table.

Ruthie kept up on fashions. He liked the mustard yellow walls of her kitchen and the bouquet of sunflowers in the middle of the table. He'd grow some of those come spring too. May-May seemed the type to enjoy the sight of a sunflower.

"What's that mean?"

"It means the electrical impulses in your heart get stuck and go round and round in one chamber, sort of, your heart speeds up to the point you can't even hear a beat, and if it's bad enough and you can't get to the hospital in time—" She ran a pointed index finger across her neck and emitted a sound like *crrrreeeek*.

"Lordymercy!"

"The good news is, the chance of that happening is slim to none."

He squeezed his bottom lip. "Well, that's a relief." He'd always had more than his fair share of good luck.

He checked on May around ten, as soon as he returned, and she looked about to stir. Her breathing had changed, and so he figured the smell of good country cooking would finish the job.

Hiking up his pants, he tried to think about what he'd like had he gone through all she did, including the heavy drinking in Lexington. Something salty and substantial.

He gathered the day's eggs, snipped a couple of ripe tomatoes off the plants, just beefsteaks, nothing fancy. His customers loved his heirloom tomatoes, so he left those alone. Back in the kitchen, he pulled from the Frigidaire a plastic bag of loose sausage one of his neighbors brought by in exchange for some of his yellow tomatoes. A good trade. Her sausage had just the right kick without setting a person's mouth on fire. Claudius really wasn't one for highly spiced food. Another reason it was good he never traveled afar, he figured.

He was laying the final fried tomato, the cornmeal crisp and browned, on a napkin-covered plate when she came into the kitchen.

"May-May!"

She had changed back into her jeans and long-sleeved shirt. "Good morning."

As much as the sight of her scars had grieved him, it was the tone of her voice that sent an arrow right into his heart. The life in it wasn't exactly gone, May was too strong-willed for that. But the liveliness, the way her tones sometimes sounded like music more than speech, was missing. In its place? Something dry and quiet, as if the creek had dwindled down to a trickle in its bed.

Beside her plate he placed a little earthenware jar filled with the whitish goop he'd spent the past couple of days working on.

"What's that?"

"My mother's recipe. For scars and whatnot."

"You saw them?" Her eyes darted from tomato to sausage patty and back again. Then they met his.

He just nodded, then sat down at the table and tucked a napkin into his shirt collar. "For the life of me, with this old shirt, I don't know why I bother! Just training, I suppose." He forked up a tomato and put it on her plate.

She didn't eat much. Claudius understood that her appetite must have dwindled when she was in hiding. Lots of people were eating grass back there in Rwanda during that time, Ruth had told him. Then again, May hadn't been given farm food like Claudius's yet. Maybe that would change things.

She went back to bed and slept until suppertime. He hoped the smell of cornbread and pinto beans would help her appetite return. Familiar food now. Claudius figured he'd bring out one of Ruth's meals the next day.

May must have slathered his mother's goop on her arms and legs, because he smelled the clover, lavender, and comfrey just before she sat down and tucked her napkin in the neck of her shirt. That same long-sleeved shirt.

After dinner Claudius set her up in an old white-and-green webbed lounge chair out in the yard. While the sun set, he read *The Hunchback of Notre Dame* aloud, his thick Kentucky accent rendering a new flavor to medieval France. May bundled her scarred appendages in a sheet. Her hair, which had been shaved at the hospital in Nairobi because it was so infested, was milky brown. Still less than an inch long, it stuck up off her head as if it mirrored the shock down in her soul. She startled at every sound and Claudius wished she was five and he could just put her on his lap and read to her that way. She needed her mother.

"What's wrong with your mom?" he asked. "Your father mentioned the doctor."

"She had a stroke, Claudius."

"I'm sorry. She's too young to have a stroke."

"Yeah. But it happens. One more thing, right?"

"At such a young age too."

Girlfriend sat beside her, looking sad at what she'd become, but remaining loyal. At bedtime when May was in Africa, Claudius had lifted that dog up in the bed with him and she stayed all night, snoring like crazy, real and warm. She'd switched back to her mistress. Hopefully May didn't mind the noise.

He found himself praying more these days. Just little snippets from a foreign land of caring for a young person.

"Serves you right," Sister Ruth said when he saw her earlier that day at the IGA. "Your life's been almost perfect for years now."

He had to admit she was right about that.

May sat in that lounge chair every day for the rest of August, allowing the sun to bleach the scars as she rested under it in a T-shirt and shorts. When she first came down in those clothes she said, "I can't dress like it's winter when it's 98 degrees. You'll just have to get used to these things, Claudius."

"It's all right, May-May."

Her legs must have been injured somehow also. He noticed when she walked, she always seemed to be a little sore. He was old enough to know those wounds wouldn't be kind when she reached his age. The arm he broke when he was eleven gave him trouble on days when the weather was changing.

The first week of September Claudius came home from the farmers' market with his backseat full of flowering plants. Elrod in the stall next to his said he was going on vacation and would just as soon get rid of the plants on the cheap. Claudius said he'd be glad to take them off his hands on the cheap.

May set down her magazine. He knew she loved fashion, so he'd purchased her a copy of some women's magazine with a gal in an impossible pose with legs and arms so long he wondered if somebody had done something to the picture to make her look like that. A bit off-looking if you asked him, but then, he wasn't used to the current ways.

"Oh, those are pretty, Claudius!"

He set the flowers down and swiped his hands against each other. "It's a bit late in the season, but they'll look pretty for a little while. And I got some mums. They'll last for years." He pinched his lower lip. "You'll be home by then, though, doing great in Lexington. Have you thought about what you're going to do?"

"Nope. I just can't."

After grabbing a shovel, he dug up the sod in a circle around her chair, leaving a grassy aisle back to the lawn for her to walk down. Inside near her chair he planted begonias, primroses, nicotiana, lobelia, and outside, zinnias, heather, and coneflowers. "They'll come back for you in the spring too, May-May."

"Can I water them?"

"I think they'd like it if you did."

Each day the tender plants grew, their root systems feathering out beneath the soil. "Growing strong and wise," Claudius told her. "The prettiest things are sometimes down in the dirt. I kinda like that arrangement. It's a little surprising, isn't it?"

On a Sunday afternoon a week later they sat out in the circle eating tomato and cucumber sandwiches on white bread after Claudius returned from his little church. "And those around the ring'll be around to remind me of you when you get back on your feet someday. Maybe my mother was right about flowers. She always said they work their own brand of magic."

"I can't imagine what is next for me."

No picture came to Claudius's mind either.

Every once in a while he'd take her down to the pay phone in town so she could call home. Late at night. Short conversations. Her mom had only improved up to a point. Dad was coping, helping her around in her wheelchair, feeding her when she couldn't quite make it.

"She does all right with soft sandwiches, so we eat a lot of tuna and egg salad. But you're doing all right?"

May related his words to Claudius.

"I am. I'll be back soon."

"Take your time, May. Mom said she loves picturing you having a good time on the farm. We can't wait to see some pictures."

"Did you bring your camera?" Claudius asked on the way home. "We got lots of flowers now to take pictures of."

"It was destroyed in Africa."

"Oh. Guess your dad just wasn't thinking."

"He's got a lot on his mind."

· 7 ·

Through the end of summer and birth of autumn that September always seemed to bring, May sat in that chair just watching the garden grow. Beyond her circle, corn grew tall, and they ate it on the cob for dinner with butter that Claudius taught her how to make from the rich milk of Eloise the cow. She'd sit in her lawn chair with a big mason jar and shake, shake, shake, while Claudius took Bill the mule out to harvest the final round of broccoli and squash. And his tomatoes. They didn't call him The Tomato Man down at the farmers' market for nothing.

Sister Ruth told Claudius he needed to do more to get May on her feet, and he told her he just didn't know how. And that was the truth of the matter. So he brought her little jobs to do right there in her seat. She even mended a couple of shirts. He told her she did well with the needle, and she seemed to like that.

One morning at the beginning of October, she sat down at the breakfast table.

"I've got a surprise for you." Claudius slid two pancakes onto her plate and topped them with a fried egg.

Her eyes narrowed, but she smiled.

—Guess Rwanda ruined her for surprises.

"Oh, yeah? What is it, Claudius?"

"I'm strapping Bill to the wagon, and we're heading out to the pumpkin patch."

"Really? When I was a kid my mom would buy a hay bale or two, some corn shocks, and five or six pumpkins to decorate our front porch. We'd sometimes go out to the apple orchard and get apples and cider. That was fun."

"I'll set up your chair there. You up for the trip?" Claudius never assumed.

She appeared to be convincing herself.

"We won't even take so much as a step off this old farm." The last trip to the pay phone had proved too stressful, and May had decided to start writing letters to her folks instead.

"That would be really nice."

She helped with the breakfast dishes—been doing that for a while now—and hurried upstairs to change into jeans and a long-sleeved shirt. She must have rubbed in some goop, because she smelled like it when she returned.

"What's that?" Claudius pointed to a length of beads and chain cascading from the side pocket of her jeans.

"My grandmother's rosary. Sometimes just holding it, and remembering that my grandmother used it to pray, gives me comfort, even though I don't think any of that does any good anymore."

Claudius wished right then he was better at talking about God. Instead he just nodded, patted her shoulder, and said, "You never know, May-May."

He helped her up into the wagon, put her chair in the back, and off they drove. "Ever been in a horse-drawn wagon before?"

"Nope. It's nice."

She was looking a little better now that her hair wasn't quite so short. And honest to goodness, he could see some little white hairs sparkling in the light brown. Poor baby. Much too soon for that sort of thing.

He set up her chair, then turned to his work.

Bend down, turn the pumpkin, whip a small hatchet out of the loop on his pants, and cut the vine. He never had to bring the hatchet down more than once, that's how many pumpkins he'd harvested.

And he never got tired of pumpkins either. He grew pumpkins like he grew tomatoes, odd varieties that struck his fancy. They were the happiest of harvests and filled his soul with a golden patina that echoed the glow the crisp air of autumn pulled to the surface of his cheeks.

"Where do you sell these?" May asked, wincing each time he cut a stem.

Sitting on her chair, she looked lost in that sweater he'd bought at Rose Brothers. He had no way of knowing size and he figured too big was better than too small, so he got her a medium. At least the sky blue color complemented her overall coloring. Ah, well.

"I sell them to a market in Lexington. He sells seasonal things, pumpkins and gourds and such in the fall, Christmas trees, garlands in December."

"The guy at Ashland and Maine?"

"He's the one. Some decorators use my pumpkins and such too."

"Decorators?"

He grabbed another pumpkin. "Believe it or not, May-May, there are people who are so rich they have other folk do their holiday decorating. Make a fine living at it too."

"I dated a boy once who thought everything was about image, but I think he probably would have at least bought his own pumpkins."

"See? It can always be worse. And, well, I don't mean to be harsh, May-May, but what was that little car all about, the one you were driving around before Rwanda?"

She nodded and pulled her sweater around her. "You're probably right."

Young people. They always had to put *probably* on things in an effort to keep you in your place.

Finally it was time to begin loading the wagon. He gathered several pumpkins in his arms, settled them in the bed, then patted old Bill on his way to gather more.

May walked toward him carrying two pumpkins at chest level. "Looks like a big orange bikini!" She laughed. "I'll bet people love these pumpkins. They seem a little more vibrant than most."

Claudius stretched his back. "They're Cinderella pumpkins. And those over there are Sugar Treats. Pie makers buy them. They do make a fine pie."

By lunchtime they had half a wagonful. The pumpkins jostled one another as Bill hauled them back home, nice old Bill who just did his job and never complained. Claudius showed May how to feed Bill carrots, and they laughed at the appreciative look the old mule got on his face.

She waved him off as he headed into Lexington, the trunk and seats of the Galaxy filled with pumpkins. When she asked him why he didn't get a truck, he just shrugged.

"My life is very simple, May-May. More space means more stuff to fill it with."

On Halloween he decided to make pumpkin soup and roasted pumpkin seeds.

"Now don't be tellin' the people at my church. They don't like such things. But I figured you'd appreciate a little celebration of the holiday."

May had just come down from a nap as the pumpkin meat was coming to a boil.

"Oh, and there's a letter for you on the table."

She opened the letter and skimmed it, then read it aloud to Claudius. A reporter had found her, interested in her story as one of two Americans who had refused to leave Rwanda during the genocide.

She threw it on the kitchen table.

"You look upset, May-May. Maybe you should get in touch with him. Sister Ruth would let you use her phone."

"I don't think I'm ready."

"Maybe talking about it would do you good. You still haven't said a word."

"I can't. I'm sorry. I know you want to hear—"

"Don't pay me no mind! I . . . well . . . I don't know what to do. I just want you to get better." He set the lid on the pot and turned the flame down to a simmer.

"Maybe it would be good to talk to a journalist. Maybe that would get me back to thinking something, planning something, I don't know."

He rinsed the pulp off the pumpkin seeds. "I noticed you don't seem to be liking those fashion magazines anymore."

She rested her chin in her hand. "No. It just seems kind of silly now."

"You could write about something besides fashion, May-May."

"I feel as much like writing as I do like sticking a fork in my eye."

He laughed out loud, drawing the bright yellow strings away from the seeds in the colander under the spigot.

"Why don't you just read or something, May-May? I'm heading into Beattyville to pick up a few things at the IGA. Want me to pick up the newspaper? Maybe that'll help get you thinking about all that again."

He wished he were better able to advise her, to help her out, but Lordymercy, he just didn't know how to do this. Grow vegetables and feed chickens, yes. Young women? He might just as well have tried to grow pineapples there in Kentucky.

And now here was the fruit of his labor in the field and at the stove sitting ready on the kitchen table. He was a little proud of himself. While May napped, he had taken down Violet Borne's cookbook, a three-ring binder scrapbook with handwritten recipes and thousands of clippings from *Ladies' Home Journal* and *Family Circle*. Or the newspaper. His mother actually had *The Lexington Herald-Leader* delivered at the house, the Sunday edition. She was brilliant, he thought. One time he asked her what would have happened to her if she hadn't had him. She told him she would have been a nurse, probably.

And then his father said, "Nurse? No way. Son, your mother, she would have been a heart surgeon. No less."

Claudius didn't know whether or not that really would have been the case, but he always felt a little bad he'd fouled that up for her, even though she told him again and again she wouldn't trade having him for the entire world.

The pumpkin soup, originally from the *Leader*, was bright orange, and a little dollop of May's butter sat on top. May's spoon sank slowly to the bottom of the bowl as she reached for the salty pumpkin seeds and threw a couple on her tongue. When she spooned it into her mouth she closed her eyes.

Yep, he'd fatten her up some.

"And later on, well, I kept back some of those pumpkins, and we're going to carve them up but good."

"Jack-o'-lanterns?"

"Remember what I said about gettin' kicked out of the church?"

She laughed. "You wouldn't get kicked out of my church."

"Is that right? Well."

They carved until nine o'clock that night, lighting candles and setting them inside. Too far out in the country for trick-or-treaters, they faced the pumpkins toward their porch chairs, some faces happy, some mean, and they drank hot, milky tea until the candles burned down. Scout and Girlfriend snoozed by the rockers.

"Is your life ever lonely?" May asked.

"Naw. Not with Bill and Scout and Eloise. And Girlfriend's fit right in with the group. But I will say it's nice having another human being around. Guess I'd just gotten used to being one of the critters!"

Yep, that would just about describe it.

He used to really believe his little speech.

8

Claudius was proud of May. She'd come a long way there in the kitchen. She'd learned to bake bread from an old recipe of Mrs. Borne's. Sourdough. No need to get yeast at the store with the good starter Ruthie provided her, one that had been going for over a hundred years.

"I had no idea stuff like this existed," May said, taking the bowl from Ruth's hands.

"You'd be surprised at all that goes on in the world." Sister Ruth handed her a bag of flour from a Kentucky mill. "Weisenberger's always does you just right. And the price is good too. I get mine in twenty-pound bags. Then a few of us split it up. Claudius included."

"This makes so much sense."

May was learning to think differently, self-sufficiently. And it sure made Claudius feel good, the way she appreciated what was grown in the earth around her and how hard he worked to bring it all forth. He had taken God's natural goodness for granted, he saw. Not in a way that wasn't thankful, but he'd forgotten the miracle of life in general. When you thought about the cold dark universe with splotches of heat and light, this green and blue jewel on which he grew, and food grew, was indeed miraculous! He'd even taken himself for granted, his work, that he knew instinctively when to put a seed in the ground. And it wasn't the same day every year either. He just felt in his bones when it was time.

A few days before Thanksgiving, Claudius rested his rifle on his shoulder, whistled to Scout, and set out.

"Where are you heading?" May called from the yard where

she was hanging out a load of clothing she'd just washed in the old machine on the porch. She actually thought running the clothes through the ringer atop the machine was fun. Hard to figure with some young people.

"Time to get us that turkey!" he called.

Her eyes widened. "I thought you meant at the store!"

"May-May, there are more turkeys in these hills than you can shake a stick at. And they're free."

Yep, she was coming along all right. And she was even doing most of the cooking for their Thanksgiving dinner. Her parents would be joining them, and May was nervous. Claudius had bartered several dozen eggs for a few pounds of sausage for the stuffing. Violet came through again with that cookbook she'd left behind.

May-May was still using her goop. Claudius had made up another batch. He wondered if those scars would ache forever. May wouldn't offer up that information on her own; that was certain.

A few hours later Claudius, his old quilted plaid jacket open to cool him after all that trudging about, and Scout, larger than life with the thrill of the cold wind and the running around, crested the last hill before the house. The turkey hung like a sack over Claudius's back, its feet held between his fingers. His jangling gait was echoed by Scout's nimble prance, and there was May on the porch, drinking a cup of tea in the cold, a book in her lap, staring at him. She waved, and he realized he was loved.

—Lordymercy! Oh, dear! Well, oh my!

Claudius could feel that rhythm in his heart from the WPW now that he knew it was there. Mostly when he lay down at night, his book on his chest, the house quiet. And there were times he felt it start up, and he'd thwack his chest with the heel of his hand and it seemed to help. He didn't know if it really did, but it made him feel better to do something.

He'd just given his chest a daytime whack, then turned and pulled the turkey out of the boiling pot hanging over a pit fire he'd built in the yard.

The poor creature landed on a couple of planks with a thud, and he began to pull out its feathers.

"Oh boy, that's awful!" May held her nose.

"Didn't know how badly it stinks when you're defeathering a turkey? Might as well dig in. It's not as bad if you've got something to keep you busy."

They plucked and pulled. Claudius handed May a pair of pliers to pull out the more stubborn feathers. She worked up a sweat, and so did he. And they laughed at the sight of one another. Finally, he burned off the filoplumes with a blowtorch.

"My goodness," said May. "Who knew it took all this?"

"Did you see what that bird looked like to begin with?"

She nodded.

"I'd say it was relatively easy to get it from that to this if you think about it. I mean, when we used to butcher pigs—"

"Oh, Claudius, no! Let's not talk about that."

She'd get used to this, he reckoned. "It makes the meat aisle of the grocery store seem a little different, doesn't it?"

"I can't even tell you."

"Tell you what. We'll finish up here, and then I'll make us a pot of coffee and we can read for a little while."

She said that sounded very nice.

The night before Thanksgiving, pumpkin pie baked, its top glistening sugary in the light of the overhead light, the bread drying in slices on the kitchen table, May sat in the living room and flipped through an old family photo album Claudius laid in her lap. He brought out his fiddle for the first time since she'd come, and plaintive mountain tunes drifted off the strings as faces she didn't know slipped beneath her fingertips. His parents, so country, with square, worn faces and pillow-button eyes, looked like they were always ready to laugh. And they were. "It's either that or cry," his dad said more than a time or two.

"I already love these people, for some reason. Did you laugh a lot around here?" she asked.

He nodded, smiled, and kept playing, wondering if she knew she'd read his mind. She was beginning to do that a lot.

"May I have a picture of your mother to take upstairs?"

He nodded again. That was nice.

She peeled off a black-and-white picture of the tall woman, boxy of figure, with white hair and an apron with fragile floral designs splayed across its surface. He knew it was yellow, and he told May that.

"And that dress she has on is the color of periwinkles." She stood on the front porch holding a bunch of roses she must have just clipped. "Those were pink." On the back it said *Violet, 1960.*

"I'll set her on my nightstand," May said in the manner of a declaration.

The next morning the turkey was already in the oven, the skin beginning to brown, when May woke up. Claudius heard her scuffling up there, and then, dressed, she ran down and began browning the sausage in Violet's largest black iron skillet. She reminded him nothing of his mother, save for the way she moved the spatula across the dark, searing surface of the pan. She swayed there at the stove, yes, but she was more graceful than poor Violet could ever have been. Violet, who should have been doing more than cooking at an old stove and raising her little illegitimate boy.

Was he overly thankful? Well, yes, he was. If a person could feel too much gratitude about that kind of love, he was guilty of it.

May began chopping up one of the onions Claudius brought up from the root cellar. "I'm not overly fond of celery, is that okay?"

"Fine by me. I can go either way." Claudius peeled potatoes and put them in a big pot of water, the starch clinging to his fingers.

In the freezer the final green beans of the season were waiting to be part of their little celebration. May thawed them under running water and proceeded to snap them into pieces, stopping every couple of minutes to stir the sausage and onions that were browning in the pan.

Claudius felt blessed. Warm and blessed and at home in his house in a way he'd never before experienced. It had always been his mother's house.

An hour later the stuffing was ready to bake and the beans were cooking with a piece of fatback on the back of the stove.

"How about a little reading?" Claudius asked as he washed his hands.

"All right."

The smells of Thanksgiving filled the house, and soon his reading of *Old Jack* sent May into that warm place of closed eyes and contentment. Mumbling, she remembered aloud Thanksgiving at her house.

"I'd eat my fill, then watch a couple of videos while the adults sat around and talked. Then I'd sneak up to my bedroom for a nap, listening to the sounds of conversation and plates and cutlery clinking in the kitchen as my mom and the women did the dishes."

He'd always liked that sound too.

An hour later Dr. and Mrs. Seymour arrived. Michael had obviously tried to fix his wife's hair, but the light brown mass hung limp. She wore an ethnic caftan type of garment—something one didn't see often around Beattyville!

May wheeled her mother up to the table, sat next to her, and cut up her food. The poor woman could hardly lift a roll to her mouth, and her speech was barely understandable. But the glisten of her brown eyes as they rested on May spoke a thousand *I love yous*.

The sounds of conversation mostly belonged to Claudius and Michael, but everyone tried to make it a good Thanksgiving. When they went around the table telling of that for which they were thankful, all but May said, “I’m thankful May is alive and well.”

When her turn came, she excused herself and said she needed to use the restroom.

“She must be having a hard time thanking God for anything,” Michael said.

“Lots of people do,” Claudius said, digging his knife into the butter. “And that’s a fact.”

A few hours later, as they were about to pull away, Claudius leaned down at Michael’s car window. “She can stay here as long as she needs.”

“Are you sure? I never dreamed she would stay such a long time.”

“It’s fine by me. I like having the company.”

“Thank you, Claudius.”

· 9 ·

He was sitting at the kitchen table cutting up Hubbard squash for a casserole. For dessert, apple dumplings. May had already cored the apples and loaded up the centers with a mixture of flour, sugar, and cinnamon. Next, having followed Violet's "No-Fail Easy Piecrust" recipe, and having rolled the dough into a thin sheet, she placed the apples on top and cut the pastry into squares. After that she pulled the dough up around the peeled apples into neat little round bundles.

"Now those are right nice, May-May. I think my mother would say you did a good job."

"That makes me happy inside."

She slid them into the oven with an easy push, straightened, and wiped her hands against each other. "There." She placed her hands on her hips.

"I'll make my mother's butter sauce just before we eat those," he said.

"Well, she's sure given me back my appetite."

"You look almost normal again."

May smiled. "Now that things are slowing down on the farm, Claudius, I think I'll make you a Christmas present."

"Just you being around here is enough."

"Don't make me anything, then," she said.

He gave a little snort. "Too late."

"Figures."

Claudius put the teakettle on as she sat down and began to help him with the squash.

"I guess I never had such good food every day like this," she said. "We ate lots of takeout. I guess everybody was always so busy."

He never mentioned she hadn't taken one step off his property since the end of August, so how could she have eaten anything else? Claudius took life as it came, and for him, it came slowly. But then, May-May was young and life was stuffed full of possibilities he'd never cared to dream about, not with what he had right there.

Claudius cleared his throat, pinched his lip. "Ever think about looking up some of your old friends, May-May? Probably some folks wondering what's become of you."

She waved that away. "Oh, I can hear them now. 'It's time to move on, May. I mean, you can't wallow in this forever. And have you gotten counseling? Maybe a psychiatrist could help you process.'"

"Process?" he asked.

"I hate words like that. As if you follow ten or twenty steps and *Bingo!* You're better! Is it really that easy?"

He didn't know. He doubted it, but he just couldn't say. He shook his head. "They might surprise you is all I'm saying."

She stood up. "But smelling squash casserole and cinnamon apples, surely that's a sort of therapy, isn't it? And knowing which tree they came from, which patch of dirt they sprang out of? Knowing, I mean, like *really* knowing they came from a little seed with everything inside it would need to become a plant that would bear fruit? Surely that reminder is enough to tell me life goes on!" Her voice rose slightly with each word, and gained in intensity too.

He sighed deep down where she couldn't hear. He thought she was right, but he just didn't know. What did Alexander Dumas ever say about this sort of thing? Nothing, that's what. And the chickens, if they knew, weren't uttering a word.

After dinner she knelt down in front of a basket of yarn his mother had collected over the years, leftover yarn from a lifetime of knitting scarves and sweaters. Oh, she'd knit some beauties that Claudius only wore on Sundays to church.

May held up the basket. "Can I use this?"

"Be glad if you did. Just can't bring myself to throw that sort of thing out. Needles are in the bottom there."

She pulled out a set. "I only know how to knit and purl."

"Two more stitches than I know!"

He watched her cast onto the needle, then slowly begin. The repetitive motion seemed to soothe her despite the uneven stitches.

Then, "Ugh! Look how terrible this is."

"I like it." He offered nothing more for several minutes, then said, "Some of the most imperfect fruit is the sweetest."

He'd said it again and again as they examined his harvest, saving the more perfect specimens for the grocery-store denizens of Lexington. The people in Beattyville weren't so picky. They knew better.

"You should come into town with me sometime, May-May."

"Maybe I should just try getting the mail first."

"Well, all right, then. You can walk down to the road with me tomorrow."

"That would be a good start."

"You ready?" Claudius asked May as they stood at the top of the driveway wearing their heaviest sweaters.

She nodded, looking like she was about to cry, her cheeks blotched, her lips white.

Oh Lord, he thought, offering up that simple prayer. This was teaching him so much, particularly, what comes so easy for some people doesn't come easily for others.

—I'm so sheltered. I'm an old man who doesn't know people.

He took her hand. "Wanna get it over with quickly, or just take our time?"

"Let's take our time." She squeezed, tightening their grip to one another.

"Now, then . . ."

They stepped forward, hand in hand, the gravel road looking

longer than it ever had before, the downward path steeper too. "You all right?" he asked.

She laughed. "We just started, Claudius."

He laughed too.

"What was it like growing up for you?" she asked. "In case you're wondering, I'm trying to get my mind off things."

He liked her directness. At least with May you didn't have to guess.

"Well, you can imagine a patchwork quilt like me wouldn't be much accepted in these parts. I got beat up so much in the first grade Mother brought me home and gave me an education here for a time."

"So you must have trouble going down this driveway too."

He looked up and realized he needed to trim that beech tree a little. "Not anymore. Those kids grew up, and I didn't leave, so I guess they figured I was here to stay and I wasn't going to bother nobody."

"That's sad."

He'd never really thought so. He had everything he ever needed on his farm.

"And I have my church. They've always accepted me. Church should do that."

"It should. It doesn't always, though."

"Maybe I just got lucky."

"Father Isaac, in Rwanda, he had a good parish there. But most of them died. One of his deacons was Hutu, and he turned into one of the murderers. Later, I saw him with the gang who came through every so often. Father Isaac didn't live to see it, though, and I'm glad. It would have broken his heart. He thought the man escaped into Burundi."

"I can't imagine it."

"Who can? So religion sure did fail in that country, if it didn't keep people from butchering their neighbors."

"People will kill others when they're scared and think God's fine with it. I've at least read enough to know that."

"I never much liked war, Claudius, but now I hate it."

"Here we are!" He touched the mailbox. "Go ahead and open it, May-May!"

She reached out, and as she did, he thought about mailboxes, and this large network of paper veins that holds people together. Lots of people. People you don't know, like the folks who do replacement windows or siding, and people you're more connected to, like the billing department of the utilities company, or best of all, a friend or relative.

He saw a familiar scrawl of handwriting on a letter-size envelope. Eli always did write like you'd imagine a spider would if able to hold onto a pen.

"Look, from Eli!" She handed him the envelope, then reached in for the rest of the mail. "How's he doing?"

Claudius hadn't told her about the wedding and all. "I'll tell you over a glass of tea."

"Here you go."

But when he tried to take it from her, she held on.

He laughed. "May-May, what are you doing?"

"Can I carry it up the hill, then?"

"'Course you can."

"What was the best letter you ever got?" May asked as they began the climb back up the drive toward the house.

"From my Aunt Cecily," Claudius said promptly. "Said she was coming from West Virginia and bringing me a puppy from her dog, Peevy. First German shepherd I ever had. And have always had them since."

"How old were you?"

"Eight. What about you? What was your best letter?"

"Hard to say. Let me think for a second."

Well, he wasn't going anywhere special. She could take all the time she needed.

Scout and Girlfriend found them halfway up the drive and made the second part of the trek with them. He knew dogs were dogs, and he never quite understood why people had to think of them as children when obviously there was a world of difference. But he had to admit he liked dogs better, for the most part. Maybe the good Lord was right in seeing fit to keep him plowing and planting.

"Mine was a letter from my father. He went to present a paper at a conference, and I was supposed to go with him and my mother, but I got strep throat and couldn't go. He said all sorts of nice things, how much he missed me, how much better it would have been with me there. It was like a paper hug."

They chattered, step by step.

"And here we are at the door!" he said.

May pulled down the striped glasses, set them on the counter of the hoosier as Claudius pulled the tea pitcher from the refrigerator.

"How old is that fridge?" she asked.

"1955!"

"Almost forty years old? Oh, my goodness." She pulled an ice cube tray out of the freezer door inside the refrigerator. The first time she saw the aluminum contraption, she thought it was one of the strangest things she'd ever seen and told him so.

She grabbed the lever running down the middle of the tray and pulled. The grids shifted, and the cubes were dislodged from the side. She put several into the glasses, dumped the rest into a bowl inside the freezer, then refilled the tray.

"So anyway, about Eli," he said, sitting down at his usual place at the side of the table.

She joined him, taking a sip of tea, then pulling over her knitting. The scarf was going to be warm at least. He smiled. Couldn't help himself. How wonderful to have somebody muscle through such a project on his behalf. Not that she'd muttered one word that it was going to be his Christmas present. He just knew.

"He's still in the service. He's a sniper now."

Her eyes widened. "Wow. He must be a really good shot."

"And there's something else you might find interesting."

"Hmm?"

"He's married now."

"Oh?"

Well, good. She didn't look that upset. Maybe he'd only thought there was more to their friendship.

"Yep. Before he left. Right after you went to Rwanda. He's got a little girl now. She was born last February. Cute little thing. Name's Callie."

"I'll bet your cousin is happy to be a granny." The needles clicked away.

"Oh, Sassy dotes on her like crazy."

"What's his wife's name?"

"Janey. She's disappeared though."

"So, the wedding was . . . shotgun?"

He nodded and took another sip. "Janey's the mayor's daughter."

"Wow."

"Into some bad drugs, so they say."

"That's sad."

"So Sassy's raising her. She's a good woman."

"I'd like to meet her sometime."

Now that was good to hear. Maybe he could start inviting a few ladies to the farm. Maybe that would be a good next step.

The rest of the day May seemed a little quiet. Bundled in a quilt, she sat outside on her lawn chair until it was time to cook dinner.

They sat in the living room later, May knitting, Claudius looking through a seed catalog once again. So many possibilities.

"You seem a little troubled," he said, leaving her room to wiggle out of talking about it.

"I was just thinking about Eli. He seems like a decent enough person. I'm sad things worked out like they did. I'm sad for their daughter mostly, I guess."

"Sassy's a good woman, though, May-May. Callie'll know a lot of love, good strong love, for the rest of her life."

"Yeah. That is a good thing, Claudius. It still makes me sad, though."

Claudius couldn't blame her. It made him sad too.

· 10 ·

They wintered on the farm, huddled around the woodstove at night, taking hot water bottles to their beds, and sleeping in the way only a cool room provides. Well, yes, a cold room.

May came into the kitchen one morning with the photo of Claudius's mother in her hand. "Poor Violet there in her summer housedress and apron looks positively blue, and I'm sure those roses she holds are frozen. Let's put her up on the cookbook shelf until spring comes."

"That's a fine idea. She'd get a kick out of you, May-May."

Being around May made him wonder why he'd been so content to stay on the farm all his life. It was interesting to see a woman move about the kitchen, sidestepping from counter to stove, that movement so feminine, so fascinating. Fact was, he knew almost nothing about women. They liked to wear hats to church. He knew that. And Ruth just didn't count any. She was more than a woman; she was a force of nature.

Oh, he and Ruthie did go way back. Her daddy's place bordered the back of Borne's Last Chance. They played along the creek during the summers, building little villages out of stones and sticks and string, making furniture and tiny cars.

Sometimes she'd come back to the house with him for lunch. His mother liked Ruthie. Showed her how to sew, and they'd sit up in May-May's room for hours pinning scraps of fabric together to somehow form a three-dimensional garment. He had to admire that sort of know-how. Seemed women could see the dimensions in things he just couldn't.

From the time he was five years old, he figured he'd someday marry Ruthie. She could punch harder than any boy in their Sunday school class, and he liked that about her. Shame Ruthie never figured it that way. But he'd never let on about his plans, and then it was just too late. She'd met Jordy, and Claudius would have never come in the way of love like that.

When Jordy died and Ruthie was only nineteen, he was the one to hold her as she cried. He had to admit, he'd been hopeful once again. Soon enough, however, he realized there was room for only one love in Ruthie's life. And there was room for only one in his. Try as he might to explain his bachelorhood otherwise, if he was honest, there it sat.

Violet tried to introduce him to suitable young women. Lordymercy, how that woman tried! He gave it his best shot, but never could overcome his overall shyness. That's what his mother always called it, "his overall shyness." And then, Ruthie. She was something! How could a fellow move on from a woman like that?

May began setting their places for breakfast. Just some oatmeal. So, a bowl and a spoon. "You really think your mother would have liked me?"

"Yes. Mother would have cried with you, and then she'd have taken you bowling or something."

May laughed. "Your mother liked to bowl?"

"More than just about anything." He ladled the porridge into the bowls. "I'm sorry I can't be more to you, May-May."

"You're all I need right now, Claudius."

They sat down; he said grace, thinking maybe it might be too soon to invite Sassy over.

The Christmas season arrived. May's parents sent her a card and begged her to come home for Christmas.

"I can't leave here," she cried, throwing her head down on

her forearm as they sat at the kitchen table one evening. "I can't, Claudius."

He didn't need to remind her how much her absence hurt her parents, who made the trip as often as they could. But with her mother's health, it wasn't as much as they'd wish.

"I know. But paying them a visit . . . maybe it would be a good idea."

"I'm not ready!" she practically wailed. Seemed she wanted nothing to do with her old life before they met, before Rwanda.

And May-May was an adult. He was here to help her heal, not pry, not take over her life.

Christmas morning she was thrilled with the rolling pin he'd crafted himself as well as a cutting board made of walnut, beech, and maple, each piece rubbed until it shonc.

"I was wondering how you'd kept yourself occupied in the barn so much during the day!" she cried, hugging him for the first time.

"It was fun. I liked having a good excuse to do some woodworking. I used to do it a lot more, you know."

"Apple dumplings!" she hollered. "I'll make us some!"

"Just the ticket. I'll get some apples out of the cellar."

"Okay," she said once the apples, four of them, were sitting in a bowl on the kitchen table. "Don't you do a thing. Just sit with me."

"I have an idea."

He shuffled into his bedroom. He hadn't done this since his mother died, and it had been one of the three or four rock-hard Christmas traditions in his family. It would have seemed silly to carry it on by himself, just he and old Scout. Just plain silly. But not anymore.

He pulled a book down from the shelf over his bed, the shelf his dad put up when he was about five years old. The room hadn't changed much. New curtains and bedspreads at various intervals. But the furniture remained the same, and in the same arrangement.

He figured he had to move his crops around so much, let the furniture stay put. Nothing wrong with that.

Sitting down at the kitchen chair, he opened the book and read aloud, " 'Marley was dead, to begin with.' "

"Wonderful! *A Christmas Carol* and apple dumplings."

"Too bad I didn't shoot us a goose, May-May."

Girlfriend and Scout dropped down for a snooze by the woodstove in the corner.

As he read, a light snow began to fall. It thickened gradually. The temperature dropped, and large flakes like tumbling Queen Anne's lace turned to something finer and more delicate, pinging lightly against the panes of glass.

He looked up from his pages every so often, watching May work, listening to his own voice. With each quarter hour that passed, with the increase of snow upon the grass and the tin roofs, the trees and the shrubs, her shoulders seemed to relax a little more.

She felt safe, he realized. Surrounded by the snow, his voice, the warmth of the stove. He did too.

The winter progressed, the chill settling in over the hills and between the trees. The chickens huddled in their nesting boxes at night, and Claudius explained over and over again to May that they were fine.

"God made animals to live outside, May-May."

But every night, May would sneak out and turn on the warming lamp just in case.

~

February came and went, May's father writing frequently, explaining how hard the cold seemed to be on Elisabeth.

But in March they prepared for the first visit in months.

"I want them to think I'm doing great, Claudius. That I'm choosing to stay here now and help you on the farm."

May scrubbed the place, Claudius tidied the winter lawn, they prepared a coconut custard pie and percolated coffee. They set the table with Violet's fine china and waited, both dressed in their best clothing.

Claudius wore his church suit, and May wore a bright green dress Sister Ruth brought her from the thrift store. Her hair just brushed the tops of her shoulders now and had grown back thick, but with a duller sheen than he recalled. And of course the strands of white, now longer, wiry and prone to do their own thing, were a recent development too.

May played the part well, sunny and chatty. She chatted more in that time than she normally did in the course of a week. So much to say about the crops, the animals, the seasons, the sun, the wind, the rain. So very much to say.

"Do you think they bought it?" he asked as they waved the two down the driveway.

"Yes. Don't you?"

"Not for a second, honey. But they know you're safe, fed, and warm. I think they know that's all they could do for you too. And your mother . . ."

"She's still not well."

"Seems very fragile."

Elisabeth Seymour still held a childlike cuteness about her, her hair long and dark with bangs skimming along her eyebrows, her brown eyes large in her pale face. Not a whole lot to fall back on, as his mother used to say, if she got sick. And she'd gotten sick.

She'd spoken to Claudius while her husband was saying goodbye to May. "I can't do it, Claudius." She wiped a sudden tear off her cheek. "I can't be there for her. I'm so sorry." And she finally collapsed under the weight of her own emotions, into his arms, where she sobbed in the chilly spring wind, helpless.

They were all helpless, he realized. Where was a strong person with the know-how to relieve this situation? How could God throw them all together to cook in this stew of incompetence, desperation, and powerlessness?

But the letters from home increased after that, and twice a month the Seymours made the drive from Lexington. They ate pie and talked about their lives, and nobody ever mentioned Rwanda.

During one visit Michael Seymour pulled Claudius aside. Claudius liked the college professor standing with him. His speech was always measured and precise, but warm. He never missed a thing anybody said, as if he stored up all that info in his long, graying ponytail.

"Should I insist she come back home?"

"She won't anyway. She's stuck."

"I don't know what to do."

"Me neither, Michael."

"Has she made any progress at all?"

"She does fine here. But just here. I couldn't tell you what she would do out in the big wide world."

"What a mess."

And Claudius had always thought everything was tidy. In a way. At least here at Borne's Last Chance. Now it was anything but neat. Not with that woman sitting in there missing her baby and not knowing what to do and having no strength for the task if she did.

Next Michael pulled May aside. Claudius, chatting with Elisabeth about the fiddle and showing her his old, handmade mountain instrument, heard their murmurs. Michael implored her to come home. But May refused on the grounds she had too much work to do and besides, she loved it on the farm so much.

For various reasons, they all chose to leave it at that.

"She's twenty-four years old," Michael said to Claudius. "I can't come in like I did when she was sixteen. I told her what I think she needs to do, and that I'll do all I can to make it happen. But I can't make her do it."

"That's got to come from her," Claudius agreed.

"Well, I thank you again for taking good care of her. I don't know where she'd be without you."

Back with you, Claudius wanted to say, because he knew May would have had no other choice. He knew he held the key. He could tell her to leave, to get away from the farm, that her time was up.

But he never would do that. No. He just couldn't.

• II •

Ruthie clued Claudius in on the importance of April 6 the day before it arrived. She caught him by the arm as he was coming out of the feed store, a bag of chicken feed over his left shoulder.

"Now you don't want to go reminding her of it, but just be aware. It was a year ago today that it all began in Rwanda. She may not realize it, but the body itself has a way of remembering."

Claudius knew what she meant. Every June 13 he felt depressed and irritable, and then he'd remember, long after supper, that it was the anniversary of his father's death.

"I'll be on the lookout. Maybe I'll make us something special for dinner tomorrow."

"The IGA is running a special on rib eyes, $5.99 a pound."

He whistled and started for the Galaxy. "I don't know 'bout that."

She looked very attractive in a pink and yellow dress covered in large daisies. She'd slid on pink shoes to match. And she'd just been to the beauty parlor.

"Oh, come on, you old cheapskate." She followed him. "You never spend money on anything and you know it. It'll do you good to expand your horizons."

"On steak?"

"If that's what it takes, then yes."

"You got a new hairdo."

She ran a hand over some curls at the back of her head, the ebony shot through with strands of gold. "I made a bold move, Claudius."

"Looks all right on you, Ruthie."

"I'm feeling a little bit restless. Been around this town my entire life."

He dropped the feed into the trunk. "It's a good town."

She crossed her arms over her chest and leaned her hip against the back fender of the car. "I've been grieving for half a century."

"Well, you never do anything halfway, Ruthie."

"True. But isn't that a little ridiculous? Jordy would have called someone who did that a fool."

"Yes, he would have."

"Have I been a fool?"

"No." He closed the trunk. "Well, I'm going to get those steaks, I reckon. What's your next step?"

She sighed. "I don't know. How much time we got left, Claudius?"

"Only the good Lord knows."

She pushed off the car and looked down at her feet. "Getting old isn't what it's cracked up to be."

"And it's not cracked up to be much."

"Maybe I should go away for a while."

Panic arose inside him. Silly old man. He shoved it down. "Never did hurt anybody."

He walked away. He had some steaks to buy. Ruthie could go wherever she liked. It wouldn't matter to him. Not really. It never did. He would still raise his chickens, his tomatoes, his pumpkins. He saw that.

"See you later, Ruthie!" he called over his shoulder nevertheless.

He put the steaks in the refrigerator and then hurried around to the scrap pile beside the barn. May-May had decided to make up her own recipe book. He'd bought her some notebook paper and a binder, and she busied herself most afternoons copying down recipes. He never asked where she pictured herself making them. Hopefully she had an idea. A little place of her own. Working at a magazine, like she'd planned to do before she went to Africa. She'd be set for a while.

At three o'clock that afternoon, he ushered her to the northwest side of the barn. "I made something for you."

A greenhouse, made out of French doors that a friend of the family, a contractor, had dropped off after redoing someone's kitchen. Claudius had made a backless cube of them, then attached it to the barn. "You love flowers, May-May? We'll grow flowers like you never seen this year."

She looked it over. "You made that in one day?"

"Oh, sure. It wasn't hard."

"Can we sell the flowers?"

"If you'll come with me."

"We'll see. Did your mother ever sell her flowers?"

"No. She give 'em away mostly. She knew how happy they seem to make folk."

May ran a hand over the side of the greenhouse. "It's very simple, isn't it? Flowers. Why is it? Why do they cheer people up?"

"Do we have to know that?" he asked.

"I guess not. Do you know it's been a year tomorrow?"

"Ruthie let on."

"I figured she would."

April 6 wouldn't be a day May could sit around and get depressed, Claudius decided. So he went upstairs to wake her up a little early.

Strange, she lay asleep with her hand in the nightstand drawer. He looked in at her fingers resting on some red fabric. He gently worked it out from beneath her fingers and unfolded a long, narrow strip of cloth, a cross embroidered at either end.

Maybe a Catholic matter.

He woke her.

Later, as he helped with the breakfast dishes, he said, "Well, May-May, I've got plans for us today."

"Well, I was planning on scrubbing the floors today."

"They'll keep 'til tomorrow. Dirt never minds waiting." He handed her the cutlery, ready to be dried and put away.

She enveloped them in the old checkered dish-towel.

"I've got some things to show you. It'll just be a nice walk. You think you're up to that?"

She'd gone further into her shell during the cold. It was time to let spring be spring. So far Claudius had let her pretend she needed to stay holed up in the house. But she was ready for some fresh air. He'd even set up the lawn chair before she awakened.

"What could a little walk hurt, May-May?"

"Maybe you're right. Sure, I'll come." She breathed in through her nose and laid her hands flat on the table.

"Good girl."

They finished up, and she slipped one of his old flannel shirts over her long-sleeved T-shirt, one of several from a Fruit of the Loom multi-colored pack Claudius brought back from Rose Brothers department store in town. Not long after she arrived, she'd come to him in tears, unable to face her own clothing.

"They remind me too much of who I was, Claudius. Who I am now. I can't stand them for another day."

He'd also bought her a pair of light gray work pants, much too large. Maybe one day he'd figure out how to judge sizes. Thankfully he had an extra belt.

Dressed in such heightened fashion—yes, he'd seen enough magazine covers at the Rite-Aid to know he had a terrible sense for clothing—she accompanied him to the far side of the yard where ivy vines grew in a great, leafy lump.

"You see that? Underneath all that are my mother's roses. I kept them up until about three years ago. The life might be choked out of them, but I was wondering if you might try your hand at bringing them back."

Violet smiled even more broadly back on the cookbook shelf, he was sure.

May nodded like a bobblehead, her grin matching Violet's. "I would."

"Well, all right then. Come see here now."

They walked to the edge of the woods behind the barn, over grass ready to grow tender and thin and bright green as it came out of dormancy. The farm was waking up.

A patch of bright purple caught her eye, and she pointed. "What are those?"

"That there is my mother's bulb garden. Mostly the crocuses and grape hyacinth are blooming now, but in a couple a weeks, glory, you'll see so many daffodils you'll have to wear sunglasses!" He laughed at his joke. He liked having someone to joke with.

She joined him. "Can I weed here? Maybe give the plants space to breathe? I mean, they need that, right?"

"They sure do. Used to keep this up too. Just so much a man my age can do, nowadays. I have to be a little choosy."

Did he ever. Had two of those WPW episodes yesterday alone. He might have to slow down more, get rid of the chickens. Aw, no. He couldn't get rid of those ladies.

They walked up the side of the woods toward the beginning of the front field. "Now I'm thinkin', May-May, that you can take the first three or four rows and plant all the flowers you want. You go through those flower catalogs and circle what you'd like, and we'll go from there."

"Really? That'll be expensive, won't it?"

He winked. "I got a little tucked away. It won't break the bank."

"If you're sure."

"Oh, it'll be nice having all that color around the place again. I'd forgotten how flowers tell me how much God loves me."

"I'm not—"

"Well, really now, honey, they don't need to be that pretty and that different from one another, do they? They could be, say, just as green as the grass and the leaves and still feed the honeybees. And now, let me show you something, just because."

He offered her his arm and she threaded hers through as they walked up the hill and into the woods, the path she'd seen him take with the dogs day after day. They soon began an upward climb.

"If you get tired, I'll stop so we can rest."

"My legs feel a little rubbery," she said. "I've been in the house too long."

"Do your knees still hurt?"

"They do a little. I figure I may never really get over the discomfort. And most likely arthritis will set in there."

"I hate to say it, but you're most likely right about that."

After about twenty minutes they arrived at a clearing atop the hill, what was, really, one of the foothills of the Appalachians. Before them an entire world spread out, the trees still bare, limbs sliding against one another in the breeze, the higher mountains bluing the distant horizon. A golden sun brightened the peaks; indigo shadows deepened the valleys. And birds. Singing and swooping above the bare treetops and diving close to the arboreal floor.

"Look at the world, May-May. It sure is a pretty sight."

"It's beautiful."

"Doesn't it just fill your heart with wonder?" he asked.

"Yes, it does."

"Wooh!" he exclaimed, and he pressed a hand to his heart doing that crazy rhythm. "I think I need to sit down for just a minute or two. That walk took it out of me."

They sat and looked before them, the dogs plopping down beside them. He knew she was feeling something. He found he could tell now and he didn't know why, or even how. It was just a sense he had.

"But it's not the whole world, is it?" she said. "Not even a mere sliver. Even less than that."

He knew she was right. He just never knew how to come to grips with it.

"Just a dot in the eye of God. And who cares about a dot?" she continued.

He felt the blood drain out of his face, and sweat broke out on his forehead.

"Are you okay, Claudius?"

"Oh, I'll be fine, just fine." He hated these strange heart things.

It didn't last long. He'd just been doing too much.

After a lunch of fried potatoes and onions, she suggested he lie down for a bit of a nap.

"I think I'll do just that, May-May. Would you mind milking Eloise?"

"I'd be happy to."

He had no idea whether or not she could. But it just didn't seem to matter. Eloise would understand. She was that kind of cow.

He was cooking the steaks several hours later when May came into the kitchen, freshly showered, hair slicked back and wet. It would dry and hang into her eyes and she'd keep pushing it back with her hand. She told him she hadn't decided whether to cut it short or let it grow out, that right now it was in that "in-between stage."

"Eloise didn't seem to mind my fumbling fingers on her udder, long-suffering bovine that she is."

"She's a sweet little cow." He turned one steak over, then the other. They'd better be good. He'd never spent twelve and a half dollars on meat for one meal in his life!

"I just rested my head against her flank, feeling the warmth of her. I never knew how much a person could love a cow!"

Yep, the meat was browning nicely, and the irony of cooking beef while talking about loving cows wasn't lost on him. "She's a good old gal."

"She seems like the nice shy woman who gained more weight than the rest of her classmates and never felt comfortable at the reunions."

He laughed. "You really are a writer, aren't you?"

"I was." She sighed. "A journalist."

"Maybe you should start up again. I'll bet that journalist is still interested in your story. Maybe you should just write it down."

"I don't know. I also threw some feed to the chickens and fed the goat. Why do you keep that little goat around? He doesn't give us milk or meat."

"Because he's funny. Got no other reason."

"Maybe I need to spend more time with that goat!"

The next morning May pulled down her new recipe book as Claudius slid into his muck boots. An envelope poking out from the pages caught his eye. The letter from the reporter. He pointed at it.

"Maybe it'd be good to finally talk about it, honey. To someone who doesn't know you."

"I don't know, Claudius. I mean, what if it brings it all back? I've been pretty good at forgetting everything here."

He knew it had to be otherwise. "It's been a mask, May-May. A pretty little mask, and I've been honored to walk along with you, but someday—"

"I know. I'll have to face it." She lifted the right corner of her mouth. "But it hasn't been so bad shoving it aside, I have to say."

"It's easy enough to do. Let's remove that ivy tomorrow and give them roses some room to grow. That might be an easier first step than inviting some writer we don't know over for tea."

She laid a hand on his arm and thanked him.

But she laid the letter from the writer, Eugene Damaroff, on the hoosier. "Maybe it wouldn't hurt to at least think about it."

Tomorrow was laundry day, so she gathered the week's clothes. A few T-shirts and flannels, work pants, jeans, and the big white granny panties Claudius just laid on her bed without a word. And Playtex Cross Your Heart bras. He guessed that was the kind Violet wore. It embarrassed the tar out of him to purchase those in town, and it might have set the tongues to wagging, but Claudius just said,

"Heard of a woman who's down and out." And Ruthie, standing beside him, bore him out, saying, "That sure is the truth!"

So much for the platinum blonde college girl with the deep tan and designer handbags, whose every move emitted a jangle of jewelry and a puff of perfume. As much as he loved her, there was a part of him that grieved that little slip of a thing who drank too much and liked to kiss the boys.

The next morning they ate a quick breakfast of Shredded Wheat, the big biscuit kind, and milk from Eloise. "Seems to me the milk you got out of her is better'n mine," Claudius said.

"You're the nicest person in the whole world."

"Well, I don't know about that."

After she set the washing machine to running, they walked toward Violet's rose garden.

12

By ten o'clock they had pulled away the vines. The poor rosebushes looked like skeletons. Claudius reached out with his penknife and cut a stem near the base of the plant. "Still green down there. There's hope."

"What do we do next?"

"Cut away the dead wood, I suppose."

Girlfriend and Scout lay belly up in the sunshine. Soon they'd both be snoring away.

"I love those animals," May said. "I love all the animals around here, actually. And I think Eloise is becoming rather fond of me."

"You're a good milker, May-May. She probably appreciates your gentle touch."

"I was thinking maybe we should get another goat. A female. Or sheep? We could raise lambs."

He was surprised. "You realize lambs turn into sheep, and then they're just more mouths to feed."

"I was thinking about the wool."

Claudius had recently brought her some wool yarn from a lady who made it at her farm, spinning wheel and everything. He saw Madge regularly at the farmers' market and showed up at her place to barter some milk for a skein of the softest gray wool he ever felt. May proceeded to knit another scarf.

"Growin' your own wool? That's a fine idea!"

"It would be a good winter project."

"I agree."

Claudius was happy she was thinking about the future, but he didn't want to risk saying so. He pulled a pair of pruning shears out of his back pocket and handed them to her. "Have at it, honey."

"But what if I do it wrong?"

"These plants can't be any worse off than they are now, can they?"

"Probably not."

"Oh"—he reached into his pocket—"here." He held out a pair of gardening gloves, brand new, just her size, on sale at the Family Dollar.

She slid them on, bending her fingers after the yellow fabric snuggled around them.

"Okay. Here we go."

She reached for a branch, a gnarled dead branch, and snipped it off. She winced. "Was that right?"

"Looks that way to me. You go ahead and do what you think is best. I'm off to water the animals."

There must have been thirty bushes, all in much the same condition. He had no idea what kind of roses they were, and in a way that was good. If they could get them to bloom, she could snip the blossoms and they'd compare them to pictures in the catalogs.

May-May loved her flowers. Maybe she could do something with them. He didn't know. But he figured it was worth a try.

By noon clippings lay all around in piles like arthritic pick-up sticks. Claudius climbed the hill with a wheelbarrow. "Let's haul these down, and we can throw them in the woodstove tonight. It's supposed to get cool."

His prediction proved correct, and that night they sat around the stove, no need for the usual heavy blanket but appreciating the warmth.

"It's nice to see those old bushes again." Claudius laid down *The Three Musketeers*. "I'd be lying if I didn't admit it."

"When did your mother pass away, Claudius?"

"About ten years ago."

"Really? For some reason, I figured it was much longer than that."

"We were a pair. She wanted so much for me to find a nice woman, settle down here. She even said she'd move off the farm and go live with her sister in Clay City."

"She was a good mother, wasn't she?"

"Yes, she was, May-May. I just couldn't seem to face her flowers after a while, though. Hurt too much." He raised his hand. "Now I don't want to be sounding like a mama's boy!"

"Of course not."

"'Cause I wasn't."

"No. I believe that."

He could tell by the look on her face she didn't.

"She was just something, is all."

"Well, maybe it's time for you to face those flowers again."

"Aw, I don't know. But you doing it for me sure is something I could use."

"Father Isaac once told me it's not bad to bear each other's burdens, Claudius."

"No, it ain't. You're right about that. That Saint Paul, as you all call him?"

"I have no idea!"

They laughed and returned to their reading, he in France with Musketeers, May in the plant catalog he'd brought home.

"I don't want to think I'm putting the cart before the horse, as you might say, Claudius, but I have a feeling those roses are going to do just fine."

"I'm sure they're glad somebody cares for them again."

The next morning an old ledger-type book with a crinkly black surface sat beside May's breakfast plate. She picked it up. "What's this?"

"It was my mother's gardening journal. She kept detailed notes every year."

May looked like she'd been given a map to buried treasure.

"I figured it would be a guide of sorts for you."

"Oh, my gosh, yes!" She flipped it open, and lines of Violet's perfect handwriting flowed across each page. "This is wonderful!" She turned to the last year. 1983.

"And it might help you narrow down what them roses are."

"That's right!"

"Why don't you take the morning off and read through it?" He reached behind him to the hoosier and lifted off a composition book, black with white speckles. "You can make your own notes and start your own journal, May-May. Some things need to be written down. It's important. And you never know who'll need it someday."

"It's true! Who'd have thought I'd be taking over Violet's gardens?"

His smile felt so wide, he wondered how it hadn't swallowed up his eyesight with it. But there she stood before him, her hair in a little ponytail now, her skin pink from working outside yesterday. And he was proud of her. So proud! "Life can turn on you in ways you never could imagine."

"For good and for bad."

"We just have to enjoy the good and recognize it, May-May."

She set down the book. "You're good at that. Maybe I'm starting to learn that too."

"That's good." He reached for his jacket hanging on the hook near the kitchen door. Time for chores.

"I mean, Rwanda happened, and it was horrible. But does it have to ruin the rest of my life?"

He didn't know. "I don't believe so, but I've never—"

"Just tell me it doesn't, Claudius! You can, you know." Her blue eyes glowed with a begging need, as if she was floating out from shore in a little boat, and all he needed to do was catch the rope she was throwing to keep her from drifting away completely.

He caught it. "No, May-May. It doesn't. The lady who grew those flowers you're bringing back to life—I'll bet she thought her life was over when she found out she was pregnant with me. But it didn't ruin the rest of her life, now did it?"

"No! You're here!"

He smiled at that. "I am indeed."

· 13 ·

Claudius headed off to the first farmers' market of the year in Lexington. He loaded up the Galaxy with crates of tender greens and jars of apple and pumpkin butter. Several sugar buckets held bouquets of daffodils, some pure white, others pure yellow, others mixed, some with bright orange centers. May had bundled them in groups of six or twelve. She'd clipped the stems evenly and tied them with white satin ribbon Claudius found at Ellen's Uniques in town, a shop with the oddest collection of craft supplies and decorative items he'd ever seen. Not that he'd seen many. Or any, for that matter. But something that hodgepodge clearly wasn't normal, was it? It sure was interesting though.

He returned from the city with the news that every single bouquet had been purchased. "You made yourself fifty dollars today from them posies, May-May."

He handed her the bills, and she handed them right back.

"You keep this, Claudius, after all the food and warmth and clothing you've given me."

He said nothing and slipped the money into his front shirt pocket.

As the spring turned into summer, those fifty dollars would turn up in the oddest places. The sugar bin, May's gardening gloves. She'd return the favor. In his book, his fiddle case. And they never said a word about it. Claudius spent too much time thinking about where the next hiding place would be, and he didn't care.

As the rosebushes struggled, the rest of the flowers grew: tulips (a big hit with the city dwellers), irises in purples, whites, and yellows, larkspur and zinnias, Jacob's ladder, daisies, sunflowers, dianthus, primroses, delphinium, snapdragons. Some raised from seed in the tiny greenhouse Claudius fashioned, others from the catalog company as promised, lilies mostly: Stargazer, Elyse, Silk Road, and May's favorite, Orange Crush. Glen the postman would deliver those all the way up the drive.

The first time Glen made a personal delivery, Claudius had made sure May stayed by the door. She needed to see someone other than him and Sister Ruth occasionally. The world was so big once, now it was so small.

"He wasn't scary," May said after Glen climbed back into his Jeep. "He was nice. He has those basset hound eyes and, I have to admit, nice calf muscles."

Claudius was glad to hear that kind of talk. Meant she was alive again, or at least starting to open up like the flowers she arranged so prettily.

And every Friday she'd sit in her circle of flowers, clippings around her, and fashion posies for the people of Lexington to grace their tables and counters with. Maybe they'd take some of them to a loved one in the hospital or the assisted living home. Maybe they'd take them to church.

"I almost don't want to know," she said one evening as she arranged the bouquets in an old five-gallon paint bucket. "Wondering is so much better than knowing for sure."

"Sometimes it's fun picturing them, though. You ever do that?" Claudius, tired, threw himself down on the grass and arranged his arms behind his head.

"I sometimes picture an elderly lady, the tops of her feet puffing up from her pumps as if they'd been stuffed with down."

He laughed. His mother had that sort of feet.

"She comes up with a purse hanging from the crook of her arm. And she tells me how she's always loved flowers, has purchased a bouquet every week for the kitchen table in the small apartment she's lived in for years since coming to the city to teach kindergarten after her husband died in the coal mines."

She sat down next to him, cross-legged.

"Sounds like a reasonable way to imagine it. You do get some old women buying your posies, so who's to say whether or not you're right about at least one of them. I can tell you this, though, most of them leave with a little smile on their face."

"But why flowers, Claudius? Why do flowers do this for people?"

"You know why yourself. You told me you were always taking pictures of flowers even though nobody else was. And you did it for you. Why?"

"I just think they're pretty."

"Well, there you go, then."

Finally, the week of the one-year anniversary of May's return to the United States, Claudius sat her down. "Now, I haven't wanted to tell you this, because I didn't want you to get a big head or anything." He smiled. "But people wait in lines to get your posies, May-May. Just tomorrow, would you drive into Lexington with me so they can meet you? I'll take your chair for you, and you won't have to do a thing. If you want something to keep you busy, we can take some flowers and you can make posies on the spot."

"But there won't be room for me in the car, will there?" Hope against hope.

"Oh, we'll figure it out. Not as many tomatoes ripened this week as I thought. Don't worry about that."

"Can I think about it for a couple of hours?"

"Suit yourself, honey."

She gathered the blooms and set them in buckets of water as he harvested his whimsical heirloom tomatoes. She whistled to the dogs, who came running from behind the barn where they'd been sleeping in the shade. The day was hot. Late July was always hot in Kentucky.

He watched as May and the dogs trekked toward the back of the property, up the hill into the woods to the clearing. She stood on the edge of the world, he knew. Maybe she picked Girlfriend up in her arms and kissed her head and face, running a hand over her soft ears. Maybe Scout sat panting, dripping lips in a grin of sorts. Nice old dog.

The foothills spread out like wide skirts of green.

She was gone for another half hour, and he wished he could hear her thoughts. What could it hurt really, she might be thinking. All she had to do was sit in a chair and smile. She'd done that plenty of times in college classes, hadn't she?

"Why not?" she said to Claudius as she sliced green tomatoes to fry up for supper. She dipped the slices in a bowl of buttermilk, then in a plate of cornmeal, salt, and pepper.

"I knew you'd see sense, May-May. You always do."

"Really?"

"Eventually. I'd say you're ready for this."

She stopped, her fingertips plump with cornmeal. "I don't know."

"I do."

· 14 ·

Loaded up and ready to set out by 5:30 a.m., they'd already tipped back two mugs of coffee and eaten two bowls of Shredded Wheat.

"You won't have time to breathe, May-May, it'll get so busy." He loved the bustle of the market, the chatting, the bright colors, the canvas shelters; he loved the aromas of fresh vegetables and baked goods. Combine those with the sizzling smell of sausages and burgers cooking from the trailer one of the local stock farms always set up, and the music of the street musicians, it all made for a feast of the senses. It was like going to a carnival every week.

"Now, usually I try to resist, May-May, but I do believe today we'll treat ourselves to some ribs one of the city ministries sets up to raise money."

"I love ribs!"

"Yep. Set up the barbecue right there. And some cornbread and coleslaw too."

He hoped that would provide a little sense of comfort or adventure. She was blazing forward, a new trail, a path that would have been tame and not much fun last year, he suspected.

"You'll see, May-May. You'll have a fine time."

She opened the door to the Galaxy. "Father Isaac would have gotten a kick out of it, that's for sure. He'd have struck up conversations with each customer. He'd definitely have found something in common or something to joke about."

"He sounds like a good man."

She slid in. So did he.

"And you know what, Claudius? It wouldn't be but a minute or two until they would open up and start sharing their pain. Father Isaac had that way about him. He never condemned me. He let me know I wasn't the first to go astray and I wouldn't be the last."

He pulled out onto Route 11. "You act like you were so bad, honey. Sounds like a typical wild youth. Not overly wild, mind you. Not a lot of drugs or stealing or something."

She laughed. "Maybe I've just got a guiltier conscience than most people!"

"Maybe it's time to move on. It's been almost a year since you've stepped off the farm. Unless you were sneaking off at night, I think you've most likely behaved yourself quite circumspectly."

She laughed a loud quick *Ha!* and turned to him, leaned forward a little, and laid her hand on his arm. "Claudius, you are exactly right!" She slammed back with relief against the seat. "You just gotta move on from some things, right?"

"Right!" He wasn't about to bring Rwanda into it. First things first.

—Maybe I should speak up more often.

"I mean," she said, "I didn't realize until just now that I could move on. It's been a long time since I let a guy—"

"Good for you!" He had to interrupt that sentence and quick.

Claudius pointed out who lived where (my old Sunday school teacher's granddaughter and her family in that yellow house there), what they farmed (soybeans and corn to the left), and where they worked (at the prison in Campton, or the Shell station near the gorge), trying his best to sell her on the outside world (and if you look up yonder on that ridge, you'll see a bitty little cabin where my great-granddaddy was born). They both waved to Glen, out doing his Saturday delivery on Route 11.

"You been to a Dairy Queen in a while?" Claudius asked after they passed it.

"No."

"Me neither. Heard down at the feed store they have things

called Blizzards. They're these thick shakes with whatever kind of candy you're hankering for thrown in and whizzed up."

"I've had them."

"They worth the press they get?"

"Yep. They sure are, Claudius."

"Well, maybe I'll give that a try. Live a little."

He pulled onto the Mountain Parkway in Slade. The divided highway flowed next to the Red River.

"Is that the Red River of that Red River Valley song?" she asked.

"I have no idea, honey. But this ain't the Red River Valley, so I doubt it's the same. Must be a lot of Red Rivers across the country."

They puttered along the parkway, most of the cars passing the old white Galaxy. They didn't seem to mind. He figured they had to admire the car was still capable of fifty-five miles per hour.

"You know, I just remembered my own little car sitting there in my parents' driveway. I don't know why I haven't thought to go pick it up."

Well, he could have told her that.

"Maybe because I didn't need it, or maybe I just don't want it anymore. I mean really, Claudius, look at me. Can you imagine me in that thing?"

He had to admit she didn't match it anymore, sitting there in oversize work clothes with wild brown hair and pale skin and hands that looked like they hadn't ever seen a manicurist at the beauty parlor.

"I haven't worn makeup since my first day in Rwanda. If you'd held up a before and after picture, you wouldn't think I was the same person."

Claudius cleared his throat. "I was wondering something, May-May. Now, as it's coming right on the heels of this big day in Lexington, I may be taking my chances, but I figure life's one big chance anyways. I mean, not in the larger sense, but every day, if you know what I mean."

"Boy, do I."

"Sometimes we have to step out a little. Take a risk here or there."

"That's true."

"Like you're doing today." He cleared his throat again. "At my church, they have a . . ." He paused and gripped the steering wheel. "Oh, never mind. It's probably a silly idea."

"Oh, go ahead. It's only me."

"True enough. All right. Well, the ladies like to put together a father-daughter banquet every year. It's just a little thing. Fried chicken. More like a picnic. And the Nada Gospel Trio usually sings."

He actually felt himself flush. And her broad smile didn't help matters any.

"Do you want me to go with you?"

"I was just thinking that maybe—"

"Do folks there know about me?"

He nodded. "Yep. Been praying for you all along."

"Really?"

"Why do you think I haven't had anybody come visit me? I'm not a recluse, you know."

"You know, you do seem too nice to be a hermit."

"That'd be about right. And you know, you could say the same about yourself."

"Hmm, maybe." She looked out the window. "I don't really have the right clothing for an event like that."

They exited off the parkway and west onto I-64.

"Did you bring all your clothes with you after you came back from Africa?"

"I left some at my parents' house."

"Thcy in Lexington, right?"

"Yes."

"Can we swing by? Would wearing one outfit from the old days set you back too much?"

She stared at him. What was she thinking? Did she feel beholden to him in some way? Wondering if she could refuse him after all he'd done. Not that he wouldn't do it again and for nothing. But he knew this request wasn't only for him. Maybe it was another step to life.

"We can go by there after the market."

He tapped the steering wheel. "Good. That's just what we'll do."

"Maybe my parents won't be home."

All the happiness he felt faded from flame to a withering tendril of smoke.

Claudius backed the car up along the sidewalk flanking Vine Street, one of the later vendors to arrive. Someone from a farm out in Scott County offered them a cup of hot coffee after they'd unloaded the produce and the flowers. The only rose to bloom so far was a big white blossom May had tucked in with the daisies for good luck.

"So you're the flower lady!" the woman who gave them the coffee said, walking over to inspect her bouquets.

"That's me."

She placed her hand on her hip, its tan contrasting with the pale yellow skirt and matching the copper buttons down the front. "I'm Nellie Poe."

"May Seymour."

"Pleased to meet you. I figured the Tomato Man here didn't make those on his own. Now, his tomatoes. You have to see them for the work of art they are."

Claudius was proud to be known as the Tomato Man once he began harvesting his heirlooms. Black Princes, Brandywines, Yellow Pears, Green Grapes, Green Zebras, Lillian's Yellow. The young business folks or those artsy kinds loved them to put in their salads. The Kroger sure couldn't compete with him on these beauties. Of course, Kentucky Beefsteaks and other nice big, round slicing tomatoes sat beside the unusual varieties.

May sat and listened to him chatting with the shoppers about each variety, almost like they were his children. He was grateful to see a cheerful look playing on her face most of the morning.

"Clearly you're well liked," she said during a lull. Lawyer-types, hippies, young people just getting started in life all wanted to talk to Claudius, laugh and joke, and usually get a sample. He was only too happy to provide them a sweet taste of earth, water, and sunshine.

"You can't expect people to buy tomatoes like these when they don't know if they taste good."

A woman came running up to May. She wore clogs on her bare feet, a pair of knickers, and an Indian tunic. Her hair, wild gray and held back in a headband, heralded her arrival better than any trumpeter ever could.

"I love your flowers!" she cried, clapping hands that sported various turquoise and silver rings.

"Oh, good!" May's face brightened even further.

"I get at least four bouquets each week and make random deliveries at St. Joseph's Hospital. And usually, I get one for myself." She scrunched up her nose. "I can't help it."

"Thanks. I'm so glad you like them."

At least ten more people came up and complimented her posies. Claudius puffed out his chest with pride, couldn't help himself. May made a few bouquets to order. But the most surprising and beautiful part of the day occurred when a young woman arrived around nine o'clock. Her long brown hair, wavy and full, swung beside her cheeks.

"I'm getting married this morning! Over at Duncan Park."

Claudius had heard of Duncan Park, a square of green in one of the poorer neighborhoods.

"Can you make me a bouquet?" Hope and apology raised her eyebrows.

"This morning?" May's mouth dropped open.

"Just something simple. It's a simple wedding. Very simple."

She looked like an Old World portrait with her soft cheeks, pointed chin, and wide brown eyes.

"Sure. Fine. That sounds like fun."

Claudius tried to act nonchalant.

—Spontaneity! This might be just the ticket!

May stood up from her chair. "First, why don't we pick out the flowers you like?"

The young woman chattered as she pulled stems from the tubs. White lilies, larkspur, yellow daisies. "I'm just going to get my favorites. It doesn't matter if they don't go together perfectly."

"I think all flowers go together perfectly." May turned toward Claudius. "If a real florist heard that, she'd probably want to hang me. But it's how I feel."

"And I like nice warm colors."

"The larkspur will set them off, won't they?" May asked, gathering each stem into the bundle as the bride handed it off. "Is your dress white?"

"Yes. My mom's."

"That's nice."

"Me and my fiancé don't have a lot of money, and we didn't want to go into a lot of debt for one day. That's kinda stupid, don't you think?"

"I wouldn't have two years ago. I mean, why not drop fifty grand? But now, I totally agree. How about some of that wine-colored dianthus?"

"Perfect!"

Claudius was enjoying the banter, sipping on another cup of coffee from Nellie. Watching May interact with another young woman made his heart soar like he was atop Natural Bridge. Maybe his prayers were being answered more than he realized.

May ran her fingertips over the top of the bundle. "Lovely choices, good job. "What's your name?"

"Maria."

"Okay. I'm May-May. I've only got white ribbon. Is that all right?"

"Great."

—She calls herself May-May.

After arranging for her return in thirty minutes, Maria sidled down the row between the stalls, stuffing produce into a couple of string bags.

"Do you think she's going to cook up reception food when she gets home?" May asked, holding up the flowers. "People really do stuff like this? I love it!"

Claudius walked over, pretending he hadn't heard a thing, hands shoved in his pants' pockets. "What'd that lady want?"

"This is going to be her bridal bouquet, Claudius. Can you believe it?"

"I'd say she's got the right idea."

She sat in her chair and tried different arrangements. "It seems to be missing something." She searched the buckets.

"A few extra blooms wouldn't break the bank," Claudius said, turning to help out a customer who held up a Black Prince like it had the Black Death.

When he finished he faced her again. The single white rose from the daisy bucket now snuggled up to the side of Maria's wedding bouquet.

Maria loved it.

"Just take it!" May flushed. "I want you to have it."

"Oh, no!" she said. "I can't do that."

But May shook her head. "It's selfish on my part. I'd like say I provided a part of your great day. Please, take it."

When Maria walked off, her hair swung against her back.

"I wish her well, Claudius." They stood next to each other, and she put her arm through his.

"Maybe it'll be the best day of her life up till now."

May continued hearing nice words from people who had been enjoying her flowers that summer, telling her where they placed their bouquets, who they'd given them to and why.

They ate ribs and coleslaw in the shade of his tarp.

"Claudius, you were right. This was good to hear."

"And this is good to eat." He nibbled the tender meat off a bone.

"You said it."

More custom bouquets found their way into customers' hands. One woman, not at all a nice lady, got May so flustered, Claudius stepped in.

"Now you need to shape up, miss, right now, or you can just go down to Barney. He's selling flowers right down there by the bank."

She threw the bouquet down and turned on her heel. May looked like she'd been slapped. She whispered, "I've read in books about people turning on their heel, but that was the first time I've seen a real bona fide heel turn."

"I was surprised she didn't overshoot the arc and turn a full 360 degrees," Claudius whispered out the side of his mouth, laying a hand on her arm. She felt shaky beneath his touch. "But she's in for it now. Barney's meaner than she is!"

May wiped her eyes with her forearm and gave a shaky laugh. "Something like that would have never bothered me before. I'm a marshmallow!"

Claudius squeezed her arm. "Don't worry about her. She does that sort of thing to everybody. Most folks are nice, though. You gotta take the bad with the good."

After he hugged her, she straightened up, sat in her chair, and arranged the remaining stems into posies. By three o'clock they were all sold.

"Oh, no!" A young woman came running up. "You're all out? Really? Shoot! I knew I shouldn't have slept so late. But last night, well, you know how Friday nights can be." She laughed. "That'll teach me." She narrowed her eyes at May. "You look familiar." She hiked her purse, embossed with a mess of Cs, further up on her shoulder.

May just shook her head. "I'm from Beattyville."

"My family's from there! Years and years ago, though."

"There's a man with flowers down by the bank." May thickened her Lexingtonian accent into something more country. Like Claudius's.

He snapped his head around to stare at her.

"You might could try there."

"Yours are *so* much better."

"Why, thank you."

"See ya!"

And off she went.

May plopped into her chair and heaved out three sighs in one.

Claudius knelt down on his haunches beside her. "What was that about, honey?"

"Did you see her, Claudius? She looked so pretty in those white shorts, that tank top. Did you see those gold flowers embroidered on there? And so tan! Most likely she spent the majority of her summer in the islands or something. Her family also owns a rambling beachfront house on the Outer Banks. When we were friends at Lexington Catholic it was like the princess and the pauper, and my family isn't exactly poor."

"She was your friend?"

"Uh-huh. Ashley Caudhill. I was crossing my fingers behind my back the whole time, hoping she'd fail to make the connection. I mean, how could she? I used to look like her, now I look like me."

"I think you're a whole lot prettier." He never did care much for those glamour girls.

"And then she was off, so free of care. Her skin all silky and shimmery and so perfect. Did you see her arms and legs, Claudius?"

—Oh, sweet Lord Jesus! We were doing so good. Why'd that girl have to show up?

"And she was wearing Eau d'Hadrien, one of the most expensive perfumes in the world. Did you know that?"

"'Course I didn't, May-May!"

She flinched. And he turned away. He could take almost anything but people feeling sorry for themselves.

His heart melted, and he turned back. "Honey, you have more to feel bad about than overpriced perfume only stupid people would waste their money on to begin with. Don't pity yourself about the wrong things. You'll never heal that way."

—I'd better watch myself. I'm starting to give pretty good advice.

· 15 ·

May's parents had moved since she'd last seen them, and she wanted to see her old house, the one in which she'd grown up, before heading to their new place. They drove east down Main Street, and then right on Ashland where soaring old houses on large lots bullied for first place in the Southern home beauty contest.

Claudius whistled. "Woo-whee."

"Up there to the right. That yellow brick house with the curved bay."

He pulled into a brick driveway. "You must have had a good time growing up here."

He liked the landscaping, lush and with lots of flowers. Mature boxwoods and holly and trellises up the side of the house with roses. "Your parents do that?"

"Yes. But my grandparents set the blueprint."

"Must have been nice. Nice big yard to run around in."

"And Woodland Park nearby." She pointed to a window on the right side of the second floor. "That was my room. We painted it sky blue, and Dad painted big fluffy clouds on the ceiling for me." She leaned toward him and whispered. "Between you and me, they were pretty bad, but he tried so hard."

"No one will ever know," he whispered back. "So where do they live now?"

"Jefferson Street." Her voice dropped in tone.

"That a bad street?"

"Mixed. I haven't wanted to think about what it might mean. Maybe they just wanted to be closer to campus."

Even Claudius knew Lexington well enough to know that it wasn't closer to campus at all.

When they pulled up to the new address, Claudius reached over and placed a hand on her forearm. "Oh, honey."

She breathed in deeply, her nostrils flaring. "I had no idea."

A sagging chain-link fence surrounded a narrow lot in which a small shotgun shack, one room behind the other, was anchored, but barely. The roof had exhaled long ago and forgotten to take a breath again. The white siding was chipped at the bottom, leaving a gap-toothed appearance; the windows, clean yet bedraggled of frame, one on each side of the gray front door, were shadowed by a front porch held up by rusted wrought iron curlicues.

She pointed to the clay pots blooming with portulaca on the porch.

"Mother threw those pots herself as a college student." Red cedar lounge chairs from the fifties—"Mother stained them every year"—also rested on the cement surface. The cushions were worse for wear, but Claudius figured replacing them wouldn't be in the budget. Not if they were living in that house.

"Is it 'cause of the medical bills, honey?"

She nodded. "I doubt if Dad's insurance pays a hundred percent. A stroke is pretty expensive."

Claudius knew that. His father had had one, and that was back before hospital stays got to be a major investment. He hoped and prayed he never had to stay in one. The vigil with his mother, who'd sustained such terrible injuries after a fall down the stairs, the same stairs he carried May up all those months ago, had been enough hospital to last him the rest of his life, however long or short that might be.

"You heard them talking about their move, Claudius. They made it sound like a sweet little adventure."

Claudius opened his door. "Well, are we going in? They've told you a thousand times to come home."

"Not since the move," she whispered.

"Seems to me they were trying not to burden you. And they were right, May-May. A few weeks ago you couldn't have handled this. But today's a different day! You came to Lexington, sold your posies. C'mon, parents are resilient."

She laughed.

He never stopped appreciating that May always got the joke.

Then her smile dropped off her face. "I don't know if I can do this."

"Then don't."

—Oh, Claudius, you fool! That's the worst thing you could have said.

He closed the car door and turned in his seat. "Naw, maybe not that. Honestly, honey, isn't it time?"

She shook her head as she gripped the door handle. Beads of sweat pushed through the pores of her forehead. "Let's go home. They can't know I know. They can't, Claudius." She swept a hand across the car window. "Look at this place. I think I owe it to them to let them decide whether or not they want me to know this."

He pulled the gearshift toward him and then slid it down into drive. "Well, all right, then." He pulled away from the curb. "But I think you're wrong, May-May. I think you should go in. I think they'd want you there no matter what."

She turned her face to the window and didn't look over at him the entire ninety minutes back to Beattyville.

His heart sagged. He wouldn't let it break, though. He couldn't do that to her, or himself. He had to be ready for whatever came their way tomorrow.

The next day, warmed by the slanted light of the evening sun, they sat at the picnic table outside Dairy Queen, May licking at a swirl cone and Claudius enjoying a Blizzard.

"These are so tasty. I think I'm enjoying the Butterfinger variety the most."

This little foray was a concession for yesterday, and he knew it.

He sighed.

So did May.

"I should have gone in," she said. "They're my parents."

"I don't know what to tell you, honey."

· 16 ·

Claudius stood in the living room wearing his only suit, a charcoal gray pinstripe he'd had tailor-made in Lexington in 1940 when he graduated from high school, the style of which had come and gone, come and gone. It had been expensive, but worth it. He doubted even his mother realized what a bargain it would turn out to be.

It was supposed to get him through college at the University of Kentucky. But he had to go to war, and there it sat in the closet. Then he didn't have the heart, after spending all that time on a submarine, to go to school. The farm seemed a fine way to make a living, already producing, a nice little house, and the animals with their breathing in and out and chewing and being let in and out of the barn . . . well, it was the routine of it all, he guessed. He couldn't say there were not surprises on the farm, but the surprises were expected. And he could stretch his limbs and enjoy his own room.

"What are you thinking of?"

He looked up from his thoughts and there May stood at the bottom of the steps.

"You didn't even hear me come down, you were so lost."

"Well, now. Don't you look a picture."

"Do your church ladies wear much makeup?"

"Never noticed. You're pretty as is, May-May."

She rolled her eyes. "I have makeup on, Claudius."

He laughed. "Well, it's not Sister Racine makeup, then. She looks ready to step on the stage!"

"So the outfit is okay?"

He was going to scoff at her worries over her appearance, then realized this was her first real outing, other than the market and Dairy Queen, in almost a year. "It sure is! I'm glad it fits."

She really didn't have anything appropriate for church, so he brought back a magazine from Jack's, one of those celebrity ones where he recognized absolutely nobody anymore and what's more didn't exactly care to. Stars just weren't what they used to be in the days Betty Grable was strutting along pretty-as-you-please or Clark Gable burned up the screen. And don't even get him started on music.

Wait. There he went again, his mind wandering. He felt a little odd, he had to admit. Somewhat observing life this morning, not participating. Well, that was enough of that! He cleared his throat. "I think that blue dress suits you more than fine. You clean up right nice. Fancy."

"You picked out a good one." She twirled, the breezy fabric tenting in a circle around her. She'd pulled her hair back into a short little ponytail and anchored it in place with some hairspray he'd purchased.

"Now you did use a little lipstick, I see." It looked nice, a sweet pink. Very youthful.

"It was still in my backpack from Rwanda."

A tube of lipstick from her old life—a survivor of sorts too. Well, there you go. He didn't know why that felt so strange to him, to think of a tube of lipstick surviving a war, but it did. A tube of lipstick should be the last thing to survive.

"I like your suit, Claudius," she said, reaching out and lifting his blue tie, feeling the soft silk. "And look at those fine shoes. Wing tips!"

She was excited about wing tips? Odd. But he'd take it.

He handed her a cup of coffee in the kitchen.

"Thanks, Claudius. So we're going to Mass first, then the picnic?"

He practically spit out his own coffee. "Well, honey, we just call it a church service."

She pinkened. "I'm sorry. I just . . . I just don't have much experience with this kind of church."

"Oh, don't you worry about a thing. The folks are real nice there."

He wished he hadn't corrected her. Maybe it would make her stay home. He would have to keep things on track. Today was a big day. He could feel it. It would change everything for her. What did Sister Ruth call days like this?

Springboards. That was it. Today was going to be a springboard for May-May.

"And you already know Sister Ruth."

"I like her."

"Well, you'll be seeing more of her. She just retired when school ended, so she'll be getting into everybody's business a bit more often."

May laughed. "You two act like brother and sister."

That sure was truer than he liked to believe.

He offered her his arm as she gulped her coffee, then set the cup back onto her place mat.

With the dogs jumping around, sensing something unusual and upbeat was going on, they slid into the Galaxy and soon were driving the mile down Route 11 into town. They crossed over the river and took a left on River Road. The church, a small white wooden building, the kind you see in model train gardens and any small town in America, was already open for business. White steps led up either side of the front to green double doors pushed open to the summer air and the sound of humming insects. Above the doors the sign *Harmony Baptist* hopefully proclaimed more than empty hopes for the congregation. Claudius liked to think it did.

He parked in one of about fifteen spaces, then turned off the car. "Now don't worry, because I've told everybody not to overwhelm you."

"Okay."

"Now you just sit tight."

He came around and opened her door, offering his arm as she slid out.

"Why some woman didn't jump at you in your day, I don't know."

"Some women are just nuts, was all I could ever figure."

She threaded her arm through his, and they walked across a thankfully unpeopled parking lot, up the front steps, and into the church. The choir was just getting up to sing.

The director said, "Well, hey, Brother Claudius."

The entire congregation swung their faces around to get a look at May.

"Wasn't welcomed down the street when I was a youngster, so Mom and Dad brought me here," Claudius whispered, feeling the need to tell her why everybody was like him and nobody was like her.

Her eyes widened, her face drained of all its color at the sight of them all.

"Oh, my," she whispered, tears now running down her face. Her knees buckled.

"She's out!" he cried, catching her beneath the armpits as she slid to the ground.

She came to within a ring of concerned faces.

Claudius leaned over. "Honey, you all right? May-May?" He patted her hand again and again.

She pulled in a deep breath. "I don't know what happened."

"You give us a scare, that's what," Sister Racine said, on her plump knees in a red suit that matched a blazing red hat the size of his mother's old wash pan. "Lordymercy, child. Let's get you sitting up. Sister Ruth is fetching you a glass of water."

She took May's hands and pulled her up with a good yank. May's eyes widened, and she gave out a little cry.

"She a plain little thing, but there's a lot of love in her eyes," she said to Claudius.

May smiled.

"See?" Racine said.

Sister Ruth ran up on her spindly bowed legs, her narrow black patent leather pumps giving her little tracking on the wood floor. How she didn't spill the glass of water she'd grabbed from the pulpit Claudius couldn't imagine.

"You all look ready to go to Churchill Downs," May said.

"Here you are, honey. Drink a little. You might just be dehydrated." She pronounced it de-hy-DRA-ted.

May let her hold the cup to her lips. It seemed everybody knew she needed a little TLC. It was written all over her face. And it always had been, Claudius realized, from the first moment he pulled his car over that morning more than two years ago.

A few minutes later they'd tucked her in the second pew from the back, Claudius on one side, big black Bible on his lap, Sister Ruth on the other, big red Bible on hers. Her black-and-white hound's-tooth skirt—his father had once had a hound's-tooth jacket—flared over the golden wood of the pew. Above the skirt she wore a white jacket with a big silk rose pinned to the lapel. Hot pink. One just like it rested above the brim of her smart straw hat.

—That woman! Such a fine woman!

"I love all the hats," May whispered.

There was something lovely about women in hats. Maybe God didn't require it of a Sunday morning, but Claudius thought maybe he looked down on all those hats and smiled. Maybe even had a laugh or two, if he noticed the woman near the front with a hat brim the size of the rings of Saturn.

The choir began "In the Garden," one of Claudius's favorites, naturally. He pictured it as the one garden on earth his toil had not brought forth, that no human toil had brought forth. God's garden, where if there were any weeds, they weren't really weeds at all. His heart sang along like it did sometimes when hearing a song that seemed to beat in time with it. Oh, and the looks on some of the women's faces as they sang. Lordymercy.

"And the joy we share as we tarry there, none other has ever known."

The pianist went right from the choir piece into the first song. "Amazing Grace."

May knew it. She sang along in a sweet, trembling soprano. "I once was lost, but now am found. Was blind, but now I see."

Well, that remained to be seen. Hopefully today would make that line true for her too.

—Oh, Lord, help my unbelief.

He just couldn't picture it: May-May up and around, getting a job at a magazine, enjoying life once again.

Still, hope seemed to stream in with the morning sun through the paned windows, casting squares onto the floor.

—Look at all these people come to worship God.

Perhaps they could help May remember God as good when bad times rolled around. He wasn't fool enough to think they hadn't seen their fair share! No, they'd had more than that. He'd sat vigil in too many living rooms and knew better. For dangling from the sleeves of their pretty dresses and suits were work-roughened hands. Above the necklines many faces were weathered and pulled down by heartache.

But there they all sat together. That was the point of it, wasn't it? Being joined with one another? Christ at the head?

Well, it seemed that way to him, anyway.

The picnic on the grounds behind the church, in the pavilion right on the river, was, to Claudius's estimation, a peek at the great feast in heaven. May should have thought so too. She was loved right away, gathered into skinny arms and big arms, crushed against meager chests and great big bosoms. Sister Ruth decided May was her charge; after all, she alone had actually met May Seymour. She escorted them to the father-daughter table, where she sat May next to Claudius and with three other fathers and their female offspring:

Chester Frank and his six girls; John Rose, an older gentleman with a daughter in her thirties; and the youngest father of the bunch, Jason Sparks, with his three-year-old spark plug, Tillie.

The chatter was loud and laced with laughter, and the ladies served them plates filled with fried chicken, short ribs, greens with hardboiled eggs, cabbage, potato salad, and three-bean salad, canned by Sister Racine, most likely not wearing the red hat at the time.

Claudius had three helpings and whispered, "I do think I'll barter some of our apple butter for some of her beans."

Sweet potato pie and coconut cake was served with either hot coffee or more sweet tea.

May leaned in toward him. "I've never eaten this much at one time. In fact, I'd have turned my nose up at this meal, counting the fat grams in my head, saving up the calories for alcohol."

"Welcome to the good life, May-May."

Upon leaving the place she received so many hugs it almost annoyed Claudius.

"Now you come back!" at least half the people said. The other half said, "You're welcome anytime. Anytime!"

When they pulled up to the house, Claudius extricated her from the car again and ushered her inside. "That was a real honor, May-May. Did you have a good time?"

"The best. It was wonderful."

"My heart hasn't felt so big in a long time. They all loved you."

"I know. I mean, I could really tell. Are they all always that nice?"

They entered the kitchen, and he laid his keys on the hoosier. "Well, it's like any church, I guess. We all have our . . . personalities."

She laughed.

"I sure am tired after all that good food. I think I'll take a nap," he said.

"I'm going to make a cup of tea and read. I think I'll look at those flower arranging books you brought me from the library."

"Do you mind telling me what happened to make you faint this morning?"

She filled the kettle with water. "When I stepped into that simple little church, it reminded me of my church in Rwanda, and then all those brown faces, all swinging in my direction, looking at me . . . It felt like I was back there, Claudius. And then I realized, they're dead. They're all dead."

"Oh, honey. Your poor mind couldn't take it, could it?"

She shook her head. "But I'm glad I made it through. I'm glad we were able to stay and enjoy the picnic."

"Me too." He headed toward his bedroom, then turned. "You truly are like a daughter to me, honey. The good Lord made me wait long enough, but it was worth it."

She ran forward, embraced him with arms grown stronger from garden work, and kissed his cheek. "I love you, Claudius."

"And I love you too, May-May."

Now those are words you can never hear too much, he realized as he took off his suit and shirt and climbed into bed. Wooh. He was so tired!

He arranged the pillow behind his head, amazed at the turns of life. For years it can go on in quiet sameness, and then *wham!* A girl enters your life, and no, maybe May wasn't the romantic relationship he thought he'd been looking for, but that feminine presence alighted like birds on corn, and he understood something: that he could live for someone else.

A copy of his new will lay on his desk under the window. He'd taken care of her. What else could he do?

17

Claudius awakened early. May was up, probably already out in the barn. Probably talking to that silly goat, or milking Eloise. She loved that cow. Yep, that's where she was. He found her in the barn.

She turned to him with a broad smile. "I'm still feeling a little glow from yesterday, Claudius. I'm going to make a big farmer's breakfast. Fried potatoes, fried tomatoes, eggs, and biscuits!"

He pulled on his bottom lip. "Now I wouldn't turn down an offer like that."

He set about his morning chores, picturing her scrubbing potatoes for home fries (leftovers for lunch, he assumed), slicing them along with some onions. With a generous slick of butter in the skillet, she'd set them frying, onions, then potatoes, setting a lid on top. Next she'd whip up the biscuit dough, roll it out on the pastry board, flour a juice glass from the cupboard and press it down onto the dough. After arranging the biscuits on a baking pan that was nonstick from years of residue, not any Teflon coating, she'd slide them in the oven, then wash and set the tomatoes aside. She'd fry those up right before they ate.

Violet's old recipe book had taught her well.

As he pulled the hose around to water his tomatoes, she hurried outside and took care of the chickens, a job she'd asked for a month before. Claudius hadn't really wanted to give up tending "the ladies," but he'd agreed. Her mental health was a real consideration in his decision, and while he knew she tried not to manipulate him into doing anything, because of the trauma sometimes it just happened that way. In the end he didn't mind. Most likely in five years May would be on her own and he'd have his chickens to himself again.

They were loved chickens, you could tell. They ran up to the gate, ready to be petted and talked to, and they gave such nice round, golden-brown eggs. How could he refuse her that? Parma-Jean the Fourth followed her around with worried clucking the entire time she fed and watered them. She picked up the chicken and rubbed her index finger along her feathery head and neck. Sweet chicken.

She waved to him as she entered the chicken coop, and he waved back. Next stop, some hay for old Bill on the Hill. But first he peeked his head in the kitchen door.

Coffee was ready, too, and she'd set the percolator on the table she'd already laid out. Life was moving forward for May. She'd even said last night that she was thinking about doing the interview with that reporter. He'd had no idea what an effect that father-daughter picnic would have!

Twenty minutes later she hollered out the kitchen door. "Claudius! Breakfast is ready!"

"Be right there," he called back from Bill's nearby pasture. He just wanted to return the wheelbarrow to the toolshed. He was planning on mending one of the fences near the road later on.

She headed back in.

My, he felt warm. His hands broke out in a sweat! He slowed his pace as he rounded the corner of the toolshed. Scout and Girlfriend ran up, begging for a scratch. He obliged, bending over, lights exploding behind his eyes, a red heat erasing them away, and then, blackness.

Two minutes later, as he left his body, seeing the welcoming smiles of his parents, friends, and relatives who had gone on before, he looked down, and he saw May running, running toward him, screaming and crying.

"She'll be all right," Violet whispered as she drew him close, his father rubbing small circles between his shoulder blades.

"Look down now," Garland said.

May sat in the circle of her flowers, the farm burgeoning with life, life, life.

"How?" Claudius asked. "Wasn't she just—"

"We're not bound to time. Be at peace for her, honey," Violet said, tucking her arm through his. "You did well. As my new friend Julian tells me here in the great cloud of witnesses, 'All will be well and all will be well and every kind of thing will be well.' Welcome home, son."

PART 2

IT IS A VERY MIXED BLESSING TO BE BROUGHT BACK FROM THE DEAD.

—Kurt Vonnegut

• I •

Eight years later

"May come in May." The first day of May never came when May didn't think of Claudius's words. It was their month, their mythic month, certainly, when he seemed close, to walk beside her as she fed the chickens and Louise, also known as "the replacement cow." She missed sweet Eloise, the large gentle dame; however, Louise was a nice cow, smaller, but with a calm temperament. She had a face May could talk to as well, and a nice warm flank to rest her cheek against when she was milking her.

The cow's coat was a little scratchy on her cheek, but warm. It was the warmth May did it for. And such massive warmth, miraculous to be sure, like cold fusion or something. Only in a cow. The energy just going on and on.

Never mind the sweet hay and clover. Those were just details.

She kept her eyes closed and milked, squeezing on the cow's teats, the milk shooting into a clean pail. May only milked Louise enough for her and Sister Ruth and Sister Racine.

"Did you know that there are only fourteen animals that have been domesticated? In all of recorded human history?"

May opened the eye not plastered to Louise's flank. "Good morning, Sister Ruth."

"Well, did you know that?"

"No."

The milk streamed in a thin line, dinging into the pail. She inhaled the sweet smell through her nose.

"Only fourteen. Think of all the animals out there."

"What animals are they?"

Sister Ruth, wearing a pair of pressed jeans, crease running down the front, and a white blouse, starched and fresh, stepped out of her tan loafers and into her pair of bright yellow muck shoes. May wore similar shoes, only hers were dark green. They'd found them together one day in a catalog Glen the postman delivered, and were just as delighted with the real things as they were at the possibility of them on slick paper.

"Well, let's see if I can remember." Sister Ruth, the official overseer of Borne's Last Chance for Harmony Baptist Church, took a basket down from the shelf to go gather the eggs she sold to neighbors and church members. The farm belonged to the church now, but Claudius had added the proviso that May could live there as long as she wanted. "There's cows, of course, goats and sheep."

"Horses."

"Yes. Dogs and cats. Rabbits."

"Chickens," said May. "And turkeys."

"I'm not sure if they included birds."

"Well, they should have! The poor ladies!"

"Pigs."

"Donkeys, llamas." May patted Eloise, then stood up.

"Ducks. And Indian elephants. They do work."

"Camels and water buffalo! I saw a painting of a pair of water buffalo pulling something. A boat out of the water, I think."

Sister Ruth shook her head and turned to leave. "That's more than fourteen. It's probably species, then."

She headed toward the coop. The woman was still skinny as a stick, still dressed to the nines, although the white had overtaken the black of her hair. May didn't know what she would do without her.

As the sun shone in small sparkles between the tender new leaves of the trees in the windbreak near her neighbors' ridge, neighbors she still had never met nor even seen (they had bought the old farm for cheap, leveled the barn, and built a vacation home), she headed toward the house.

On the stoop May stepped out of her muck boots, stepped inside the kitchen, then slid into her slippers. Well, Claudius's old slippers, moccasins, the leather of which now shone with slickness from years of scuffing around the house. She liked the *whooshy-whish* sound they made when she walked across the wooden floors. It sounded like he was walking by her side.

She turned on the oven to heat.

Oh good. The percolator had finished up. She poured herself a cup of coffee and set out a mug for Sister Ruth. Yesterday's mail sat on the hoosier.

A fresh loaf of bread sat on the counter, and Sister Ruth had remembered the jar of mayonnaise and the tuna fish too. May loved looking at the circular from Jack's IGA each week and making up the shopping list from the specials. It was almost a challenge. Could she eat just what she grew and what was on sale? She didn't make much money from the flowers she grew and Sister Ruth sold—and half of that she gave to Harmony Baptist—so she had to be frugal. So far, she'd done a good job conserving and saving a dollar here, a dollar there. And she didn't need much, not with all the books Sister Ruth brought her from the library.

She put away the groceries as Ruth entered, basket of eggs tucked under her arm. "What's for breakfast, May-May?"

May pulled out a mushroom quiche from the top shelf of the fridge. "Is this all right?"

"Of course."

She cut two generous portions, set them in a pie pan, and slid them into the heated oven.

Sister Ruth poured herself a cup of coffee, then sat down in the seat opposite May's. The day after Claudius died, May had put the salt and pepper shakers, napkin holder, and sugar bowl on his place mat, and nobody had sat in his chair since. Well, the only person that ate at her table was Sister Ruth, who wouldn't have dreamed of trying to fill in for Claudius.

Eli used to come by every so often, after he got out of the service, limping a bit from the knee replacement surgery he received after sustaining an injury in Afghanistan. It had got him home, at least. But that had not proved, in the outcome, to be a blessing. Poor Eli. She could barely think about what had happened to him. At least twice a week she wondered what she could have done to prevent the tragedy, and came up with nothing.

"And I went to the utility company and paid this month's bill as well as settled up at the IGA," said Sister Ruth. "So you're all set for another month."

"Great. Thanks."

"Now, when is that reporter man coming?"

"Next week."

Sister Ruth laid her hands flat on her straw place mat. The mats were almost completely tan now, the afternoon sun that fell across them having bleached out the green dye completely over the years. "We have to talk about something, May."

Oh, boy. May took a sip of her coffee, hoping to hide behind the brim.

"Your hair."

"No."

"Look at it. It's down past your bee-hind. And all that gray. And it isn't a pretty gray either, honey. It's that iron gray with yellow around the edges."

"It's easier this way."

"'Course it is! It has no style. It's ridiculous. No woman your age should wear a braid that long. I just think if you got back a little style you might—"

"Keep trying." May stood up. "I think the quiche is heated up."

"Well," Ruth sighed, "at least you've finally agreed to meet with that Mr. Damaroff. Only took you nine years. Maybe talking to him will help expunge something, maybe help you sleep a little better. You sure you're ready?"

May stood up, walked over to the oven, and peered through the window. "Don't act all soft and concerned now. I just can't stand your harping on it anymore."

"Good. Maybe I've done something then. Even without a haircut."

The quiche needed a few more minutes.

"One of these days, Sister Ruth, you're going to realize what a hopeless case I really am."

"Nobody is."

May pulled the toaster off the refrigerator and plugged it in. "I don't know about that. Think about poor Eli Campbell."

"Who would have thought him capable of that?"

"Not me."

"And you should know!" Sister Ruth's eyes glinted.

"How about handing me the bread?"

Sister Ruth reached behind her and opened the bread drawer. "Here." She held out the bag of rye bread, and May grabbed it. "Well, at least you didn't freak out like Eli. You know, the past is the past, honey. Can't do nothing to change that, and you know it. You got to move on."

May slid the bread in the toaster and pushed down on the black button. "How many times have you said that to me, Sister Ruth?"

"I don't know, honestly, I don't. At least once a week for the past eight years."

"And you don't have to come here every day."

"I like the work. I enjoy the flowers. I enjoy the people down at the market and at the flower shops. So don't think I'm doing it for you, May. I've got my own reasons, and they don't include Harmony Baptist Church."

"All right then."

They'd been doing this song and dance for years.

"Are they still okay with me being here on the farm?" she asked, warming her hands atop the toaster.

"Who knows what they're thinking? Got to tell you, though,

the church is growing. After all these years snuggled up to that little river, we can't seat everybody now."

"You don't look happy about it. I thought that would be a good thing." She leaned back against the stove and crossed her arms, then uncrossed them, noticing a piece of straw from the barn on her work pants. She picked it off the gray fabric and twisted it between her fingers. "Aren't churches supposed to grow?"

"I suppose so. It's just different. We had such a tight-knit community, and now that's going away with young people who want Jesus and his people on Sundays but have no understanding of what it means to really follow Jesus together day by day, heartache by heartache, joy by joy . . ."

She kept going. Sister Ruth could have her own church and be a darn good preacher, May had decided a long time ago.

Claudius, for some reason, had been reticent about his faith. Sister Ruth had made up for that in the first six months after his death. May didn't mind, though. It was all the religion she got nowadays.

Sister Ruth left after breakfast to take care of her "accounts." She did the bookkeeping for the farm and the church. She probably had lunch plans with someone, either a nice ladylike salad plate in her small dining room, or a sandwich at Dooley's Purple Cow.

May shook her head and walked toward the bathroom, the final pit stop before driving the tractor out to the spring field, as she called it. Seven years ago she'd planted her flower fields according to their blooming season. It was easier to harvest them together and made the whole operation make more sense, from her perspective.

As she washed her hands, she heard a knock at the front door.

Glen stood there in all his mailman hunkiness. All these years later, and he hadn't aged at all. Whereas she, with her gray hair, skin tough and tan all the time now, blue eyes resting in a crinkled setting, hadn't stood up so well, as Ruth had just that morning been pointing out.

Maybe his face wasn't exactly the kind of good-looking she appreciated in college, that Easter Island square of a face all the model agencies must have deemed handsome. Glen was more cheerful than that. His eyes, blue like the morning sky at the beach, drooped down. His lips were too thin to be a model's, but they smiled all the time, resting above a rounded bulldog jaw that couldn't grow much of beard to save its life.

Eye candy. That's what Sister Ruth said they were calling it these days. Good enough for May.

And apparently for the other unmarried women in the area, according to Sister Racine, his neighbor, who said he went into Lexington at least two nights a week and didn't get home until at least two a.m.

"Here's a package for you, May." He held out a small box from a place called Amazon.

Sister Ruth was always ordering stuff from there. May suspected it was the new pair of pruning shears she had been talking about the week before. Ergonomic. Summertime and the squeezing is easy, up to the minute. Sister Ruth liked anything up to the minute. May had put her foot down, however, when she'd suggested a television and satellite TV. May didn't even have a phone! What business did a woman without a phone have owning a television?

She didn't have the money for that either.

"Thanks, Glen." How dingy gray her socks had become. She tucked one foot behind the other.

"And your mail."

She took that too. "Great."

"You doing okay?"

"Yep."

"Ruth driving you crazy?"

She laughed. "Not yet."

"Good. Tell her I said hello."

"Okay. Well, I don't want to keep you."

"See you later, May."

He climbed into his van and drove off with an easy guy-wave. And thus her life with Glen.

May riffled through the letters. Familiar handwriting scrawled across an envelope made from a newspaper. Dad. It opened easily and, sitting now at the kitchen table, she read about his life in London. His little reports had become her picture window on the world at large. He made her feel like she was right there with him in that little enclave where he lived "in Christian community" with a group of people from his parish who were set on "loving God and our neighbors as ourselves." He taught during the day at London Metropolitan University.

And Lord knew he'd needed to throw himself into something after her mother died six years ago. He knew the name of every kid in his neighborhood, helped them with their homework, and kept a pocketful of hard candy.

She laughed at his tales of Father Xavier, a retired Jesuit priest who took it upon himself to be their spiritual director, an ancient man who made daily prayers last twice as long, "teaching us a lot about patience and bladder control," Dad wrote.

She finished reading about them readying the beds in their community garden and preparing for their summer tutoring program. His thoughts on his classes and students were ripe fodder for his letters as well.

May set down the letter, written on the back of a bright pink flyer advertising nail tips. She'd write back tomorrow.

She clipped blooms from the many varieties of irises banked together, white, golden, purple; she pulled down the branches of her poplar trees and gathered their sturdy yellow cuplike blossoms; she pruned flowers from the azaleas she'd planted years before. And the clematis vines gave up their flat flowers, the viney stems perfect for wrapping around the other stems.

As the afternoon waned, she sat in the redwood lounge chair her father had brought by before he left, the webbing of the old aluminum chair having given way beneath her the year before, and arranged her posies. The circle of perennials hugged her tightly, most of them still green but promising blooms soon. She never used these for the farmers' market—they were Claudius's way of communicating to her all these years later.

A quick supper of tuna salad on toast and Sister Racine's three-bean salad led to knitting her father's Christmas sweater, then reading in Claudius's chair, then bedtime in the room upstairs, where nothing changed except the sheets every Wednesday.

Eyes getting heavy as she read about Laura Ingalls Wilder cavorting on the banks of Plum Creek, May turned out the light, opened her nightstand drawer, and fell asleep, her hand resting on the stole Father Isaac's hands held so long ago.

• 2 •

At five thirty the next morning Sister Ruth pulled up in her giant old Suburban, that same red entity that had been frustrating Beattyville motorists for centuries. She and May loaded up the bouquets, the gentle blossoms shivering in the breeze, the stems drinking the water at the bottom of the old sugar buckets. The land welcomed the vapor settling over the fields and between the tree trunks; the sun, just painting the horizon with pale light, promised to burn it off by ten.

"I talked to Sassy yesterday," Sister Ruth said, hefting a sugar bucket into the back of the vehicle. Today she wore pressed khakis and a bright red twinset with sparkling beaded jewelry. Was it any wonder their flowers always sold out?

"Has she heard from Eli?"

May remembered Eli's visit soon after Claudius's death. He had become a highly trained sharpshooter, his wife had disappeared, and his daughter, Callie, was being raised by his mother. He'd tried to put a good face on it all, but underneath, May could see the light had gone out.

"Yes. She was wondering if maybe you'd write him a letter or something. Death row gets pretty lonely."

"I'll bet it does."

"Do you think you could? Maybe it would be good for you."

May smiled. Lately everything Sister Ruth suggested seemed to have the ulterior motive of moving May along. At least she wasn't anything but forthright about it. May couldn't have stood it if Sister Ruth thought her that stupid. Agoraphobia, post-traumatic stress disorder, depression, anxiety disorder . . . the list could go on and on. May knew what she was. After all, Sister Ruth had diagnosed her years ago with the help of Sister Racine, a registered nurse. Only her nonsuicidal tendencies and her refusal to be admitted anywhere saved her from full-scale intervention after Claudius's death.

"Let me think about it."

"All right. I guess that's about as good as I'll get from you for now. But let me tell you this: he's decided not to appeal his sentence. Sassy says he's depressed as all get out."

May couldn't blame him. "I'd be too."

"Still, he's her son, and she doesn't want him to die. What mother would?"

"That's true." May placed the last bucket into the back of the Suburban and shut the doors. "I'll *really* think about it."

"Good girl."

"The last time I saw him, I should have done something drastic."

"We've all told ourselves that, honey." Sister Ruth fished her keys out of her pocket. "You were so low yourself, you weren't capable of helping anybody in that way."

"Maybe if I'd been a little more sympathetic."

"You were sympathetic."

He'd come to May eight months after he was released early from his third tour of duty, knocking on the door of the farmhouse around one a.m. He looked like he'd been coughed up by death, if death was a cat. When he put his arms around her, she could barely stand the stink of his unwashed clothing and body, and he felt wiry, no longer the large football player she'd slept with years before. She'd known that body, not this one.

"I can't find a place to sleep, May."

"I'm sorry, Eli. Come on in."

He'd come home from Afghanistan, stayed at his mother's and tried to be a good father to Callie. But left untreated for the "emotional issues," as Sister Ruth called them—PTSD, as Sister Racine said—he picked up from warfare, he wore out his welcome, failing to find a job. What was there in Beattyville anyway? And poor Sassy and Buell, who, respectively, drove the school bus and cleaned vacation cabins on Thursdays and Fridays, couldn't afford another mouth to feed there in that little frame house down the road. Travis, a friend from high school, let him sleep on his couch and threw in drugs for free.

Everybody figured that was where it started—the drug and alcohol abuse escalating exponentially.

"I've seen this before," Sister Ruth said the next day, after Eli had gone, showered and in a set of Claudius's old clothing. "It breaks my heart. It's like he's had a complete personality change. He was such a good boy."

May had wanted to laugh. Sister Ruth didn't know him at UK! He could outdrink everyone at the Fishtank, night after night. Then again, Sister Ruth didn't know May at UK either, and May was glad for it.

It was the very next week the killings had taken place, leaving them all in shock. Eli Campbell? And now he sat on Death Row at the penitentiary in nearby Campton, refusing to appeal his sentence.

May waved Sister Ruth down the drive as she drove their flowers off to Lexington, where she'd sit on a bright blue sideline chair with the UK Wildcats screen-printed on the back. In the last few years Sister Ruth had become a raving Wildcats fan, listening to the AM radio station that discussed the doings of University of Kentucky sports with the same fervency as the talk radio crowd discussed taxation, the war, and whatever else May chose not to care about anymore. Sister Ruth still dabbled at the lottery too.

Poor Eli. Maybe she should write to him. But when she thought about how frightened his victims must have been there in that convenience store in Clay City on a windy fall evening, she couldn't imagine communicating with him. She knew how that man and his daughter must have felt when he turned on them from his position at the counter where the attendant was scooping together as many bills as quickly as he possibly could.

Two shots.

And down they went.

Poor Eli?

She knew she should feel compassion. She knew the basic series of events that had led him from decorated vet to someone killing two people while committing a felony. She knew you couldn't use up a person then cut him loose.

But May couldn't forget his victims, either. And when she thought of Eli, she thought of them, a father and his eight-year-old daughter, and fear gripped her throat, strangling her with feelings, reminding her of events she was still desperately trying to forget.

She entered her kitchen, made a cup of tea, and sat down to write her father. Maybe he'd suggest a way that might give her the strength she needed to reach out. If anybody could do that, it was her dad.

3

Pastor Marlow sat back in Claudius's easy chair and rested a wing-tipped shoe atop a wide pinstriped knee as May settled with a stiff spine onto the arm of the sofa. Used to be, Harmony Baptist only came out to the place once a year. May figured the rest of the time Sister Ruth told them everything they needed to know. She didn't ask for any further information. She only had so much room left in her brain these days.

Changes were afoot at Harmony Baptist, though. Sitting catty-corner from her now was not the old pastor who'd waved his handkerchief over her face when she fainted years ago at the back of his church. Pastor Jenkins had died the year before of heart disease. He and May used to sit and chat for a couple of hours during his visits. He was an interesting conversationalist, a generally caring person, and May always enjoyed the fact that he was content to leave her alone there on the property.

But Pastor Marlow, sipping on his iced tea, brought heat to her scalp like she imagined people on trial felt when they entered the witness-box.

He'd come in with plans just two months after Pastor Jenkins's death. Sitting right in that same chair, he'd run a hand over his shaved head. "You can't live here for free. I do not believe that's what Brother Claudius meant. You at least need to tithe with the money you make off your business."

May had no idea how much he thought she made, but she was relatively sure his guess was way out of proportion.

"But I'm already giving the church half the proceeds."

"Are you tithing personally?"

"What does that even mean?"

"Ten percent of your income must go to the Lord."

"But I don't attend your church."

"You live on our good graces." He set his foot down and held up the palms of his large hands. "Not that we mind reaching out to a woman in need. But you'll need to keep a careful accounting of your expenses, and we'll need to look them over every couple of months."

"Okay."

And now, every few months, Pastor Marlow, gold-frame glasses winking in the light, sat in Claudius's chair, drilling her about productivity and still expecting a few dozen eggs at the end of it all. For free. Made her mad. But she presented him with a tithe to keep him happy.

May knew what Claudius's will said. Basically, she was to treat this farm as her own until she left or died. She paid the property taxes, too, in order keep as much autonomy as possible. She didn't have to split her proceeds with the church. Legally she could have just stayed here and run her own business, but she didn't want to be beholden to anyone, so from the beginning she had given the church half of what she made.

She'd never told Sister Ruth about Pastor Marlow's demands. Ruth would fly into such a snit, that poor little church on the riverbank would never be the same. And Ruth would make May stand up to Pastor Marlow, thinking maybe this would be good for her, help her to realize she had a lot left in her, and so on and so forth.

She'd rather just deal with Marlow her own way.

Hmm. She liked that. She'd just call him Marlow from here on out. In her head, at least.

"I want to tell you something about the plans the church is making for the farm."

May sat up. "I didn't realize there could be changes. According to the will—"

He straightened the knot on his claret silk tie, though it had sat there perfectly beneath the evil twin of his Adam's apple. "Well, the church, as you must have heard, is growing. Beattyville needed a dynamic, Spirit-filled ministry with powerful anointing. It isn't any surprise the people are flocking in and giving all they have. We need to build a new church."

"Here?"

"It's land we own. On a good road. The board thinks it's just the right place to do it." He set his tea on the side table.

"Well, I don't use all the fields. I'll bet we only use about ten acres out of the forty."

"We've talked about that." He waved her words away like a fly. He still wore his college football ring. University of Louisville.

"And?" She set down her glass and pulled the knees of her work pants into her fists. She missed Father Isaac right now, and Claudius, such a fine Christian man, even more. She'd even give Pastor Jenkins a big kiss if he showed up from beyond the grave.

Powerful anointing. What did that even mean, coming from a person who'd drive you off your farm, steal your livelihood, and buy a nice suit with it?

"It simply wouldn't do for the members to have to drive through your farm to get to the church. And we'd like to remove the trees there"—he pointed out the window to the wooded, downward slope that hid the farm from Route 11—"and place the building in such manner as to have good visibility from the road."

"Where the barn is, I'm assuming."

"No. That would eventually be the activities building. Where your house is."

May pulled at her bottom lip. "When?"

"We want to begin demolishing the place a year from now. Next June."

"Where am I going to live?" She had no idea why she was asking the man.

"You have to admit, the church has given you plenty of time to build a new life, May. Maybe too much. You haven't been off the place—"

"Yes, I know! I know that better than anyone."

He cleared his throat. "We have our doubts."

"Who's we?"

"Me. The board."

"So, let me get this straight. You've known I was here in spiritual and emotional distress, and you've actually talked about it, but nobody came up to care for me except for Sister Ruth and Sister Racine?"

"I'll admit, we've enabled you. And those two are more than capable."

"Enabled me?" May rose to her feet. "What does that even mean?" She grabbed her glass, then set it back down again. "Here's the deal, Pastor Marlow. You can't get me off of this place without going against Claudius's will."

He settled more firmly in his chair. "We've thought of that. We have to do what's best for the church. And we're fully prepared to do what needs to be done. And May, we'll help you find a new place."

"But my livelihood! Where will I find a place to grow flowers?"

"There are a lot of other things you can do."

"This isn't right."

"Yes, it is, May. You're not seeing sense. More people will be helped with this church than by your flowers. Don't you want to be a part of that?"

She couldn't believe this. "You can't do this without breaking the terms of the will."

"You going to take us to court?"

"I might hire a lawyer, yes."

"With what money? I know how much you make here now, don't forget. Frankly, I've got to admire your thriftiness. You live pretty well even though your profits keep you below the poverty level."

"Somebody will help me pay."

"Who? Who do you know now?"

"Okay. But I don't want you on this place until June 1 of next year. Can you at least let me make as much as I can without your intervention, so I'll be able to move on?"

He hesitated.

"Come on!" May said. "Use some of that powerful anointing to meet me in the middle here."

He sighed. "Oh, all right. I guess it's what Jesus would want us to do."

May wanted to lift him up by his lapels and give him a good, full-footed Holy Spirit kick in the pants right into the back of his Ford SUV, an arching missile flying headfirst in a suit and tie like something in a cartoon. Yep, that would feel just right.

She had known this day would come. But she'd hoped.

She sat down to write her father. While she asked him about good advice on reaching out to Eli, she would also have him list some good ideas on how to move on.

Move on? If anyone had ever felt sick at a thought, it paled to the dread that settled in May's stomach at that moment.

May thought Sister Ruth was going to have a stroke right on the spot. She almost wished she hadn't told her. She had thought about keeping it a secret, as she had Marlow's other dealings, but she couldn't.

"I just can't go through this alone, Sister Ruth. I'm sorry to put this on you."

They sat on the back stoop, bowls of melting French vanilla ice cream in their laps, not eaten, just swirled around with their spoons.

"Oh, hush! I can't believe he's been treating you like this for almost a year and you never said a thing! And calling it a tithe! More like the lunch money bully is what I say. He doesn't know how many flowers you give away to the hospices and assisted living homes, does he?"

"I wouldn't know." Her mother had always taught you don't advertise those small acts of charity. "Let God and you have that secret between yourselves," she told May every Christmastime when they'd shop for baby clothes and diapers for unwed mothers.

"No. You wouldn't tell him. But I'm glad he doesn't know; he'd want to take credit for that too. Mercy, child! I'm so mad at that man I could spit. He's always talking about money and faith and equating how much you give of one with how much you have of the other. He makes twice as much money as poor Pastor Jenkins and still isn't satisfied."

"He's done a lot for that church, though. Sister Racine's pretty fond of him."

"Bigger isn't necessarily better. Sometimes it's just bigger. That's all." Sister Ruth stuck out her bottom lip.

May laughed and put her arm around her, squeezing her closer. "Look at it this way. Maybe this is the opportunity for me to 'move on' you've been praying for."

"I still don't like it. He had no right."

"No, he didn't. But he could. You know what my father says?"

"I like that man. Tell me."

"He wrote to me once that sometimes when people think they *can* do something, they *ought* to. Just because we can doesn't mean it's right."

"What was he talking about when he wrote that?"

"Torture. Embryonic stem cell research. Nuclear arms. Cloning." May blushed. "He's Catholic. They're against all that stuff." She knit her brows. "At least I think so."

"Ahh. I see. He's right." Ruth set the bowl on the concrete next to her. "There's always people who make bad decisions for good reasons. Or even the opposite way around too. But God always calls his children back home, doesn't he?"

"I don't know." May knew Sister Ruth was going to funnel the broad down to the personal.

Sister Ruth patted May's knee. "Don't worry. I won't preach at you, honey. I'm still too mad at Pastor Marlow."

Marlow.

"Thanks. Tomorrow morning we'll start making plans on how I'm going to figure all this out."

"You can count on me."

"One thing I've never doubted." May squeezed her arm again and laid her head on Sister Ruth's shoulder. Her best friend in the whole world.

It was big out there. But she had a year, right? A year was a long, long time. Anxiety began tunneling through her chest cavity.

"You know, Sister Ruth"—she raised her head—"Claudius didn't think I'd be here this long. Really, I think he's probably a little shocked up there that I'm still here. Maybe I shouldn't be mad. Maybe I was wearing out my welcome and just didn't realize it."

"I don't think our brother would have looked at it that way at all."

"No. But he'd be sad I've come no further."

"Yes. That he would. Neither he nor I has done you a bit of good. We're too soft."

"You just don't know what to do with me."

"It's more than that. It's like what a doctor must feel when she has to decide to amputate."

May winced at the word.

Sister Ruth continued. "What if you decide too soon? What if there was the slightest chance it was going to heal on its own, and you cut it off before you needed to?"

"I'd hate to be a doctor, for those very reasons. I think I'd lie awake at night second-guessing everything I did."

"I *know* I would!"

"In my case, I'd say healing *hasn't* happened on its own."

"No. You're right about that. Definitely right about that."

May took a couple of bites of the ice cream made from Louise's tasty offering and one of the chicken's eggs. A neighbor's honey too. Everything from their ridge.

"I'm dead," she whispered later, as she wiped down the kitchen sink for the night. At the very least, turned to stone.

And how could a stone get up and walk?

4

Long ago Violet Borne asked her husband, Garland, to build her a small, ladylike writing desk for their living room. It sat on a small hooked rug to the right of the front door, beneath a window, and always had, according to Claudius. Violet liked to sit in the ladder-back chair, her spine taut, and write letters to friends and relatives who'd moved on from Beattyville, copy her recipes, or write in her gardener's journal.

May followed in her shoes. Every afternoon around two, chores finished, a bit of time before tending the animals for the evening, she sat in Violet's chair. She wrote her father, of course, and copied recipes from Sister Ruth's copy of the *Lexington Herald-Leader*—recipes she rarely made. The gardening journal, naturally, took first priority.

Today, however, she slipped out a pad of paper—one of those flip-top pads, bright white paper with blue lines that inhabit the stationery section of the grocery store—and set it on the walnut surface beneath her hands.

All right.

Eli Campbell.

Maybe this was a good first step in leaving the farm. She wasn't sure why, but it seemed, at the very least, like it wasn't a step backward.

May 15, 2003

Dear Eli,

I'm sure you're surprised to get this letter. I wonder if you get many letters. I suspect you don't. But Sassy told Sister Ruth that you were feeling lonely there and that maybe I should write to brighten your day.

I don't know how much this is going to brighten your day, though. I'm not exactly a ray of sunshine these days myself, but I figure, why not? Isn't it strange that our paths have taken us to such places? You're a murderer, and I'm an agoraphobic. There, I wrote that "out loud." But after what happened to you, I'd be foolish not to take this opportunity to be completely truthful. I haven't been off the farm in years. Did you hear about what happened to me in Rwanda? I know we didn't talk about it when we saw each other after you got out.

Guess maybe I am the right person to write to you. We're both in prison, right? Remember that night our senior year? We looked hot, didn't we? The hot girl and the football player laughing and dancing, and we were going to graduate and do cool things with our lives. I still remember what you were wearing: jeans, faded atop your thighs, and a Western-style shirt, but not too Western. Just right. You always had nice hair, too, Eli, so thick, and it just went the right way; you weren't one of those jokers who blow-dried and gelled. Sister Ruth says they call those guys "metrosexuals" these days. I'm so out of things now, I don't even know why that's so funny, but she laughs her head off! Now look at us. Pretty pathetic and eerie the way life will spin you around and kick your butt in a direction you never intended to go.

So anyway, I'm sorry for what has happened to you. Sister Ruth says you've decided not to appeal your sentence. I can't say that I blame you. I know you're not a monster, and I know you're dealing with a lot of the fallout of being in a war. Believe me, I know what war feels like. But still, it's got to be the worst kind of guilt imaginable. I don't know exactly what happened, just the bare facts, but don't feel you have to tell me one way or the other.

Well, that's enough for now, I guess. Feel free to write back.

I've got loads of time here. My flowers keep me busy enough, and the animals, but other than that, my life is quiet.

Sincerely,
May Seymour

It was common knowledge around town that Eli couldn't come to grips with what he'd done. He'd fallen into a deep depression, not that anyone could blame him. May wondered how all those people who murdered their friends in Rwanda were feeling these days. Whenever she longed to go back there, she thought about all those murderers walking around, felt like she wanted to wretch, and realized she'd never return.

At six she brought Louise and Flower the goat in from the pasture and settled them in the barn. Flower was looking a little rough around the edges these days. She was old, which was why she didn't climb her way out over the fence. Her sister goat, which May had purchased with her, died several years before, and goats need another goat. That's what Claudius always said. Poor little Flower.

The chickens were clucking around in their run. They ran to the gate when she opened it, just as they always did, squatting down to receive her rub on their feathery backs. And then, when she entered the coop to make sure they had enough water, they chirped in the worried way that made them sound like old women at their bridge game talking about their wayward grandchildren.

"Good night, ladies," she said. "Thanks for the eggs."

Glen knocked on the front door at ten the next morning. "Got a package for you."

"Is it from Amazon?"

"Nope." He smiled. "Sister Ruth must be behaving herself."

May laughed, wishing she'd not chosen to wear the old red, black, and blue plaid shirt Claudius left behind. But she was missing him extra that morning. No ideas yet for moving on. Not a one.

She took the package. "Thanks."

Glen cleared his throat. "I heard about what the church told you."

"From who?"

He scratched his calf. "Word gets around. I'm really sorry. Do you know what you're going to do?"

"No. Not yet."

"A year's a long time, right?"

"Uh-huh."

"Well, good luck."

"I'm going to need it."

"We're all pulling for you."

"Thanks."

"And if there's anything I can do . . ."

"I'll keep that in mind." What could Glen possibly do? He was "eye candy." Eye candy. May still wanted to laugh. Sister Ruth said she got an e-mail every day called Urban Word of the Day. She sure came up with some funny expressions.

A minute later Glen was heading back down the drive, his tanned arm resting on the windowsill of the Jeep.

"Well, all right," she said, wondering what Glen could really do that she wasn't willing to do for herself. At the very least he could help her load her stuff into Sister Ruth's old Suburban for transport. She prided herself on the fact that it wouldn't be much.

She opened the box in the kitchen. From her dad, for her birthday. A short note sat atop wadded-up newspaper.

> Happy Birthday, May! May born in May! I still remember when you came early. Your mother was horrified. "We can't name her May now. It seems so cliché!" But I said, "No way. She's May. Just look at her. Ready to bloom into something beautiful and good." And you have.
>
> I love you. Dad

P.S. The community was given two of these recently, and we only need one, so we all agreed it should go to you. I guess you could say this is a Happy Birthday gift from all of us. Especially Abbess Mary-Frances. She prays for you every day.

The Beloved Community called Mary-Frances, a deep caramel-colored woman who'd been to hell and back in her youth, their abbess, though they weren't really an abbey or anything that official. Of course Father Xavier would have something to say about that, so at her request they never called her *Abbess* around him. But Mary-Frances was their spiritual backbone, leading them in their fixed-hour prayers and walking the streets of their London neighborhood every day.

May riffled through the paper and pulled out a smaller box.

A camera!

Immediately memories of wandering around campus, parks, the arboretum, flowed through her. Just she and her camera off on jaunts on nice spring mornings or autumn afternoons. Lexington was so photogenic. And she didn't care what she looked like on those walks. Jeans, a T-shirt, a ball cap. It just didn't matter.

She lifted the box. Nikon D-40. May always liked Nikons. Most Americans preferred Canons, but her father always liked Nikons, so she did too. It was as simple as that.

Digital.

Digital?

What was a digital camera?

Sister Ruth would know.

But for now, she had cleaning to do. Tomorrow that reporter was coming. For years he'd been writing to her, begging for that interview. And finally May had written back, and then talked to him on Sister Ruth's cell phone.

"Isn't it a little late now?" she asked him. "It's been years."

"Things this horrible never go away. People will always want to read about Rwanda." His voice wasn't overly deep, but a resonance vibrated around the edges. Not enough to be on the radio or anything. He sounded like somebody content to be behind his camera, behind-the-scenes in general. Just two little words, *Eugene Damaroff*, up at the top of the column of words he'd sweated over. She hoped for his sake all of his articles didn't take this much persuasion from the interviewee.

"Didn't seem like anybody cared too much when it was happening," May said. She'd been sitting on the front porch, legs folded up beneath her, braid falling down her chest to rest curled up on her thigh.

"No. You're right. But unrest is growing there again, and maybe a retelling would be good. I know you've been reticent, but it's been nine years now. I was thinking about going from that angle. Talking about how you've been going about your life."

May wanted to laugh. "Come on down to Kentucky."

"Can you come to New York?"

"You're kidding me, aren't you?"

He laughed, and it was a warm, chuckly laugh that made her feel like she'd just stepped into the warmth of the kitchen after gathering the eggs on a cold morning. "Can't hurt to try."

He was coming tomorrow afternoon at three, flying into Lexington and renting a car like a big person to drive over. She tried to picture what he would look like, and she realized he hadn't aged in her mind for the past nine years he'd been begging for the interview. She always pictured him as one of those guys who still parted his hair in the middle and wore sleeveless down parkas. He probably no longer wore the imaginary ponytail she'd fashioned for him. Maybe he had a little gray at the temples. Of course he'd be wearing long pants, but in her mind his calves were every bit as nice as Glen's.

She grabbed the broom and began to sweep the wooden floors of the living room and kitchen, ready to mop them until they shone, reflecting the squares of the window and the open door.

• 5 •

The butterflies in her stomach annoyed May. Eugene Damaroff was an accomplished journalist who had won awards, traveled to dangerous places to get his stories. Sister Ruth had, of course, researched all about him on the Internet. Since May had at one time wanted to be a journalist, and had obviously cast that aside, he felt to her like the embodiment of an impossible dream.

She shook her head. The embodiment of an impossible dream? Where did she come up with this stuff? Obviously she wasn't fit to write anything anymore.

The embodiment of an impossible dream. Ugh! She shoved her foot into a pair of jeans, shimmied the fabric up her leg, then repeated the process with her other foot, more shimmying, up over the hips, a quick button . . . Okay, not so quick—she'd gained some weight.

And not even a baby to use as an excuse.

Surely there was something appropriate to wear on top. Sister Ruth brought her clothes from yard sales and thrift stores from time to time. "Honey, you'd wear Claudius's clothes for the rest of your life if I'd let you."

"Well, they *are* comfortable."

And Ruth waved an impatient hand, accompanying it with a *tsk*.

May slid the hangers over one by one. Sister Ruth preferred blouses, obviously, and May liked tops. She'd never cared for buttons, actually, even as a child. Her parents used to laugh at how much she hated buttons. But seeing them lined up, those little holes ruining their flat, pearly plane—yuck.

Nevertheless, she chose a blouse. With buttons. Just a simple, three-quarter sleeved white shirt designed to stay untucked. She shrugged it on, still trying to remember what you do when a man is coming over. Okay, no booze. She smiled. Opening her jewelry box, she lifted out her mother's string of pearls, sent to her by her father after the funeral. She fished around and retrieved a matching pair of pearl earrings, just two big pearls on golden posts.

Understated.

Elegant.

—Oh, boy.

When she brushed her teeth, she cursed herself for having let her hair go gray. How hard would it have been to put a rinse on it? And Sister Ruth wasn't coming by today, so she couldn't ask her to run down to the Rite-Aid and pick up some Clairol.

—Okay.

She tried to summon the college girl in her who took an hour to get ready, who rubbed her skin soft with nice lotions, who wore perfume and eye makeup. Well, there was no makeup in the house, so she could forget about that.

At least she could look classy! She clung to that. A lot of women, older women with money and horses and all, didn't wear makeup, and they put *their* gray hair back into buns. Chignons! Always a good idea. And better than a long braid, right?

She rebraided her hair, slicking it back with a black comb and some water, and wound it into a large bun at the nape of her neck. May found herself zinging a little bit in the pit of her stomach.

Back up to her closet, she stared at her shoes. Work shoes, every pair. Her father had boxed up a few of her mother's things and sent them on for memory's sake. She dug through it. Not much there, but one pair of shoes her mom had worn when she was a young woman in college and May had worn for dress-up rested at the bottom. Elisabeth Seymour had bought them in a thrift store to begin with. Black patent leather pumps with pointy toes and midheight heels that whittled down to a dot. Very 1950s.

May sighed. This was as good as it was going to get.

Heels jiggling back and forth, wondering how she'd ever worn heels so much back in college, she put on the kettle to make some iced tea, then sat on the steps out back. How nice it would have been for the dogs to come running up just then. They'd know all that primping was to hide the fear that raged like a black spark inside of her, that she could wear a classy chignon and pearls but the story would remain the same. It would always be the same story about a girl who knew nothing, went to Africa, and came home a different creature with scars inside and out that refused to heal completely.

Eugene Damaroff didn't have a ponytail. He didn't have any hair at all. His scalp sprouted a bit of five o'clock shadow, the tiny dots of freshly growing hair hinting at typical male pattern baldness. A pair of charcoal gray jeans encased a wiry bottom half, and a black shirt with gray stripes hid a slender torso. One of his loafers was supported by a thick sole, at least two inches higher than the other shoe. He'd sounded a lot younger on the phone.

May liked his sleek black glasses.

He was on his cell phone as he walked without a limp toward the front porch, and his mouth, surrounded by a white goatee, was smiling as he spoke. He stopped in the middle of the walk, set down his bag, and finished up the conversation, circling his hand as the person on the other end was obviously dragging out the conversation. May read his lips.

"Great! See you then!"

He shut the phone, picked up his case, then strode up to the door and knocked.

May, peering through the curtains on the front window, waited some five seconds before opening the door. "Hello, Mr. Damaroff. Would you like a glass of tea?"

He started just a bit, then smiled. "Hello, Ms. Seymour. Why, yes, thank you, I would."

"Do come in."

She swung the door open more widely and let him into her home.

At the kitchen table they sat, and she told him her story, front to back, without a break other than to switch tapes. It took hours. She began the story the day Claudius found her on the side of the road. Eugene Damaroff didn't say a word, but he looked her in the eyes, straightforward, and in them glittered the sympathy of a stranger.

6

Eugene Damaroff wiped his head with a bandana and turned off the tape recorder. "Thank you. I know that was unbelievably hard for you."

May stared over his shoulder as his words finally reached her as though they'd arrived in a little wooden boat through a heavy mist. She shook herself back to reality. Yes, she was here, in Claudius's house.

"I'm sorry it took so long."

He unplugged the recorder and lifted it from where it sat between them on the kitchen table. The windows framed a moonless night.

"When will the article appear?"

"In a couple of months. I'll let you know."

She stood up. "Would you like to stay the night?"

He looked at her, gaze snapping up. "Um, Ms. Seymour . . ."

"I mean sleep here. In the other bedroom. You're not flying back to New York tonight, are you?"

He shook his head with a nervous laugh. "Sorry. Leave it to me to jump to conclusions. No. There's no red-eye out of Lexington. But I have friends I'm staying with."

"Oh. Of course. Sorry. It was a little silly of me to think otherwise."

"Why? It's Kentucky."

"Who knows anybody here, you mean?" She smirked.

"Exactly."

She sat back down as he packed up his computer.

"Do you ever miss Lexington and your life there?" he asked, wrapping the cord around his charger.

"Sometimes. But no, mostly not."

"It's a beautiful little farm you've got here. But not beautiful enough to never leave it."

"How did you know that?"

"I'm writing a story on you." He slid the computer into a black leather case. "You don't think you're the only person I've interviewed, do you?"

"Sister Ruth?"

"Ruth Askins?"

"Yes."

"Uh-huh. I did."

"Lordymercy."

"That sums it up. She's quite the character."

"Oh, you'll find plenty of characters here in Kentucky."

He clicked the latch. All set to go. "That you will. I also talked to your advisor at UK."

"Dr. Clausen? I haven't thought of her for years."

"She said you showed great promise as a student. Why didn't you mention your love of journalism when I contacted you?"

She shrugged. "I didn't love it by then."

"Fair enough. You think you'll ever get it back?"

"I may have to." She didn't feel like explaining further, and he didn't ask. Guess somebody had told him about her ticking clock.

She walked him to the front door.

"Thank you, Ms. Seymour."

"You're welcome."

They shook hands. He turned to go, then hesitated, turning back. "Ms. Seymour, may I make a suggestion?"

"All right." She didn't know what else to say.

"Find a priest, a minister, somebody."

"What?" The only person that came to mind was Marlow.

"That's all. I've talked to your old high school religion teacher too. Wasn't there a time you seriously thought about being a religious sister?"

May laughed out loud. "Oh, Mr. Damaroff. It was one of those school assemblies, emotions were high, the nun who came to speak was young and pretty. We all considered the possibility for at least five minutes."

"She said other things about you too. At least go to church. What could it hurt?"

"I'll think about it." She would not.

"Have a good evening, and thanks again. I'll be in contact."

The next day Sister Ruth sat down on the edge of the bed. "I've taken care of all the animals. You think you'll be all right tomorrow to get the flowers ready for the market?"

May, curled on her side, heard her. But all she felt like doing was staring, eyes straight ahead, right into Sister Ruth's cherry-silk-covered stomach.

"You had anything to drink since he left? Anything to eat?"

May shook her head. "I just can't get up yet."

"All right. I'm bringing something up to you. A sandwich or something. And some juice. You just stay here today. I'll see to everything."

"Thank you."

May hadn't told Eugene anything she hadn't thought about over the years. But assembling those memories together like a string of beads made it easier to put them around her neck, and now here she lay, feeling strangled, just trying to breathe.

She closed her eyes, the story unraveling itself over and over and over behind her eyes. Father Isaac dying over and over and over again. She missed him every bit as much as she missed Claudius.

She opened her eyes again as night was fading. A turkey sandwich rested on her nightstand, accompanied by a glass of orange juice. May sat up against the headboard and ate.

What did that journalist mean by telling her to find a priest? How could he begin to think he knew what she needed? Why should she want to find a priest? If she found a priest, she'd find a church, and she already knew that wouldn't do her any good.

Now the village was different. Because of Father Isaac. But then, Father Isaac realized the true nature of Christianity, that it was Jesus. She had loved Jesus so much there with him. It was because Jesus suffered with the rest of humanity. Suffered and suffered and suffered, and enough already! When was Jesus going to stop suffering and just make it all stop? Hadn't he had enough yet?

The next morning as she was making breakfast, she took a chance and told Sister Ruth about it. She knew she'd latch onto it. Sister Ruth had been trying to get her to church for years.

"He's right. You got to take care of your soul, honey."

—Oh, boy.

"I don't know." She sighed. "I've been doing okay without all that."

Sister Ruth laughed and laughed.

"Okay, okay! You're right." May cracked an egg into the frying pan. Then another.

"I've met the minister down at St. Thomas Episcopal. His name's John, a casual kind of pastor. A good man. You'd like him. Want me to ask him to come see you?"

"No!"

"Oh, all right."

May pushed two pieces of bread down into the toaster. "Give me time to get used to the idea."

"Please, child. You won't do anything about it until, one, somebody does it for you, or two, it just happens and there's nothing you can do about it."

"What do you mean?"

Sister Ruth sat in her chair and straightened the cuffs on her yellow cotton blouse. "Your life lives you. You don't live it. Do you understand what I'm saying?"

May turned her attention back to the eggs. "So did you hear anything at church about the decision regarding the farm?"

"Most of the congregation is upset about it. But Pastor Marlow is the type of man who seems to get his way."

"That's sad."

"Well, in the end it'll be good for the church, they say, and they'll forget about how it all came to be, and Reverend Marlow will be called a man for his time and season. That's always the way it works. But somebody has to pay the price somewhere."

May scooped up the eggs onto two plates and laid slices of toast alongside. She sat down opposite Sister Ruth, who held out her hand so May could place hers inside. She said grace, but today she didn't pray *at* May like she sometimes did. She prayed *for* her, for strength to do what she had to do this year.

After breakfast, Sister Ruth took off for the beauty parlor, and May gathered flowers—as many as she could. She'd give some away if she had to.

As May was finishing lunch, just some egg salad on a bed of the spring lettuce she had planted, Sister Ruth came back looking beautiful, her hair cut very short on the sides and back and teased into a pleasing arrangement of curls on top.

"My goodness, Sister Ruth! That's quite the change. I love it!"

"It was time to get into the twenty-first century. If I had to scrape my hair back one more time, I was going to scream. Now we're going to have to get you going into something more stylish."

May had thought the bun looked pretty good the other day, actually. Maybe she just needed to fix herself up a little more.

Sister Ruth spied the camera box on the hoosier. "When did you get that?"

"My father sent it to me for my birthday."

"Lordymercy, that's a nice one!" She picked it up and turned it in her hands to get a good look.

"I guess it is. I don't know about this digital stuff, Sister Ruth."

"Well, you're going to need a computer to download all the pictures you take."

"Yeah, right."

"Oh, I'm sure you got some money saved up for a rainy day." She lifted up the camera, spied some other black thing with a cord coming out. "This is the battery and the charger. I'll get that charging for you, and then we'll take it out for a spin."

"You know how to work it?"

"Well, maybe not completely, but I'll look at the manual first."

"Please."

While Sister Ruth sipped her tea and read, the battery charging on the hoosier, May cleaned out the bathroom sink and shook out Claudius's clothes hanging in his closet. For an hour she rambled about until Sister Ruth hollered, "It's ready! Green light! Let's go take us some pictures, May-May!"

Sister Ruth slid the battery up out of the charger. "Now see here? This little door on the bottom? That's where you slide the battery in." She picked it open with her thumbnail. "And see those silver squares? They line up with those other silver slivers in there. And never, ever touch them!"

"Why not?"

She shrugged. "That's what Brother Ben told me."

"Brother Ben? You all have a Brother Ben at your church?"

"I tell you no lie. But you can believe him. He's a very technical sort."

She turned on the camera, pointed it at May, and pressed the silver button on top. May winced.

Sister Ruth flipped the camera around and there May was, on the screen, looking like a monster was about to attack her.

"Lordymercy! That's horrible! Is that what I really look like?"

Ruth looked at it. "It's not so bad. I mean it may not be your best day, honey, but you've been worse. A lot worse." She held it forward. "Want to give it a try?"

May received it into her hands, held the viewfinder up to her eye, and clicked. And there she graced the screen. Sister Ruth. With a dazzling prepared smile.

"You look great. Figures."

"That's 'cause I was expecting it. Oh, I do like this new hairdo!" She took the camera. "Let's try another one!"

"No!" May yelled, holding her hands over her face. "Now that's going too far, Sister Ruth."

"All right, party pooper." She frowned. "How about if we go outside? I'm sure the trees won't mind, even if you do. Or the chickens either, for that matter."

May started clicking as soon as she stepped out the back door. It had been so long since she'd held a camera. She liked the feel of it, the perfect heft—not too heavy, but not light either—as it snuggled in the heel of her hand.

"And don't be shy. I have the resolution set low, which means . . ."

May spaced out while Sister Ruth sputtered technical jargon.

" . . . so you can take about a thousand pictures."

"Oh. Wow. Really? That's awesome!"

—Awesome? Did she just say that? Really?

So she fired away, picture after picture, hiding her face behind the black box, yet seeing. Really seeing. "This is wonderful! I'd forgotten!"

"I know. There's nothing like a camera, May. It's the best way to see the world. And then you get to see the world again and again when you look at the pictures."

A thousand pictures without worrying about the expense? Amazing the things that happen when you store yourself away on a farm for a decade.

· 7 ·

Eli took his time writing back.

Glen had to come to the door to hand May a package, but he raised his eyebrows at the letter sitting on top.

"Eli Campbell," May said, though he didn't utter a word.

"Can you believe that? Who'd ever have thought Eli had that in him?"

"I know. Doesn't it make you wonder what you yourself are capable of?"

"Not that! I'd never gun somebody down."

But May shook her head. She knew what otherwise decent people found themselves compelled to do. "I don't know."

"Gotta go. It's nice you're writing him, though, May. I mean, he may deserve to rot, and maybe even rot alone, but it's good you're reaching out." Glen reached out, too, and touched her upper arm.

She said good-bye and watched him climb back into his Jeep.

August 25, 2003

Dear May,

Your letter came as quite a surprise. I'm glad you wrote, though. You're right, I don't hear from many people. Mom sends me letters and visits when she can, but she's busy raising Callie now. You should see that girl. She's the most wonderful nine-year-old in the world.

I don't really know what to write about. I know we knew

each other once, to put it mildly, but you must be having some doubts about writing to a convicted killer. Just know you're safe with me. I'm not going to get somebody outside to stalk you, and I have no romantic designs. Those days are gone. Well, the romance part. I've never sent stalkers on anyone. If all goes as planned, I won't be here a few months from now anyway. But letter writing does pass the time. We watch TV sometimes, too, and I read a lot.

My crime was horrible. I admit that and don't blame anybody but myself, just so you know. Not even the military. Most guys with my training don't shoot an eight-year-old and her father while robbing a convenience store, even if they are high like I was. I've been clean now since I've been in prison, and that's about all I can say for the experience. I deserve far worse, so I'm not complaining. You'll hear lots of complaining in here, that's for sure. Almost every guy on my block is a repeat offender, and I keep wondering why they did what they did knowing what it's like in here. I guess it's more complicated than that. I mostly try to keep to myself though. They gossip too much for my liking.

I've never been raped or committed any act like that here either. They all know I'm a little crazy, highly trained, and they stay away, thank God. Or maybe God has protected me in a way I don't deserve. I've been thinking a lot about those sorts of things now that execution day is set to be scheduled. I know God has forgiven me, but I can't forgive myself. What I wonder though, is my failure to enter the appeals process suicide in the eyes of God? Don't people go to hell for that? I really don't want to go to hell. I know I'll have some sort of punishment to face, but hopefully I'll skip out on an eternal measure of it. Honestly, I hope God just annihilates me. How merciful that would be. But I don't believe that's the way it goes. My conundrum is theological. People call it "eternal security." Do you believe that, May? That once you're saved, you're always saved?

Anyway, thanks for listening. Upon rereading this, I see it's a little odd. I don't get out much, you know. You can write back again, but don't feel you have to. I have such fond memories of you, May. We could have been really good friends. You were always easy to be with.

Sincerely,
Eli

~

May set the letter on the kitchen table. Oh my. Eli was getting all theological on her! *Once you're saved, you're always saved*? She'd never heard a sentence like that in her life! And talk about God and suicide. Shoot, she just figured she was going to cheer the guy up a little.

Maybe she wouldn't write him back. Who was she to say anything to him about his standing before God? She doubted God gave a rotten fig about what was happening to Eli Campbell anyway. If he didn't care what happened to Priscilla and Yvette, who never murdered anybody, why would he go the extra mile for a child killer?

8

Monday morning dragged itself over the horizon, bringing rain along with it. August was waning; nine months to go and she'd only had one visit from Marlow, thank goodness, and she'd refused to answer the door. Not much to do outside, and May hated rainy days. Usually she saved up all the major scrubbing of the house for rainy days. It kept her busy.

Rainy days, rainy days.

The rainy days in Rwanda were the worst.

Sister Ruth came around nine thirty, her old Suburban bounding over the potholes like a bucking bronco. It made no sense whatsoever that a woman who could barely see above the steering wheel drove such a behemoth. She saved the speed for May's driveway and slowed traffic to a standstill everywhere else. *Putter, putter, putter.*

May opened the back door before she could knock. "Hey, Sister Ruth!"

She cried with a start. "Lordymercy! You frightened the daylights out of me, honey!"

"I heard you coming up the drive. Come on in. You want a cup of coffee?"

Sister Ruth stepped inside, removing her raincoat from her shoulders and the plastic rain bonnet from her hair. Monday was her beauty parlor day, and that new haircut looked just as good the second time around. Why that prissy, neat, pin curl of a woman ever took May on, May just couldn't say. Maybe Ruthie Askins felt the need for penance.

May poured her a cup of coffee and set it down by her place at the table.

"What brings you here on a rainy day?"

"Well, I was thinking it rained last week and you scrubbed this place from top to bottom. I was coming to save you from doing all that again."

"Too late. I've done the upstairs."

"Oh, honey. You're too much!"

"I like that shirt." May felt her sleeve, peacock blue silk.

"I got it at the thrift store for a dollar fifty last half-price Wednesday. You really should come along sometime." She lifted her mug and blew on the hot coffee.

"I've already got more things than I could possibly wear in a week."

Sister Ruth raised an eyebrow. "So I guess going to the beauty parlor is still out too?"

May couldn't blame her for trying.

"Time's a wastin', honey. You got less than a year. You've got to start with baby steps, and cutting that string mop hanging down your back would be a fine place to begin."

"Hey, it's a horse's tail, and you know it. You still haven't told me why you've come. I doubt we're going to sit here in the kitchen all day."

Sister Ruth set down her mug on the left upper corner of the place mat, the perimeter of the mug bottom exactly at the edges. She smoothed out the fringe and looked at the window, the rain running down the panes. "I looked up Eli's address, and I thought we might just take a drive over to Campton."

"Sister Ruth, I don't think I—"

"Oh, not to visit him, you silly goose. Lordymercy, do you think I'm a fool? I'd just as soon try to gain a hundred pounds in a night as get you to visit anybody. No, we'll just drive by and look at the new prison. I hear it's state-of-the-art."

"Sister Ruth. Seriously. A prison field trip?" May sat, no cup in hand. She'd already had too much caffeine for one day.

"Now, now. What can a little drive hurt? You been here on this farm for almost a decade. I've been comin' and comin', and heavens but you're getting to be a chore. Buying your groceries, getting the money orders for your bills, picking out books. I've been patient—"

"You've been a saint!"

"Yes, I have. So just humor me. Get in the truck and sit your bottom down and let me take you for a little ride. That's all."

Nine months left. Baby steps. "Okay."

Ruth tapped the table with both hands. "That's it? That's all I had to do?"

"I guess so."

"Lordymercy!" She stood up and headed into the bathroom to powder her nose, as she always called it.

May figured she'd better clean up a little herself. It was a big day in an odd sort of way, and why today was the day, of all days, she chose to leave the farm, she couldn't say, but she was going to go with it. So she grabbed a pair of clean jeans, a blouse Sister Ruth brought her several years ago, and a gray cardigan sweater she'd knitted last winter.

She figured she'd try doing that bun hairdo again.

She opened her nightstand drawer and touched Father Isaac's red stole, lifted it to her nose and breathed deeply, and hoped for the best.

When May joined her in the kitchen, Sister Ruth's reaction was much like Claudius's all those years ago, only this time her dressing up was several steps down from the getup for the father-daughter picnic. At this rate, next time May got off the farm she'd be in pajamas.

"Well, don't you look nice!"

"Thanks."

"See? You just needed a little encouragement, and I was the one to do it."

—Oh, boy.

Five minutes later they headed down Route 11. Things hadn't changed much at all in the last eight years.

"Wow. I haven't missed much, have I?" May shoved down the feeling of nausea threatening to take over.

"Keep telling yourself that, honey."

"Maybe I will."

"Lots of new cabins and things down further."

"That's nice."

A few of the beech trees lining the road were beginning to turn a little golden around the edges, and as they continued farther, the cliffs of the Red River Gorge, a rock climber's Mecca, towered over them.

—Just think about nature, May. The trees, the rocks, just like on the farm.

They passed by the spot near Natural Bridge State Park where Claudius found May that long-ago day. She pointed to the side of the road. "Right there is where I met Claudius."

"He never would tell people how that happened."

So May filled her in, glad for the distraction.

"So you've been lost from the beginning, honey."

"Yes. I guess you could say that." She hated it when people were right about such things.

Sister Ruth sighed. "I sure do miss him. He was a good friend to a lot of us. Many a time a family couldn't buy food, and he'd show up in that old car, unloading eggs and vegetables and milk. Don't know what people do without him now."

"What I do, I guess. Try their best to get along."

Ruth took a right onto Route 15.

Vacation cabins and chalets clung to the hills surrounding the exit off the Mountain Parkway. A visitors' center, even a wedding chapel, combined with a couple of gas stations and a Subway, dotted the scene.

"I do love that Subway place," Sister Ruth said. "The meatball subs are delicious."

A meatball sub. May wanted to cry at the thought of it, imagining her teeth sinking through fresh bread, sauce, and cheese and into the soft ground beef of the meatball. She must have moaned just a touch, because Sister Ruth agreed.

"Mmm, hmm. Very tasty, indeed!"

"I used to eat a lot of Subway in college. Cheap food, and there were a couple of them near campus."

—Keep talking, May. That way you don't have to think that you're actually *in civilization*!

"I loved college. I don't know why I never went back and got my PhD."

"Do you have your master's?"

"I worked on that back in the seventies, honey!"

"Wow. Claudius never told me that."

As they wound down the road, May couldn't take her eyes off Sister Ruth. Actually, she *wouldn't* take her eyes off her. Much easier that way.

"Claudius said you were married once."

"Yes, I was. Years and years ago. Jordy was killed in the coal mines, honey. The chain on the drill, the machine that grinds coal off the face of the mine? You know what I'm talking about? Well, it snapped off its gearing and took the left half of Jordy's face off. He was killed instantly. Twenty-three years old."

"How old were you?"

"Nineteen."

"And you never married again?"

Her face softened. "If you'd have known that Jordy, you'd know why. Not another man like him in the universe. And he was mine. For just two short years. But I'm so glad the Lord gave them to me."

May couldn't begin to fathom that kind of gratitude in such an obvious tragedy. Sister Ruth must be a little crazy.

"No children?"

"Not until you came along!" And she laughed some more.

They finally turned onto Main Street in Campton and headed out of town for about a mile before taking a left at the sign reading

Campton Correctional Institution. The prison rose out of the ground, surrounded by walls topped with razor wire. May had seen a lot of razor wire in Rwanda. She pulled up her sleeve and looked at the scars on her arm.

Sister Ruth *tsked-tsked*. "My great-nephew is in there right now, God help him. He was such a nice little boy too. I pray for him every day."

"That's good." She hoped so anyway. Maybe Sister Ruth's prayers rose up to where they were intended.

They sat about a hundred yards before the guardhouse, stopped along the side of the road, just staring.

"He's in there," said Sister Ruth. "That man. Right in that building. Wanting to die. I can't imagine it."

"I can."

She turned to May, eyes wide. "Why do you say that, honey?"

"The same thing? Day after day?"

"Well, that's true." She stared forward at the prison walls. "I wonder what it's like on death row, knowing you're going to die."

"We all know we're going to die. Just not the when."

"That's true. Thank goodness. I don't want to know that!"

"I kinda do."

"Honey! You aren't serious!"

"I am. Maybe I'd try to do something different if I really knew I didn't have much time, Sister Ruth."

"You and a billion other folk. And you don't have time. Pastor Marlow is going to make sure of that!" She started up the car and began a three-point turn.

"That's true." May rested her elbow on the armrest and set her chin in her hand.

"And besides, if we knew death was around the corner, we'd be scared to death and wouldn't be able to do much of anything. That's what I think."

She was probably right.

"I'm thirty-three years old, Sister Ruth."

"That so? You were just a little thing when you came."

"I feel a million years old."

Ruth turned back onto Main Street. "You'll have to tell me about that sometime."

"Maybe I will."

Her right hand left the steering wheel and grabbed onto May's. She drove that big old truck all the way back to the Mountain Parkway exit without letting go, all the way into the parking lot of the Subway.

She squeezed May's hand as she shut off the engine. "How about a meatball sub?"

"I don't know, Sister Ruth."

"Oh, it'll be fine."

The folks behind the counter knew her as Ruthie. Ruthie Askins.

"Why, Ruthie Askins, where you been?" said a large woman with pink rouge in slashes on her white cheeks and large doses of mascara on her eyelashes.

May was glad to see those claw hair clips were still in fashion like they were when she was in college. She loved those things.

"Oh, I been busy as usual, Yvonne." Only she pronounced it Why-Vonne.

May felt a giggle rise up in her chest.

"Meatball sub on Italian?"

"Make that two."

"I'll make them extra good!" Why-Vonne raised the bread knife with conviction.

May placed her hands on her head, ducked under a table, and screamed. And screamed and screamed and screamed.

She couldn't have told you how Sister Ruth got her back to the Suburban. All she could do was cower as close to the door as she could get, her body shaking all over.

It was hot, it was cold, and definitely not in-between.

"We're getting you home, honey," Sister Ruth cooed over and over again. "Just hang on in there."

And she prayed out loud in a soft voice, asking for Jesus to comfort May with his Holy Spirit. By the time they arrived back at Claudius's farm, May was breathing normally but still feeling like a person out of time and space.

"You go lie on the couch, honey. I'll take care of everything. I'll make you a hot cup of tea too."

"That would be nice."

"*Shh*. Don't say anything. Just rest."

May wandered into the parlor and lay down, resting her head on an orange crocheted throw pillow. Sister Ruth grabbed an afghan off Claudius's chair and covered May. She fell asleep under red, green, pink, purple, and yellow squares before the teakettle screamed.

When she woke, Sister Ruth had been gone and come back. "I'm sorry. I truly am," she announced, looking up from a book on the kitchen table in front of her. "I should have known better than to get you off the farm, go to the prison, *and* stop at Subway."

"Like any of this is your fault." May leaned against the doorjamb.

"And Rwanda made that knife make sense."

"Yeah, but I use knives here."

"Not like Why-Vonne. She raised that thing like one of those men now, didn't she?"

May shrugged. "How about that cup of tea now? Want one?" She went for the kettle.

"No, I'd better go now that I know you're okay. For now."

—For now. Why did Sister Ruth always have to say it like it is?

· 9 ·

Thank goodness the sun shone the next two days, and day three after the stupid Subway meltdown dawned bright and clear as well. May thought she might buzz through her chores, work up a good sweat, and sit in the sunshine with a book. And not *The Awakening*, she could tell you that. Sister Ruth brought that by a few weeks before. Usually she'd pick something fun and insincere. *The Pirate's Sultry Ladylove* or something like that. Or a mystery. She enjoyed Ellery Queen mysteries. But she didn't need a book about a woman in misery.

And she'd wear a short-sleeved shirt today too. After all, she wasn't setting foot off this farm for a good long time. What a disaster!

Eight o'clock rolled around, and no Ruthie Askins.

—Hmm.

There weren't many flowers left anyway. So May entered the toolshed and gathered ten coils of chicken wire, thirty flat green metal stakes, long twist ties, and a hammer. She loaded them into the wheelbarrow and headed toward the rose garden to begin putting the plants to bed for the winter. She eyed the rusty corral where Bill the mule used to graze away the days. She missed the old beast.

The sun shone warm on her head, heating it up into the roots, and she shook her hair, having left it loose, feeling pretty good. A beautiful day on a beautiful farm. Why not enjoy that?

The barrow bumped over the ground, jarring her arms. Thankfully it didn't hurt her scars anymore. They'd turned white, not as frightening as they used to be. And her knees only bothered her when the barometric pressure dropped suddenly.

Wait.

She was just going to relax today.

Oh well. Might as well do it. She could relax tomorrow.

So with the hammer she drove three posts into the ground around each bush. She'd brought enough for about ten bushes. She had sixty now, having doubled Violet's amount in order to make more posies. Ten dollars apiece for those posies! And the occasional request for wedding bouquets too. The job would take several days. But it didn't need to be completed until after the first frost. Best to get a good head start.

The last blooms were drying and turning to seed, letting the bush know to stop producing. Violet's journal told her it was good to help them into dormancy. May stopped pruning mid-August so new green growth wouldn't be damaged by the frost.

Once the stakes were driven, she unrolled the chicken wire around them, attaching it to the posts with long twist ties. A wire cylinder, about two feet in circumference, stood around each bush.

She checked her watch. Two hours. Not bad.

Not time for lunch yet, so maybe May could relax. The breeze was a bit cool. She hadn't even broken a sweat. Oh well.

After depositing the wheelbarrow in its place beneath the toolshed window, she headed back inside to make some iced tea. While that was brewing she picked out a gothic romance mystery book and made for the garden circle. The mums would be blooming soon, their buds just beginning to loosen at their tips.

Within a quarter of an hour she was sitting down, sun on her arms, glass of tea beside her, *Kirkland Revels* in hand. She had to admit it; she liked Victoria Holt and her mysterious passageways, darkened corridors, and brooding relatives. She could read in the sunshine for hours a day if she chose. Why she didn't do it more often was beyond her.

Two chapters and half a glass later, a car pulled up in the

driveway. May sat up and swung her legs over the side to get a view of the Suburban as it stopped, wondering what Sister Ruth was going to say about being late. But it wasn't the Suburban. It was a Chevy maybe, compact and tidy.

She stood as a man in black pants and a gray shirt emerged, a white, square patch blazing at his throat. Oh boy. A priest.

A priest?

A priest had come to visit? Here? With her wearing a short-sleeved shirt?

Sister Ruth! That rat! She had better not show up here for another two weeks, was all May could say! She couldn't believe it!

Okay, maybe she had gotten a little cranky, come to think of it.

"Ms. Seymour?" the priest called upon seeing her.

"Yes?" She extricated herself from the garden circle. "Can I help you?"

"I'm John Richards, rector over at St. Thomas."

"Oh." The Episcopal church.

He approached and reached out his hand. "Sister Ruth suggested I drop by."

"That doesn't surprise me." She shook his hand, noticing the dirt under his fingernails. "Do you garden?"

"Yes." He withdrew his hand. "And I hate those gloves."

"Me too."

"I love the feel of soil."

"I know exactly what you mean."

Her Kentucky-bred hospitality took over. And he was a man of the cloth, for heaven's sake. "I was just having a glass of iced tea. Would you like one?"

"Is there sugar in it?"

She liked the mischief behind his hazel eyes and way the folds beside his mouth stayed when his smile left, which wasn't much so far. His hair was as gray as hers, overgrown, but not looking like it had done so on purpose. He didn't seem much older than May.

"Lots of sugar."

"Count me in, then."

"Come on in."

He followed her into the kitchen, obviously not feeling the need to talk. She should have felt a little uncomfortable but she didn't. He had that easy air about him, like he visited with strange recluses every day. Shoot, for all she knew, maybe he did. Maybe there were recluses all over Kentucky, and he was some kind of missionary to them.

Saint John of the Hermits.

Did Episcopalians have saints?

She handed him the iced tea.

He winced after he sipped. "You're right! That is sweet!"

"Oh—"

"No! My wife thinks I eat too much sugar. This is a treat." He leaned forward and whispered, "Don't let the news out."

"I won't," she whispered back. She liked this man, she almost hated to admit, since she would tell him not to come back as he left. "Would you like to sit in here or outside?"

"It's a beautiful day." He slid a finger between his collar and his neck and pulled.

"Let's go out on the front porch then. We've got a couple of rockers out there."

She sat in Claudius's chair. Father Richards sat in hers and fiddled with the collar again.

"Feel free to take that off. I get it," she said.

"Thanks." He pulled the white strip out from around his neck, slid it into his pocket, and unbuttoned the top button of his shirt.

"So what did Sister Ruth say?"

"She told me about the incident at Subway."

—That rat!

"Oh. Yeah, that was pretty weird."

"I minister over at the prison. I see a lot of weird." He sipped, then set his glass beside his chair. "You were in Rwanda?"

She held out her arm and rubbed it.

"That's horrible!"

"Tell me about it. Hang on for a second, I'll be right back."

She ran up to her bedroom and pulled an issue of *World Conscience* magazine off the corner bookshelf. "The Remaining: The Americans Who Stayed in Rwanda, Ten Years Later."

She hurried back down and held it out. Father Richards looked at it, then handed it back. "Wow."

"Yeah. Anyway, this writer had been trying to interview me for years. I finally let him. It's an interesting article, according to Sister Ruth. I haven't read it. He said the only other American there was never attacked like I was. He didn't understand what it was like to be at the losing end of a machete, but I still admire him for staying too. He must have been frightened like me, but unlike me, he saved the lives of a lot of people."

"That must have been difficult."

She sat back in the rocker. "So, honestly, I thought after telling this guy all about it, I would be over it. I thought I was, until the 'Subway incident,' as you put it."

"People relapse into flashbacks years later. Sometimes years lapse in between."

"Do you go over to the prison regularly, Father Richards?"

"Yes. And call me John."

Maybe she should bring up Eli Campbell. But not today. She still wasn't inclined to visit him. He shot a child. She didn't care how much PTSD he had from the military. She needed to write him, but lately she just felt angry that he was no better than the men who had tried to kill her.

She and Father John chatted about the farm, her flowers, even how hard it was for her to move on, back into the mainstream of life.

"Not that I blame you. This is like a little piece of heaven right here."

"It's true."

He drained his iced tea, then stood up. "Thanks for your hospitality, May." He held out the glass.

She took it with a nod. "You're welcome."

Following him to his truck, she said, "So that's it?"

"I find it's best not to bog people down with a long visit the first time." He opened his car door, then rested his forearm on the roof. "You going to be okay today?"

"I was okay yesterday."

"All right. I'll see you later."

She held her tongue. It would be rude to tell him not to come back. Still, she wasn't about to thank him for his visit. He was a nice man, but if he decided he didn't need another sad-case project, she wouldn't mind a bit.

When Sister Ruth arrived the next day, May handed her Eli's letter.

She read it, then followed May around while she fed the animals. "Well, I gotta say, he still sounds like a straight-up fellow, honey."

"I guess it won't hurt to write to him again."

"No. It's a way to reach out beyond yourself. At little cost, I might add."

"Thanks."

"How's that camera going?"

"I love it. But I'm up to nine hundred pictures. I've deleted some of the bad ones." She poured chicken feed in the feeder. The ladies flocked around and started pecking away. Golden Comets were such pretty chickens, their feathers a warm red-brown. They weren't broody either, letting May take their eggs with barely a cluck, and never a peck.

"I'll pick up a computer for you. You can get them for around three hundred dollars now."

She hated to admit how bad she wanted one. "Is that a desktop?"

"Yessiree. Laptops are a little bit pricier."

"How much?"

"Another two hundred or so."

Four months' electricity, and winter coming up. "Let's spring for the laptop. Then I can take it up to my bedroom. I don't want to have to sit at the same desk all the time."

"Good thinking, honey."

May opened a little wooden box that said Coffee in scripted writing and pulled out five hundred dollars. She wanted to cry but felt powerless to stop what she was doing, and she didn't know why.

Marlow's June deadline was coming. Maybe she could see this computer as a step toward something else. More like a tentative gesture, if she was honest.

It wasn't six hours later that Sister Ruth returned from Lexington with a box in her small brown hands.

"It took me a little while because I had to stop at Chick-fil-A for a sandwich. I never go to Lexington without getting a Chick-fil-A." She pulled out an HP laptop with a lime green cover.

"Wow. It's actually pretty."

"Honey, I know! Let's get this set up."

Thirty minutes later, May still dreaming about a Chick-fil-A sandwich, Sister Ruth worked the mouse. She'd pulled up a program called Photosmart Essential and got the pictures "downloading" from what she called a USB cable onto the computer. Whatever downloading meant.

When the words *Delete from camera?* came up, May panicked. "What if something happens to the computer?"

"Then you'll take more pictures to replace them. You can't just keep that camera around with no more pictures left."

"It just seems so permanent a decision."

Ruth laughed and pulled up another screen. "See here? This will help you organize your pictures, and someday you can edit them."

"Like how?"

"Oh, I don't know. Brother Ben does great stuff with his. Special effects, words, and when the skin is too dark and the shirt is too white, he can balance it out."

May thought of all her hours in the darkroom, the quiet there, the dim peacefulness of dodging and burning. "Well, there's something to be said for developing photos without all those chemicals, I guess."

"Well, you're all set." She kissed May's cheek. "See you tomorrow, honey."

May scrolled through her photos again and again and again. What a pretty little farm. How did she get the pictures *off* of the computer, though?

One step at a time, May-May. It was as if Claudius whispered the words right into her ear.

· 10 ·

By mid-October the frost still hadn't arrived, but she was ready for it. A local nursery had delivered a load of compost to put around the bottom of the rosebushes, and she'd raked leaves over there to dump inside the chicken-wire cylinders, providing a nice cozy winter coat for the roses.

Believe it or not, she looked forward to raking the leaves. The smell was worth all that work. The breathlessness. The sweat. Reminded her of those times after school when the kids in her neighborhood would get together for a game of SPUD, everyone out of breath and laughing, finally unzipping their jackets and throwing themselves into the leaves on the ground.

May was just closing the door on the yard around the chicken coop when Glen pulled up in the drive, but in his pickup, not his mail truck. He reached into the back and lifted out a large cardboard box. Little yips and yelps squeaked from inside.

May ran over. "What do you have there?"

"A couple of charity cases I'm hoping you'll take in." He opened the lid, and two heads popped up. "May, let me introduce you to the front-running contestants in this year's world's ugliest dog contest. Or they should be. They have one every year, you know."

"I had no idea."

And yes, they were the ugliest dogs she'd ever seen. "Oh. Wow." She tightened the knot on the gray bandana she had tied around her hair.

He cocked an eyebrow. "They're a mixture of Chinese crested hairless and dachshund."

"They're so little. Have you asked anybody else to take them in?"

"Pretty much everybody."

May crossed her arms.

"I know you like bigger dogs. Scout is a hard act to follow," Glen said. "Girlfriend, too, although she wasn't big. Just had a big heart. And believe me, I know dogs. Too well!"

"Occupational hazard."

But May's heart melted when they both rose up, placing their sleek front paws on the edge of the box. Little fur covered their wiry bodies, more of a grayish-brown down, but from their ears and around their heads sprouted longer, blondish hair, almost like a monk's tonsure. Their eyes shone like dachshunds', Coca-Cola brown shot through with sunshine, and their noses were longer.

He touched the head of one. "This is the bitch." Her coat, if you could call it that, was a warmer shade than that of the other dog. "And this is the male."

May picked up the girl first, to honor Girlfriend. She was warm and wiggly and snuggled into May's jacket. "Sweetie. That's your name." Then she picked up the other dog. He passed gas. "Oh my!"

Glen waved his hand in the air. "Ugh! That's nasty!"

"You're Stinky, then. Sweetie and Stinky." She cocked an eyebrow at Glen. "All right, call me a sucker, but I'll take them."

"Perfect!" Glen reached into the back of the truck. "Gotta get to work, May. Brought you a bag of dog food too."

"Thanks."

He carried the food and Stinky around back, and she let him into the kitchen, Sweetie in her arms straining to get down.

Glen whistled long and low, his gaze spanning the room. "This is like stepping back in time."

"I know. I love it."

He shoved his hands in his pockets. "I do too. I like the stars on the cabinets."

"Thanks." May had made them a few Christmases ago and hadn't taken them down yet.

The dogs skittered around the kitchen, their toenails clicking on the old linoleum, sniffing at everything. She laughed, couldn't help it. "They're as funny as the goat!"

"Crazier, that's for sure." He nodded. "Okay, I'd better get. See ya, May."

"Thanks, Glen. I appreciate it."

"No, thank you for taking them. I just knew you loved dogs. Now, you know they aren't going to be able to be left outside for long when it gets cold."

"Stands to reason."

She watched from the front door as he walked to his car. "Glen!"

He turned.

"Thank you. I mean it. I know what you're doing. Or at least trying to do."

Lifting his hand in a wave, he said, "Here's hoping."

After he left, May poured food in their bowls, set out water, and fixed a pot of coffee. She watched those two crazies all morning as they zipped around the bungalow, up and down on furniture, still sniffing up a storm. And May had the time of her life.

So how sad was it that "the time of her life" had been reduced to that? And it got worse. For the next two weeks she knitted Sweetie and Stinky sweaters for the winter. And truthfully, it was already a little cool in the house. At least sixty degrees. Gray and navy blue for Stinky. Gray and red for Sweetie. She looked like one of those weird sock monkeys when May tried it on her. Maybe the winter wouldn't be quite so bad.

October 26, 2003

Dear Eli,

Well, I've got two dogs now. Sweetie and Stinky. They're uglier than a pile of worms, but I like having them around the house.

I've read about your case a little more. Sister Ruth brought me some copies of newspaper articles. She also told me that the family of the people you killed don't want you to die because they figure if you want to die, then you don't deserve that out. Sister Ruth said your mom wants me to try to talk you into appealing, so that's why I told you about that. I can at least say I tried. Maybe you'll just decide to live on in misery for their sake. Then you'll still be alive and I'll have done my job and Sassy will be satisfied.

Sister Ruth, by the way, takes care of me in many ways, and has ever since Claudius died. I guess I am somewhat of a hermit, though I'd never use that term exactly. Recluse is my title of choice. Anyway, she brings me supplies from Beattyville, groceries and whatnot, and she delivers the flowers from the farm to the market.

My father sent me a camera for my birthday, and I bought a laptop to download the pictures onto, but I have no way of getting prints or I'd send you'd some so you could see this pretty place. And Stinky and Sweetie might make you laugh like they make me laugh.

Regarding your theological questions, I have no idea. I asked Sister Ruth about it, and she says since you all are Baptists you believe in eternal security, whatever that phrase means. I asked her to show me all this in the Bible, but every time she's here I never remember to get out Claudius's old Bible. Anyway, I'd just go with what you've been taught. I don't think Catholics take that view, but don't quote me on that. Sister Ruth says Methodists don't think that way either. Presbyterians do. To be honest, she's confusing the dickens out of me. And all that to say, I'm no help. I have to wonder about the whole thing (Christianity/God/the Universe and Everything) anyway, so a particular like that isn't even at my level of questioning at this point.

Now, with the suicide factor, and would it be suicide or not. I don't think so. Wouldn't that be like telling a cancer patient who refuses treatment they're committing suicide? But something you might want to take into consideration is the nurse who's going to put the IV in and the executioner who sets the machine in motion. Even if they think they're not committing a sin with what they're doing, they still will lie awake at night knowing they ended your life. That's a heavy load to put on someone if you don't have to. Just something else to consider.

Sincerely,
May

May set down her pen and reread the letter. Death and life, so clinically discussed. That's all she had. If it wasn't enough for Eli, oh well. If she started ranting and raving she might never stop.

The first frost finally arrived, so May set to work. She steered the wheelbarrow toward the compost pile and loaded it up. As glad as she was to get the roses to bed for the winter, she always felt a little sorry for them, having to weather several months of cold out there.

First she pruned off the roses that had dried up like little brown paws. That took a few hours. Then she mounded a few handfuls of compost around the roots. Another hour. Finally she filled the chicken-wire cylinders half-full with the leaves the trees provided. As Claudius always said, "Nature takes care of its own."

"Have a nice sleep, lovelies."

She wiped her hands on her jeans, turned her back, and headed to the pumpkin patch. No Bill to hitch to the wagon anymore, the wheelbarrow just had to do. She'd get several barrows full, use some for the ritual jack-o'-lantern arrangement for the front porch and the rest for the year's batch of pumpkin butter. The house would smell like cinnamon, nutmeg, and cloves for days.

• II •

November 2, 2003

Dear May,

I guess the best part about a letter from you is that you never hold anything back. That's a good thing, believe me. You sound so different from the person I knew in college. Mother says Sister Ruth tells her you're still sweet, but I guess it's hard to hear certain things in letters.

Not to mention I'm a murderer now, and you were around murderers in Rwanda. Believe me, I get the connection. One more way to realize the depravity of what I did. I'm no better than those machete-wielding monsters. Boy, that can't make the needle come fast enough.

Regarding the photos. You'll either have to buy a photo printer to hook up to your laptop or just go on the Internet where you can upload the prints you choose. Then they'll print them off and send them to you by mail. That would be my advice. Unless you get a high-end printer, it's probably going to spit out two pictures and then break down. Stuff is made so cheaply these days.

The dogs sound crazy. I always thought dogs would be fun to have around, but my mother had allergies. It must be nice to have them around, though. There isn't a day goes by that I don't wish for a pet. Even a fish would do.

Maybe Roger and Faye's family think they want me to stay

alive and miserable, but I know they'll be relieved deep down when I am dead. To use psychological jargon, their need for closure is most likely greater than their desire for justice, even if they don't realize it. I want to give that to them. It's the only thing I can do for them now. I'm not under the delusion this will make up for what I did to them, and it doesn't give me even a small measure of personal peace. I simply believe it's the honorable, even the right, thing to do.

I'm still pondering whether or not this is actually a suicide. I probably think about that too much, but what else have I got to do? I try to read a lot, but it seems a little ridiculous to further myself that way. Kind of like a ninety-year-old getting braces. But I've got to pass the time somehow. If you have any books you want to get rid of, send them on over. The more inane the better.

Anyway, thanks for the letter. I appreciate it.

Sincerely,
Eli

P.S. Nice reference to *Hitchhiker's Guide*. I love Douglas Adams.

Sister Ruth read the letter as May peeled the rind off a slice of pumpkin. "At least the man has a sense of humor."

"I thought so too."

"He's right about the Internet and your photos."

"How do I do that, then?"

"You have to get a phone line, honey."

Great. Another bill to pay. That free camera was costing her a fortune!

"I don't know, Sister Ruth. Would it be worth all that?"

"Sure it would. You can upload your work on various Web sites, and you might even make some money from them."

"Really?" Now she was interested.

"Uh-huh. And to be honest, with a phone, you could take care of your accounts yourself, arrange for deliveries from the nursery and such, order from seed companies. You could do all that online."

"On the phone line?"

"On the Internet. That's what 'online' means."

"I can see the Internet has come a long way since I left college. The last thing I remember was CompuServe."

Sister Ruth fished in the knife drawer and slipped out another paring knife. She started peeling off the bright orange rind of a sliver of pumpkin. "Oh, yes. You can do everything online. You can even order pizza, and you don't have to talk to a soul until the delivery person comes to your door."

—Sign me up!

"Would you mind setting it up with the phone company?"

"Not one bit. Then, honey, you'll be on your own."

Nice. Hadn't she been since Claudius died?

Sister Ruth crossed her arms. "At least in who you can persuade to deliver. I still wish you'd get that Galaxy repaired. It would make my life a whole lot easier if you could run your own errands."

May cut the pumpkin meat into cubes. "Watch it, Sister Ruth. You know what they say about too much too soon, don't you?"

She cast her a glance filled with good-natured scorn. May didn't know how she did that sort of thing.

The crazies were sleeping in a basket near the woodstove that May had going at a muted, gentle heat. Glen split wood for her and kept some for his fireplace, so he was coming by Saturday after work. May was wondering if she should put on real clothing, try to look at least mildly attractive.

"How's the lottery going, Sister Ruth?" She filled a pot half-full with water and set it to the boil.

"I won two hundred and sixty dollars yesterday! I'm getting luckier and luckier."

It was the woman's only vice. What could May say? Sister Ruth could be doing a lot worse.

"How about if I go in on a ticket with you sometime?"

"Oh no, honey! You've got some of the worst luck of anybody I've ever seen. I might as well just throw my money in the garbage can."

Glen came in from chopping wood. Despite the fact that it was only fifty degrees, he'd removed his shirt for a while, and May was glad to see she could at least still find a man attractive. Really attractive.

But he slipped back into decency as she poured him a glass of iced tea.

"Thanks for doing that. I can do a lot, but some things still hurt me."

"No problem. The deal works for me."

She'd just labeled the last jar of pumpkin butter. Three hundred jars at six dollars a piece. About four dollars profit each. That would keep the lights on a little longer.

"Would you like to stay and have a bite of supper?" she asked. "Just in thankfulness for bringing me the crazies."

He laughed. "Normally I'd love to, May. But I've got a date tonight."

"Okay! Just thought I'd ask. It probably wasn't going to be that great anyway." Just homemade biscuits and homemade jam, fried chicken, green beans, and mashed potatoes, was all.

He slugged back his tea, and after he went May decided every dog needed at least two sweaters. And she'd make the fried chicken for herself. So there, Glen.

12

A light snow fell during the night, a little early for that time of year. May hurried out with her camera before the sun rose completely and melted it away. The cold immediately nibbled the tip of her nose as well as the tips of her fingers, but it was worth it the way the light dusting on the coop, the barn, and the toolshed looked like powdered sugar and the low rays of the sun sparkled it up. It looked like a gingerbread farm.

One thing she'd learned in the first photography class she took at UK was that the shot was the thing. Or something like that. The point was, you had to do whatever it took to get a good one. They usually didn't happen by accident.

By the time she was almost finished, having knelt on the wet ground, sat, and even laid down on her stomach and her back, she was a mess. But it didn't matter. It was nice quick hit of achievement.

Remembering an old wreath in the toolshed, she grabbed it and took a few more shots with it in the frame. She'd upload the photo and see if anybody wanted it for Christmas cards or something.

Last week she'd made ten dollars on some photos for some country magazine publishing an article on chickens. It helped to enjoy your subjects, and when you appreciated them, it was even better. Those feathered ladies fed her like she fed them. Hard to take a bad picture of your food source.

If she could sell ten pictures a week, that would make the difference she'd need to use some heat this winter, and she could put a little away to save up for first month's rent and security deposit for her coming life.

She couldn't picture anything about that new life. Not an apartment, not a job, not a city, not a person beside her. Not a thing.

After throwing a couple of logs into the woodstove, she uploaded her pictures onto the computer at the kitchen table, then logged onto iStockphoto and selected the pictures she wanted to put up on the site. Three of the wreath shots, with the sun rising and that warm light, were filled with holiday sentimentality. In a good way. Had she kept those buildings painted and pristine, they wouldn't be nearly as good.

Yep, that's what she'd tell herself. And honestly, she wasn't about to go painting them now for Marlow.

In her bedroom, she peeled off the damp clothing, her skin rising with goose bumps, covered herself in a robe, and ran down to take a shower. The water heated her fingers and her nose, and she took an extra couple of minutes in the stream. It felt so lavish. She had more in common with her dad's austere community life than she realized. May just didn't do it for God.

After slipping into thermals, jeans, and one of Claudius's flannel shirts, two pairs of socks, and his old fleece-lined moccasins, she set the kettle on the stove.

The screech of tires in the driveway sent her running out the front door.

Sister Ruth jumped out of the Suburban. She raised her hands in the air, hooting and hollering with joy. "May-May! Honey baby, I won! I won!"

"Sister Ruth, what on earth are you talking about?"

She rushed up, hand on her panting heart. "I decided to play three times instead of my usual one ticket, and I won the lottery! Thank you, Jesus!" She raised her hands again and danced in a little circle.

"How much?"

"Two hundred thousand dollars!"

May screeched, too, and pulled Sister Ruth into a giant hug, and they twirled around like the crazies right there in the driveway.

"I came right over. Woo!" She breathed in again. "I can't believe it. I never thought. I just had a little fun with it, gave me something to dream about here in this godforsaken town. You know what I mean. I thought about traveling, or buying a nice little house somewhere, or even just a small shopping spree at Dillard's. Nothing big, maybe two complete outfits, everything brand-new."

—And she'd deserve it.

"Or maybe even buy a new car. Nothin' fancy, but with a lot better gas mileage."

"Sister Ruth, you just can't help being practical, can you?"

"No, I can't! You're exactly right."

"So what are you going to do? And can we go inside? I'm freezing, and the kitchen should be nice and warm."

The kettle had been screaming for who knew how long. "How about a celebratory cup of tea?" May asked.

"That sounds like just the ticket!" Ruth set her purse on the table. "Get it? Ticket? Lordymercy! Honey, I cannot be*lieve* it!" She danced again, this time the crazies joining her, yipping and barking and turning circles.

Having those two ugly dogs was worth it, they made this scene so perfect. In an odd sort of way. But why should May expect anything else?

"Do you know what I think you should do?" She set Sister Ruth's tea on her place mat and they sat down.

"I'm open for any and all suggestions." She peeled off her coat and bared a Thanksgiving sweater with a colorful turkey in desperate need of a diet program.

May imagined the bird, when he wasn't decorating sweaters, driving a semi up and down I-75 and stopping at every Waffle House along the way.

"You've been talking about a Florida vacation ever since I've known you. Which means you've probably been talking about it longer than that."

"I won't contradict you there."

"So why not do it? It's getting cold now."

"I have family down there. My father's cousin Mary's girl lives near St. Petersburg."

"Would she let you come?"

"I think so. I don't know why not. We're family."

"But we're in Kentucky, we do things differently. Family means something more here."

"No, she was always a good girl. We had fun together as children when we got to see each other."

"What's her name?"

"Oella."

May winced.

"Now, now," Ruth said. "Now, now."

"Just be back by Christmas," May told her.

Sister Ruth drained her cup. "Got to go, honey. There's so many people to tell." She stood up and waved her hands again. "Lordymercy! What a day!"

May saw her to the truck and waved her down the driveway. Sweetie and Stinky ran around her in their sweaters. She picked them both up and headed back to the kitchen, logged onto the Internet again, and decided to see if *Vogue* had a Web site.

"Years ago," she said to the dogs, "I wanted to be editor in chief of that magazine."

Stinky passed gas and ran into the other room. She couldn't blame him there.

November 13, 2003

Dear Eli,

Well, I still don't know how it can be called a suicide. I've been thinking it over too. Now, I dislike capital punishment as much as those people who are trying to fight for your life, but they're the ones calling it a suicide. I mean, not that I'm the greatest Christian in the world, but Jesus didn't open his mouth when they were laying all those charges on him, did he? His plan all along was to be killed, and nobody calls that a suicide. I think, and I've got no expertise in either theology or criminology or the law, as you might guess, unless you stick that needle in your own arm, you're good to go as far as suicide goes. I'd offer to be there for you, but I can't even go to Subway without freaking out.

I've been taking a lot of pictures and got the Internet. The other day I ordered a few shots of the farm to send you. Don't expect any pictures of me, not that you asked for one, because I'm not exactly what you'd call photogenic these days. Years ago, I wanted to work at a fashion magazine and had all the latest clothing and hairdos. Now, well, I'm just going for clean. The animals probably don't even care about that! Sister Ruth sure would get on me, however, if I developed body odor and bad breath. She's a clean freak.

Do you get any kind of Thanksgiving dinner there? It'll just be me here again this year. But I make a turkey anyway and then a big pot of soup to freeze. That'll last me until the end of January if I eat it for lunch every day. I didn't know how to cook before I got here, but I do pretty well now, so at least there's that.

I think I'm going to have to get Claudius's old car fixed. Sister Ruth won a bundle in the lottery and is heading to Florida for a nice long visit with family. She leaves tomorrow, and I don't want to bother her with a phone call, but I have no idea where to get the darn car fixed. I've lived here for nine years and don't know anything about anything. All I know is, it won't start. Not even so much as a rumble.

Those prints should be here next time I write, so I'll send them on. Happy Thanksgiving. Oh, here are a couple of really sappy books that will leave you as intellectually and emotionally bereft as you were when you started. I don't know how stuff like this gets published, and I'm not all that deep.

Sincerely,
May

May only gave out her new phone number to a few people. Sister Ruth, of course, Glen, and Father John from St. Thomas. The last one was a mistake because he called at least twice a week if he didn't visit.

He was coming a few days before Thanksgiving, and May was sure his visit would include an invite to his house for Thanksgiving dinner.

Glen knocked on the front door at mail time. "Look, May! I think you got a check from iStockphoto!"

She snatched it out of his hand and ripped it open. "Fifty bucks! Wow!" She didn't check her account every day, because that just seemed like asking for bad luck.

"Congratulations. You might be able to make a go of this."

"I don't need much."

"What about articles?" he asked, leaning against the porch post. "You can write those, and Web sites will buy them." He looked good that morning in his winter uniform. Probably because of that girlfriend of his.

"I have no idea what I'd write about."

"Well, how many women do you know that run their own flower farm?"

"Farmette. And how many women do I know, period?"

"Good point. Gotta fly. Here's the rest of your mail."

The electric bill and a letter from Eli. She tore open the bill first. $35. The advantage of not having central heat. Guess the hot water bottle in bed at night was worth it. If it got bad enough, she could sleep in a sleeping bag in front of the woodstove in the kitchen. She generally spent most of January in front of the woodstove. But it hadn't been that cold yet.

November 19, 2003

Dear May,

I wish I could help you with the car. I have no idea what to tell you. It was an old car years ago, and sitting for a decade, well, I doubt there's hope for it. Hopefully something will work out before you have to take your flowers to market. It's probably best to sell the Galaxy for parts and at least get something out of it if you can.

You're right. Those books you sent did nothing for me intellectually, spiritually, or emotionally. I'm indebted.

I'm sorry you won't have anybody for Thanksgiving there with you. It's always been my favorite holiday. My mom always cooked up a ham and a turkey; she'd save up a few dollars here and there from her grocery money throughout the year, and that day she'd pull out all the stops. She'd let me help her in the kitchen.

I'm actually a pretty good cook, though I haven't made a thing in years. Before I went into the service even. What about you? Do you have any good holiday memories? I remember the Thanksgiving when I was eight. It was before we went to live with my grandfather. My dad was a lazy bum who my mother supported ever since I could remember, and my grandfather wasn't much better but at least he could hold a job, which was more than I could say for a lot of the men in my family who sat by the mailbox and waited for their crazy check to come in.

At least she finally ended up with a good man, and when I went away to UK I knew she'd be okay. But then I came home, and this area, Beattyville, everything, it's depressing. I don't know how you stay. I went into the military as a way to try and get beyond all that, and it worked for a while. But I should have never come back home after I got out. That was my big mistake. Anyway, that Thanksgiving it was just the two of us. No angry men.

I'm glad my mom found Buell, though. He's a good man and he does right by Callie too.

Hopefully you grew up in more stable circumstances, but with you being a hermit (excuse me, recluse), I have to wonder about that. You didn't really talk about your family much.

Well, at least you don't go to bed thinking about the people you've killed. I don't just think about Roger and Faye. I think about all the people I killed in the military. Law-abiding citizens are thankful for us, but they rarely think about how those deaths wear on a soldier's soul no matter who the fiend is that gets it.

I'm looking forward to those pictures. I remember seeing you one day in Woodland Park snapping pictures of the flowers near the restrooms and tennis courts. It was before we met at the Fishtank. I thought you were beautiful. I just wanted to say that I never meant to use you. I didn't think I had. We met at the Tank and went back to my place and you were gone by three a.m. I was hoping to catch up with you at school but never ran into you. We hung with such different groups too. And then the summer before boot camp, I thought maybe we had a chance, but I'd already fooled around with "the mayor's daughter," and the wheels were set in motion. Wow. How different life would have turned out if I'd had you to come home to.

Do you think God was giving us a lifeline and we didn't recognize it?

Eli

Thinking about Eli, May made up a pitcher of sweet tea for Father John and set it in the fridge to cool before he arrived. She cared for Eli, sure, but he had obviously felt a little more strongly about her than she had him. May had to admit he'd never been a jerk like some guys she'd gone home with. In fact, he'd been rather sweet.

She'd stopped feeling guilty about all of that. It was over and done with, she'd confessed it to Father Isaac and to God, and those days of recklessness were over. She was amazed, even all these years later, she hadn't ended up pregnant or with a disease. A thankfulness remained. That was all. Done.

Now Father John, having arrived with his happy attitude, gratefully took the glass from her.

"May?" he asked, settling at the table, "is there anything you want to ask me about, spiritually speaking? I've been coming for a while now, and I was just wondering."

"Well, let me ask you this, Father. Is God ever out to get certain people?"

"I guess that depends on who you ask."

She sat and pulled her knitting onto her lap. "True. I remember this kid in my CCD class when I was twelve or so. He loved talking about hell, and the more people that ended up there the better."

"I've met some people like that myself. But I assume you're speaking about you, Rwanda, and then the death of your friend Claudius?"

"Pretty much, I guess."

"Hmm. It certainly would seem that way if you didn't take into account the fact that if you hadn't have gone there, you would never have met Father Isaac. And I'm sure having that year with Claudius was worth it, wasn't it?"

"Yes."

"Would you go back and not come to the farm if you'd have known he was going to die so soon?"

"No. I'd still have come."

"So, there's that. Now back to Rwanda—"

"I don't know how you're going to make any sense of that one." She crossed her arms. "But I'd like to see you try."

"Well, there was meeting Father Isaac."

"Yes, but if we'd have escaped the war, that would have been better."

He pushed his tea further toward the center of the table. "Well, that's a different question, and one that doesn't have a good answer other than everybody wants free will for themselves but not for other people."

"Those were evil people!"

"Right."

"And God could have stopped them!"

"How?"

"I don't know."

"Me either," he said. "All I know is he didn't. And he doesn't usually, even though we think he should."

"So do I just accept that?"

"Not at all. You participate in making things better. The only way we can see how God works is when we join in. I tell you the truth, the people who do the most to bring about mercy and peace in the name of Christ aren't the ones who question God the most. It's usually those who aren't doing anything but getting mad on behalf of people they themselves aren't willing to lift a finger for."

"I still don't get it. Why was I there? Why can't I move on?"

"Maybe you're stuck in the senselessness of it all."

"No kidding."

"I guess that's obvious, isn't it? And you surround yourselves with living things. The flowers, the animals." He pointed to the dogs asleep by the stove. "The crazies."

"My life wasn't complete until the crazies came."

"Obviously." He lifted a brow. "Let me ask you a question." He sipped his tea. "What did you bring to the people of that village before they died?"

She thought about it. Father Isaac was doing everything she did before she got there. "Well, I don't know. Other people came and served there with Father Isaac. I wasn't the only one who came."

"You were the only one who stayed."

She could feel her eyes smarting.

He took her hand. "Maybe, May, you told them the world

cared. That God cared in a bigger, wider way than they knew before then. Maybe God wanted them to know that before they died."

"But why did I have to live? I feel stupid even saying that. But Father John, they'd suffered so long, and I was just a spoiled kid. Why was I allowed to keep going and they ended up—" A sob escaped her. She squinted.

"No!" he cried. "Don't hold it back, May. For heaven's sake, and yours, if there's a time to weep, it's now."

He stayed until May stopped crying. She didn't rant or rave, or wail. A river had found a straight stretch and she allowed herself to ride along. Finally she lifted her head.

"Survivor's guilt. It's so cliché."

He hugged her tightly, then let go. "It wouldn't be cliché if it didn't happen to so many people. To tell you the truth, May, life is cliché. We seek after love and acceptance in almost everything we do, from people, from God. If that isn't cliché, I don't know what is."

When he left, he invited her to Thanksgiving dinner and she said no, thank you. "But if you want to come over for some turkey soup on Sunday after church, you're invited. Bring your wife too."

"Are you sure?"

"Positive."

"I have two kids."

"Them too."

"I'll see you then."

He slid into his coat, and she walked him to the door. "May, just something else for your consideration."

"Okay."

"Maybe God stops things a lot, but we don't know it and never can know it because the event just didn't happen or didn't even come close to happening."

"Maybe. Hey! I've got a question, real quick."

"Go ahead."

"What does 'once saved, always saved' mean?"

"Depends on who you ask." He scratched his temple. "You've been talking to a Baptist?"

"Eli Campbell. We're pen pals." Oh boy. Talk about cliché!

He nodded. "Good. I'm glad. Well, it's the belief that once you make a commitment of faith, you'll never have to worry about going to hell again."

"Even if you murder a father and his daughter, or a hundred of your neighbors?"

"It's always a little more complicated than that, May. I don't think there's a Christian in the world who believes a person can commit themselves to Jesus one day, and then murder and not feel bad about it, and 'once saved, always saved' still be true. It's always about the heart. Repentance. We're going to sin. For some people it's going to be horrible. But the sinner always can repent and turn to God."

"But what if Eli had murdered those two people and then walked outside and been struck by lightning and died?"

He laid a hand on her arm. "But he didn't. And right there, May, is the grace of God."

· 13 ·

November 24, 2003

Dear Eli,

Thanks for telling me about your childhood. It's funny how we can get to know somebody and really know so little. My childhood was pretty typical, a professor married to a music teacher. They got along well. No siblings. Lots of time in my bedroom reading or walking around the neighborhood with my camera or playing with the kids on our street. I used to spend all of autumn making the Christmas newsletter for our family to send out with the Christmas cards. Always got rave reviews. Okay, on to your letter.

I don't care how many people you've killed, but if you want to tell me the number that would be fine. Maybe someone should know that besides you. It seems like something you should get off your chest before you die.

And regarding our "thing," well, you shouldn't feel at all guilty about anything as far as my feelings are concerned. First of all, the fact that we didn't see each other after the Fishtank, well, there are thirty thousand students on campus. That speaks for itself. Second, I really enjoyed our week together after graduation before you went off. I don't have any regrets in getting to know you better and there was nothing to be ashamed of, which is a miracle in and of itself. I think you're right, maybe if Janey hadn't gotten pregnant, we might have had a little something nice between us. Maybe it would have gone further and matured into something deeper. Who can know these things? Don't forget, either way I would have gone to Rwanda. I'd probably have been in no shape for a romance anyway.

The pictures came today, so I'm dropping them in with the letter as you've probably already noticed. I had to include one of the crazies because they defy explanation. Sweetie sleeps curled around the top of my head now. I honestly don't know how I can still sleep with her like that, but I do.

Thanksgiving being Thursday, I'm going to bake tomorrow. Claudius's mother left behind a wonderful recipe for pumpkin pie. Do you get to receive care packages? Because I could send you something sometime.

Sincerely,
May

Any other year the aroma from the roasting turkey would have been wending its way around the bungalow by nine in the morning. May always started it too soon. She didn't know what she was thinking, telling Father John about that soup. Who did she think was going to bring her a turkey this year? She hadn't got groceries in since Sister Ruth left for Florida. And she wasn't sure how she was going to get any because she'd tried that old Galaxy again and it was deader than poor Eloise the cow. But Sister Ruth would be back in two weeks, and May would survive until then. Fresh eggs, milk, and vegetables she'd canned the previous summer were hardly staples to complain about.

No way would she ask Glen to start caring for her. He already found her pathetic enough. And she couldn't imagine what she could offer him in return for doing the shopping. Fresh eggs? That would hardly be worth his time.

She made a pot of coffee, refusing to get out of her pajamas until ten. You can't pretend things are fine on a Thanksgiving morning with no turkey. That's just ridiculous. The woodstove warmed the room at a nice roar and she kept the door open to mimic a fireplace.

As she poured the first cup the phone rang.

"Happy Thanksgiving, honey!"

"Sister Ruth! Same to you. How's Florida?"

"Couldn't be one bit better. We're having a reunion time, living in our second childhood. I'm not even worried about you, that's how good a time I'm having."

"I'm fine. The dogs are fine. The animals are fine. Even the minister you sent over is fine."

"Well, that's a relief!"

"So only a few more days!" May said.

"That's one of the things I'm calling about. I'm extending my stay until mid-March."

"Really?" May set down her cup. "That's great! You must be having an even better time than you're letting on."

"I love it here, May. The warmth is so good for me. I forgot how much I hate the winter there. It's depressing."

—Yeah.

"Well, good for you, Sister Ruth."

"You're going to have to get along without me."

"I'll manage." If she could only arrange for some groceries.

"That's what I'm afraid of."

"I'll be fine."

"That's better. How about, 'I'll take this opportunity and get on my own two feet before June'?"

"Okay."

"That's what I want to hear."

May didn't doubt that.

"Well, honey, Happy Thanksgiving and I'll check in every so often."

"You have a good time."

"Can't help myself."

Wow. Well, she'd lived through three months alone in a burned-out village. A winter in Kentucky? Child's play.

But after bundling in her jacket and taking care of the animals, her mind settled to the truth of what was going to be a long winter. She hoped Eli would write back soon.

Sunday afternoon around one, Father John and his family pulled into her driveway. She pretended she wasn't home even though she knew he knew she had no place else to be. She peered down from her bedroom window. There was no soup! No soup!

What a sweet family.

His wife's hair soaked up the sun in a shining auburn ponytail, and she held a Tupperware container in her hands. She was slender, dressed in a simple skirt and sweater set, pearls and pumps, and her face registered sadness when Father John shook his head. She handed him the container. As she ushered the two kids, a preteen boy and a girl not much younger, down the walk and loaded them back into the little white compact, Father John set the container on the porch.

He turned the car around and pulled slowly down the drive.

May felt like the lone pioneer who sits on his claim as the rest of the wagon train rolls away. She remembered the UN Jeep as it pulled out of the village, leaving her behind. And where there was the cry of the villagers, now only silence remained.

· 14 ·

It was the coldest January she could ever remember. The snow had blanketed the ground for about a week, and nights were dropping into the single digits. She had to feed the stove several times a night to keep the cold at bay. Poor Sweetie and Stinky looked positively blue with their fuzzy skin constricted by the chill. She let them sleep inside the sleeping bag with her, and with Stinky, well, it wasn't the most pleasant experience. She just couldn't bear to think of those naked creatures shivering all night, even if they wore both their sweaters.

She slipped out after the sun rose to feed the animals. She'd hung a warming lamp in the chicken coop for the ladies, set a heated base under their waterer, and hoped the barn with the doors shut nice and tight was warm enough for Louise and Flower. May felt so sorry for them, her heart wanted to bring them into the kitchen for the night.

The days passed in a blur, collecting upon themselves in a chilly mass, each day the same, each day leading her down into the melancholy she'd never allowed before. The promise of spring, of planting and growing and picking and arranging and selling, had brought hope the many years before. But this winter? What would spring bring?

Sister Ruth called every so often and asked about her plans. But she had none. It was like asking someone who didn't know how to write how her poem was coming along.

She gathered the mail when Glen came, their normal banter cut short by the chill. She stood at the kitchen door and eyed her gardens that would be no more. She shooed Father John away in a blurt of anger in early December, telling him she wasn't ready for his prodding. That one good cry didn't mean they were best friends. And every Wednesday when he knocked and she refused to answer, she picked up the zippered baggie of cookies or brownies or potpie or chili he left on the rocking chair out front. On Tuesday night, she put the container on her stoop.

May stayed in her sleeping bag as much as she could, thankful Glen was still chopping wood and leaving some for her. She read or listened to the radio. She hadn't taken pictures since Christmas.

So this was what it felt like to give up.

And the coffee and tea were gone.

Day into night. Night into day.

February arrived. She could tell she'd lost weight by the way her pajamas hung on her. Glen offered to run to the store, but she wouldn't take him up on it. It was humiliating enough having Sister Ruth do all that. So she put on her smiley face and acted like everything was fine. All that was left to eat was rice and eggs and the weekly offering from Father John's wife. She heated up Louise's milk to drink something warm. It wasn't as cold now, but it was still freezing in her bedroom, and she was conserving on heat. She hadn't taken a shower in a month. She didn't want to be naked and cold in that bathroom. She didn't want to wait for the water to heat up. The kitchen sink would do just fine. Sweetie and Stinky sure didn't care. And the chickens never had.

Eli wrote faithfully, twice a week, telling her about the history lessons he finally decided to take, as if writing it to her would cement the information in his brain. And he told her about God and stuff, which was probably why she felt unable to respond as she should. It wasn't that she didn't want to hear it. She just didn't know what to say. Maybe she wasn't supposed to say anything. Her return letters consisted merely of little quips and quotes.

She hurried through the chores and jumped back inside the

sleeping bag. When she felt like it, she read. Maybe she was a bear in hibernation. That seemed like a much better explanation.

She waited for that one balmy weekend in February to arrive where the crocuses threatened to bloom. But now it was the twenty-fifth of the month, and she safely surmised that weekend never would come. They were all alive, though. They were surviving. It's all she really knew how to do. By the last week of February, she was down to just eggs and milk. Everything else was gone.

She brought Father Isaac's red martyr's stole downstairs on February twenty-eighth and wrapped the narrow crimson fabric around her neck. It just didn't seem right to leave it deserted up there in the nightstand any longer. Outside in the dark, sleet clicked against the glass of the windows, on the tin roofs of the farm structures, and softly against the wood siding.

Snow at least lulled a person into believing all was well, because of the gentle beauty. But this seemed dangerous and slippery. Dark and cold. She added more wood to the fire, wrapped the stole more tightly around her neck, and slid into the sleeping bag. Only seven thirty, but time really was relative during the winter.

Sister Ruth would be home in two weeks.

She woke up! Sucking in her breath, she opened her eyes. The fire.

The fire.

Father Isaac! Patrice! Yvette! Where are you?

She gasped in a breath. As her eyes focused she reached for the stole. The woodstove. The woodstove was the fire.

No cross, no bodies. A woodstove. Just an old woodstove.

Her skin prickled as if a shower of rubble ran down between her skin and her muscles. She couldn't breathe.

Oh God.

Oh God.

—I need Claudius.

She unzipped the sleeping bag and threw it back, the heat that had collected around her like a cloud dissipating into the red darkness.

She shoved on her boots and her coat, pushed open the door, and ran for the fields.

Into the woods. Limbs tore at her hair and clothing.

And up the hill to the clearing, where the spirit of her friend really lived. He's not in the graveyard. No. Not there. And he never has been. He's here. Oh yes, oh no, he's here.

Atop the ridge she folded in half, landing on the stiff winter grass as the cold wind shifted its way through the trees and across the grass, and the sleet continued to fall.

Smashing the grass with her hand, the sideways view of black mountains blurred with the water from her eyes coming more from the cold than anything else. Her cheek felt the ground.

Her heart began to slow back to normal.

"I'm so tired of eggs," she whispered, closing her eyes.

Claudius whispered back, "I don't rightly blame you, May-May. I'd be sick of them too."

And he didn't tell her to walk to Beattyville and get some groceries or ask Glen to pick some up for her.

She woke a second time. She couldn't move.

Freezing rain covered her, soaking through her clothing. She opened her eyes, the whisper of light over the mountains in the distance, the great domes gray in the pale shimmer of new morning.

Memory gushed from her brain to her limbs. She sought to move her legs. So slow. Rolling onto her belly, she groaned. Lordymercy. Onto her hands and knees. Oh, her knees! So tight and throbbing. She rocked, hoping for momentum. How had she stayed asleep?

She took a few deep breaths.

—Get up, May! Come on!

She sat back on her heels, then slammed a foot onto the ground, leg bent at the knee. Her hands clutched at tufts of grass as she tried to straighten, her behind high in the air, every muscle screaming at the sudden movement. And her scars ached. Oh, Lord. Her knees hadn't felt like that in years.

May stumbled home.

The woodstove glowed with coals. She threw in a few logs as Stinky and Sweetie scampered about her feet. Letting them out for just a few minutes to do their business, she made a quick cup of hot milk. What she wouldn't do for a cup of tea right then.

She couldn't stop shaking, shivering as she stood at the door watching the dogs until the milk simmered. While it cooled a bit, she filled their bowls extra full, changed their water, then hurried upstairs to change her clothing.

Oh! The chill of her bedroom hit her full force, and May could barely peel off her wet clothing. Getting into a fresh pair of flannel pajamas was even more difficult. Cold clammy skin and fabric? Not exactly a smooth combination. Three pairs of socks next, the second and third pair easier to negotiate.

Soon the dogs were scratching at the door, looking almost blue with cold and wet.

May let them in and dried them off with a tea towel.

She sipped her milk and climbed back into the sleeping bag, shivering and shivering and shivering. The woodstove could never be hot enough even if it was glowing white.

May had a cough. Big surprise. But it was the second of March, and the warm should be arriving soon, right? The freezing rain changed to snow and it lasted all night and into the gray of the morning. She awakened feeling a little feverish and achy. But she'd be feeling better tomorrow most certainly. She slogged through the chores, the snow slipping into her shoes and wetting down her socks and, good grief. Really? What part of her brain stopped functioning when she chose not to wear boots, but instead slid her feet into an old pair of muck shoes?

May filled Louise's manger with hay and repeated the process for Flower. She opened the door to let them wander out into the barnyard if they so chose.

Next the chickens, all huddled together in a feathery circle beneath the light in the coop. She poured food onto the feeder and filled the waterer with the hose she'd dragged over. They gathered around her, the friendly lot, little *chip-chips* coming from their throats. Claudius had taught her to pick the chickens up when they were little chicks and talk to them.

"Hey, ladies," she cooed. "How are you girls doing this morning?"

Parma-Jean the Fifth squatted down to let May pet the feathers on her head.

March 2, 2004

Dear Eli,

I'm not much of a writer during the cold months, I'm afraid. Life slows down tremendously here, and I thought I'd take more pictures, but right now I only leave the kitchen when I have to. I took your advice and always keep plenty of wood out on the stoop. I've added that to my daily chores. All the animals are fine, but I don't know why or how. It's comforting though. We do all we can to escape nature, and they live in it just fine. I wonder why God made us like he did, having to survive by our wits since he didn't seem to equip our bodies to simply just be. Unless you live in Hawaii or something. Do you ever think about how much different life would be if we had fur?

I'm glad to hear you met with Father John. I ran him off a month or two ago. I just can't face things at the moment. I don't know why I'm even writing this to you, but I figure you're the safest person I know right now, which is pretty ironic considering why you are where you are. The ironies of life never cease to amaze me. I feel like I'm living the most ironic existence in the world. Hiding from the world amid so much life. Weird.

The days at UK seem really far away, almost like a dream. I've never really known who I am, at least not in any sense of fullness. And I didn't there either. But that's only become worse with age, so much so that those days feel almost as if they never happened. Except for you. And you've changed as much as I have. It's odd.

I got caught out in the freezing rain and have quite the cough now. So I just do the chores as quickly as I can and get back in my sleeping bag. I don't even feel like reading. I don't know why I'm even writing this, to be honest. I guess I feel sad you're there all alone with nobody to really communicate with. That must be terrible. Most likely, my defenses are down because I'm not feeling good. I've been thinking about what you said, how different life might have been had Janey not become pregnant. Maybe I would have come home from Rwanda before the killings. Maybe we'd be living in a house in Lexington, or an apartment in some big city somewhere, you teaching school (perhaps you'd have an advanced degree by now) and me, most likely, doing a more serious form of journalism. I think even a couple of months in Rwanda would have removed aspirations of *Vogue* from my desires. I must be a little hazy to be writing all that. Sorry.

Hopefully the warm weather will come sooner this year. I haven't checked the almanac. Claudius always did that sort of thing, but I'm lousy at anything that smacks of being official. He was a farmer. A real farmer. I just grow flowers. There's a big difference, don't you think?

Okay, that's all for now. I'll get this out front before Glen gets here with the mail.

Sincerely and with frostbite,
May

—Oh, boy.

The color of her phlegm had deepened, and the chills coursing through her were only rivaled by the raging heat that erupted two minutes later. Hot and cold, hot and cold. May just wanted to sleep. She couldn't eat. The thought of an egg made her more nauseated than she already felt. There was a thermometer somewhere around, but she hadn't needed one before and even if she did have the strength to go rooting around, she couldn't remember where it was.

The crazies eyed her from where they lay by the woodstove. She eyed them back. What a life for them. It was bad enough for a human to live like this, but those little pups deserved better. She laid Eli's letters on the kitchen table next to her cot and read them again and again. He'd switched from medieval history to funny stories about the various jobs he had in high school and college.

Every time May got up she searched the yard for a sign of spring. Shouldn't the crocuses be poking up in the bulb garden? Usually they took her by surprise, but she realized they'd slipped into the mode of that proverbial watched pot.

—Just want a cup of tea, no more, no less.

It was *all* she wanted. But hot milk was better than nothing, and it soothed her throat a bit, the length of it so raw from all the mucus dripping down.

Her lungs contracted in a spasm of coughing.

—Lordymercy, my chest sounds like rusty bedsprings.

She burrowed down further into the sleeping bag as the day lightened the farm. There was enough food for the animals today. More than enough. Still getting deliveries from the feed store as usual, she'd just loaded it on the evening before. Knowing how it was packed with protein, she'd have been lying if she'd said she wasn't tempted to try some of it a time or two. She really didn't need to go out there. They needed water, though. And Louise needed milking.

Heaving sighs, she milked Louise, then dragged the hose out to the chickens and made sure Flower and Louise had enough water too. Her coat flapped in the breeze. She just couldn't button it. It was ridiculous, in that state, not to bundle up. But she couldn't. She'd leave a note for Glen asking him to water the animals after he got off work for the next couple of days. Milk the cow too.

In and out and in and out of sleep. Back and forth. Dream to home. Home to dream. Time liquefied, so did night and day. The most May could do was let the dogs out and drink a glass of water. And cough, the pain stabbing her.

—I must have pneumonia. But it will be warm soon, won't it?

She eyed the phone. Who would she call? The feed store? Sister Ruth? She wasn't going to bother Glen anymore. She heard him knocking yesterday, and anyway, she didn't want to go to the doctor's.

Lifting her shirt, she viewed her abdomen. She looked almost like she did post-Rwanda, her stomach dipping below her hip bones as she lay there. Ridiculous. But she survived that, didn't she? And she lived to literally tell the tale. What would that journalist think of her now? The pictures of her would be even better, more skeletal and dramatic.

She threw some more wood on the fire. The pile on the stoop was getting low, but the thought of dragging herself over to the woodpile to get more?

—I just can't.

Another spasm of coughing assailed her, and she wondered who lit the fire in her lungs.

—I'm so cold.

She burrowed down into her sleeping bag again.

May dreamed she was dying. She dreamed she was dead. She dreamed she was walking through a land of walking corpses, some with missing limbs, yes, but others with gunshot wounds, or tumors; some had nothing showing, but May could only imagine. All she passed touched her sorrowfully and shook their heads sadly as if to say *How sad for you.*

And Father Isaac appeared before her, but he was whole, and beautiful and full of grace, and said the words nobody else would. "You had people who loved you, a safe, warm place, good food, and the work of your hands." He cried for her, weeping and wailing. "What more could God do?"

"I don't know," she whispered. "I just . . . I can't . . ."

His eyes pierced hers. "You can. You must. It really is now or never, May."

She closed her eyes against his gaze, and he shook her lightly. "What are you waiting for?"

May jolted out of sleep!

A knock shook the back door. May jerked the bag off her face, cold air hitting her nose. Oh no, the stove had gone out. The dogs shuffled at her feet. She could barely lift her head. Her clothing was stiff from sweating and cooling and sweating again. It didn't matter.

She eyed the window. By the light she guessed it was mid-morning. "Glen, is that you?"

A coughing spasm hit her.

"May!" the muffled holler filtered through the glass.

"Come in," she called, not very loudly, but she tried.

She just wanted to close her eyes again. Just for a minute. She was so tired.

The door swung open in a gust of cold air.

May gasped.

"May!" Glen threw the door shut and ran over. He knelt down beside her, took one look at her, and said, "I thought something was wrong when you didn't even pick up your mail for the last three days." He touched her forehead. "You're burning up."

May shook her head from side to side. She wanted to talk, but it was just too much effort. So she moaned a little. And the coughing began as she took a deep, painful breath.

"The animals?" she whispered finally. "Go check."

"They're fine. I've been taking care of them like you asked. Come on. Let's get you to the clinic."

"Okay." More coughing.

Glen scooped her up, sleeping bag and all, and carried her to his truck. The heater blew hot air into the cab. Oh, so nice. He gently arranged her on the seat, hurried around to his side, and turned up the heat full blast. "Oh, May. What's going on?"

She laid her head against the window and closed her eyes. "I'll be fine."

15

Lynn Richards entered their yellow guest bedroom, holding a tray balancing a cup of tea and a saucer of toast. "I don't blame you for not wanting to go to the hospital, May."

"I don't have health insurance."

"Any other reason?" She arched a brow.

—She doesn't seem like the wife of a clergyman.

But she didn't *not* seem like one either. Dressed in loose jeans and a mint green pullover fleece, her clothing told May absolutely nothing about her, other than she wasn't flamboyant in nature and she liked to be comfortable. And warm. May appreciated both of those things.

"Has John said much about me?"

"Only what he thinks he can without breaking your confidence. But I fill in the missing spots. He says your farm is lovely." She handed her the cup, a deep blue china teacup with roses painted on the white interior. "Plenty of honey."

May laughed. And erupted into more coughing. "Ouch."

"I know. I had pneumonia once. It's painful. But I'm glad you agreed to come here."

May calmed down and took the tea. She breathed in the lemony scent, then sipped.

—Oh, boy.

Tea! What she had been wanting for almost two months. The dark liquid, sweet with honey and lemon, slipped down her throat; it didn't ooze down like milk or race down like water. Perfect. *Thank you, thank you, thank you* thrummed through her mind.

Lynn sat on the side of the bed.

May came up for air, then settled the teacup on her lap. "Glen called John right away."

"Glen felt terrible. You'd been talking to him at your door, and he thought you were okay." She lifted her arms and began redoing the barrette holding back the front of her auburn hair, which in the light shone strawberry. May could see her as a little girl on roller skates who probably skinned her knees a lot and wasn't afraid to fight with the boys. "Ruthie probably told him to check."

"You know Sister Ruth?"

"Darlin', everybody knows Ruthie."

May wasn't surprised.

She sipped again. This tea was the best tasting thing to ever go in her mouth, better than anything she ate when her parents took her to France for one of her dad's academic conferences when she was fourteen. Better than Denny's at two in the morning with friends after a lot of beer. Better than good chocolate, not that she really remembered what that tasted like. "Oh, thank you."

"You're welcome. Now you just rest. John called one of the parishioners who's going to take care of your animals every day until you recuperate. I told him to bring your dogs over."

"Thank you."

"I hear they're quite . . . unusual."

"That's putting it mildly."

She stood and brushed the creases out of her jeans. "Well, finish your tea, and if you need anything just holler, or clap your hands or something. I'd give you a bell to ring, but my maidservant is polishing it. Do you want something to read?"

"Not right now. I'm tired."

"You're on quite a heavy round of antibiotics. Okay, I'll leave you be."

May drained the tea, then pulled the white down comforter up around her neck and turned toward the nightstand. The martyr's stole rested by the lamp.

She decided John was her man of God. Eugene Damaroff was right. How he knew, she couldn't fathom, and didn't care. Closing her eyes, glad for the warm bath she'd just had, the cup of tea, and a soft bed with an electric blanket, she slept.

May had been recuperating at the rectory for a week, given love and good food and time. The kids, Julia and Luke, entertained her when they came home from school. Lynn drank tea with her and taught her how to crochet. The dogs loved it there too. Her body was getting stronger and stronger; each day something inside mended just a little.

May was sitting outside watching the crocuses bloom near the back door when John came out and handed her a piece of hot apple pie. She was beginning to suspect the iced tea business had been a ruse to put her off her guard. She told him so.

He laughed. "It wasn't then, I assure you. But I guess Lynn realized with all the stresses of the ministry, and loving my sweets like I do, she needed to give it a rest."

"I'm glad for you. And you're not really heavy at all." She stabbed the pie and lifted a forkful to her mouth. "Oh boy, this is good. Lynn sure can cook."

"Why do you think I married her?" He pulled up a black metal chair, the feet scraping along the cement.

"I hope it was more than that."

"Oh, it was. Believe me. She was the kindest, calmest person I'd ever met. I knew I'd need her."

"For your parishioners?"

He shook his head. "For me."

"That's nice. So what do you bring to the table?"

"My charm and good looks?"

"Try again."

More pie. The apple slices perfectly tart and sweet and soft melded with the golden crust as she pressed the bite to the roof of her mouth to spread across her tongue.

"Maybe you should ask her that. I've been wondering for years. I completely got the better end of the deal."

"I'm thinking you're right about that, John."

He ate his pie, too, and they sat in silence for a while, Sweetie and Stinky rolling around on the lawn and chasing birds almost as big as they were, having a great time.

—Must be nice to be that free.

Finishing, Father John set his plate beside his chair and reached into his jacket pocket. "I brought your mail."

"Thanks."

"You got a letter from Eli Campbell."

"Oh, good. He wants me to take a picture of the Purple Cow in town. He said he used to hang out there."

"Want me to bring over your camera?"

"Thank you. I think I might be able to venture out a little bit."

"You look so much better."

"And I feel a lot stronger. Thanks for bringing me here, John."

"I'm glad you're feeling better. We love having you."

—What a nice thing for him to say.

"It's about more than the pneumonia, you know," she said. She picked up the outer edge of piecrust.

"Just getting off the farm?"

"Yes. And it only took starvation and near death to do it!"

"But you came. You took the first step, May. That's important."

She couldn't rest in that for long, though, she knew. If she was moving forward, she had to keep going. "Now I really have to consider what I'm going to do come June. I can't wait any longer."

"Good thinking, May."

—Well, finally.

Dear May,

It sounds pretty bad there. You need to call someone. I know you have a phone line now. You've met Sassy, my mother.

Call her. Her number is 555-3579. I know she'll help you out.

Father John visited me again a couple of days ago. I asked about you running him off, and he was pretty good-natured about it. I think, if you'd like to repair the relationship, he'd return. You probably need to have a spiritual person in your life. We all do really. I know after Rwanda you have trouble viewing God as merciful. I did, too, for a long time. Unfortunately I didn't ask questions of why evil happens. I know why firsthand being the evildoer. But I wondered why God didn't stop me. Why Roger and Faye had to come through those glass doors at that precise moment.

Write when you can. I'm sure you're glad it's finally warming up a little.

Warmly (ha, ha),
Eli

No better time than the present. Her heart sped up. She willed it to back down. Her life depended on this.

Heading down River Street toward Main, the breeze blew warmer than it had yet that spring, bringing with it a hopeful shimmer as it moved the bare limbs of the trees that filtered the sunlight onto the grass. All those walks she had taken with Girlfriend in Lexington! May would be dressed so cute, her legs bare and shaved and tanned. *Honk! Honk!* There'd be plenty of that.

Now she resembled something like a bag lady benefiting from a morning shower. She passed Jack's IGA, thinking how much food she'd eaten from that place and never stepped a foot inside; didn't know where the milk cooled or the bread loaves lay in stacks on shelves. How weird. Then Rose Brothers Department Store where the clothing she was wearing came from—which, she had to admit, was a bit more fashionable than when Claudius bought things for her. The thrift store too. She liked the olive green and orange lamp in the window with tassel fringe on the burlap shade. How groovy would that be in a college apartment?

The camera bag bumped on her hip, and nobody looked at her askance. It wasn't like Beattyville was Fashion Central or anything. She was just another backwater country person who rarely got off her farm.

—My farm?

That Marlow!

There was the joint. On the corner of Circle and Main. Dooley's Purple Cow. Who thought that was a good idea? And where did a name like that come from? The children's rhyme? "I never saw a purple cow . . ."

And what does that have to do with hot roast beef sandwiches, cheeseburgers, and meatloaf?

Nevertheless, she stood on the far corner and snapped off some pictures of the low-slung brick restaurant with the large plateglass window looking out onto the sidewalk. Stepping across Main she snapped more . . . some close-ups of the sign proclaimed that inside she would find "home cooking at its finest."

Sign her up for that! Maybe next year or so.

A boy, about fourteen, pushed through the door and onto the sidewalk. "What you taking pictures for?"

"I'm a journalist," May said, the words falling out of her mouth. "I might write a story about this place."

"Okay. Just so long's you're not doing anything shady."

"Not even a little bit. Can I take your picture by the door?"

"Will I be in the paper?" He scratched his dirty-blond crew cut.

"Maybe." It *could* happen, right?

He puffed out his chest, looking proud of himself there in his jeans, long-sleeved UK T-shirt, and a white apron. She fired off several pictures. He was a great subject.

"Thanks. Wanna see?" She turned the camera around and showed him the pictures.

He grinned. "That's cool."

"You take a fine picture. What's your name?"

"Wayne."

"Okay, Wayne. You want me to bring you one by after they're developed? I live just up the way."

He nodded and headed in as she turned around and walked back in the direction she had come. In a manner of speaking.

May stopped along the way, taking pictures of whatever took her fancy. So much to see. So much to make her own.

—Is that what I'm doing?

The pool joint, the town stage, a butcher shop, a gas station, a big brick church, and yes, a lot of places closed up and rotting, sad to say.

It felt like a little dying town, but to May it throbbed with life.

Yes. This was her town. And Marlow wasn't going to take it away from her.

· 16 ·

May sat at the tile-topped kitchen table with Lynn, peeling potatoes. It felt good to use her hands like that again. All the potatoes she'd peeled with Claudius! Lordymercy!

"Please let me give you some money for the food you've given me. At least the tea," May said. "I bet I've used up three boxes' worth!"

"Not at all necessary. Although I was going to use that extra grocery money to go have some Botox injections."

"What's Botox?"

Lynn laughed. Then told her.

Oh good, she wasn't serious. It felt weird not getting the current jokes. But botulism? People injected botulism bacteria into their faces to make their wrinkles disappear? May realized things had gone absolutely over the top out there. It was like smoking a cigarette to keep your bowels regular.

It was like hiding on a farm for a decade to keep sane.

"I need to go back home," she said.

"You sure you're ready?"

"Yes. I've got work to do."

Dear Eli,

I'm going to fight to stay on the farm. It's my farm. That man has no right to take it out from under me.

Can you see the spring flowers from your window? I doubt it, but I thought I'd ask. I thought I'd tell you I hope so.

May

She'd been dreading this day and yet looking forward to it for a long time now. Out for the afternoon stroll that Lynn named "May's Camera Constitutional," May walked up the hill to St. Thomas church and followed the signs to the church office.

Father John, dressed casually today in khakis and a blue flannel shirt, welcomed her into his church study. He'd finally got his hair cut, and Lynn had taken to calling him Father Hedgehog. "What's up, May?"

"Hi, John. Well, it's time."

"What for?"

"Do you have some time to talk?"

"For you? Sure. Let's go sit in the pews."

"Okay."

He chose the third pew. "What can I do for you, May?"

"I want to make a confession." She held up a hand. "I know you're Episcopalian, but please, I need this. It's time."

"Oh. Well, of course, May. We have a rite of confession too. Just a moment."

He rose and hurried back to his office. He returned wearing a thin white stole, the sign of his priesthood. He sat back down next to her. "Are you ready?"

May nodded. "The question is, are you?"

"'I can do all things through Christ who gives me strength.'"

May remembered her confessions of years ago.

—Oh, this will be so good. Such a relief!

She was already anticipating the freedom of knowing somebody knew, somebody besides God. And once it all was voiced, out there in the real airwaves, she couldn't take it back. She couldn't fool herself that she'd never felt and thought the things she did, or behaved in the manner she did. It would solidify everything, make it real enough to be dealt with once and for all.

"Bless me, Father, for I've sinned. It's been ten years since my last confession."

"The Lord be in your heart and upon your lips that you may truly and humbly confess your sins: In the Name of the Father, and of the Son, and of the Holy Spirit. Amen."

She crossed herself and uttered, "Amen."

She paused and examined her conscience, praying for the Holy Spirit to enlighten her mind to recall where and when her heart had wandered far from God. Where *she'd* wandered.

"I hated God. For a very long time. I let it blacken my heart and pull me from the world he loves. I let my anger help me lie to myself. I've been lying to myself for so long. And you know what? I figured being angry at the horrors that go on was enough. And I figured maybe if I threw it all onto God, I could walk away free."

"Don't be too hard on yourself. It's easy to do."

"Don't give me an out. I questioned God's love and thought if he was choosy, then I could be too. I chose to love selectively, people who would ask nothing of me, people who would love me lavishly even though I refused to do the same. I used them. Over and over. And that was wrong too."

He gave a nod.

"I turned my back on my mother in her hour of need and refused to support my father, who had to care for her."

He nodded again.

"I'm tired, Father."

"I know, May."

And she continued, revealing the depths of her heart to this man of God. Belligerence, lack of charity and understanding. Each word lifted a string of the iron netting that had bound her heart, ever constricting with each passing year.

Finally.

"But I feel like I'm coming out of it. Like I see God again. I mean, I know he's always been there. But I recognize it now. And I'm thankful. Finally. I'm giving thanks again."

"Gratitude is always a good place to start."

"I fell back into the spoiled teenager category. Like, if I couldn't have everything exactly my way, I wouldn't play."

He nodded again. "May, it was more than that. You were the victim of horrible people."

"I didn't have to stay that way."

"Maybe not. But now it's time. And that's it."

"No going back."

"I doubt you ever will."

They sat in silence for a while. Finally he whispered, "Are you finished, May?"

"Yes." She knelt down, pressed the palms of her hands into her eyes. "Jesus Christ, Son of God, have mercy on me, a sinner," she prayed.

He settled his hands on her head. "Our Lord Jesus Christ, who has left power to his Church to absolve all sinners who truly repent and believe in him, of his great mercy forgive you all your offenses; and by his authority committed to me, I absolve you from all your sins: In the Name of the Father, and of the Son, and of the Holy Spirit. Amen."

Father John took both of her hands in his. "The Lord has put away all your sins, May."

"Thanks be to God."

"Abide in peace, and pray for me, a sinner."

May couldn't move. Still on her knees, peace washed over her because once again, she'd drawn near to the God who was never far away to begin with.

"I love Jesus, Father."

"I know you do, May."

She reached into her jacket pocket and pulled out the martyr's stole. "I want you to have this. It was Father Isaac's."

"Oh, May. Are you sure? This must mean so much to you."

She pressed it into his hands. "Please. You came when no one else would. I can talk to you like I could him. I would rather you have it than anyone else."

He put his arms around her shoulders and hugged her, just for a minute. "Thank you, May."

· 17 ·

The words of the church service flowed over her in warm waters of consolation and love. And when Communion began, May listened to the words, really listened to them, aching for them, for the first time in her life.

She wanted to close her eyes and breathe it in, but she couldn't tear her gaze from Father John. He seemed so different in this light, the priestly calling settling on him, around him, through him, swallowing him whole, and she loved him more. He connected her once again with Father Isaac, who she knew was looking down, don't ask her how, only that she knew how happy he was that she was there that morning.

—Jesus would surely let him take a peek at this, wouldn't he?

Maybe Jesus was right there beside him. May wanted to believe that.

She used to love Jesus so much.

Her own voice, making the responses, soothed her. The voices of others, responding with hers, wrapped around her like a prayer shawl. May's grandmother used to wear a head covering at Mass, the gray, soft lace brushing the broken-in skin of her cheeks. She passed away when May was five. A small corner of May's heart curled in on itself at the memory of a woman who lived a quiet faith.

May remained in her seat as the congregation filed up to receive the Eucharist. They knelt at the rail around the altar, heads bowed until the server reached them. Reaching out for the bread, they dipped it into the wine and ate.

Jesus filled her heart. And the words *Come home, May* filled her soul. *Come and dine.*

She sprang from her seat and ran down the aisle, receiving the Body and Blood, strength and life and blessing and movement.

—Yes, Lord.

Back in her seat, she thought of flowers. Flowers, flowers, and more flowers. She'd plant more than she ever had.

God would have to work out the details of the harvest.

March 12, 2004

Dear May,

My mother visited me today with Callie. It was so good to see my daughter. But I know how hard it is for her to see me like this. Oh, May, it's all so useless. I look back over and over and I try to think about "that moment." What was the exact moment, the decision, that set my feet on this path? Was it going into the military? Was it my first joint at sixteen? Was it walking through Travis's door after I got out of the military, knowing what he was into? I don't know. Maybe it's the collection of decisions. We like things to be neat and tidy, and one fateful moment is a whole lot more dramatic. But there is that point of no return, isn't there?

Mama's still trying to convince me to appeal, but honestly, I just don't see what good it will do. If I don't die, it's not like it's really going to change the system in the State of Kentucky, will it? I'm not sure about that. Just thinking things through. Is it wrong for me not to take advantage of the full extent of the system in order to give others hope that they might do the same? I don't know that either. It's tricky. I never thought one could have so much effect from a jail cell.

I've been reading the Bible more, at the encouragement of Father John. Are you reading yours? You should. Man, I'm being bossy. But I don't want to start this letter over, so you can make of it what you will. I take it all back if you want me to. If not, there it is. Anyway, Father John says that Israel had pretty stringent requirements as to when they would administer the death penalty. Three eyewitnesses were necessary. Only one person saw what I did, so I guess biblically my execution would be unjust. So I'm thinking about that too. If they came to get me right now, I'd still go forward with the needle. That much is sure today, and each day I wake up I realize today is all I can count on.

If you could have seen my daughter . . . That's where it all gets the most difficult.

Take care,
Eli

May felt her heart tear in two.

—Seriously. What if things had worked out differently between us?

What if he hadn't gotten Janey pregnant, and she'd come home from Rwanda and they'd embarked on something more than a few dates? She thought how different his life would be, mostly. But then, what about hers? A nice daughter like Callie to raise and love. A little house or apartment with dishes she'd picked out when she registered for their wedding.

Oh, they'd still have had an extraordinary life. Eli wouldn't have encouraged her to do anything less than something brave and amazing. She would have traveled the world with her camera, captured blazing, shattering images, somehow escaping the bullets, and she would have returned home to strong arms, some lovemaking, and smiley face pancakes the next morning before walking the kids to school.

Time to do some chores.

A strange car pulled up just as May was gathering eggs. The chickens had rotated their time to about three in the afternoon for the final egg count to be in. She'd forgotten her basket, so seven eggs nestled in her T-shirt, scooped up to hold them.

It wasn't really a nice car. May didn't know much about cars, but she knew the old Lincoln had been a great car probably at least thirty years before. Rust spots bloomed on the fenders, and black flecks pitted the chrome. The engine sounded fine, though. At least to her. She'd only recently started riding around in cars again.

Sassy emerged. At least that's who May guessed it was, judging from the fact that she bore Eli's face. She favored happy colors, including the yellow blonde of her hair, gathered into a high ponytail and held in place with a hot pink ribbon coordinating with her stretch pants. She waved, the sleeves of her lime green sweatshirt almost leaving a visible flare across May's visual field.

May waved back with her left hand, her right hand still cradling the eggs.

"Sassy?"

"Yep! It's me!"

A girl slid out of the car, tall for her age, big boned but without any extra flesh, with a wide jawline and sandy hair, just like her father.

"Come around the back to the kitchen while I put away these eggs!"

May quickly rinsed them off and set them in the bin in the fridge.

Sassy and Callie walked in, the wind catching the screen door and banging it against the side of the house.

"Whoa!" Callie jumped and quickly caught it.

"Thanks."

Sassy set her purse on the kitchen table, then picked it up again. "Sorry."

"Don't be. Make yourself comfortable. I was just about to have some tea. Would you all like a cup?"

They agreed and sat down.

"I just wanted to bring Callie over," Sassy began. "She heard you were writing Eli and wanted to thank you. I do too."

"Did Eli tell you?"

Callie nodded as she slipped out of her turquoise hoodie, revealing a yellow Hello Kitty T-shirt. "We write letters all the time." Her voice came out in a soft whisper, directly opposed to her form. "It's meant a lot to him."

May filled the kettle and set it on the flame. She sat down. "It must be hard for you."

"It is."

"How do you feel about him not appealing?"

"I'm completely against it!" Sassy said.

"Not me," Callie whispered.

"Really?" May asked.

She shook her head, her dirty-blonde hair skimming the tops of her shoulders. "I love my dad. He shouldn't have to live with the kind of guilt he suffers just for me." She patted Sassy's hand. "Not that you shouldn't feel the way you do, Granny. He's your kid. Nobody wants to lose their kid."

The shock of such maturity in a—what, ten-year-old?—hit May like a baseball.

Was it any wonder, though, being raised by her granny because her mother was a druggie and her dad was away all the time? And then . . . the murders. It was too much, surely.

"You two have each other, it's obvious," May said.

"Oh, yes." Sassy nodded. "I don't know what I'd do without my granddaughter."

Something gripped inside May's heart, that usual fear that she'd love too much, too many people. Her confession came back to her, her words about her own choosiness, loving only those who were safe to love, who expected nothing in return. That would change right here, right now.

"I'm glad you came," she said.

March 14, 2004

Dear Eli,

Well, I'm working my way back to life. I think. Now I'm wondering how to keep my farm. Claudius's farm. Okay, the church's farm. There must be some way I can stay and everyone be happy.

I'm going to have to get a vehicle. There's no two ways about it. I came home to another letter from Sister Ruth, who's prolonged her trip yet again. She's living it up with her cousin, going to supper clubs and dinner dances with other senior citizens. And since she's such a smart dresser, I'll bet she's the belle of the ball. Anyway, the Galaxy's dead, as you supposed.

Walking the streets of Beattyville didn't kill me, so I figure I can darn well do my own grocery shopping.

Regarding whether or not your execution is just, well, I think there are two theories here at war. We're a people. A people who belong to our country. And at times society decides these things. What's right and what's wrong for it. A lot of people say that's a valid way to figure out morality. I don't know. I mean, if you take that to its logical conclusion, slavery was okay then because society said so, the laws said so, and therefore, according to some folk, God said so. It's like the Iraq war. Although I'm sure you being a Marine think that was all right. Which might go to make my point fall down in your favor. That your sentence is indeed just because society says it's so.

Then again. Are some things just right and wrong regardless of society's take on it? And does your sentence fall into that category? Is it okay to use the Bible, either one way or the other, regarding this? You can say that Israel used the death penalty (can you tell I've been talking to Father John about this too?) to justify your execution. But then, like you said, you can go further and see how Israel decided to employ it, which isn't what we do here in the United States.

Oh, man, Eli! All this clinical talk of death I just spouted off! I hate it! I hate death. I hate the way mankind takes the very life of other people and justifies it! I saw that firsthand, to its ugliest extreme. Where does it all begin? Where does it end? Why must it be so? Maybe I'm the wrong person to talk about this with, because if you want to know how I feel, how I really feel, it's that I DON'T WANT YOU TO DIE!! Okay?! I can't imagine even for one moment what good it will do anyone.

Callie understands, though. I finally met her. Sassy brought her by. She's wonderful, Eli. She deserves to have a dad. You've learned so much there. It's not like she'd be better off without you. Don't fool yourself for a moment that that's the case.

Okay, I'm done.

So tell me what your days are like there. Would you mind? It will help me picture your life better.

Well, I guess I'd better go out and make some bouquets from the bulb flowers. I can't take them into Lexington to the farmers' market without a car, so I might have to force myself to walk downtown and see where I can set up a lawn chair and a bucket of posies. I'll show that Marlow!

Oh, and Louise died! She choked to death on the wire fence. More death. It still makes me mad. She was such a nice cow.

May

· 18 ·

March 18, 2004

Dear May,

I have to admit, I didn't realize how much of a thinker you've become. Wish we'd have had conversations like this years ago. Do you ever wonder why some younger people, like we were, dumb themselves down? You were the cute little blonde and I was the hulking football player, and all along we had some good thoughts to share. Why didn't we?

I've been trying to think of what you said regarding society deciding morality, and I think there's something to it. John gave me a book about the teachings of the early church, and divorce comes readily to mind. Early Christians wouldn't have thought to do such a thing except under certain circumstances, and now the practice is pretty widely accepted. War is another area. You're right. Many of the early Christians were killed rather than go to war and kill another human. And now killing is thought of as righteous. In a way that parallels my situation. But didn't your church draw up a whole just war doctrine? Obviously they decided some circumstances were okay. So, does God give us all latitude to work out what is right and wrong? I mean, yes, some things will always be wrong. But what about the gray areas?

Why is it the most vocal of Christians are gleeful at the thought of my death? Don't they realize that I could be going to hell that very night? Aren't they even a little bit sad at that thought? It doesn't seem so. And yet, who am I to judge them? Do I have any right to even think such thoughts? I guess I'm just letting my mind meander.

I'm glad you're going to fight for the farm! What's your plan of attack? As for me, I'd start by planning what you're going to plant this year. But you might want to start visiting Harmony Baptist, get to know the people there, get them on your side.

They've given me a date of May 29. So that leaves a little over two months. I'm relieved, but at the same time, somewhat terrified. Although I have to wonder, can a person be "somewhat" terrified? Does that even make sense?

Take care, May.
Eli

March 23, 2004

Dear Eli,

You never did answer me about your daily routine. Is that some sort of penitentiary secret or something? If so, that's okay. You don't have to answer. As for my daily routine, it now includes walking into town to do my own grocery shopping at Jack's. Can you believe it?

Thanks for the good suggestions about getting the farm back. I took your advice and went to Harmony Baptist yesterday. Marlow's jaw dropped when I slipped into the back pew. I sat next to Sister Racine, who, by the way, makes a great three-bean salad. Something strange happened, though. I went in there as strategy, you know? But after the service, the folks gathered around me, and I thought of Claudius. I felt really close to him then. Sister Racine and Brother Ben invited me to have lunch with them at Dooley's Purple Cow, and I did! I got a bacon grilled cheese sandwich, and I just sat and listened to them critique the pastor's sermon for the next forty-five minutes. Sister Racine drove me home. All in all, it was good, and I'm praying again. I still have a lot of questions for God, and I'm looking for his explanations on a lot of things.

I'm getting ready to run this business. Case in point, I sold my flowers, bulb flowers, downtown on Saturday and sold out. But nobody came up when I was sitting there. So I saw the busboy from The Purple Cow get off after the breakfast shift and asked him if he wanted to make some money. His name is Wayne, and he said yes. So he sat there and sold out in an hour. $150. I gave him fifteen, and he said that was more than he'd ever made in an hour. Obviously I'm going to have to beef up my image. Or beef it down. Something new, that's for sure.

Do you have e-mail? I finally figured it out! Glen showed me how to open a Hotmail account. So far I only get offers for the weirdest things, some I can't even name—me, the reformed college bad girl! That's how weird it is on the Internet. Oh, boy.

On that glorious note, I'll close. But despite that, I feel like I'm doing better than I have been in a long time.

May

· 19 ·

May picked up the phone, which seemed to be jangling extra loudly for some reason.

"May-May, honey!"

"Sister Ruth."

No wonder the ring was so loud. May laughed.

"What's so funny?"

"Just you. It's so good to hear your voice."

"I've got news!"

"You're staying in Florida."

Silence.

"Well?"

"You took the wind right outta my sails, honey."

She'd just had a feeling. "I'm happy for you, though, does that count?"

Sister Ruth sighed. "I guess it'll have to. I heard you were trying to sell those flowers downtown. And you been going to Jack's too!"

"You sound proud."

"Honey, I am! Oh, I sure am."

"Maybe your leaving was one of the best things that could have happened to me."

"Now, now. Don't go too far."

March 26, 2004

Dear May,

Glad to hear you've been walking to town. It's about a mile, right? How do you carry your groceries home, or transport your flowers up that killer hill? Please don't tell me you take the wheelbarrow. You do, don't you? Another word of advice, get your stall back at the Lexington farmers' market. Quick!

It's true you may have to beef up your image, although I can't imagine you look as bad as you say. You were a knockout in college. It would be hard to ruin those kinds of looks no matter how hard you try. Don't think I'm being creepy or anything, just thinking you're probably too hard on yourself, like most people. Well, strike that. Some of the guys in here aren't hard enough on themselves and haven't been for a good long time.

Okay, my daily routine. It's pretty bland, as you might expect. Up at seven, breakfast soon after. Around nine we're let out to either go into the yard or to the activities room. That's where I paint. I've been painting for a while now. Almost since I got in here. My mom and daughter have a bunch of my pictures. They started out pretty chaotic, which isn't surprising, but they've gotten increasingly more orderly. I can't control much about my life, but I can control my art, so I work hard at it. (I always liked to draw as a kid.)

Then back into my room for a couple of hours. I've heard some death row inmates are in their rooms as much as twenty-three hours a day. It's not like that here, and I'm thankful. We have another time in the afternoon where we can either exercise or go to the activity room. Usually I just stay in my room and read. The gossip gets a little wearing to say the least, and it's not even good gossip. Dinner. Back to the room. Lights out at ten. That's pretty much it.

You're probably going to ask if I've made any friends, and the answer to that is no. Best to keep distant. I've had no problems like you imagine in prison. We're kept on constant surveillance. Still, I try to remain brooding and crazy-eyed just in case. I figure it can't hurt.

So back to your spiritual journey. I guess I can't blame you for wanting God to explain himself. We all do, to a certain extent. Most of us don't come right out and say it, though. I'm sure the relatives of Roy and Faye ask those questions too. But we're talking about you here, not me and my situation. My question to you would be how do you think God should go about explaining himself. In my experience, God's spoken more times than not through circumstances and people. If you've spent a decade out of circulation, and haven't gone anywhere or done anything outside of what makes you comfortable, how do you think God should explain himself? Maybe you haven't given him a chance. It seemed like he was trying with Claudius. Do you think it was a coincidence that the person who took care of you after Rwanda was someone like that? And then when Claudius's time to depart came, Sister Ruth was there. Two people who seemed to understand what walking with God meant, and neither of them got through to you in that way. And then, Sister Ruth left and Father John showed up. Maybe God was telling you he was taking care of you, because all you went through happened through no fault of your own. Now I realize that doesn't answer your questions about Rwanda, but it might help you realize the answer to some of your questions about you, and that's as good a place to start as any, don't you think?

Glad to hear you're praying again. Is God talking back?

Well, I'll close for now. Tell Father John I said hello next time you see him. And regarding your farm, you might need a little help now that Sister Ruth is in Florida. Maybe Callie could help you out. She'd sure be cute selling flowers too.

Eli

Sassy thought Callie and May would do just fine in Lexington together. May agreed. The girl dressed in jeans and a hoodie, and tucked in the pocket was a sandwich and a baggie of Cheetos. May wore the same, her old UK sweatshirt sent years ago by her dad. She bought a pair of regular old jeans at Rose Brothers too. Nothing weird about those!

She'd called at the last minute and arranged to get her old stall back at the market. And Sassy's husband, Buell, offered the use of his old pickup. He'd dropped it off the night before.

"Let me help you load up those flowers," he'd said, climbing out.

May liked him instantly. He looked a little like Santa Claus, only fatter and with aviator glasses and a T-shirt.

"We're behind what you're doing, May." He grabbed a couple of sugar buckets full of daffodil posies. "Whatever we can do to help you, we'll do. You should keep this farm."

It encouraged May. Maybe it wasn't such a far-fetched idea.

Then again, Buell and Sassy didn't know Marlow the way she did.

"Let's head 'em on out, Callie." She opened the door of the black pickup truck, and Callie hopped in. May had acted to Sassy like it would be a fun outing, but she knew she needed the responsibility of having Callie along to keep her from another freak-out.

—Who'd freak out in front of a fragile ten-year-old?

Not even May. At least that's what she was counting on.

She slid into the driver's seat. "So, you ever been to the farmers' market, Callie?"

"Nope. I only been to Lexington a few times before. But I'm game to do anything that gets me away from Beattyville."

"I'm kinda nervous," May confided.

That was easy enough to do. Callie was that type of girl with a very innocent, round face, soft and pink of cheek, but the smoky brown eyes in her sockets were about thirty-five years old. According to her grandmother, she wasn't the most popular kid at school and had learned to keep to herself years ago.

Callie split her ponytail and pulled, tightening the arrangement. "Well, I imagine it's going to bring back memories for you too. Mama told me you went to UK."

"Yeah. That seems like forever ago."

"Oh, it was!"

The girl's nod was much too effusive for May's comfort, but she had to laugh.

She backed out of the driveway, put the truck in drive, and headed down Route 11. She could picture herself walking along the road with a wheelbarrow full of flowers; it was an odd sight. Five minutes later she realized *she was driving*! And it was fine. All the instincts had remained intact.

—Well, good then.

May shoved down the fear that surfaced with the recognition of her accomplishment. She could do this. People had done much bigger things after trauma. She was just driving a big old pickup truck. That was it.

She'd renew her driver's license later, stick right to the speed limit for now.

Callie asked if she could turn on the radio.

"Please!" May almost screamed the word.

Callie looked at May, then touched her shoulder. "Mama told me you're a hermit, kinda. You sure you're gonna be okay?"

"I'm going to have to be."

"I know what you mean." She leaned forward and worked the buttons. "I feel like that every day when I walk into school."

May couldn't have been prouder of Callie had she been her own daughter. The child ran the table, interacting with the customers with a warm politeness, giving suggestions, and how did she learn so much about flowers?

"Oh, I researched things at school when I found out I was coming with you," she said as they ate their sandwiches and drank Cokes from a nearby stand. "You know, if we added greens to some of the bouquets, we might could charge a little more. They'd be more like arrangements."

May sighed. "I know I should learn to arrange flowers better than I do. It would be fun to open a little shop, wouldn't it?"

Callie nodded. "I could help you run it."

"You'd do a good job of it, that's for sure."

"I love putting stuff together."

May didn't have a hard time believing that.

"You're back!" a happy voice yelled.

May wheeled around. Who could forget the lady with the wild gray hair and the turquoise jewelry?

"I am!"

The woman ran around the table and pulled May into a hug. "There hasn't been a Saturday market go by that I haven't thought of you. Where have you been all these years?"

"It's a long story."

She pulled back. "Well, it's good to see you, sweetie."

May gave her three free bouquets. Somebody remembered her. She could hardly believe it.

The customers came and went, remarking on the flowers even if they didn't buy. She'd forgotten what a boost that was. Thankfully, nobody she knew came by, except an English teacher from Lexington Catholic she'd never had.

Sold out a few hours later, they packed up the truck.

"What do you say we head over to campus after we eat? My treat." May slid the last bucket into the back. "I brought my camera. Maybe your dad would like to see pictures of his old haunts."

"Okay."

An hour later, after a hamburger from Triple J Farm's trailer, they parked by the student center. May unpacked her camera on the lawn by the Young Library, a lightly imposing building built after her time. "I guess I should show Eli some of the new stuff too."

"Do you think that might make him feel bad?" Callie asked.

"I think he'll be glad things are moving forward, don't you?"

"Probably."

After she snapped off a few pictures of the massive brick structure complete with arches and a large cupola, they ventured onto the older part of the campus. May felt herself grow younger with each step, as if all the years collected between her shoulder blades and rolled down her spine one by one.

On that bench in front of Funkhauser—she clicked off a few frames—she'd sit with her girlfriends and they'd drink soda and talk about boys and dreams and they'd laugh out loud, a little too loudly, to garner a bit of attention from the other passing students.

Callie and May strolled on down Rose Street, the evening sun red on their necks and the aroma of Thai cooking drifting from the restaurant on the corner as they passed the Singletary Center for the Arts. They turned left onto Avenue of Champions and stopped in front of Memorial Coliseum where the women's basketball team used to play.

"I watched a lot of games here. And down at Rupp Arena."

Callie just shrugged, and May snapped off a few shots of the slightly Art Deco, blond brick coliseum. The memories rolled by in her head. Screaming their heads off and jumping up and down and wearing Kentucky Blue and shouting "Go Wildcats" over and over. "You know, I didn't always have to have a date to the games. Sometimes I'd just go with girlfriends."

"That's good. Granny's already told me not to be too dependent on men for everything."

"That's real good advice."

"I mean, not that they don't have their uses," she said. "It would be terrible if you had to always be the one to carry the heavy suitcases."

May laughed out loud. "Men are just fine. Good ones, anyway."

"Did you ever have a nice boyfriend, May?"

She shook her head. "No. I didn't go steady with guys. I just went out on a lot of dates. I was more about having a good time in those days."

"Did you ever love anybody?"

"No." They continued on down the avenue so she could take pictures of the student center and the old gymnasium.

"That's so sad."

Amazing she couldn't see that then.

May sighed. "Too late to worry about it now, though!"

"I don't know. I read on the Web the other day about a couple, ninety-five years old the bride was, who just got married."

They snapped some shots by the student center, and May remembered sitting on the sofas there sometimes, reading or studying by herself. She wasn't always with groups of people. Sometimes she could be quiet and centered and focused. She'd forgotten about that.

"I graduated with pretty good grades," she said.

"You seem really smart."

She lowered the camera. "Really?"

"Uh-huh."

—She said it so matter-of-factly she must really believe it. Huh.

"Do you ever think about going back to college? Mama says she'd love to go to college sometime."

"Not really. I guess there are lots of way to learn things."

"She says you can make more money with a good education."

May changed the camera setting to auto. "Depends on what you're learning to do!"

"What did you study?"

"Journalism. I loved it."

"Then why aren't you doing it anymore?"

"That's a long story."

"You ever going to do it again?"

"Hmm. Don't think so."

Callie flipped back her hair. "What a waste of time and good money!"

"Oh boy, are you ever right about that."

"I've already started saving up for college. I want to get away from the kids in my school as quick as I can."

They took more pictures of the campus, weaving along on the paths between the buildings. May took pictures of Callie too. She'd look back at those pictures someday and think *My dad was still alive then*. And then she'd look at others after the execution and think *Now that was taken after he died*. When the time came, it was going to be all over the news. It would be horrible.

They stood in front of a stainless steel sculpture that looked like a praying mantis. Callie imitated the pose.

"Just think, Callie, maybe someday you'll be a student here, and you'll look at these pictures and remember your first visit."

"That would be nice, all right."

"Let's head back to the car and drive to the stadium. Eli would definitely want to see a picture of that."

Callie agreed. "He was a good football player, right? Did you see him play?"

"Yep. I sure did."

May remembered him there on the football field, blocking, pushing, all manner of manly brutish things. The roars of his teammates, the accolades, then finishing the game, showering and heading out with friends for the evening. Having beers bought for him, being the college athlete. He wasn't the best player on the team, but he was solid, always dependable to perform to the level everyone needed him to. May guessed he'd been like that in the military too.

—And now, look. What a lifetime can bring to someone.

She took a few frames. "Let's go," she whispered. This was just too sad. Classrooms were one thing. But the stadium? The contrast was unbearable. "The light is fading too much now anyway."

May remained quiet as they loaded themselves and the gear into the truck.

"Are you okay, Miss May?" Callie asked thirty minutes later as they sped down I-64 in the dusk.

"I was just thinking that there's more than one way to waste a perfectly good life. Eli did it one way. I'm not going to pretend you don't know. We both love your dad. But we both know what he did."

"Thank you," said Callie. "Everybody wants to hide it. They

think they're being mean to him in front of me if they bring it up. But I need to talk about it sometimes. I don't really have anybody to do that with."

"But there are more ways to waste a life." She turned on the cruise control. "And that just makes me sad, Callie."

"Me too," she said.

"Your granny tells me you're quite an artist."

"I do love art."

They pulled onto Mountain Parkway, the road a wide, flat plain taking them if they so chose deep into the heart of the mountains. Just to Beattyville for them, though.

"What are you going to do come June?" Callie asked.

"I don't know. But maybe we could do it together? I'll need your help to keep this farm." Let her know how wonderful she was, so the message of the snot-nosed brats at school didn't get through to her for good. May had always wanted to give kids like that a good punch in the nose.

Callie smiled a wide grin. "Okay! I'd like that."

They were going to need each other, and May was fine with that.

20

April 1, 2004

Dear Eli,

An image change is underway. Callie and I went into town to Rose Brothers Department Store. As a Lexington girl, I'm used to Dillard's, so I guess the Brothers Rose use the term department loosely. But never mind about that. I figured I'd get something a little more suitable than work clothes to build my business. It makes me a little mad that people don't want what appears to be an indigent bag lady around, but hey, I remember enough from my advertising classes that sometimes it's the image as much or more than the actual product . . . Claudius could go into Lexington looking practically homeless because he sold vegetables, and people expected a farmer from out east not to care about his attire. At least that's my guess. But a young woman looking like she's been living in the woods all her life? Nope, that won't do.

So anyway, I bought two sundresses, a light cardigan sweater, and a pair of sandals. I decided to cash in on the Easter crowd who might have forgotten to buy Mom flowers, and I still need the money, so I clipped more daffodils and tulips, and I sat right there at Main and Broadway. I French braided my hair and wore one of Claudius's mother's old Easter hats, a wide-brimmed straw hat with violets on the crown. Honestly, I don't think anybody recognized me, which was a good thing. I brought extra bouquets and sold out in three hours. Four hundred bucks! In Beattyville.

Sassy brought over a pan of lasagna last night! I hate to admit it, but after she left, I heated it up in the oven and ate half of it! A 9 x 13 pan. And you know what? I could have eaten more. I'll tell you what, the lasagna at the hot food bar at the IGA can't hold a candle to hers. I'd been getting a piece of that every week as a treat, but now I think I'm ruined. The pickled pigs' feet may end up looking like an option soon if I'm not careful. And actually, the fried chicken wings are delicious.

Okay, so I've spent more time with Callie and, oh, Eli! She's a beautiful girl. So tall and with all that dark blonde hair! She got all the good parts of you. Ha!

She's so kind too. She carried in the lasagna and asked if I'd like it in the refrigerator, then sat at the table and listened while we talked. She took out a little sketchbook and created the most beautiful, whimsical flowers and curlicues with a pack of markers she took out of her purse. I'm getting her to design a business card! I know a good thing when I see one.

She'd laugh at Sassy's jokes, and when she asked if she could see the animals, I gave her a tour of the farm. She thought my goat was funny, which racked up the points for me! You should be so proud of her. Sassy says she gets made fun of in school. Bullies seem to hone in on the nice kids and make them targets even if there is nothing at all odd about them. I'd say it's jealousy on their part, because she is just something. If you want me to go down to the school and threaten those no-goods, I will.

She wants to come help me on the farm after school and will continue accompanying me to the farmers' market on Saturdays. Thank you for that suggestion. We're going to do well there.

Eli, please think again about your appeal! Don't you want to stay alive to see how Callie turns out? I mean, don't you want to see one of the good things that came out of your life? She's going to do such lovely things someday; I just know it. I'm appealing to your emotions again with a heavy hand, but maybe it's something you should think about, you know?

You're right, of course, about not giving God the chance to explain himself. I've been thinking about that, which is why I'm going to church. I mean, it can't hurt to let him try, right? I have to admit there's something to your idea of God sending Claudius and Sister Ruth at just the right time. And maybe you're right. The best way to try and figure out why he let Rwanda happen is to first figure out why he let it happen to me. That seems a little selfish, though, Eli, because those people in the village were my friends. They saved me from myself in so many ways. Well, at least temporarily.

I went to church again Sunday. Sister Racine actually invited me over for dinner, but I had to get to planning my beds. So we're having lunch together this week. I'm going to talk to her about the farm and see if I can get her on board.

Glen's about to get here so I'll close and get a stamp on this thing.

Love,
May

May sat up late in Claudius's chair thumbing through Violet's old gardening journal. She had it practically memorized by now. It used to comfort her, make her feel as if she was just continuing a work, adding to it, maybe. Making it something more?

Yes. That was it exactly. She'd do what she could, build the business back up, and hope somehow she could convince Marlow to let her keep the farm.

Her eyelids grew heavy and she padded up the steps, looked in the nightstand drawer and felt the emptiness. No stole. But it was where it should be. And strangely enough, she realized, so was she.

21

April 7, 2004

Dear May,

I had a great idea! Start bringing in bunches of flowers to decorate the church on Sunday. Corsages too. How can the good folk of Harmony Baptist appreciate your flowers when they don't get to enjoy them on a regular basis?

I always get updates from Sassy about Callie, but hearing it from your perspective, well, I haven't been that joyful in a long time. It felt like Christmas at Grandma's. Ugh! How corny is that? But I can't help it, that's the way it is. She is beautiful, isn't she? And yes, I'm really proud of her. As far as staying alive for her, I see what you're saying, but she's young and vibrant and she'll move on. I never was in her life much, especially after I got so drugged out. Poor Mother, I was living with her right after I got back from Afghanistan, and two months in, she had to kick me out. Less than a year after that, I murdered Faye and Roy.

Callie's never had me as a father, May. Not at all.

I've been praying for you a lot lately. I'm not sure why, but I'm wondering if you're okay. Are you? Father John told me the Holy Spirit will tune our hearts to pray for those we love, even if we don't know what's going on with them. You seem to be doing so well, it's probably just stupid worry on my part. The weird thing is, I haven't even seen you in years. Don't get that I'm hinting at a visit. That's something you have to want to do all on your own.

May 29 can't come soon enough. The waiting these last months or so has been excruciating. I have to admit, I hope to see you making giant leaps by then. Have you thought about visiting your mother's grave? That might help you heal too.

Your friend,
Eli

Eli was right. She didn't make it to her mother's funeral, had never really laid to rest that lovely woman who played Yahtzee and made pumpkin pancakes and tried to make her into a good person. She'd done her best not to think about her.

The grave was bare. Back at the farm, Claudius's grave was a riot of color right then—oh, how she was going to miss just walking up there and having a talk with him, if she couldn't keep the farm—but her mother's sat there like an island almost, so forlorn and deserted, in a sea of flowers.

ELISABETH MEADOWS SEYMOUR

She sat cross-legged next to the tombstone and leaned her cheek against it. "I was an idiot," she whispered to her mother. "What was I scared of with you? What did I think you were going to ask of me? What did I think I was going to ask of you?"

She didn't know, couldn't answer.

Tears pricked. Why so much sorrow? Didn't those men with machetes realize their actions didn't stop on that day, with those people? Didn't they realize that those acts were stones in the river of space, thrown, and broadcasting ring upon ring for years, until, never ending, they passed stars, galaxies?

"God, don't make me become so introspective. Can I just move forward and worry about the whys later?" she whispered.

She gazed around her at the beautiful flowers planted in beds all around. She wondered if any of her posies had ended up here and figured they must have. So much color and life. And yet, death seemed to follow her. Her mother, Claudius. Eli was coming.

—I'm a walking angel of death, leaving people and villages in my wake.

Poor Claudius, to have found her by the road that day. That sure sealed his fate. It was a good thing Sister Ruth got out while there was still time.

She lay down next to her mother, folded her hands across her stomach, and fell asleep in the sun as she muttered "I'm sorry" over and over again.

Oh, good grief. This was too much!

May sat down in the middle of the carnage and cried. All her ladies were gone. Some had been killed by whatever it was that managed to get into the chicken run. The rest were missing. Probably eaten now back in the woods. Had she really forgotten to latch the door? She'd been taking care of them for years!

It was horrible. The three inside the run were half-eaten chunks of feather and bone. She couldn't imagine what the noise must have been like.

Eloise. Bill the Mule. Girlfriend. Scout. Louise. Now the ladies.

Only that darn goat was left. And she didn't do anybody a lick of good.

Was the farm itself telling her it was time to move on?

April 10, 2003

Dear May,

Sassy told me about your chickens and your subsequent question of whether this was a sign. Well, let me just offer another outlook. Maybe it's a sign to make the farm your own. What would you do differently at Borne's Last Chance if you weren't worrying about preserving Claudius's memory? Maybe that's something to think about.

I'm sorry about your chickens, by the way. I know how much they meant to you. Why don't you get online and see what kind of chickens you would like to try raising next? A friend of mine in elementary school had Araucanas, and they laid the prettiest blue and green eggs.

As the time shortens until my death, I've been praying especially for you, May, for strength to do what you have to do. Callie seems to be taken with you, and I'm grateful for that. She's going to need you. God will help you.

Love,
Eli

~

May set down the letter on the kitchen table. Her life was just beginning as Eli's was slipping away. She prayed, head down on the place mat.

It was time for it because this world was so beautiful and so horrible at the same time that to try and make sense of it on your own would land you on a farm for a decade. But nobody can make that a life, can they?

So May prayed for Eli. And she prayed for Callie and Sassy. And she prayed for Roger and Faye's family. They'd probably heard about May 29, and if they were happy, she could hardly blame them. But she prayed for a peace to alight upon them before then, because she knew Eli's death wouldn't bring it.

—Oh, Jesus. Jesus, Jesus, Jesus.

Anger. Sadness. Frustration. Sorrow. Nothing straightforward or singular came over her. She stood up, agitated, and looked out the kitchen window toward the empty coop.

—Poor little chickens. They kept me alive this winter, and that's the protection I gave them?

She gazed out on her little spread.

Make it your own, May-May. Her head resounded with the sound of Claudius's voice.

When Marlow showed up, she gave him the last dozen eggs in the refrigerator and told him she was just leaving. She strode down the driveway to the river and watched the glittering curves as the water rushed through town.

22

May had taken the last five hundred dollars of savings and bought herself a small pickup truck. A little white Mazda from years gone by, the back of the driver's seat had to be propped up by a milk crate, and the small cab had the general smell of thousands of hours of bodies stuck inside.

On Sunday morning she put on one of the sundresses, a black-and-white toile, and pulled her hair back in a bun. Pearls, those old heels, and a little perfume, and she was ready for church. Earlier that morning Callie, who'd been experimenting with floral arranging utilizing tips she'd read online, crafted a beautiful arrangement for Harmony Baptist. It sat next to May, perfuming the odiferous cab as she headed down River Road to the little white church.

Everyone praised the arrangement, talked about the cheerfulness it brought to the old church. And Marlow just fumed, preaching on "sowing seeds of discord."

May had no idea what he meant until the next day, when he showed up on the farm. She'd already let him in and seated him in his chair in the living room when he pounced.

"Don't think I don't see what you're trying to do, young lady."

"I'm older than you are, Marlow."

It felt good to call him that out loud.

"Be that as it may—"

"And I know exactly what I'm doing. In fact, I'm doing exactly what you think I'm doing."

"I want you off my farm!"

"*Your* farm?" She shifted in her chair; he shifted in his. "Look,

Pastor Marlow, there are forty acres here. Surely we can subsist side by side."

"But the roadside view . . ."

"We can work with that."

"I don't know."

"Just give me a fighting chance! Do you have to be so pigheaded about it?"

"That does it." He stood up. "Find another farm. It would be easier for us that way. We've got plans."

"What does the congregation think?"

"They'll do what I say."

—I wouldn't be so sure about that, May thought as he stormed out.

She picked up the phone and called Sister Racine. "I just want ten acres, Sister Racine. And I'm prepared to pay full price."

"How? Not that I'm against it, baby."

"I haven't figured that out yet." She squeezed the receiver. "But I will! Can you help me?"

"I'll do what I can."

"Is this going to cause problems in the church?"

"Honey, there's always problems in the church. The fact is, Pastor Marlow has been doing too much too soon. Us older folks have been left in the dust. Now it's not that we can't see the future needs tending to, but where's the love? That's what I keep asking."

"I don't want to cause a rift."

"Oh, you won't. Trust me. I'll just grease the wheel for you. But I think you're going to have to turn it yourself with that offer. That's got to come from you."

April 12, 2004

Dear Eli,

I don't think Marlow is going to budge. My only course of action is to buy the land, and I have almost no money. But I've been thinking about what you've said about making the farm my own, doing what I'd like with it, and, well, I want to share it. Not only with the church, but with the people I love. I don't know what that will look like yet, but we'll see what I can come up with. Ideas appreciated.

Here it is, my last-ditch effort to get you to appeal. You have six weeks left. I have to give it one last shot. I thought of an old Rwandan saying that I think fits both of us. "You can outdistance that which is running after you, but not what is running inside you." Can't you find some reason for your life to go on, Eli? Callie loves you. Sassy loves you. And you've helped me to figure out my own life. Please, please, please appeal! Is a life that's free the only one worth living? Can you possibly be so unimportant, so non-vital because you are locked up, that you have nothing to offer anybody? It's just not true! I can't tell you how hard I'm praying you change your mind. So is everybody else that knows you.

I've got to go. Callie's coming over. I'm going to teach her how to make Violet's biscuits, and then we're going to walk the farm and see where our dreams take us.

Love,
May

Sassy combed the last of the brown tint through May's hair. She'd picked May up earlier and brought her to their home, a tiny clapboard house clinging for dear life to a hillside in town. "I had to use three bottles of Clairol on you, May! You have a lot of hair, despite the twelve inches we cut off."

Callie nodded from where she sat near the bathroom sink, a pink porcelain square set with a stainless steel rim in a sparkly white counter. She'd done the cutting herself, and now it rested about halfway down May's shoulder blades.

"Callie, you did such a good job," May said. "You are so talented."

It was true. Callie was one of those girls who'd try anything crafty or handy or artistic. She could already sew throw pillows and embroider napkins. She could make jewelry out of wire and hardware (which she sold at one of the gift shops in town) and whip up a pan of brownies from scratch. Eli should be proud.

While Sassy was a wonderful grandmother, the fact that Callie would be, for all practical purposes, parentless come May 29 tugged down at May's heart and soul. But what could she do?

"Oh, I almost forgot to tell you!" Sassy said, combing May's hair into a big gooey dollop atop her head.

May looked at herself in the bathroom mirror. "I look like they could sell me at Dairy Queen."

Sassy laughed. "You do! Anyway, I was at church the other day when one of my friends was talking about her daughter's wedding, and I recommended you and Callie to do the flowers. I've got her number in my purse."

"Isn't that neat?" Callie's eyes sparkled.

May agreed. She could hardly imagine picking up that phone and making the call, though. The feed store was one thing. But a regular lady on the other end? She was going to end up stammering and stuttering. She knew it.

"I also told her you were a wonderful photographer. She said she wanted to see your work."

"Really? That sounds like a lot of fun."

"We don't have a photographer around here. It might be a good way to supplement your income."

Night had fallen and Callie was long in bed when May rose to go. Sassy had told her all about Eli as a child, and May hadn't laughed so much in years. Or cried.

"Buell lost his job," Sassy said as May put on her jacket. She gripped her hands together, and May realized she'd been wanting to tell her all evening.

"Oh, no!"

"I don't know what we're going to do. We're already a couple of months behind on the mortgage."

"I wish I could help. I just spent my last penny on that little truck."

"I wasn't asking for your help, May. Just hoping you'd pray for us is all."

May drove home with Sassy's request in her mind. She couldn't remember the last time somebody had asked her to pray for them.

Poor Sassy and Buell. And Callie. This was just what that poor girl needed. A dead father and losing the only home she remembered.

May was about to vent her anger at God, but the words of Father John resonated in her heart, the words he'd spoken about those who join in on doing God's goodness seeing his care for his children. Sassy hadn't asked for help, but May was going to give it to her. May had plans.

April 16, 2004

Dear May,

I put the Rwandan quote on my wall. I've tried to face what's inside me since I've come to prison. But maybe there's more. I'm praying God will show me whether or not he wants me to appeal. I've never asked him. By the way, Father John gave me that idea. He's pretty shifty, isn't he? I like the man, though. He's really been the only pastor figure I've had since I've been here.

I've got six weeks left, so your pictures of UK were especially wonderful to see. For a good fifteen minutes I remained in a world of good memories, and the glow of old times seemed to follow me throughout the day. I look at them at least twice a day and try to capture who I was then. Not that I was all that wonderful, but it was better than who I turned out to be. Thanks, as well, for taking some pictures of Callie. I imagine you two have a great time together, the way she smiled so easily into your camera.

I got an idea about the farm. (Again.) What if you raised money for the down payment? You don't have much time to save up the cash. I know that probably seems impossible, but you do have people who love you: Callie, Sassy, even Buell. Glen would probably help out, some of your friends at Harmony Baptist, and maybe Sister Ruth would return. Callie told me about those biscuits and Violet Borne's recipe book. Maybe you could cook a big feast to raise money. What do you think of that idea? Assuming, of course, Pastor Marlow agrees.

Well, enough of me telling you what to do. Pray for me in these last weeks.

Love,
Eli

May put on her best dress, a pale green cotton shift, and headed over to Harmony Baptist. The church office, gussied up with silk flower arrangements and a wallpaper border, anchored the basement. The heels of her sandals clicked on the white linoleum squares. She came with an offering in hand.

Sister Racine, who said the pastor was ready for her request and who wouldn't reveal her persuasive secrets, had assured her that Pastor Marlow loved pie. May had picked up some apples at the farmers' market, rolled out some of Violet's No-Fail Easy Piecrust dough, and with Callie's help cut out fancy leaves and swirls with a paring knife.

"That's the way to get to any man of food," Sister Racine said. "And Pastor Marlow is a man of food."

His status as a bachelor helped her cause. The man didn't go home to a home-cooked meal each night. He had to be sick of Dairy Queen and Dooley's Purple Cow, his two favorite haunts according to Brother Ben.

May loved Brother Ben, a loud, blustery man who'd give you the shirt off his back while telling you why you didn't deserve it. Both he and Sister Racine were on board for the feast and had offered to help in the kitchen at St. Thomas. Of course, John and Lynn had jumped at the prospect. They'd all kept it a secret so far, but now it was time to get

Pastor Marlow on board. May wanted the front ten acres; that was it. According to the appraisal she'd need fifty thousand dollars, due to the fact the barns and the house sat on that part of the property. She just needed five thousand of that for a down payment. Easy, right?

Pastor Marlow took the pie. "You want something, don't you?"

"Yep. And whether or not you get to keep that pie depends upon your answer."

He looked down. Looked up and stared hard at her. Then he shook his head and laughed. "You want that farm bad, don't you?"

"Just a little piece of it. Ten acres in fact."

"So Sister Racine says. Have a seat, May." He set the pie on his desk, a simple gray steel desk, and she sat down facing him.

"Here's the deal, Pastor Marlow. I've got a nice little business going, and thirty acres is plenty of space for Harmony Baptist. The land will be free and clear to you, of course, but I'm willing to pay you a good price for what I want. Do you realize what fifty thousand dollars would do? It would be a great help for the new facilities. Have you talked to the bank about financing yet?"

"Yes."

"And do you have enough down yet?"

"That's the church's business."

"Oh, come on. We're not enemies, are we?"

He sighed, then rubbed a hand over his bald head. "No, May. We're not."

"Then tell me what's going on."

"No. We don't have the down payment in hand. This is a poor church, May. We're growing, and the giving is enough to keep things going here, but no. We won't build on that for another three years without some help."

She crossed her arms and waited. "Think of all the powerful anointing that can happen with fifty thousand dollars."

He shook his head. "Oh, May. I don't know . . ."

"Please! This is the perfect solution."

"I know. But I've been thinking, doing a lot of soul searching."

"That's a good thing, isn't it?"

"I'd like to think so. Do you know this is my third church in six years? Did you know I get hired to build up a congregation and then move on to the next struggling church?"

May shook her head.

"But I'm tired, May. I'm tired of growing churches. Tired of giving empty pep talks every Sunday. Tired of tickling itching ears and telling everyone about all the good things and forgetting to mention we have to take up our cross."

—Take up our cross.

Was that what she was doing in Rwanda?

—Oh my! Oh my goodness!

She folded her hands tightly. "Then do that on the farm," she whispered. "Tell people how to really follow Jesus."

Father Isaac did that. Every Sunday. Every day.

"At what more beautiful place could that happen? Every time they come to church they'll see fields of flowers and cows and chickens. Please, Pastor Marlow."

"I'll take it before the board," he said.

"Do you know what they'll say?"

He smiled, the real man—tired, a little disillusioned, and in need of a real church family—shining in his eyes. "They'll say yes and amen, May. In fact, it will most likely be the loudest amen I've heard since I came."

May jumped up from her seat, ran around to his chair, and gave him a hug. And before he could take back what he'd said, she shot out the door, leaving a beautiful pie ready to be eaten.

April 19, 2004

Eli,

We have less than six weeks left. I realized just the other day that these letters won't go on forever and I almost broke down right there in the kitchen. I need you to send me a visitor's form, Eli. If it's okay with you, I think we should meet face-to-face. I can come once a week as soon as the paperwork goes through.

We're going for the fund-raiser. I'm really excited. So are Sassy, Callie, and Buell. I don't know if you know it, but they're about to lose their house. They're going into foreclosure. But here's the silver lining around the cloud. If it all works out, I've invited them to live with me. Callie's still going to help me with the flowers, and Buell (he grew up on a farm) is going to grow a big garden and take produce to the farmers' market. We'll get more chickens and another cow! The goat's still around. Little Flower will get to stay on, providing us with laughs, and we're getting her a companion too. If we raise the money, that is.

I couldn't have done any of this without you.

Don't forget to send me the form!

Love,

May

23

May was heading to prison.

She looked in the closet. A sundress, of course, the black-and-white one, and her white sweater and black sandals. She'd been wearing those sundresses all the time, but it wasn't like Eli had ever seen them before. He didn't know most likely everybody in Beattyville and beyond was sick to death of them. Even if she wasn't.

She hadn't felt nervous about seeing a man in years.

—Yeah, May. A dead man. Dead man walking and all that, remember?

She shoved those thoughts down. Maybe she just didn't want to look homeless anymore. But nerves filled her as she recalled his letters, the tattered papers she'd read over and over again, though she'd never told a soul. The letters that had kept her company during the long winter in the kitchen.

May fed the crazies, gave them plenty of water, picked them up and hugged them. She climbed into the truck, threw it into first gear, and set out.

A guard ushered May into a sterile room with some tables and chairs, plastic and beige. The floor was tiled in linoleum squares in a shade of chilly gray, and they shimmered under a coat of wax, or whatever it was they used these days. May doubted it was wax. That just seemed kind of old-fashioned, and yet she could see prisoners in their jumpsuits spreading it with fraying mops. Yep, it was a fraying mop kind of room.

"Just a few minutes," said the guard, a corpulent, tired man with red hair and a terrible case of conjunctivitis. He looked wearier than twenty-year-old chicken wire, and May didn't blame him. What little child ever dreamed of growing up and working in a prison? He probably felt as jailed as the inmates at times.

In her bag she'd arranged all the pictures she had printed from UK, the farm, Beattyville, and loads of shots of Callie. She figured if they got tongue-tied in person, the pictures would help keep the conversation going. But unfortunately, she had to secure her purse in a locker in the lobby.

He entered the room. Clothed in black sweatpants and a gray T-shirt, Eli definitely looked older, the skin of his face slightly broken in like hers, but the same boy-next-door good looks had clearly hung around the neighborhood.

"May!"

"Hi, Eli."

A guard stood by the door as Eli crossed the room and embraced her. And May realized something in that moment. Eli Campbell was her friend. Not just someone with a pen and good ideas, Eli Campbell actually cared. She felt it in his arms.

A broad smile split her face as she pulled back. "It's so good to see you."

He returned the grin. "Yes, it is, May. It really is."

She felt herself blushing. Darn it. "Want to sit down?"

"Sure."

"So what did you have for breakfast?"

He laughed. "Scrambled eggs and toast. I forewent the turkey bacon. You?"

"Rye toast."

"Very nice."

"You look good."

"So do you, May. I like the brown hair."

"It's my true color. Well, before it went gray."

"It suits you."

"I didn't know what to expect at seeing you. You've gained a little weight since the last time I saw you."

"You mean I look healthier than when I was a drugged-out skeleton?"

"Something like that."

They sat in a corner where two large windows met to welcome in the midday sun streaming through, heating the air around them. Combine that with nerves, and sweat began to break out on her brow. She wiped it off with the sleeve of her sweater.

"Why don't you take that off?"

"You sure?" she asked.

"Why not?"

He wasn't thinking about Rwanda.

She slipped it off.

He whistled and reached out, running his hand along the scars. "Wow."

"Yeah."

"I mean, I knew it would be bad. But without a picture . . ."

"I know."

"I'm sorry."

"For what?"

"I don't know. It just seems like all of us might be a little guilty somehow."

"I'm not sorry."

Did she really just say that? She was sorry it all happened, yes, but if it had to happen, she wasn't sorry she was there.

—Oh, God. Finally! Thank you!

The guard shuffled a little. Everything sounded so loud in the room.

"Why?"

She held up her arm, allowing the sunlight to glisten along the pale stripes. "I guess I realize something. These stripes connect me with the people I left behind. The people who first showed me how to live. Really live."

"I'm happy for you, May."

They sat in silence for a minute or two, the sunlight growing and the heat collecting. May figured she might as well get the first order of business over with.

"Are you still set on the execution?"

His mouth formed a line. "Yes. It's too late for an appeal now anyway."

"Are you sure?"

"No."

She batted his leg. "I didn't think so."

He shrugged. "When you live into something long enough, it's hard to turn it around."

"Oh boy, is that the truth."

"I took Father John's suggestion and prayed about it, but God hasn't said anything one way or the other."

"Maybe he's leaving this one up to you."

"You seem to be doing well, now."

She allowed the subject change. "You don't know the half of it." She began relating her plans. "Buell's going to build a new, larger coop. Four times as many chickens, and Sassy's going to sell the eggs. Buell's going to grow an acre or so of tobacco. And over behind the barn, soybeans. But mostly he'll grow produce for us and the market. An old friend of his from high school is going to help him get Claudius's tractor up and running."

And on it went.

"Well, you've got a month left, May. Can you get everything worked out by then?"

"I'm going to try my best. If all goes well, I'll get to stay in Beattyville."

"I sure wish I hadn't stayed!"

May reached out and took his hand. "Me too. Maybe things would have turned out different."

"How's Callie?"

"Fantastic!"

She thought of the pictures she'd mailed. Callie making biscuits. Callie drawing, tongue at the side of her mouth in concentration. Callie holding both crazies by their bellies, high over her head.

"Isn't she something?" he asked.

"How are you feeling about dying?"

It seemed like a terrible question, like one asked by those boobish reporters who shove a microphone in front of the face of someone who just lost his family in a monsoon. *How do you feel?* they ask as the masses sit back in their living rooms and groan, pointing to the screen and saying, "How do you think they feel, you idiot? Do you really have to ask?"

She wanted to shock him. She wanted to contrast her question with the images of lovely, sweet Callie.

"I'm ready." His blue eyes glittered in the sunlight across his face, the same light warming his blond hair. He almost looked exactly like he did in college.

"How can you be sure?"

"You've come on the scene, May. You're a survivor. You'll make sure Callie's okay from here on out. Your pictures prove that. And Mother too. I wish I could see that farm."

"Me too."

"Even if I didn't die, I would never get out of here. I deserve this life, but that doesn't make it any less unbearable. Imagine a life that will never change."

"But that's not true. We've become friends again!"

"Correct."

"And that's not enough?" Even as she said it, she realized how lame it was. "Never mind."

"Thanks. I didn't want to answer that one truthfully."

"Well, I don't know where I'd be now without you. You have to realize how much you've changed my life."

He began to wave that away.

"No!" she said. "Don't do that! Don't take that away from yourself or from God's uncanny ability to use people most of the world would deem hopeless."

He squeezed her hand. "Your heart has always been bigger than that."

"And you know that because . . . ?"

"You wrote to me while you were dealing with your own sorrow. I'm the only guy here who gets letters from someone other than family, and most of them don't even get those. Can you believe that?"

—Not really.

She shook her head, but deep down she knew it was true.

"Yeah. Not many people want anything to do with us."

"I guess they're scared."

"Probably. We're the lowest of the low. By anyone's standards. Even our own, if we'd admit that. And still, you put your pen to that paper and reached out."

"We're two of a kind, Eli. I figured that out before I went to Rwanda. And while I wasn't in love with you then, I think I might have been able to go that way had we been given the opportunity. I sure did enjoy being around you those couple of weeks. I felt like we connected. I guess you could say I reached out because I loved you. Or the memory of you. I don't know."

"Whatever you mean, you reached out because your heart told you to. When we give through love, that's what will sustain us. It's what makes our lives good. Truly good."

"Because love doesn't seek for itself."

He nodded. "I wish I'd have learned that a long time ago."

"Eli, don't take this the wrong way. But I love you. I mean, these last few months, writing and all, you've become more than a friend. You've been a lifeline."

"You've been a lifeline to me too." He pressed her hand between both of his. "I have an important question to ask you."

"Well, if you're asking my hand in marriage, it's no way!"

He laughed. "No. I wouldn't ask that of anyone! Can you be here the twenty-ninth? I don't want to die alone."

His words punched her in the heart. "Yes," she whispered. "I'll be here."

"Thank you."

His face hardened, then crumbled. And Eli cried like the innocent baby he once was, so many years ago.

—How does this happen?

She knew the story. But that didn't explain much. This was Eli in front of her. How did this happen?

· 24 ·

May sat atop Natural Bridge in the afternoon sunshine, her legs dangling over the side. She loved the view of the treetops, the hills and valleys spread out before her eyes like a gathering of flowers not yet turned brilliant. The copy of the Rwanda article rested on her lap, and she figured it was finally time to read it.

It had to be good, though, to see the experience written down cogently, almost clinically, by someone else.

She began, amazed at how easily her eyes sipped up the words.

Adding the story of Carl Wilkins, an Adventist missionary who refused to leave, to her story settled her soul. Did he know about May the way she knew about him? Most likely he did now. What a brave man.

The sun beat down upon her neck as she read how Carl watched his wife and children ride away in the convoy sent to transport them to Burundi. How he hid in his house for three weeks with the two Tutsi domestic workers who'd been with the family for several years. How he saw the body of his neighbor draped over the fence of her yard.

May had seen many such sights. She thought of dragging all those bodies from houses, gardens, one lying over the hood of his car.

And then Carl emerged, procuring a permit to travel the city roads. He kept an entire orphanage alive, saving all those children, as well as the director, Damis Gisimba, a Hutu who wouldn't align himself with Hutu power, who said because he'd stressed unity between Tutsi and Hutu with his children, he couldn't turn back.

May felt a heat spread beneath her scalp.

—Oh, God. I just didn't know. I didn't know how you were showing up.

Six Tutsi neighbors of the orphanage stayed alive in the storage closet and the lavatory. For three months! Carl kept them fed and brought water each day.

And miracles happened again and again, because someone was around. Someone was there.

Her accounts weren't at all heroic, she realized, not with shame but with a sense of relief. She survived. Yes, she was loyal to her friends, but she could do nothing to save them.

You suffered with them, May-May. Claudius's voice uttered the words. *And isn't that what Jesus did for us?*

—Oh, but he did more than suffer. He rescued us too.

One step at a time, May-May.

She felt a tap on her shoulder and turned. "Glen!"

"May! How are you doing today?" He reached into his pocket and wiped the sweat from his face and neck with a red bandana. He was just way too cute dressed in running gear. But he was no Eli, really. Of course, there were other ways he was no Eli either.

He took a sip from his water bottle. "You're looking really nice these days, May. And you're up here on Natural Bridge? What's up?"

"Life's too short?"

"Does that mean I won't have to chop wood for you anymore?"

"Pretty much."

"Really?" He grinned. "So you're really going to make it?"

"I really am."

"Yes!"

—What?

"Wait. You were all taking bets, weren't you?"

He clipped his bottle back onto his belt. "Somebody tried. But I nipped that one right in the bud."

"Thanks."

"Hey. A mail carrier feels a certain loyalty to the people on his route." He breathed in. "And I'm glad I didn't bet against you! See you later, May."

And he set back to his jog none the wiser to the place he'd held in her healing.

She continued through the article, wondering now, all these years later, how she had made it. There was only one reason.

May climbed to her feet and walked around to Lover's Leap, where she sat against an outcropping of rock and watched the sun go down. She let the love of God wash over her, cleansing away every drop of blood, every scar, every fear and failing. At least for today.

She decided she'd let Jesus do the same thing tomorrow if she needed him to. And the next day. And the next after that. Until she awakened one morning to find that it was gone for good.

The sun set and the chill dropped in. She was alone.

May walked back to the bridge, stood in the middle, and looked up at the stars. She held up the magazine, a pulpy offering, toward the sky, and with a grateful sigh, hurled it onto a breeze that caught it in its arms and carried it away, beyond where she could see.

May visited Eli every chance she could over the next couple of weeks. They fit years of conversation into six total hours, and he wrote to her of his fears as well as moments of peace and breakthrough. So now that the time had come for him to die, May realized a part of her would go right along with him. And that was all well and good. Truly. It was part of being human. The pieces we lose to others, God might replace with something better and more useful to the next person who comes along the path.

Eli joined her in the visitation room. He took her hand as they sat. "Well, I got some bad news. Or maybe it's good news. In any case, it's what I figured, but I wasn't sure."

She squeezed his fingers.

"You won't be able to witness the execution, May. Only my

family, Roy and Faye's family, spiritual advisors, prison personnel, and the media can be there."

"Oh, wow."

"I know. I don't want my mother to come, and nobody else will. So"—he exhaled heavily—"I guess I'm on my own."

"Father John will come."

"Yeah. I guess he'll have to do."

"I'll tell him you said so!"

Despite the conversation, he laughed. May loved that about Eli.

· 25 ·

Father John crossed his arms and leaned back in the pew a bit. "I knew you weren't quite like everybody else, May, but this takes the cake."

She plucked at her sundress. "I know. But it's the only solution I can think of."

"Well, there are worse reasons to want to marry a person. What's today's date again?"

"May 20."

"Nine days. We can do it, I think."

"I'll get the marriage license. And get Eli going on what he needs to do at his end. As long as we can get this done by the twenty-seventh, I think we'll be okay. But I'll make sure."

After calling the warden and the prison chaplain, May set a date in her mind, started up the truck, and headed over to the prison to ask Eli Campbell if he would be so pleased as to marry her.

He shuffled into the room. With each day that came and went, yet another string that held Eli to this world snapped in two. If it kept up, by the time the execution arrived, there would be little left.

"This is a surprise, May."

"I've got a proposition for you. Have a seat."

She'd dressed up for the occasion. She'd bought a flowing, brown gauze skirt and an ivory shirt with an empire waist. The copper embroidery around the scooped neck shimmered in the light.

"You look nice. What's the occasion?" He sat.

"Well, I figure I'd better look nice if I'm going to ask you to marry me."

Several seconds stretched between them.

She slid her fingers along his. "I know. I know it's strange. But I've got it all worked out." She pushed the paper sitting on the table between them toward him. "All you have to do is sign the license. Father John, if you don't mind it being an Episcopal wedding, will preside."

"Wait a minute. I don't even know what you're doing here, May. Okay, I mean, I know what you're doing. What I don't know is why."

May hunched down on her knees beside him. Not marriage-proposal posture, but one of imploring. She took both of his hands and held them against her heart. "I'm not going to let you die alone, Eli. So I'm asking you to marry me so I can be in that room when the time comes."

He closed his eyes.

He cleared his throat.

He bowed his head.

"So what do you say?"

Eyes still closed. "I think you're crazy, May, but this gesture means more to me than you know."

"It's not a gesture, Eli."

Something holy imbued the moment, as if they were suddenly wrapped in air and light. She laid her head on his lap, closing her eyes as his hand found its way atop her head.

And she loved him.

Father John donned his robes for the occasion, and May wore a white sundress she found at Rose Brothers. Her scars glimmered on her arms.

Of course, the bouquet was the prettiest thing in the room. Callie made it, zinging with excitement. Sassy baked the cake, slices of which only Eli, Father John, and May would enjoy. It sat over on the table near the corner window of the rec room, one layer, white icing, with real daisies—from Borne's Last Chance, of course—ringing the sides.

Eli wore gray pants and a white shirt, and was freshly shaved. Though the marriage was definitely offbeat, he made a handsome groom.

—So why am I doing this?

Because Jesus had taught her how to love again through this man, and she loved Eli for that. She wanted to honor him, be with him through sickness and health, and till death parted them in four days. As Father John told her, "Those are the best reasons for marriage I've heard in a long time. The length of your union is irrelevant."

Their heads jerked toward the door as it was unlocked and opened. Pastor Marlow bustled through.

"Darius!" said Father John. "I was thinking you wouldn't make it. Glad to see you!"

"Thank you, John."

"What?" asked May.

"He's your pastor. I thought he'd like to be here."

May nodded. That Father John. Father Hedgehog turned Fox. "Come on over, Pastor Marlow."

"When John told me what you were doing, I found it hard to believe," Marlow said.

"It's true." May took Eli's arm again.

"But I think it's wonderful, May. You're really something."

Father John opened his prayer book. "Shall we proceed?"

They all nodded, then he stopped. "Wait! I forgot." He opened his briefcase, pulled out the red martyr's stole, and hung it around his neck.

May's hand flew to her mouth as she gulped back a sob. "Thank you," she mouthed.

He dipped his head, then looked up.

Did Father Isaac see? She hoped so.

So there they stood, pledging themselves to one another, arms linked, hands joined, united in Love.

She couldn't help it; she felt as if a light glowed from her heart and out through her eyes. If that was corny, well so be it. She'd eat it right off the cob. Eli folded her to him after they were pronounced husband and wife, after he kissed her softly on the lips when Father John said, "You may kiss the bride."

"Thank you," he whispered, his breath skimming across her cheek.

She pulled her head away from his chest and cupped his cheek and jaw with her hand.

So many of the people she loved in her life were taken away from her by death. But she chose to give herself to him knowing he would be gone soon. She realized just then, that's the way it always is. We live, we die, and to love in those circumstances, all we can do is take a chance. But no matter how long we get to love, every second of that is a blessing.

He hugged her to himself again, and in the antiseptic visitation room, the noontime sunlight heating up the glossy tiles and the plastic furniture, they clung to life, their own, and each other's.

· 26 ·

Eli emerged from the deathwatch chamber into a small room where May waited. Here he would have his last meal and visit with those he loved. The guards had put him in last night.

"Welcome to Motel 6," he said with a shaky laugh.

"This makes the visitation room look like Buckingham Palace."

They sat at a small table. It seemed they were always sitting at tables.

"Father John will be here soon," she said. "But I'm here all day, if you'd like."

He'd already said good-bye to Callie and Sassy a few hours before. "It was the worst moment of my life," he told May. He placed his hand on her forearm, then absentmindedly traced her scars with the tip of his index finger.

"How are you feeling?"

"Nauseated. Nervous. How about you?"

"The same. I don't want you to die."

"I know."

She watched his hand move along her arm, and she touched the tendons along its back, webbed like a duck's foot, as they moved beneath his skin.

This time tomorrow no life would remain in his body.

"So," she asked, "would you appeal now if you had the chance? Now that it's so close?"

His hand stopped, and he curled his fingers around her arm and gave it a light squeeze. "Do you mind if I don't answer?"

She moved around to his side of the table, squeezed in tightly beside him on the attached bench, and laid her head on his shoulder. There they stayed, neither of them finding anything worth saying that would improve the silence.

Father John visited awhile and prayed with them, then left them alone. May had cried the entire time, listening to the words of this man so in tune with the suffering of the people he came in contact with.

Eli forewent his last meal, instead asking for a Coke that he sipped to help tame his upset stomach. "It's good that Roger and Faye's family will have closure. That's what keeps me from going crazy right now."

"Forgiveness is the only way they'll truly put this behind them. But I can't pretend to know what they feel like, and I sure know it wouldn't be easy."

"No." He sighed. "It's best this way."

May doubted that. Perhaps Eli was just providing an already grieving family with just one more thing to be disillusioned about. They thought his death would heal, but it wouldn't. Then what?

—It must be so horrible.

"You all have five minutes." The red-haired guard poked his head into the room.

May wondered what it felt like to utter such ordinary words in such extraordinary circumstances.

"Wow," Eli whispered.

He drew a breath deeply into his lungs, and May wondered how many more breaths he had left. Most think it would be impossible to count the breaths they have left, but now Eli couldn't say that. Five hundred? A thousand?

She glanced at the clock over the door. Eleven thirty p.m.

In a little over half an hour, Eli would be dead.

She put her arms around him, and they stood body to body, their lengths supporting each other. There was nothing to say other than *I love you*. And *Thank you*.

And they said these phrases. Over and over again.

She tried to soak in the details of every inch of his face, each hair, each fleck of color in his irises. This man who saved her life, who picked it up from the dirt, brushed it off, and gave it back to her again.

And of all the pictures she'd taken in her lifetime, there was one that would always be missing.

—I must remember. I must remember. I must remember him.

There were so many people she remembered now. Claudius, her mother, the villagers who had died. She would be faithful to that.

The guard returned. "It's time."

One final kiss, their lips pressed in a tenderness she'd never known, and he was led back into the deathwatch room to get dressed.

It was good-bye.

Eli told her he would walk to the chamber instead of having to be strapped to a gurney. "They know I'm not going to try anything."

Heaviness descended and filled in around them as he walked away and the cell door clicked shut.

"Ma'am. Let's get you to the observation room," the guard said.

"How old are you?" she asked.

"Twenty-four."

"Lordymercy," she muttered, and accompanied him down the hallway.

He ushered her into a white room furnished with the usual plastic chairs, a large plateglass window the far wall's centerpiece. The curtains on the other side were closed.

Others were already gathered. She didn't know who they were. Roy and Faye's family? A couple of reporters sat in the back row. Big news, this execution. Who in his right mind refuses to appeal?

Outside the prison protestors were gathered, holding a vigil for Eli and against the death penalty, candles in hand, singing "Dona Nobis Pacem" or something. And they were praying.

Father John hurried in and led her to a seat. "As his wife you should sit up front."

Heads turned, and the stares from their eyes burned into her skin. She gazed back at them, her eyes filling with tears for their pain, knowing death only stops the pain for the dying.

She took Father John's arm, head bowed, and slipped into a chair. The reporters murmured, and so did the other occupants of the room. May tried to block out their conversations as she prayed over and over again, "Give him peace. Give him peace."

The cry of "Dead man walking!" echoed in the hallway, slipping under the space between door and floor.

"Oh, dear Jesus," she whispered. "This is really it, isn't it, Father?"

"Yes, May. I'm afraid so."

They whispered as quietly as possible.

The best thing she could do was be brave. Eli wanted to give the family closure. Her slobbering all over and making this about herself wouldn't be doing right by Eli.

"Do you know how this is done, May?" Father John whispered.

She shook her head.

"Well, they'll lay him on the gurney, secure his wrists and his ankles, and get the IV started. They put one in each arm to administer the drugs. What's strange is that the tubes go through a hole in the wall into another room where the medical personnel are."

"They're not right in the room with him?"

"No. A doctor will be with him to verify he's died and proclaim the time of death."

"Is it a one-way window?"

"No. He'll see you, May."

"That's good."

They sat for a couple of minutes, listening to the victim's family talk about the terrible Eli Campbell, the maggot who was finally getting what he gave. And she couldn't blame them. But they didn't know Eli. And they honestly couldn't, really *could not* care that he'd become a good man, a kind man, the man who wrote her faithfully. To do so would dishonor the deaths of their relatives. At least that's the way most people would see it. Or so she thought. How could she know what they felt any more than they could understand what was going on inside of her?

"Now, I'm not sure about Kentucky, but in some states, they have several people administer the drugs, but only one set ends up in Eli's veins, the others go into a dummy bag. That way the executioners don't know who was the one to end his life."

"Great. So they can *all* think they probably did it."

He cleared his throat. "Well, I suppose that's one way of looking at it."

Her blood pounded the sidewalls of her arteries, and she was so aware, so aware, so aware of being alive, and knowing she was going to be alive in ten minutes, because the clock said 11:55 and in five minutes it would be May 29.

The curtains swished to the sides as if it was early morning and somebody was opening them to let the sun in as the coffee brewed.

There he lay, the head of the bed raised, a sheet covering his body.

The warden said, "Mr. Campbell, would you like to make your final statement?"

"Yes, sir." Eli Campbell, thirty-three years old, cleared his throat, the back of his sandy hair mussed against the pillow, the recessed lighting catching the blue in his eyes and warming his skin, paled to the shade of skim milk. "I realize that I can never bring back Roger and Faye, so all I can do is offer myself up. It won't make Christmases any better, it won't stop you from you weeping on their birthdays, especially Faye's, or keep you from wondering how big she'd be, or what she'd look like."

Faye's mother sobbed.

"I know I'll never have your forgiveness. I haven't forgiven myself, not that that matters. But the only way I can let you know how truly sorry I am, how I'd give anything to make up for it, is to give everything I can. May God grant you all peace. That's all I can ask for any of us, I guess." He looked at the warden and nodded. "That's it, I guess."

The pencils of the reporters behind her scratched furiously on their small writing pads.

Eli looked May in the eyes, nodded, and slowly blinked a *thank you*. She didn't know how she knew that was what he was telling her, but she was sure of it. She tried to fill her eyes with love and gratitude. She laid her hand on her heart.

He settled his head back and closed his eyes as the doctor approached the gurney. The warden checked his watch.

Two more minutes.

Every part of May's body stiffened, waiting for the death of the man who brought her back to life.

"We live in one great big paradox, Father," she whispered.

"That we do, May."

"Come on, come on, come on," a young man nearby grated through his teeth at the clock. "Let's wipe this scum off the face of the earth."

She curled her fingers around Father John's arm, the only sign of her strain, the tears drawing slow, wet stripes down her face. She swallowed again and again as the seconds ticked down. Eli kept his eyes closed, and she wished she could crawl inside his head and know his thoughts, or crawl on that bed, curl around him, and hold him as he died.

Several minutes passed.

A nurse ran in from the next room, where people were waiting with drugs to stop a life. She pointed to the door, gesturing as if she didn't know what was going on.

The doctor leaned down to Eli's face, pulled out a penlight, opened his eyelid and checked his pupils. Eli didn't move. It was like he didn't even notice the examination. The guards remained in position as the warden followed the physician into the next room.

Eli lay there. Serene, still, an expression of peace on his face. How could he remain so calm?

The warden poked his head through the doorway, motioning to a guard who hurried over to the window and snapped the curtains shut.

"What happened?" She turned to Father John.

"I have no idea. Maybe there was a malfunction in the equipment. I don't know."

The angry young man let out a string of expletives while Roger's wife sobbed into her hands. "I shouldn'a come. I knew I shouldn'a."

An elderly woman, her mother, May supposed, put her arm around her. "Let's go, Becky. Come on."

"She's come all the way from Chicago, Ma," the young man snapped. "Leave her be."

The woman mumbled something back, but they settled back into their chairs, the fluorescent light greening their complexion further.

The door to the observation room opened and the warden entered, his face red with stress. With knit brows above pursed lips he stood by the window. "Well, folks, there'll be no execution tonight."

"What?" the young man yelled, standing up and tugging on his UK sports jersey. "Did the governor call at the last minute?"

"No." He turned to me. "Mrs. Campbell, I know you were expecting your husband to die tonight, and he has. We don't know what happened. After his statement, he lay back, and while the minutes were ticking down, he . . . well, he just died, ma'am. His heart just stopped."

Father John placed his arms around her as she wept. "God took him," she said into the black of his suit. Tears of sorrow mixed with tears of joy.

When May returned to her home around one o'clock, Pastor Marlow was waiting on the front porch.

"May." He stood up.

"Hi, Pastor Marlow."

"Call me Darius."

She put the key in the lock and turned. "Come on in. If I ever needed a cup of tea, it's now."

He followed her into the kitchen and leaned against the counter as she set the kettle to the boil.

"John called. Told me what happened," he said.

"It's strange, isn't it?" She pulled down two teacups from the cupboard.

"Have a seat, May. Let me take over from here."

She took his offer. "Thank you."

A few minutes later they sat face-to-face at the kitchen table, cups of tea between them.

"I need to apologize," he said. "To you and to God."

She remained silent, wanting to hear the rest.

"Here you were, up here on this farm, suffering in sorrow, and all I could see was the property."

"I didn't make it easy for anybody to reach out."

"That wasn't your job."

She sighed. "I guess not."

"Even when you started coming to the church—"

"For totally selfish purposes."

He laughed. "Well, yes. But it's not that anymore, is it? You sit with old Brother Ben every Sunday, and you don't have to. Sister Racine even told me you asked about joining the choir."

"She was supposed to keep that a secret until I decided for sure."

"Be that as it may, it still proves my point."

"Okay. I'll concede. I love the people at Harmony."

He drained the small cup in one go. "I've talked to the board and the congregation, and everyone agrees. You can stay on the land, May. Keep your part in Borne's Last Chance, and we'll move to the back of the property. In fact"—his eyes danced—"we're thinking of building right atop the ridge, the world spread out like a map outside the windows."

May knew she should dance and sing but, still drained from the events of the evening, all she could do was press her hand on top of Pastor Marlow's. "Thank you."

"I figured you could use one good piece of news today, May." He stood. "I'd better go. We're praying for you. All of us."

May believed him.

· 27 ·

Three months later

The hall of St. Thomas Episcopal Church was filled to the brim with Episcopalians, Baptists, Catholics, and even the Methodists, all hearing about May's plans. They came to feast.

Callie rushed into the church kitchen. "Can you believe it? Three hundred people!"

The women of Harmony Baptist bustled from oven to worktable, plating fried chicken (the birds donated by a farmer up the road from May), sausage stuffing, and corn pudding. Savory greens simmered in pots on the stove, and Buell was frying up tomatoes by the dozens. Arranged down a long table in the hall were pies of every sort, donated by Father John's parishioners.

Sister Ruth had flown back for the occasion. She grabbed May and wrapped her wiry arms around her, kissing her on the cheek. "Violet's recipe book delivered once again, honey! The biscuits were perfect!"

Callie had taken May's favorite recipes and made a beautiful booklet she titled *Violet's Recipes from Borne's Last Chance*, filling it with her artwork and selling them for five dollars apiece. "Five dollars!" she said. "Can you believe people would pay that much?"

But after they tasted the meal, they did indeed. Every book was gone by the time they cleaned up and turned out the lights. They'd made enough for the down payment on ten acres. Harmony Baptist said it wasn't necessary, but May knew better. She needed her own place to grow and become and sow and gather.

Father John and Lynn greeted the guests, Pastor Marlow in their wake, shaking hands and refilling glasses of tea and lemonade. Even Glen showed up with his buddies from the post office. She heard more good wishes and promises of prayer in that afternoon than she'd heard her entire life.

"I wonder if my skin is glowing, the way it feels?" she said to Callie. They'd both dressed in white dresses and wore flowers in their hair. Callie now lived in the other bedroom upstairs, next to May's.

"Oh, it is, Miss May. It really is!"

Returning home, May walked what would soon be her land. Already the new coop housed forty chickens of at least five different breeds, since May couldn't decide on just one.

She made sure the new cow, Weezie, was in for the night, and she counted her chickens, thankful for each one. Flower seemed to grin and so did Laurel, her new buddy. She'd made it through, watching as May and the old place came to life once again.

May laughed.

She walked up to the ridge where the fresh grave of Eli lay beneath the night sky, next to Claudius.

The stars looked down upon her, and when they flashed she knew that all the people she'd loved who had come and gone were still with her, living on, not just in the faith they knit in her heart, the rosebushes they planted, the barns they built, or the children they sired, but they went on and on, like the universe God held in the palms of his hands.

· acknowledgments ·

To all who serve the work at Thomas Nelson, especially my editor and friend, Ami McConnell, whose input made this book so much the better, my sincere thanks.

With gratitude to Chip MacGregor who helps me remember what's important.

I'd especially like to thank Phillip Elmore, on death row in Ohio, who wrote many letters and gave of himself in the midst of a death sentence. I pray your appeal comes through and that God keeps you in His tender care.

To my friends and family, especially Will, Ty, Jake and Gwynnie, well, you bring me resurrections daily, and for that I'm most grateful.

With thanks to the triune God I serve inconsistently but with hope.

LISA SAMSON is the award-winning author of twenty-six books including *Quaker Summer*, *Christianity Today's* Novel of 2008, and *Justice in the Burbs*, which she co-wrote with her husband, Will, a professor of Sociology. When not at home in Kentucky with her three children, one cat, and six chickens, she speaks around the country about writing and social justice, encouraging the people of God to "do justice, love mercy, and walk humbly with God." She loves nothing better than sitting around her kitchen table, talking with family and friends, old and new.